THE CASANOVA EMBRACE

Also by Warren Adler

OPTIONS
BANQUET BEFORE DAWN
THE HENDERSON EQUATION
TRANS-SIBERIAN EXPRESS
THE SUNSET GANG

THE CASANOVA EMBRACE

୶ବ

By Warren Adler

LIBRARY
LINCOLN MEMORIAL UNIVERSITY
Harrogate Tennessee 37752

G. P. Putnam's Sons, New York

105246

PZ4
A239
Cas

Copyright © 1978 by Warren Adler

All rights reserved. This book, or parts thereof, must not be
reproduced in any form without permission. Published simultaneously
in Canada by Longman Canada Limited, Toronto.

SBN: 399-12107-2
Library of Congress Catalog Number: 77-18423

PRINTED IN THE UNITED STATES OF AMERICA

To Don M. Wolfe
who ignited the flame

. . . and who hath fully understood how
unknown to each other are man and woman!
—Friedrich Nietzsche
Thus Spake Zarathustra

THE CASANOVA EMBRACE

I

Covert intelligence agents and security men in the various embassies along the tree-lined street knew instinctively that it was a bomb blast that had intruded on the chilly morning calm. It was hardly an automobile's backfire. Windows nearby were shattered. Bric-a-brac fell from shelves and tables in the elegant houses innocently included in the blast's periphery. A pervasive, unfamiliar odor flumed invisibly upward through the usual pall of pollutants hanging in the heavy air of Washington. Someone who not only surmised what had occurred but actually saw the twisted wreckage of the gray Pinto, floating, it seemed, in a cloud of smoky afterblast, called the police.

Spectators, hovering behind heavy draperies, contemplated with fascination the block-long wreckage. A hubcap had been blown, like a discus, into the trunk of a tree. A tire lay on the doorstep before the heavy wrought-iron door at the entrance of the Greek Embassy. A trail of upholstery stuffing, white, like heavy snow, lay on the black surface of the road.

11

Experienced eyes, familiar with the impersonal ruthlessness of explosives, picked knowingly among the rubbish of the violence seeking pieces of a human being. A foot, the shoe still carefully laced and reflecting on its shine the glint of the shrouded February sun, lay on a patch of grass, fifty feet from the car's mangled remains. A ringed hand rested eerily on a piece of deformed chrome ornament. Patches of red materialized adjacent to the main wreckage, adding a grisly highlight to what might have been a surrealistic performance for an avant-garde art show.

Officer Bryant of the Executive Protective Force, a tall man with a craggy face, felt the backwash of bile in his throat as he tamped down an involuntary retch. It was the worst, most horrifying scene he had ever beheld. The first detail he was conscious of was that of a man's mangled torso in the front seat jammed against the remains of the dashboard. Actually, it was the sight of the head that had made him want to vomit. It was cleanly severed at the neck and lying like an errant basketball on what might have once been the car's back seat. The eyes were open, the silvery-gray surrounding the black pupils oddly clear and glistening, not at all dull, as one might have expected of dead eyes. A thin mustache, neatly edged, lay perfectly centered above a thickish angel-bowed upper lip. The face was ivory smooth, the fleshtone dark, not tanned by the sun. The mouth was set in a broad sardonic smile, showing even white teeth.

"I'll be a sonofabitch," Officer Bryant heard himself say after he had assured himself that he had conquered his urge to vomit. He stared at the face in the isolated head, fascinated, compelled to absorb the horror of it. He had no idea what to do. Officially, he was paralyzed.

Sirens screeched as both marked and unmarked official cars swarmed into the area. Materializing suddenly were wooden horses blocking both ends of the affected geography. Police began to reroute traffic. A white ambulance from the Georgetown University Hospital was quickly passed through the cordon. Two pale white-coated doctors stepped out, surveyed the scene, hesitated, went back into the ambulance and reappeared wearing surgical gloves.

A group of uniformed police with gold braid on their caps talked quietly with men in civilian suits as they clustered around the main area of wreckage. One of the men in civilian clothes waved the doctors forward. Behind them came two uniformed attendants carrying a stretcher and a package of transparent bags.

"Looks like a single corpse, male Caucasian," one of the men in civilian clothes said. He was from the FBI, a take-charge type, from his bearing, obviously the acknowledged senior of the group. "Be careful," he whispered to the doctors. "There may be prints."

"They should leave their shit at home," another man in civilian clothes said. His complexion was sallow, his hair completely white. He was Alfred Dobbs, CIA. Flashbulbs popped as two FBI photographers recorded every detail. An acetylene torch appeared suddenly in the hands of a policeman. He wore welder's glasses. The flame of the torch bit into the mangled metal and cut a long rectangular gash in the wreckage, large enough to remove the remains.

When he had finished, the doctors knelt, poking their arms into the opening, and gently removed the torso. Part of it seemed to disintegrate in their hands as they deftly edged it into a large plastic bag. Securing it with a length of tape, they placed it on the waiting stretcher. Sliding half his body through the opening, one of the other doctors saw the head.

"Oh, my God," he said, lifting it by the hair. He put it in another plastic bag and handed it to the other doctor, who placed it on the stretcher with the remains of the torso. One of the attendants was searching the area for other signs of human remains, a plastic bag in his hand, like a garbage picker gathering rubbish after a county fair. He picked up the severed hand, found

13

the foot, as well as pieces of unrecognizable parts, and put them quickly in the bag. He was a young man, had been a medic in Vietnam. He was used to this, he told himself. He had seen worse. He sensed that people were watching him from behind the tall windows of the big houses and he liked the attention.

The doctors, too, continued to find bits and pieces of flesh and bone in what was once the interior of the car. They moved methodically. They knew that the FBI would want the pathologists to get everything that could be found and they wanted their efficiency to be commended.

A beeping sound grated the ear, and the FBI take-charge man drew a compact walkie-talkie from his pocket and quickly extended the antenna.

"Grady here," the FBI man said.

"What is it, Jack?" He recognized the voice of the director.

"A white male Caucasian, sir. Looks foreign. Probably a Latino or Italian, maybe. About thirty feet from the Chilean Embassy on Massachusetts Avenue. He bought it from a homemade, emanating from the interior of a 1974 Ford Pinto. The medics are picking up the pieces."

"A real mess, eh?"

"Better believe it."

"No identity?"

"The prints will be over shortly. Wait a minute, sir."

One of the doctors handed him what seemed to be the remains of a District of Columbia license. He held it up at a distance to assure the focus of his farsighted eyes.

"I've got a license make," Grady said into the walkie-talkie. He gave the director the number, heard the sound garble as the director repeated it to another person. Static crackled as Grady waited. He knew the information banks were being sent into action, the electronic probes activated. Waiting, he watched with some annoyance as the CIA man approached, the competitive animosity surfacing as he recognized the gray-haired man. It was Dobbs. Pretty high up, he thought with contempt, knowing how swiftly they would move in when they smelled a foreign involvement.

"Eduardo Allesandro Palmero." The director's voice intruded over the static. His pronunciation was amusingly inaccurate. "The car was registered in his name."

"Any ident yet?" Dobbs asked.

"What was that?" the director asked.

"I've got a spook here, sir," Grady said. His contempt was undisguised.

The director sighed. "Who?" he asked.

"Dobbs," the CIA man said. Grady repeated the name. "He wants to know." There was a brief pause. He knew what was in the director's mind. Hoover would have told him to get lost.

"Tell him," the director said.

"Eduardo Allesandro Palmero," he said, proud of his pronunciation. He wondered if the director had overheard.

Dobbs heard the name. It was the confirmation he had dreaded. His stomach had lurched. How could he have not foreseen?

"Is the name familiar?" Grady asked, the contempt hidden, professionally alert. The answer from Dobbs was spare, crisp.

"A Chilean. He was in the Allende government. We gave him asylum." There was more to tell, Dobbs knew. But this was all they would get. Grady sensed the sparseness. They would dole out only what was officially necessary. He conveyed the information to the director.

"Shit," the director said. The foreign aspect meant CIA interference, bureaucratic competition, aggravation and chicken shit. "Keep me up on it."

"Yes, sir," Grady responded, hearing the sign-off click. He put the walkie-talkie back in his pocket.

"That's it," one of the doctors said, tapping Grady on the shoulder. Grady motioned to two of his men who jumped in behind the attendants. The ambulance backed out of the street and moved swiftly down Massachusetts Avenue, sirens turned

15

on, the message of urgency, frightening to the many ears who could hear the shrill agony of its sound.

The street was crowded with police, FBI and other officials and experts. Many picked meticulously through the wreckage, carefully retrieving any object that might be potentially useful. They combed the length of the street, peering, hawklike, on the ground. Some worked on their hands and knees placing material in plastic bags with tweezers. Official photographers continued to snap pictures. Technicians tenaciously brushed all available surfaces for prints. Samples were taken of everything—blood, dust, the upholstery stuffing. Everything.

Men with small pads, ball-point pens scribbling, paraded up and down the street. Some went in to interview people in the big homes and embassies nearby. They talked to servants, staff, ambassadors, their wives, children. Reporters, forced to remain behind the wooden horses, yelled questions to the men working in the street. Flashbulbs popped. Television and motion picture cameras whirred.

Everyone worked swiftly. Grady was satisfied with the cooperation of the D.C. Police, the Executive Protective Agency, his own men and the specialists with their sophisticated equipment who sought to gather every scrap of evidence that might tell them who had noisily separated Eduardo Allesandro Palmero from his life on this chilly morning in February. Amid the bedlam, he occasionally cast an annoyed glance at Dobbs. Damned spooks, he muttered, knowing that they would, as always, withhold pieces of the puzzle. Dobbs, Grady sensed, was already deep in speculation, which was an accurate bit of insight. Dobbs was the Langley wizard on terrorist groups, the resident expert on the sub-underworld of competing gangs who waged continuing war between factions and ideologies. This battleground respected neither national boundaries nor human life. It was an ugly, brutal, maddening war of unparalleled intensity, with many casualties, waged far from the prying eyes of the media. There were rarely any wounded. Combatants were wasted. Only the innocent were occasionally maimed when, by some odd misfiring, they were not killed.

This was Dobbs' arena. Under his supervision were hundreds of analysts, technicians, agents in every country of the world, covering people of every persuasion, all on the payroll—hired guns, mercenaries supplying bits and pieces of knowledge—so that Dobbs could observe this war and synthesize it for the President and his advisors. Essentially, he was the information filter and he knew his own power, the power of word control.

Sometimes, with luck, he could track a hit in advance. The Palmero thing, he knew, was an aberration. Who could believe it? His mind was already manufacturing logic, rationalizations, the coverup. On the surface, it could appear to be a logical Junta hit. Was anything awry, out of focus? Where was the currency for the Junta? he asked himself. Every specific wasting had a purpose. Nothing was without design. Perhaps, though, at the moment, it might be useful to let the obvious prevail.

Watching the scene, now winding down, as the men efficiently disposed of their assignments, he grew restless to be back at his desk in Langley to read the Palmero files, to reach into the information banks, to comb through the forest of information gleaned from the monitoring of the Chilean counter-insurgents, an arm of DINA, their vaunted intelligence apparatus. For Latinos they were a marvel of organization, a long and ruthless arm that could pick out and set up anti-Junta agents with superb dispatch. Probably the German influence, with their passion for thoroughness. They had destroyed their enemies in Europe, Africa, the Middle East with great skill. A quick hit. Then fadeout. He wished their own "Capos" could be half as efficient. Capos, he called them, borrowed from the Mafiosa. They would now see him only as a bungler.

Grady moved closer. The man was in his fifties, but still retained that clean FBI Irish look. You could spot it coming at you almost before you saw the face, as if they threw out some special scent.

"Well," Grady said, "how do you read it?"

"Could be a Junta hit," Dobbs said. He wanted to seem sincere, wondering if he had successfully achieved the role. Grady nodded, as if he understood. "It obviously seems political." Did he seem suspicious? Dobbs wondered. Bits of information retrieved themselves in his mind. Palmero had been a strategist in the Allende inner circle. He had been Allende's Minister of Interior, but that was merely to give him a handle. In actuality, he was the propaganda man, the ideological brain, and the Junta had put him in prison. They had given him a bad time, very bad.

The CIA had gotten him out, ostensibly, as part of a barter for United States aid. Actually, he was set up to be one of their pigeons, a lure, carefully marked bait. They might have intervened, prevented this act. Had he been mesmerized, Dobbs wondered, wanting to see how Palmero's last act would unfold. That would make him an accomplice. He shrugged. Guilt was a wasted emotion in his business.

"It has all the earmarks," Dobbs said, feeling the need to reinforce Grady's naive suppositions.

"Do you think it will be the beginning?"

Dobbs understood. The United States was a kind of neutral territory. Even the most ardent fanatics shied away from performing their bloody business on American soil. Setups were difficult. Officials were less corruptible. Surveillance was sophisticated.

"I hope not," Dobbs replied. In this case, it was still neutral, he knew.

"They should do their bloody shit elsewhere."

"What kind was it?" Dobbs asked. He knew the answer to that as well.

"Plastic stuff. We found the timer. It looks like it was placed

18

in the back seat, set to go when he hit this area. Where was he heading, you think?" Grady was fishing now.

"Who knows?" Dobbs shrugged, on his guard. The symbolism was clever, the blast so close to the embassy. A lucky stroke? Or well planned? Either way, it was a useful device.

"You think we'll get them?" Grady asked.

"Nobody ever does."

"We'll get them," Grady said with an air of conviction.

"Good luck."

"They'd better not start this shit over here. It'll open up floodgates. Palestinians. Irish. Cubans. They'll drive us up the wall."

Their naivete was incredible, Dobbs thought. The FBI was stupid, he told himself. Too macho. Too worried about their own image. Too simplistic. This business happened in the shadows. It was his war. The FBI was out of its league and he was grateful for that.

The crowd in the street began to thin out. The wooden horses were removed and a crane and truck appeared. The crane quickly lifted the wreckage of the Pinto into the truck while the remaining litter was removed and bagged. Then it, too, was put into the truck, covered and driven out of the area. Reporters pressed around Grady as he moved toward his own car, but he said nothing and drove away.

Dobbs moved slowly out of range of their probing voices. He liked to think of himself as invisible, an observer, when he was in the field—a rare occurrence. Shrouded in the mist of anonymity, he surveyed the scene.

The large embassies on either side of the street had borne witness impassively. Another one of man's silly brutalities, they might have said if they could talk. Dobbs could see eyes still watching in the shadows beyond the large windows. The street emptied. The last traces of the twisted Pinto had disappeared. Even the bloodstains on the asphalt had been removed, and the janitors of the various large homes and embassies had already swept the shattered glass. Glaziers were on their way to replace the shattered windows.

Soon cars were moving normally and people had ventured back into the street, observing the spot where it had happened, then moving on to accustomed chores. The men of the Executive Police with their blue-trimmed uniforms resumed their posts. A recall of the morning events would chase boredom for a few hours, then it was back to the stultifying emptiness of their official duties.

Dobbs walked to his car. So far, he had observed nothing amiss. But it was still too early to be sure.

What was there in Eduardo ... he began to think of him as a companion ... to inspire such ... he hesitated ... awesomeness? He needed to refresh his mind, consult the files, review the total picture. It was not the conclusion he was concerned about. That had already been determined. What had this man possessed? Why had it eluded him until it was too late?

He was still turning it over in his mind as he suddenly discovered that he had mistaken a turn and was heading the wrong way on the Beltway.

II

It was one of Marie's special private pleasures to recall the exact moment of her first observance of him. Later, it would become a ritual of their lovemaking, like an after-dinner drink savored with all the concentration and subtleties that the taste buds could muster.

It had happened at a crowded affair at the Roumanian Embassy. There was always an eclectic group, since Roumania could bridge the invitational gap of ideologies. One could find representatives of antagonistic countries and factions calmly sipping champagne together as if what was happening in the real world was merely a fictional device for a movie script. It was politically appropriate, she later agreed, for Eduardo to be on their invitational list, since it gave him the opportunity to continue to provide visibility for the ill-fated Allende regime.

He was standing in a corner of the ornate room, deftly removing tidbits from the buffet table, searching swiftly but carefully, with a practiced eye for the most interesting culinary concoction. Then, with special grace, he had propped the plate on the tips of the fingers of his left hand and proceeded to eat with the calm assurance of one who had obviously had long experience at the buffet tables.

She had watched him from across the crowded room, an idle curiosity, since she was stuck with a most boring man from the Department of State whose words she could barely hear above the social din. Her husband, the Minister Plenipotentiary of the French Embassy, gesticulated with his usual intensity in a group of other foreign diplomats. There goes Claude again, she remembered thinking, turning slightly, spilling a drop of champagne on her pink Cardin, the one that was lent out of his collection to publicize French wares. She had looked up swiftly, caught his eye, then with feigned embarrassment but real relief she excused herself and went off to the ladies' room. She had felt his eyes watching her as she moved away.

"And then?" It was his ritual response whenever she recalled the moment, her head nestled in the crook of his bare arm, the hard muscle a pillow, as she played with the hairs of his chest.

"Then you passed completely out of my mind."

"Completely?"

"Well, I was concentrating on the removal of the champagne stain."

"But I did notice that you had disappeared."

"How could you? You were so busy stuffing your face."

"My digestion has nothing to do with the male antenna."

"And what a beautiful antenna."

Her hand reached down and fondled his penis. She felt its awakening response. Then she removed her hand.

"It was the furthest thing from my mind."

"But a seed was planted."

"Perhaps I loved you then, from that moment."

"You romantics. You exaggerate everything."

"How then can you explain this?" She reached again for his penis which had hardened now. She looked downward and

22

watched it grow, fill out with its mysterious movement of blood, an enigma. "I was an innocent. I had never been unfaithful. I have been married fifteen years. I felt myself grow wet with yearning."

He reached downward for her organs, confirming the result of suggestion.

"You see. I am still that way."

"Purely chemical. Purely a physical reaction." He chided her playfully as two fingers massaged her nipples.

"When I came back you moved toward me. I saw you from a corner of my eye. Then I looked at Claude. I don't know why. Perhaps it was guilt. Perhaps I knew what was happening. But he was busy being intense and impressive. He is quite impressive, you know, quite eloquent."

"I'm sure he will be an ambassador at his next posting."

"He will be important someday. Quite powerful and influential. I must never embarrass him. It will destroy him." She felt her eyes begin to mist and a throbbing in her chest, a sob urgent to be heard. But she held it in, crushed it with her will.

"I brought you a glass of champagne."

"You came over with two. I could barely catch my breath when you came near me. My knees began to shake. I swear it. I wanted to refuse your offer of the glass. I felt that my fingers would be clumsy and I would spill some more on poor Monsieur Cardin's creation."

"But you took it and your hands didn't shake."

"It was a commitment even then. I must have subconsciously wished to take anything you had to offer."

"I said something silly," he responded shyly as his body moved downward, his lips brushing the soft skin of her belly.

"You said: Come we must toast beautiful women."

"Isn't that ridiculous?"

"I felt myself blushing and I knew that something was happening."

23

He moved downward further, his lips touching her pubic hairs. She reached for his hard organ, caressed it, kissed its head and shaft. She felt him tense, the hardness increase.

"It was the beginning of a madness. I hardly knew myself. I am a woman now," she said. "You have made me a woman."

He kissed her organs, titillating her clitoris with his tongue. She responded in kind, reveling in her newly found animality, this volatile chemistry that she had not thought possible. Then he was over her, maleness incarnate. She waited with quivering expectation, a bit of flotsam on an angry river, following the crashing tide. She wished she could stand outside herself and observe what was happening, what he was doing to her, so that she could enhance the experience of it. The sob began again, turning into a low moaning as his hardness entered her, filled her, and her heartbeat accelerated, the joy of it suffusing her body, her soul, every nerve end alert to his maleness. She floated on the rushing river, feeling the surge of ecstasy, a repetitive thrash of waves, washing over her as he continued to plunge inside of her. I do not deserve such a gift, she imagined she was telling herself, vaguely acknowledging the guilt of it, but no longer caring.

Actually, what she had been reobserving was the reality of the moment of their meeting, not the surface details. He had, indeed, offered the toast, duly made and ritualized. But, standing there in the crowded room, he had been quite ordinary, merely, she had thought then, following the protocol of the event. Of course, she noticed his eyes, silver specks in the gray, luminescent. How could she have avoided the compelling eyes?

"I am Eduardo Palmero," he had said. His English had little trace of accent, although the precision revealed it had been studied and was not an original tongue. Holding out his free hand, he took hers. She remembered the light pressure, but felt the fingers' strength. The touch was delicate but powerful.

"Marie LaFarge." She had hesitated, looking again over at

where Claude was standing. "My husband is the French minister."

"Ah, Madame LaFarge."

"Don't say it," she said, laughing, knowing she was showing her good white even teeth. It seemed a breach of the formality. But she had already begun to feel his closeness. "I don't knit."

He smiled. His teeth were also good and very white, against a skin slightly dark in tone, softened by the trim black mustache and the flared nostrils, another enigma in the dark face. These were details she was absorbing consciously. The touches of gray at the side of his head of full hair, slightly curled, the thin nose, a median size between aquiline and patrician. He was approximately six feet, slender, a man aging with grace. One might say oozing with charm, an errant thought at the time, since she did not want to think of his spontaneity as contrived.

"Italian?" she asked.

"My father's side. My mother was Spanish. Actually, I am a Chilean."

"With the Embassy?"

A brief cloud seemed to pass over his face, dulling the eyes, wrinkling the forehead, tightening the lips.

"No," he said coldly. "I am, for the moment, *persona non grata.*"

She knew at once. The wife of a diplomat is trained to understand. And living with Claude one dared not even seem ignorant of the games of nations, as he called them.

"Roumania," she said, sipping the champagne to mask embarrassment. "Yes, I see."

"Brothers under the skin," he remarked cheerfully with a slight movement of the glass toward his Roumanian host. "At least the exile gets a chance to eat and drink." He smiled again, moving closer, his eyes probing deeply now. She knew now she had fully gained his interest and it was flattering to her. She was being a flirt again, she realized. Claude would

105246

chide her about that, especially after a party when he had had too much to drink, which triggered his jealousy but made him amorous. The idea of it apparently excited him. "You flaunt yourself," he would say in French. Their intimate moments seemed to demand it. "It is all in your imagination," she would reply, but he was already close to her, his breath coming swifter, his face flushed. "There is a limit." It seemed a game, as if he were deliberately bringing himself up to a boil. "I am a true and faithful wife," she insisted. "You should be proud that men find me attractive." By then, he was fondling her. "You are a woman. You do not know what is in men's minds." What occurred was swift, violent, and, on his part, passionate. She wondered why nothing he did moved her. It was the major disruptive influence in their lives. She had mothered two children for him, did his bidding as a dutiful diplomatic wife, surely did not embarrass him, was supportive and outwardly loving. But he did not move her. For many years she had resolved that this is the way it really is. That there was something in her that could not be moved, a patina of cement, beyond which feeling could not penetrate. It was not only with Claude. No man had ever really moved her. The fact of it had made her seem dry and brittle to herself. Frigid. It was terrible to live with such an idea, she had decided. What was all the fuss about, she wondered. It was nothing, empty.

"There are many of us in this town," Eduardo had assured her, perhaps sensing her interest. Her eyes roamed his face. It intrigued her to see the moods flash across it, like lightning on a midsummer afternoon.

"Chileans?"

"Exiles. Mostly American citizens now. The world map has changed so radically in the last thirty years that the exiles can hardly tell from which country they have been exiled. At least, we in South America know where we are from."

She wondered if there was an edge of humor to his remarks. Tempted to enhance it, she nevertheless remained silent. It was

26

her diplomatic training. One never knew the cast of mind of a person of different nationality, Claude had warned. Different languages created different nuances. Words might be easily translatable, but not the value of the words in emotional terms. Guard yourself, he had warned. You might be speaking English, but you are thinking in French and he is thinking in his own language.

"We are revolution-happy," he said, smiling. Then the lightning came again and the smile faded. "Ours was the only real revolution since the conquistadors were thrown out. Sooner or later, we will win. We have just lost the first round." She noticed that his hands had balled into fists and he seemed to be wrestling internally with his rage.

She was fascinated, she admitted to herself, but she had no desire to hear his story now. It was inappropriate to be heavy in an event like this. Diplomatic receptions were essentially for surface talk. One nibbled at the leaves and left the roots alone.

"And you, Madame LaFarge?" he asked, unwinding, his anger fading.

"I am a diplomatic wife. We have spent the last fifteen years roaming the world. West Germany. Canada. Hungary. Cambodia."

She noticed that guests were beginning to leave and that Claude had glanced her way, nodding, the thin smile a harbinger of what she might expect later. This man was monopolizing her attention and it was getting obvious. She must excuse herself and reach her husband's side, a diplomatic maneuver. She held out her hand.

"It was so nice to meet you, Mr. Palmero," she said. He took her hand in his and she felt the power and electricity of his touch, an unmistakable surge of sexuality. This is absurd, she told herself. But her knees did shake and she could not deny the flow of her juices. What is it, she wondered, a wave of confusion breaking in her mind.

"We must meet again," he said, holding her hand and

27

looking into her eyes, the invitation blatant. It was the moment to deny it, to exercise deliberate indifference, to pour water on the hot coals.

"Yes, we must," she responded, knowing that she had exposed her essence. It was a totally new sensation, an enigma. My God, is this me, she wondered, withdrawing her hand and moving across the room to her husband's side. He introduced her to his companions while she watched Eduardo Palmero cross the room, graceful and confident, hardly the defeated exile that he wished to portray.

Later, when they arrived home, Claude admonished her playfully for her flirtatiousness. But he was secretly proud, she knew. Luckily, he had not taken much liquor.

"Who was that fellow?" he asked.

"Some South American," she said with feigned indifference.

Claude took her in his arms and pressed his pelvis against hers. She felt his hardness and she was imagining that it was Eduardo, and there was, she knew, more feeling in her response. Despite this, she remained unmoved.

Weeks passed and it still would not go away. She performed her daily tasks by rote, her mind fogged. The children were cared for and fussed over, suitably swathed in what she imagined was motherly love, disciplined, and otherwise parented. At times, they must have sensed her strangeness.

"What is it, Mommy?" Susan, her ten-year-old, would ask.

"It?"

"You have hung my skirt in Henry's closet."

"I can't imagine what I was thinking."

But she knew what she was thinking since she carried in her head always the graceful image of Eduardo Palmero, probing the message that he carried in his gray eyes with their flashes of silver. At times, when she was not pursuing some task, his image would become more animated as if he were calling to her from somewhere inside her brain. I am thirty-five years old, she would tell herself, not some dumb teen-aged ninny. I am a woman of the world, she assured herself, although secretly she knew that she had remained an innocent. Claude LaFarge had not been her childhood sweetheart. Actually, she had considered herself quite experienced with men by the time she had met him. She was a student at the Sorbonne, living with her parents in their big house on *Rue de Lyon.* Her father was a prosperous surgeon. Her mother was totally devoted to him. They entertained frequently and lavishly and it was at one of their soirees that she had met Claude, a rising young diplomat with the foreign office in Paris. Even then he was intense, totally immersed in political matters, but in those days she had been attracted by that and, of course, he had, by every standard of class and position, the impeccable credentials for a perfect match.

They had been married in the Cathedral of Notre Dame and spent their honeymoon in Marrakesh. Quickly, she rationalized the trauma of her sexual indifference. Her mother had hinted of it. Satisfy your man, she had confided. What more was there? Actually, she enjoyed being the wife of a diplomat, enjoyed living in foreign places, enjoyed her children. She enjoyed a happy marriage, she told herself. Claude was not indifferent and she sensed he was faithful and honorable.

If there were secrets they were those special ones that mates normally kept from each other, glossed over, sometimes forgotten, rarely violated. Sensible people forgave them silently. Nor had she ever dared confess them to the priests when she was still religious. She could not tell him, for example, that her cousin Michel, thick-witted and dull, was the first male she had seen in full sexual excitement. To this day, Michel might have felt that he had seduced her, but she knew that it had been she who had been the aggressor, her curiosity that had gotten him into that state. She had even let him put it part way into her and had watched; his eyes were closed when he had his climax and she was fascinated by the sight. Nor would she dare to tell him about the other young men at school

29

whom she had learned to satisfy by masturbation and some-times orally. In those days, the guilt had been deep, although the pleasure to herself illusive. Actually, her hymen had been ruptured by Pierre Damon, an intern who worked for her father, in the back seat of his car, but it had—like all the other experiences—been relegated to secrecy. Looking back, as she sometimes did, she concluded it was nothing, hardly worth the expense of energy. Actually, as time passed, the secret memo-ries took on an unreality, events that had never really hap-pened, and she hardly thought about them, going for years without consciously remembering.

Now she was remembering every detail and it annoyed her. This is not being me, she told herself. But what, after all, was "being me." Is this all, she wondered, reviewing her life with Claude and her children. And yet, it seemed so pedestrian a position to be in, a stereotype of the yearning, dissatisfied women in those American magazines geared to attract readers from those searching for "fulfillment." Am I like them? she wondered. A Frenchwoman was supposed to be different. She refused to let herself be depressed by such thoughts. Then why was she longing for another glimpse of Eduardo Palmero, and why was she experiencing physical signs of such longing? She would nervously survey the crowd at social events, at super-markets, at restaurants. And when she walked the streets her eyes were always fastened on the people on both sides of the street, looking for him. She had even looked up his name in the telephone books of the District of Columbia, Virginia and Maryland. It was not listed.

But she did enjoy fantasizing about him, picturing him with his arms around her. Kissing her face. There was something terribly exotic about her imagining that he was kissing her face, little pecks at her eyelids, her nose, her cheeks, her ears, then a long lingering kiss on her lips. Occasionally, she had caught herself staring into her mirror, mouth open, the image in front of her blurred, feeling wonderful.

"You seem so preoccupied, darling," Claude said to her one

evening when they were having dinner at home—a rare occasion. She felt it odd that he had noticed. It must really be showing, she thought, determined to be more guarded.

"Not really," she said, feeling her sudden need for secrecy. "Perhaps I am coming down with a cold."

It was while she was consciously being more guarded that Eduardo came back into her life, a disembodied voice on the telephone. It startled her, coming as it did in the middle of the day. Actually, she had heard the ring as a faraway intrusion in her mind as she lay on the bed taking an afternoon nap. Later, she would insist that it was *déjà vu*, that she knew it was he at the other end of the line.

She was cranky when she reached for the receiver, feeling weights on her eyelids and a heaviness in her arms and legs, a frequent aftermath of her afternoon naps.

"Mrs. LaFarge?" the voice enquired. It was deep and resonant with a touch of humor. Always, even in her memories of him, there was a touch of humor. The recognition quickly activated her adrenalin and she was fully alert in a moment.

"Yes, this is Mrs. LaFarge."

"I hope you will remember me. The Chilean fellow at the Roumanian do." He said "do" with a British lilt as if he were reading lines from a Noël Coward play.

She hesitated deliberately. Was it merely coquettishness? Or fear? She felt a sudden flush of' warmth and she actually looked into the mouthpiece as if she might see his face.

"Of course," she answered. "The Chilean." She had wanted to add with the silver-gray eyes and white teeth. Her hands began to shake.

"I never distrust first impressions," he said. There was no uncertainty. No wavering. He had been that sure of her from the beginning.

"I have always been taught to beware of first impressions." She was conscious now of being deliberately flirtatious. It is delicious, she felt.

"I thought perhaps we might have lunch."

31

She thought for a moment. It was not the first time that men had called. Lunch? It was a euphemistic term for tryst, a delicate first probe. Her response had always been: I never have lunch with men. Sometimes she actually had told her husband about it, knowing he would be secretly flattered. But not always, although she had turned down all offers. She had hesitated too long.

"I suppose you think it rather forward," he said. She wondered if his gray eyes looked innocent. Yes, she said in her mind.

"Is there any particular reason?" she began. She marveled at her own ability to prolong the titillation.

"Reason?" She pressed the earpiece closer. She could hear his breathing. "I suppose we must have a reason. All right then. I am seeking a French response to the Chilean question."

She had wanted to say: And what is the Chilean question? The problem, she giggled inwardly, is what is the answer to the immediate Chilean question?

"My husband would be far more knowledgeable." He must not think that I am easy, she told herself, shocked at the idea.

"I am interested in the woman's viewpoint. This is something peculiar to Chileans. Our women are extremely important. They have attained much in Chile." He had suddenly become political. Was the moment slipping away?

"Well, I suppose that is quite harmless," she said.

"Why are you talking about harm?" he asked. But the message had already been delivered, sealed and dropped irretrievably in the slot.

"All right," she said with finality. She had heard someone at the door. The children. Claude returning early.

"Tomorrow?"

"Tomorrow."

"La Niçoise in Georgetown. Twelve o'clock."

"Yes."

"Wonderful." The word seemed sincere. She hung up, lay

32

back, closed her eyes, picturing him again. Then it occurred to her that she had not said his name. Eduardo, she whispered. Eduardo Palmero. The door opened and her daughter burst into the room, rushing into her arms. She smelled of the outdoors, fresh and chilled.

Expectation and anxiety made it impossible for her to function smoothly. She forced herself to keep her mind on the business of her life. The children. The meals. Her husband's problems. He was fond of long monologues about what was happening at the office, the imagined slights, the little successes and glories. He had a tendency to brag about his prowess as a manipulator of people and he reveled in his calculated moves.

"I was born for intrigue," he would say, looking toward her for the expected supportive response. There was no end to his need for flattery. What a child, she thought, conscious now that she was already looking at him quite differently.

"You are very clever, Claude," she told him, putting more into it than she had ever done before.

"They are all jealous of my influence with the ambassador," he said, encouraged by her remarks. "The State Department calls me to get a reading before proceeding with him. Of course, I tell the ambassador and he is quite prepared to play the game."

"I never have doubts about my Claude."

"He is quite thick with Paris and he is talking more and more of pushing me for an ambassadorial post."

"Soon?" she asked, with what she imagined was wifely innocence. Her heart began to beat heavily. Not yet, she thought.

"Soon enough," he said testily. "The question is where. The right post. Someplace with contemporary importance. It is no good to be an ambassador to anywhere."

"Of course, Claude." She reached and patted his sleeve as he lifted his wine glass in what seemed like a toast to himself.

She managed to get through the night, spending nearly an

hour in the bubble bath before going to bed. She could not bear the thought of Claude touching her and was thankful that he was asleep when she crawled in beside him. She lay stiffly, not daring to move, as if the slightest movement would acknowledge her presence and trigger his desire to make love. But nothing could still the agitation of her mind and she forced herself to recall events in her life to calm her anxieties and keep her thoughts from Eduardo Palmero.

She remembered summers on the Riviera. Her parents had a summer home in St. Tropez and she and her girlfriends would spend their days on Tahiti Beach making sandcastles and teasing the beach attendant by hiding the beach pads behind the restaurant. The waters of the Mediterranean were deeply blue then. She recalled the restaurants along the quay, remembering each one as she walked past them observing the beautiful ladies and handsome men talking animatedly over their drinks. She had felt so unattractive then, gawky. She would stare at her reflection in the mirror for hours. "You will be beautiful one day," she assured her image, "and exquisite men will love you." The anticipation of all that would then fill her with joy.

"Still at the mirror," her mother would admonish. "What do you see in there?"

"Nothing," she would lie, guilty about her vanity, but reveling in the imaginary future. "Please, God, let me be beautiful," she said in her mind. That was long ago. Having grown up, she was not as certain that her prayers had been answered. Perhaps she looked beautiful, but she certainly had never felt beautiful.

The next morning, after she had gotten the children ready for school, she went up to her room and began to dress. She had forced herself to be particularly attentive to them, even to Claude.

"Wear the striped tie," she had said as he tied the knot in front of the mirror. Obediently, he loosened the knot and took the proffered striped one, reknotting it.

"Better?" he asked.

"Much."

Then he had kissed her on both cheeks and left the house. Soon after, the maid came in and she could hear the whir of the vacuum in the living room.

She could not still her excitement and her fingers shook as she applied her makeup. Taking particular care with the process, she looked at her face from many angles, finally finishing the job in the natural light near the bedroom window where the sun streamed in on this clear winter's day. During the night's restlessness she had decided on her costume for the day, but changed her mind as she stood in the sunlight, choosing a tailored skirt and white blouse instead of the beige pantsuit.

There was nothing special or symbolic about the choice, she told herself with a lack of conviction since the special cut of the blouse showed off her fine, still uplifted bosom, the nipples of which had been unaccountably hard all morning. Don't be such an innocent, she admonished her image in the mirror, seeing herself giggle like a young girl, enjoying the wickedness of it. There were other signs of involuntary sexual yearnings as well, but she put that out of her mind, concentrating instead on getting into her clothes, dabbing her perfume, patting her hair in a final survey of herself. She smiled into the glass, showing her even white teeth curling against the delicately rouged lips, wondering if others might think her as beautiful as she thought herself at that moment.

It was not until she had headed the car in the direction of Georgetown that she began to think of consequences. Suppose someone sees her? "Saw Marie the other day at *La Niçoise*, Claude," someone might say, a sneer of malevolence behind the mask of innocence. "Very attractive fellow she was with." "A man?" Claude might say, but with exquisite blandness, revealing no less an annoyance than at a fly resting on his arm. But inside, he would begin to churn and she would pay the price in pouting and moodiness.

35

"A perfectly innocent lunch," she could respond. "A wonderfully humorous fellow. You simply must meet him. He is planning a visit to Paris and was simply hungering for information. I told him to look up Mama and Papa."

Stumbling across this cover story restored her confidence, although arriving in the restaurant she nervously scanned the room for familiar faces, noting with relief that he had ensconced himself in a far corner in the shadows. How ridiculous, she thought, as she moved toward him, realizing that that was the first place the gossip seekers would look.

He stood up as she approached. He was actually taller than she remembered and his figure was slim and graceful in a well cut gray suit. He wore a tie with flecks of silver that matched his eyes. Reaching for her hand, he kissed it, but she was too nervous to respond with grace. Besides, her hand felt clammy and she was embarrassed.

"So good of you to come," he said, moving behind her to slide her chair. He seemed so confident, his manners impeccable. He is well-born, she thought, a bit of snobbery that she had once despised in her mother.

"And so good to see you again, Monsieur Palmero."

"Such formality. I am Eduardo."

"Yes, Eduardo." She hesitated. "And I am Marie."

He bowed his head and smiled. The eyes crinkled merrily in the corners. The waiter came over.

"Campari and soda," she said. He put up two fingers.

"So," he said when the waiter had gone. "I have you to myself at last."

"It is a small prize," she said, flattered, of course. She had always been modest, even deprecating, when confronted with effusiveness. Claude had remarked that she was fishing for compliments when she performed this little affectation. He was correct, of course. She felt Eduardo watching her and averted her eyes, looking at her fingers instead.

"I have thought about you often, Marie. I hope you will forgive my forwardness, but I felt that I must see you again, if only to talk. I feel privileged that you have come." She felt an odd kinship with him as she caught the foreign inflection in his flawless English.

Her eyes rested on his hands, the white skin and ridges of black hairs that covered them. Watching them, she felt a surge of electric excitement, wondering if the Campari she had just sipped had too quickly gone to her head.

"I am always delighted to be in the company of an attractive man," she said, knowing it was her voice, but hardly recognizing the words as her own. She was flattering him.

"Sometimes—" he said, eyelids flickering. There was a brief excess of moisture in his eyes, a glistening mist. "—I am assailed by an overpowering loneliness. They tell me it's the exile's syndrome and it attacks with great subtlety when one least expects it to occur. At that point, one feels entitled to a brief fling." He paused. "An innocent peccadillo. For a Latin," he assured her, "that means being with a beautiful woman."

She smiled. This is all so contrived, she thought. Then why am I loving it? Because I am vulnerable, she decided.

"You have no family?" she asked. The question reflected her own guilt.

He lowered his eyes and looked about him with suspicion.

"A wife and child in Santiago." She saw his lip quiver, more like a grimace than a sign of longing. Perhaps it was a subject too painful to broach. She remembered again Claude's admonishment. People of other languages and cultures react differently to emotions. She felt a sharp stab of jealousy and resisted the temptation to inquire further.

"And do you like Washington?" she asked. It seemed a logical question.

"It is necessary for me to be here." He laughed suddenly. "And I am easier for them to watch."

"Them?"

"The CIA. The DINA. Everyone watches everyone. It is a game."

"And are they watching us now?" she asked, frightened but

37

willing to be brave, feeling the sense of danger. Would Claude one day discover an account of this in some musty intelligence file?

She looked about the restaurant at the other diners. He watched her and smiled.

"We are having an innocent lunch." Reaching across the table, he placed his hand on hers, squeezing lightly. She looked into his eyes.

"Absolutely."

"Mostly," he said, pausing, cautious. "The anger sustains me. It can almost dispel loneliness."

"Anger?" A nerve palpitated in his jaw. He gripped her hand.

"We will destroy them one day." His eyes had narrowed. "We are assembling our weapons." A sense of danger thrilled her. She placed a hand on his.

"It will all work out. You'll see," she said, the inanity of the remark galling, as if she might be talking to a child. She had not expected her own reaction. It had thrown her off guard and she was annoyed with herself.

"We will make it happen." He drew in a deep breath, then watched her until, she assumed, the anger had drained. Then he smiled.

"There. That is better."

"What a beautiful gift you have given me," he said after a long pause.

"A gift?"

"The best gift of all."

"I don't understand." She was being a coquette now. He was making love to her and she was reveling in the pleasure of it.

"The gift of you. What could be more delicious? A sweet winter's day. The hint of culinary delights and a beautiful lady. My ecstasy is complete." He was surely mocking her with this stilted language, this contrived charm, she told herself. But it is irresistible, like something in an old-fashioned play.

They chatted lightly, the waiter refilling their drinks. She was relaxing now, telling him in detail about her children, her life, although she admittedly left gaps when it came to her husband. In fact, she barely mentioned him. They ordered fish, sole, after an elaborate explanation from the waiter on the ingredients of the sauce, and a bottle of icy Chablis.

"As cold as possible," he told the waiter. They continued to talk. She felt herself chattering away about her childhood and he hung on every word. What am I saying that is so important, she wondered, unable to stop herself from going on.

"My father was, still is, a rather pompous-looking fellow, a doctor. He wears a pince-nez, but once he walked into the house he never took himself seriously. He was, is, a marvelous mimic, making fun of his patients and everybody he had met that day and we would laugh until our sides split." She was remembering her most joyous moments and sharing them, wondering suddenly why she had never really done so with Claude. He is a perfect stranger, she thought, and I am telling him things I have not discussed in years. Finally, when the waiter had poured the last drop of wine she noticed that she had been doing most of the drinking. Surprisingly, she discovered that she didn't care. She was happy. She was alive. Then she felt his leg pressing against hers under the table, the touching an unabashed sexual signal. Vague stirrings were coming into focus. He seemed to sense them and his leg began to move rhythmically, stroking her. She could barely swallow.

"You are a flower," he said.

"I am a woman," she whispered. Again, she berated herself for her inanity. Her breath came swiftly now and her heartbeat was accelerating.

The restaurant had begun to empty. He called for the check, paid it, and they stood up. She felt a brief dizziness at the sudden motion, but it passed quickly. Outside he took her hand. It seemed so natural.

"Where is your car?" he asked.

She had forgotten.

"We will take mine."

"Where are we going?" she asked, knowing it was a formality that needed no answer.

She followed him across the street. He opened the door of his small car and she got into the front seat. Sliding in beside her, he took her in his arms, kissing her neck, drawing her face to his, pressing his lips lightly on hers, then suddenly with pressure. His lips felt soft, but strong and demanding, and his tongue darted into her mouth. She had no illusions about her body's demands, had known this would happen from the beginning. When he released her, he started the car and he drove silently toward Massachusetts Avenue. His hand held hers, tightly. It was a five-minute drive to his apartment. He found a parking space in the lot. Still holding her hand, he led her through the lobby. In the privacy of the elevator they embraced again and she felt the hardness in his pants and felt her voice screaming inside her. I am alive. I am alive. Later, she would not remember the first impression of his apartment, only that when the door closed behind them, the urgency of her sexuality made her tremble with pleasure. Her hands reached out to him, extensions of her nerve endings, groping for his flesh, the feel of it, the mysterious invisible pull of it, as if her body were in some magnetic field reacting to the beckoning of unseen forces.

Who am I, she wondered, an errant thought that intruded, as she actually got on her knees before him, unloosening his pants, kneeling before his erection, like a supplicant before a shrine. You are beautiful, she heard herself say, her eyes greedy for the sight of him as she kissed and caressed his manhood, feeling his hands on her hair. She was growing shivery with pleasure, the orgasmic urgency beginning, a sensation so rare in her life that she cried out with pleasure, unable to control the sounds in her throat.

Then she was being half-lifted to the bed and she felt his fingers undressing her, removing the pantyhose that she so

40

ceremoniously had put on just a few hours earlier. She lay back watching his body loom over her, saw the depths of the silver flecks in the gray eyes, the wonderful smile. A gift, she thought. It is my gift. And then she drew him inside of her as he plunged, gently at first, sliding inward, filling her up with a largeness that perhaps she had longed for, suffered for, wanted. The power of it, the pleasure of it made her gasp as he lingered for a moment and she moved her body to meet his, waited, drew back, returned again until he was moving into her with a hardness that she knew had never touched her experience before. I am being born again, her mind told her, as she began to tremble and shake, waves of pleasure unfolding like some vast repetitive surf responding to the cosmic pull of the moon. Inside of her, she felt his throbbing, the beat of his blood as it gained strength, then hesitated, like the tremulous flight of a predatory bird who glided, then moved downward toward its prey, an explosion of energy. She heard some inchoate sound, felt his shudder and the receding surf, feeling the inner spring of her body lose its tension, uncurl, search for silence and repose.

When she had recovered her sense of self, she wondered whether he had watched her and was suddenly ashamed.

"Look what you have done to me," she said, conscious now that her dress lay creased above her waist. He, too, was still wearing his shirt, the tie still neatly knotted.

"I don't know myself," she said, despite her disarray, feeling beautiful nestled in his arms, his hardness disappearing now, her mind responding to the details of hygiene.

"You are wonderful," Eduardo said.

"It is you who are wonderful." She was determined now to tell him. "I have never been moved like this. I swear. Never." She watched his face. Then he turned away.

"I meant it," she said. She had expected him to respond. But he said nothing, watching her, almost clinically. Had she moved him? she wanted to ask.

41

"I want to stay here forever," she heard herself say. I need this man, she told herself secretly. He was disengaging, now standing up, immodest about his nakedness. She looked at his penis, a beautiful gladiator in her imagery, glistening in repose, and she lifted her hand to caress it.

"You are beautiful," she said again, rising to kiss it. Then he moved away into another part of the apartment and she heard water running. Lying there, she could not believe she was the same person who had awakened in her bed that morning.

She looked about the apartment. It was sparsely furnished. The double bed on which she lay was actually a mattress on a Harvard frame. A bridge table piled high with papers, and books were everywhere, a forest of odd-shaped columns. There were bookshelves along one wall, crudely made, brackets stuck into the wall with shelving painted the dull white color of the walls, which were barren of pictures. Beside the bed was a night table with a reading lamp, and along the windowed wall, three piles of newspapers nearly reached the ledge. She noted that some were written in Spanish, some English. The blinds were slightly awry, furthering the transitory impression. It seemed incongruous and she could not place the neat handsome man in such a tumultuous environment. It was a cell, more like an animal's cage. On one of the chairs at the bridge table was a grease-stained box which once had contained a pizza. She noted, too, that no telephone was visible. She was so absorbed in her survey that she did not see him return.

"The den of an exile," he said. His voice startled her. Recalling her modesty, she stood up and primly patted her dress. He had apparently showered and his curly hair had blackened with the dampness. He looked younger.

"It needs a woman's touch," she said, suddenly embarrassed as he stared at her. She saw her shoes, like stray bricks from a ruin, on the carpetless wooden floor. Beside them, her pantyhose lay in a crumpled heap. Gathering them up quickly, she went into the bathroom. It was damp from his shower and the

42

one towel on the rack was wet. A ring of dirt circled the white porcelain sink, above which lay a thin sliver of soap from a tiny bar, perhaps from some hotel. A single toothbrush, the bristles worn, lay in the porcelain holder. In the mirror, she saw that her eyes had filled with tears. Everything is changed, she thought. Her old life was dead. Removing her dress, she washed with great fastidiousness, as if the careful cleansing might erase the guilt that had begun to tug at her.

When she had put herself together, repairing her makeup, she came into the room where he was standing against the wall. He had raised the blinds and was staring into the street, watching the cars move along Massachusetts Avenue. She caught him in profile, deep in thought, intent on some probings. Hesitating, she watched him, a stranger. There was an illusiveness about him, something uncapturable. Perhaps, she wondered, it was because she had only received enough information to sense him, not yet to know him, which is what she wanted now. To know him. To really know him. She moved beside him and kissed his earlobe. He put his arm around her, still staring into the street. She followed his eyes, wondering what was absorbing him.

"What is it?" she asked.

"Occasionally, I think I see the Cordillera."

"The what?"

"The Andes. The spine of Chile. Sometimes, I see a mirage."

She looked out the window.

"It is only a parking lot." She wished she could also see the Cordillera.

"Yes," he sighed and continued to stare out of the window.

She reached for his hand, kissed his fingers.

"I will make you happy, Eduardo."

He looked at her, his eyes clear and bright.

"I feel..." she hesitated, feeling again the pang of guilt, remembering her children, Claude, her neat and ordered life. She had betrayed them all. A weight materialized in the pit of

43

her, lay there, temporarily formidable, indigestible. I must not think about it, she warned herself. I must separate my life, my needs. . . .

"I feel like a woman," she whispered. "For the first time in my life. I feel like a woman." She remembered her pleasure now in his arms, the waves of ecstasy. Moving away from her, he looked at his watch. The gesture made her sad. Time is the enemy, she knew, sighing as her mind filled with the impending details of her ordinary life. The children would be coming home from school.

"I must go now," he said, looking at his watch. The act pained her. "They will be wondering." She wanted to ask 'who?', the sudden sense of possession compelling, the urge to be curious an irritant. Who dared to preempt "her" time?

"Yes," she agreed, searching for her pride. She did not want to mention her children, her home. Like his, it was another world, not theirs.

"We must have more time together," she whispered as they walked toward the door. It was another unintentional articulation. Why must I put a voice to every thought, she wondered. Claude would have been more calculated, subtle, choosy in his use of words. There seemed a great void between them. It was as if she had taken the first bite of a beautifully prepared and delicious concoction and someone had taken it away from her. It had titillated her hunger and she wanted to finish it.

"When?" she asked as they stood in the elevator.

"I will call you," he said.

"When?"

"Soon."

"But you have no telephone," she said, feeling instantly ashamed of revealing what she had discovered, as well as the illogic of her response.

"In my business, the telephone can be an enemy," he said with an air of finality.

She watched as he hailed a passing taxi, then opened the

door for her when it pulled up the sloping driveway. She had expected him to drive her back to her car. But she shrugged off her disappointment and slid into the back seat, lifting her hand in a half-hearted wave of farewell. Again she felt a pang of loss, but she forced herself to concentrate on the problem of finding her car and she gave the driver directions to the restaurant.

III

Knowing what he knew, Dobbs felt a rare sense of anticipation as he looked at the formidable materials strewn across the table that dominated one side of his office. He had asked for every available bit of data on Eduardo Allesandro Palmero. He was after the distilled essence of the man, the core of him. Before, it had only lapped at the edges of his consciousness, as if his mind were a remote ocean beach. Now the waves were crashing, dominating in their power. He wanted to know more, if that was possible.

He did not merely want summaries. He wanted raw data as well, information gathered routinely or in white heat. Was he being professional, he wondered, or was there something in himself demanding the knowledge? Or was it pique at his own miscalculation, his inability to understand the real motives of the human animal? Is this what they call a crisis of confidence, he speculated, a reflection of his own impotence, or ignorance? It was not the wasting of a human life that burdened him, only his blindness to the possibilities of how it might occur.

Three women. Eduardo's women, Marie LaFarge, Frederika Millspaugh, Penelope Anne McCarthy. Moving a chair closer to the table, he settled comfortably and fingered the material. Then he sighed and began sifting and shuffling until he found something that triggered a response—a tiny landmark, a detail in a map, something that might synthesize his own mind and heart with those of Eduardo. It was important to know what had gone wrong. He had been so sure of his actions. The surveillance. The entire scenario seemed so logical. Why had this happened? He looked at the mass of files before him. One must always go back to the beginning. He broke a seal, opened the file.

Born in Santiago in 1936, weight eight pounds, completely bald at birth, skin pink, healthy, a moneyed family, landed aristocracy on his mother's side, a huge home in Santiago's suburbs where the ground sloped upward to the Cordillera and the view of the Pacific was spectacular. The wealthy always took the best locations to build their monuments and pursue their diversions. The father, Manuel, had been also born in Santiago, his father before him a Neapolitan fisherman who arrived penniless in 1901. A migration of necessity, Dobbs mused, noting that the DINA analyst had suggested an escape from the Carabinieri rather than a legal immigration. In those days, one did not bother with the fine legal points of immigration.

There was also the hint of another family, left in a Naples slum, but, if true, that did not stop the grandfather from finding solace in the arms of Rosa, who at fourteen seemed to have been bartered for the grandfather's labor aboard her own father's fishing boat. He was fifty at the time. Dobbs imagined himself, fifty-five now, already dry. Comparisons were odious, he knew, wasteful. It was, in addition, unprofessional. Rosa had been the mother of Manuel, but she had died of diphtheria before she was twenty and somehow her husband had wound up with her father's boat.

The Latin mind could embroider lavishly, Dobbs knew. But

48

antecedents carried clues and they were beginning to emerge.

The DINA material told of still another wife, Concetta, sixteen. So, he is getting interested in older women, Dobbs chuckled, the thought dispelling for the moment the odd self-pity aroused in himself. Four additional children emerge, half brothers and sisters, duly recorded by the birth registrar at the Church of Cabrine, honoring the saint of the fisherman. And there are two additional births recorded. Two different mothers. Apparently, the grandfather was an honorable man, accepting the responsibilities of his fornications.

Energies apparently remain to acquire a fleet of fishing boats, a moderate monetary success, enough to send Eduardo's father to the University, then to law school, to gather expertise in marine law—no small thing in a land with little else than copper and two thousand miles of coastline.

Dobbs had never been to Chile, but he had read enough to imagine it, the Cordillera stretching into the infinite blueness of the sky, the incredible blue Pacific and, in between, the lush land in the south and the dry craggy earth to the north. It is the mountains, the diet, the iodine in the fish, and the earthquakes that make them crazy, he had been told.

The father, Manuel, had married Carlotta Ramirez. The DINA analyst included clippings from the leading paper of Santiago, evidence of the lavish fanfare of the event. There is a picture of Eduardo's mother, stiffly resplendent in her bridal gown, and a report of a reception for three hundred people. So, the son of the Italian fisherman does pretty good for himself, Dobbs thought, shifting in his chair. The analyst describes their house, a gift from the bride's parents, their beachside villa, also a gift. There is an element of envy in the report. The bureaucrat's eye-view of the gentry. They are newlyweds. He is twenty-four. She is eighteen and they have six servants, the analyst says—bitterly, it seemed to Dobbs, who wondered whether it was his own inner voice that had embellished the sarcasm.

So, the stage was set, Dobbs thought, getting up to stretch

his legs, as if he needed some respite before plunging again into the mists of Eduardo's past.

Eduardo, like his father, was the first son. Other children follow, three daughters. Obviously, the DINA had interviewed all the servants, gardeners, and maids, who gave their version of the early days of the Palmero household. Can one reconstruct a man's essence from this, Dobbs wondered, continuing to read. The mother was indulgent, spoiled, materialistic, short-tempered, aloof, cruel to the servants. The father was away on business often. The young Eduardo was bookish, withdrawn, but athletic, excelling in sports and scholarship. Dobbs pictured him in his mind, the tanned skin glowing, the lean body graceful as it moved in the woman-dominated household.

The prince of privilege was given anything he wanted, including the indulgence of his mother, whose meager fount of affection began and ended with Eduardo. Even the sisters were indulgent through their jealousy. Did he manipulate them even then, Dobbs wondered, feeling his figurative nose warm to the scent. Then as the daughters disappeared into convent schools, the mother began to travel.

There was one maid, Isabella. The interrogators found her in a mountain town where the Trans-Andean Railroad chugs over the Cordillera to Buenos Aires. Dobbs paused, knowing that he had reached the first clearing in the trail, searching the woman's words, so scrupulously recorded by the DINA agents. Mutual enemies make strange bedfellows, Dobbs observed, his mind floating into the past, seeing Isabella's skin soften, lighten, grow supple, young. . . .

Eduardo had not noticed her at first. Perhaps it was simply that at thirteen it did not occur to him to notice her since the house was always filled with women, sisters, his mother, multitudes of female servants, and his life was filled with other things. Not that he was oblivious to the female form and the stirrings it could arouse. But he lived mostly in his imagination then, and the women in his dreams were those that he had met in his books, sweet and lovely, while the women in the household with their pots of creams, their manufactured scents, their hairpins and curlers, their sloppy bathroom leavings, dampened any ardor he might have felt in his adolescent heart. Attendance at a boy's school gave him an even more distorted view, and watching the older boys masturbate confused him further, although his curiosity deepened as his body matured.

She seemed to have been employed in a single role, to keep fresh flowers neatly arranged in vases throughout the house. He hardly had ever looked at her, although he seemed always to come across her heavily laden with either fresh-cut or decaying flower stems as she padded barefoot, like a frightened kitten, through the house. She was taller than most of the other young servants, with jet black hair which fell madonna-like and glowing from a central part.

They were at the dinner table, the long polished rectangle laden with overabundance, his father's chair empty, the sisters chattering, while his mother sat sullenly at her end of the table. It was school vacation time and the girls had brought home friends who raised the decibel level with their endless high-pitched patter. Squat uniformed servants scurried about, pouring, serving the varied menu, carrying deep steaming dishes from which the family helped themselves in turn. When his father was absent, Eduardo was always served first.

He might have seen her peripherally as she puttered at a vase at the far corner of the room, one of his mother's prized Mings in which she was placing bunches of yellow autumn flowers. His gaze, he remembered, had just floated upward as his mother reached, with the long silver spoon, into a bowl of steaming vegetables. Her general annoyance and ill-humor, combined with her abstracted indifference, caused some of the vegetables to drop from the spoon onto the bare feet of the serving woman, who promptly dropped the dish with a resounding crash. It might have been a simple accident if it had not triggered a reaction in Isabella, who turned suddenly, her fingers caught on a stem, and the Ming vase crashed to the polished tile floor.

The sudden explosion and the reality that it was a priceless Ming seemed to draw all the anger and annoyance that had been congealing in his mother's mind. She stood up, the cords in her neck bulging as she stood towering over Isabella, from whose face the blood had drained, turning the pink glow to an ashen white.

"You dirty little bitch," his mother screeched, slapping the girl repeatedly on both cheeks.

"Forgive me, mistress," the girl mumbled, lifting her face as if welcoming the blows as penance.

"That was priceless, you whore," his mother cried. "Look what this monster has done!"

"That clumsy little devil," one of his sisters said.

His mother grabbed the girl by the shoulders and began to shake her, the silken hair flowing as if caught in the eddy of a heavy wind.

"I will not have this! I will not have this!" his mother cried. Eduardo could see the harried faces of the servants poking out of the kitchen.

"You illiterate, incompetent little whore!" his mother screamed, repeating "little whore" until her anger reduced the epithet to a long piercing shriek.

Finally, Isabella's stoicism crumbled and a low cry seeped from her chest, stirring him to compassion. He assumed it was compassion, since he empathized now and could feel and understand the girl's pain.

"Enough, Mama!" he cried, standing up and banging on the table. Perhaps it was the sound of a male voice or simply the emphatic crack of his fist, but it was enough to cause his mother to take her hands off the girl. She must have been frightened by the outburst and had run screaming from the room while Isabella slumped to the floor like an injured animal whimpering with mortification and fear. Finally, one of the older servants lifted her from the ground and led her away through the kitchen door.

That night he relived the incident in his mind, feeling again the empathy and compassion for this girl who was hardly more than his own age. But beyond the pity, beyond the knowledge of her suffering he recognized in himself for the first time a kinship with the servants. He felt ashamed for his mother, his sisters, and he determined that his father must intervene to stop any further abuse. What was a vase compared to a human being?

The next day he searched the grounds of their estate for her. He found her puttering in a flower patch, kneeling in the soft earth. When she saw him, she stiffened and burrowed deeper in the earth with a trowel, ignoring his presence, her long hair spilling over her face, the ends almost touching the ground.

"You mustn't be afraid," he said kneeling beside her. She continued to work, ignoring him.

"I apologize for my mother," he said gently. "Really, she will forget all about it soon. I know she will." He doubted that. His mother held an endless supply of scorn and vindictiveness, especially for servants, a fact well known in the household. Whatever enmity was left was reserved for his father, whom Eduardo adored.

"She will send me away," the girl said finally, swallowing hard to keep back her tears. Life in the poor villages was a terrible struggle. In a rich household, one ate regularly.

"It wasn't your fault," Eduardo said. He patted her arm. The touch of her flesh warmed him, confusing his motives. She was bent over and her full breasts pressed tightly against her blouse. Despite his compassion, he was conscious of searching the fabric for the outlines of her nipples.

"I was not careful," she said.

53

"It was an accident."

He felt the power of his own protection, seeing her even now in a different way, confused by a new implication. She is beautiful, he decided, as she glanced up at him, her large dark eyes reflecting her vulnerability.

"It will be all right," Eduardo insisted.

"She will send me away," the girl repeated. "Nothing can stop it." Servants were always being discharged, some for cause, others out of pique, or simply to reinforce the authority of the family over their lives. For Isabella, the fear was both tangible and logical. He stood up, towering over her. Still on her knees in the flower beds, she looked up at him.

"I will not let them," he said. It was a solemn commitment. "I swear on my life." He had actually put a hand over his heart. Then he turned from her and walked swiftly back to the house. For the first time in his life, he felt the power of his manhood. Without turning, he knew her eyes were following him.

That night his mother did not come down for dinner and he took her dinner tray to her bedside. It seemed a perfect ploy for ingratiation. She was always especially vulnerable when she was wallowing in self-pity. Reclining on a bubble of pillows, she was doing her nails. She wore a brocaded bed jacket and her hair had been fastidiously done in an upsweep by one of the servants. Actually, she was quite beautiful. And she always pretended to be sick on the eve of his father's return. He was still not of an age when he could grasp the complex relationship of his parents. When they were together publicly, they were stiff and polite. Privately, behind their bedroom door, they shouted and argued. Finally, his father's absences became increasingly longer and his mother's irritability increased. Dutifully, Eduardo kissed his mother's cheek after he had arranged the tray securely over her blanketed thighs.

"How sweet, my darling," she said softly.

"Are you better?" he asked, perching himself carefully on the foot of the bed as she sipped her soup.

"Better, yes," she said between sips. "That incident with the vase unnerved me, I suppose. I am calmer now."

"You must not get so upset. It was only a vase. A material thing."

"An old possession is not to be taken lightly," she said, pointing the spoon at him. "Considering that one day you will be the head of this family, we will all look to you to protect our possessions." Like his father, she was obsessed with the idea of family responsibility. The family, the blood, ownership . . . that was her principal obsession. The idea of it had been drummed into him very early.

"I understand that, Mama," he said. He waited for her mood to change. "It wasn't really her fault," he said finally, his throat constricting despite his strong attempt to appear nonchalant. He knew he was testing the waters.

"Not her fault?" Her spoon, poised in mid-air, dropped back into the soup. He had badly miscalculated. "Eduardo, you do not know about servants. Don't be fooled by their apparent humility. They would cut our throats if they could get away with it. Nothing is ever done by accident. It is all deliberate. In my father's time, they would be whipped."

He had heard that all before, but for the first time the imagery was clear. He shivered, thinking of the small, helpless Isabella kneeling in the soil. Behind his eyelids, he could feel the well of tears begin.

"We must never forget who we are," said his mother. "And we must never forget who they are."

He stayed for a while longer, then left, kissing his mother on both cheeks. He had bungled it. He had failed her. He cursed his stupidity and lack of courage. He should have demanded mercy for her. He was, after all, a man.

Those among the servants who had chosen to protect Isabella kept her out of the house and handled the flower arrangements for her. It was not uncommon for them to wait out their mistress' wrath. Keeping her out of sight might save her, although it was doubtful. Mrs. Palmero had the memory of an elephant, and she was brutally vindictive and unmerciful. Meanwhile, Eduardo visited her in the garden, reassuring his commitment.

"As soon as I am noticed, she will send me away."

"Not as long as I am here," he bragged.

"You are still only a boy," she mocked gently.

"I am a man."

His father's return was always an event in the household. They had been told he was away on business. Since he was Chile's foremost authority on marine law, and much in demand, it was a logical story. Much primping and polishing would ensue and his handsome father's appearance at the end of the long polished table was always celebrated. However, it was not long before the tension between his mother and father would begin to emerge beneath the surface of their public attitude.

"Rio is glowing," his father said, describing the city from which he had just returned. "At night the skyline looks like a mass of fireflies."

"Fireflies are not the only insects that come out at night," his mother would snap and the girls would lower their eyes in embarrassment. His father's eyes would smolder and he would pat his lips nervously with his napkin.

After a few days of accelerating domestic warfare, Eduardo knew that his father was contemplating another trip. His lips had grown tighter than when he had arrived and the pinched look under his eyes was more noticeable.

But while he consciously measured his mother's and father's temper, he spent most of his time with Isabella, either sitting near the remote flower beds that edged their property or accompanying her on trips to gather the wild autumn flowers that crept up the foothills of the massive Cordillera. In the distance, the craggy frost-tipped peaks watched over them like sentries.

56

She was a simple girl from a small village in the remote upper reaches of the Cordillera. She could not read or write, but she was intelligent and quite beautiful with her long silken hair and dark eyes that peered up at him from under heavy curling lashes. She insisted on calling him "Señor Palmero."

"I am Eduardo," he would say proudly, holding both her hands as they paused in their walk, looking into her eyes.

"I cannot call you that," she said shyly, her head bowed.

"But that is my name."

"I am Isabella, but you are Señor Palmero."

"I am Eduardo." He brought his face closer to hers. Their noses were almost touching. "Eduardo!" he shouted. "My name is Eduardo!" When she did not respond, he shook his head and smiled. But he could not keep his eyes off her, watching her effortless walk as she moved swiftly up the slope trails.

He was, he knew, unable to relate the romantic notions abstracted from his books and the crude talk and actions of his schoolmates. His physical reaction was not unlike theirs, but his thoughts seemed quite different. There was another element, too, to his relationship with Isabella.

". . . and you must stay away from the servants," his mother had warned, concentrating her most formidable admonishment on him after one of her numerous lectures to her daughters. She had drawn him aside. Vaguely, he could remember an incident preceding her warning. A servant girl had been dismissed for pregnancy.

"They are filthy and diseased. They will make your parts rot."

He had only been ten at the time and it was a long time before he would know what "parts" meant. At the time, he thought it might be his eyes.

"Do you get it by touching?" he had asked innocently. His mother had contained a smile for a moment, then burst out laughing.

"Not by touching," she said, between side-splitting howls, further confusing him.

So there was some element of danger in consorting with this girl, he knew, although he was still not completely certain how one crossed the Rubicon to this physical hell. He knew by now what "parts" meant. Isabella, too, sensed the fear in him and the danger to herself.

"You should not be with me," she would say, when sounds of others could be heard on the trails, and they would hide in the brush, their heads close, their hearts pounding, as the footsteps would come toward them and fade again. Once he had kissed her hair and an elbow had brushed her breast, an action from which she recoiled in fear.

"No!" she had hissed, like a cornered cat.

"I meant no harm."

She began to cry lightly. He wondered what had upset her.

"They will surely send me away," she whispered between sniffles.

"Never!" he vowed, enjoying his sense of bravado with its implication of manly protection. Tentatively, his arm reached out for her shoulders and she let him briefly caress her. Then, standing up, she led him back to the trail. But the touching had profound effects on him.

"Will you be my girl?" he asked as they paused again on the trail. She put a finger on his lips.

"They will send you away as well."

"Me?" he chuckled. He turned and looked back at the house and the Pacific sparkling in the distance. "I am the firstborn," he said with imperial seriousness, as if the idea had been intoned by his parents. He beat his breasts like Tarzan and shouted across the expanse, "I will be the master here."

"You are frightening me, Señor Palmero."

He turned toward her.

"I am Eduardo," he said. He reached for her. Whatever resolve she might have had vanished. He gathered her close to

58

him, feeling the mounds of her breasts against his chest. "And you are Eduardo's girl." She nestled closer for a long moment. He felt the hardness begin. She must have felt it as well. Then she broke away and ran swiftly down the trail. He could not catch her and both of them slowed as they drew closer to the house. Even then, he knew why. The act of chasing a servant girl was, after all, inappropriate to the firstborn.

But that did not stop him from thinking about her and wanting to fulfill his commitment to protect her. He determined to enlist the help of his father to prevent her dismissal. Indeed, it was his father who selected the opportunity one night at dinner.

"I do not see the Ming," his father said, as his eyes searched the sideboard where it had stood for years. Eduardo felt his heart stop.

"Oh, so you noticed," his mother said. "One of our clods of a servant dropped it and it broke into a million pieces. Now you see what I must go through in your absence?" She began to work herself up. It was an accident, Eduardo wanted to scream, but he held his peace. "If I ever see that little snip, I will kill her!" his mother cried.

"Well, it was quite expensive," his father mumbled, as if the outburst required a reply to assuage it.

"Expensive? It was priceless!" she said maliciously, as if his father's observation had merely been perfunctory. "I simply will not put up with such conduct."

His father lowered his head and shrugged, his mother's venom continuing to spew in an endless cacophony, actually the litany of her own frustration in which Isabella was only a handy, vulnerable and dispensable conduit.

Later his father retired to his heavily ornate study. Finding his courage, Eduardo followed him. The study was his father's sanctuary with its endless rows of law books and high windows which, when opened, as they were now, brought in the sounds and smells of the Pacific Ocean.

59

"Father?" It was, he knew, the voice of the supplicant. When he entered the study, which was sacrosanct, it meant that important things were afoot.

"Eduardo?" His father looked up over his glasses. He had been slumped over his desk scratching at a pad, an opened law book at his elbow.

Noting his son's seriousness, the father removed his glasses and leaned back in the heavy leather chair. Eduardo, following the direction of his father's extended palm, sat on the straight-backed chair beside the huge carved desk. In that position, his father looked kingly, a god, with the power to grant mercy. He must, Eduardo decided, make a clever presentation.

"I must talk to you about the Ming," Eduardo said, his voice cracking, as it was doing frequently these days.

"The Ming?" The father nodded, remembering. Eduardo noted how quickly he had put the subject out of his mind.

"It is a matter of simple justice," Eduardo said, knowing that such a thesis would draw his father's attention.

"I saw it happen. It was purely an accident," Eduardo said, the words coming too fast. He urged himself to slow down, but he could not control the flow. "The serving maid had dropped this dish and the crash frightened the girl who turned and a stem caught on her sleeve and the Ming fell to the floor and broke."

His father's eyes narrowed over thick eyebrows, a sign of his concentration. He has been engaged, Eduardo thought happily. Indifference had been his principal fear.

"And Mother attacked the person." He was studiously avoiding the use of her name, attempting to simulate his own distance as an observer only. "It was wrong. Unjust." He emphasized the word, letting it sink into the salt-tinged air. "It is our responsibility to deal with the matter justly," he concluded, mimicking his father.

His father smiled, perhaps proud that his son had absorbed the lesson.

"Has she been dismissed?"

"No," Eduardo said, hastening an explanation. "She has stayed out of sight and the housekeeper has not yet acted. But there is no doubt that Mama will erupt when she sees her again. Mama does not forget."

"And have you discussed this with your mother?" Eduardo could sense the lawyer's mind turning over.

"How could I?" he answered helplessly. Then quickly: "It is a matter of justice. There is genuine fear in this house. I am sure all of the servants are troubled and the poor girl must be living in hell."

His father pondered the young face before him. Eduardo was conscious of the clear eyes caressing him. He loves me, he told himself. Not that the matter had ever been in doubt. And I love him. He wanted to tell his father the truth, but held back.

"I am asking you to give this woman justice, Father," Eduardo said, warming to the request. "To do what is right." He knew that, despite the growing animosity with his mother, his father's word was law in the house. No servant would dare go against his orders, regardless of what his mother might do.

"I believe you should speak to her," Eduardo pressed, hoping that his father, seeing Isabella, would observe her helplessness, understand her vulnerability. And, more important, it would prove to Isabella that Eduardo had kept his word, that he had protected her.

His father stirred, stood up and pulled the bellrope to summon a servant, who arrived quickly.

"What is this person's name?" he asked.

"I am not sure." He wondered if his hesitation had been duly noted. "Isabella, I think." His father turned to the servant.

"Send Isabella here." The servant looked at Eduardo briefly, a stab of fear in his eyes, then hurried away.

When he had gone, his father embraced him. He was still a

head taller than Eduardo. He pressed him close, kissing him on the cheek.

"I am pleased with you, Eduardo," he said, patting his back. "You have the sensitivity to understand. We are all God's creatures and He laid down the rules for our meting out justice. I understand."

He wanted to kiss his father's hands but hesitated since he had often seen the servants do that. Instead, he settled for an *abrazo* and left the room quickly, heading out to the long patio that adjoined the study's high windows, settling himself in the shadows, braced in a corner against the chilly breeze floating in from the ocean.

He did not have long to wait. His father had resumed his work, replacing his glasses on the bridge of his nose and scratching his pen along the pad. Isabella's knock was furtive, barely audible to his father, although Eduardo had heard it clearly. Then it came again, a bit more assertive, and his father raised his head. "Come in," he called. He looked over his glasses as the pale and frightened Isabella entered the room. She had apparently put on her best dress, although she was barefoot, and brushed her long hair. Eduardo's heart lifted when he saw her. His father waved her forward and contemplated her. Her head was lowered, her eyes watching the floor shyly. But her carriage was straight and her young breasts strained against the tightness of her dress. If only he could hold her now, Eduardo thought. Surely, when she sees how I have protected her, she will let me hold her in my arms, he thought with excitement.

"You are Isabella?" his father asked gently.

Isabella nodded. Señor Palmero watched her for what seemed like a long moment. It was a look of contemplation. He took off his glasses and moved slowly in front of his desk, standing over the frightened grl. Reaching out, he put a hand under her chin and lifted her face.

"You are quite charming," he said. Isabella stood rooted to the spot. Her face was visible now, the eyes still lowered.

"You must not be afraid," his father said gently. "I am here to help you, to protect you."

Why doesn't he mention me, Eduardo thought. His implicit faith in his father's wisdom was not shaken. He will tell her soon.

"I believe it was an accident," his father said. "Am I correct?"

Isabella nodded, her eyes still lowered.

"I believe it was not your fault."

Isabella moved her head from side to side.

"And I know that you would not like to be sent back."

Isabella moved her head from side to side again.

Señor Palmero paused, his eyes moving furtively around the room. He stepped away and slowly moved toward the door, securing the latch to it, talking as he walked. Eduardo was confused.

"Sometimes the mistress becomes overwrought when she sees her possessions broken. It is perfectly natural," Señor Palmero said, returning to face the girl, who had lowered her head again when his palm had removed its support.

"You must not be afraid," he said quietly. "I am the master of this house and will not hurt you. Do you believe that?"

Again he reached out and cupped her chin in his hand.

"Do you believe that?" he repeated.

Isabella nodded. What is he doing, Eduardo thought. A panic seized him as he saw his father's hands touch Isabella's breasts, cupping them, pinching them lightly. Isabella's eyes continued to look downward. But she did not move. Father, please, he shouted within himself.

"You understand I will not hurt you, Isabella?" Señor Palmero said. She could not nod now, his hand under her chin prevented it. Then his hand moved downward to her crotch, caressing her, slowing lifting her dress, showing her bare legs.

Eduardo felt his heart pumping. No, he wanted to shout, but the word was lost in the gurgle in his chest. He watched, riveted, as his father lifted the girl's dress over her head, revealing the small body, the flesh like light burnished copper, the thatch of hair at the crotch jet black. His father worked his hand between the girl's legs now and she began to undulate, hesitantly, then with greater abandon.

"I will not hurt you, Isabella," his father repeated again and again, unhitching his belt, then lowering his pants, revealing a huge phallus in full erection.

"Do you know what this is?" he said. A deep flush had risen on his face. He did not wait for her response. "Have you ever had this in you?"

The girl shook her head. Her eyes were open now and she looked at the object with some interest.

"You must kiss it, then," the father said, as the girl got on her knees and began kissing and stroking.

My God, Eduardo shouted within himself, sensing his brutal betrayal. He wanted to run, to hurl himself over the cliff to the crashing ocean below. But his legs would not move. He wanted to cry, but tears would not come. He wanted to shout, but he couldn't find his voice. Worse, he could not tear his eyes away from the sight. His father's eyes were closed now and the girl was moving instinctively, mesmerized, her tongue licking the shaft of his father's penis. Finally, he turned away, sensing the superhuman effort of his will and the beginning of emptiness in the pit of his stomach. Justice, he sneered, spitting into the wind, feeling the moisture return, sensing the essence of his disgust.

Dobbs shook his head. Was there some clue here, he wondered, moving the file away with the tips of his fingers as if it were an object of some revulsion. He stood up, walked across the large office, returning only when he felt the press of time.

IV

It was not easy for Marie to separate her two lives. Her mind was filled with thoughts of Eduardo. She fantasized about being with him, relived her experience in his apartment, tried to feel and touch him in her imagination, sometimes with uncanny success. But her main fear was that someone, her children, Claude, would see into her thoughts. If only she could tell them how beautiful it was, tell someone about it.

Perhaps it was a form of compensation, but she seemed to work harder at being a mother and companion for Claude. She marveled at her own toleration of her husband's egocentricity and bad temper. When anything had gone wrong with his day Claude had a tendency to bring home his hostility and edginess. He would pick fights with her, criticize her, insult her. Normally, she drew on practiced reserves.

"You mustn't take it out on me."

"I'm not. I'm merely stating the obvious. You are not informed. You don't read the newspapers enough. It is frustrating to come home to a wife who is ill-informed."

This was a familiar refrain. But she had her defenses.

"My job is to take care of the children. Maintain our home. My priorities are different than yours."

"I will outgrow you," Claude would warn, his eyes blazing with anger, focusing his wrath and frustration on her. The implied threat had always struck a note of fear.

Now, she was more tolerant when this theme surfaced again.

"I will try to read more, Claude," she would say, defusing his anger by her feigned contrition. She would be amused by this line. What does it matter, she thought. I have my other life.

At night, before she could empty her mind and fall asleep, she would think about Eduardo, his loneliness and the power and strength of his sexuality. But if there was happiness in the memory, there was sadness in the yearning.

After three days, when he did not call, she began to grow anxious. Without a telephone, he was simply unreachable, and it took a great effort of will on her part not to return to his apartment house, although she would deliberately plan her chores to drive past it. She had had lunch with him on Tuesday. Finally he called on Friday. Hearing the phone ring, she knew instantly that it was him.

"Marie?"

"Eduardo?"

There was a whisper in his voice, as if he were frightened that he would be overheard.

"I called you yesterday, but left no message."

"I was out," she said. "That was very wise." There was a long pause. She heard his breathing.

"Can you see me?" he whispered. The words seemed furtive, exciting her interest with their urgency. He needed her. The assumption filled her with joy. She had actually made plans for a luncheon with the wives of her husband's colleagues. But that, like everything in her life now, was tentative, a charade, filling the time between Eduardo.

66

"When?" She had also lowered her voice. Was it possible that her phone was tapped? Claude had warned her. "Be careful what you say," he had confided. "We cannot assume that they are not listening in."

"Who?"

"The CIA. It is a standard practice with us in Paris, although we have equipment to detect it. But it is not foolproof."

"What could I say that would have value?" she had responded. Now, she knew. The telephone, indeed, could be the enemy.

"Today. At noon." She thought for a moment, hesitating, her mind filled with the logistics of refusing to go to the luncheon.

"Of course." She had wanted to say "my darling," but held back, proud of her cunning. The phone clicked off. She dialed another number, apologized, talked of special chores that had come up. She had rejected the idea of telling them she was not feeling well. It might get back to Claude. In this way, she would be telling them somewhat of a truth. Some chore, she thought, laughing gaily as she sprang up the stairs.

As she drove to his apartment house, her mind and body filled with anticipation, she found herself looking into the rear view mirror. This is ridiculous, she told herself. How could Claude know? How could anyone know? Nevertheless, she parked a block from the apartment house and walked the rest of the way, turning quickly as the eyes of the deskman washed over her briefly. Not wishing to be announced, she quickly reached the elevator, thankful that she was the only one in the cab.

He was waiting for her in the apartment, had apparently heard the elevator and opened the door. Although her agitation had increased as she came toward his apartment, she calmed herself in his initial embrace, which set off all the triggers of her sexuality, an instant reaction. He was wearing nothing above his waist and feeling his bare flesh so unexpectedly gave her a warm surge of pleasure. She felt his breath against her ear, then a whispered, "I have missed you," which made her press more tightly against him, reaching for his erection, feeling the wonder of its hardness. She admitted now that part of her anxiety had been that it would not be the same this time, that what she had felt during their first meeting was merely the explosive tendency of a pent-up, frustrated woman. I have been dormant for fifteen years, she had insisted to herself, knowing that she meant dormant since birth, unrealized, a neuter. These new feelings had resurrected the search within herself. Feeling him now gave her the validation that she was, indeed, still alive. Someone. A woman.

"You are my man," she told him, running her fingers through his hair, down over his bare back into the envelope of his trousers at the small of his back, down over his hard buttocks. Again, as she had done last time, she knelt before him, unfastened his trousers and pulled them down, then his shorts, kissing and caressing him. "My beautiful man," she cried, feeling tears rush down over her cheeks. "My beautiful man." It seemed, even then, like some primitive litany. She felt his hands on her hair, but he said nothing. In the midst of this act so foreign to her experience, she observed herself, a spectator. And the spectator, marveling at the total loss of her inhibitions, nevertheless felt pride in the participant, in her humanity and passion. I want him to come in my mouth, she told herself, her tongue compelling and urgent on his erection. Such an idea had always inspired a sense of nausea.

Then she felt the throbbing as he neared the moment of his pleasure, which increased her own passion, the wave beginning inside her again, as it had done the last time.

"Yes. Yes," she heard him say as she repeated to herself, my man. My man. My beautiful man. Then she tasted his libation. It was the way she thought of it, his libation to refresh her body and her spirit. Like wine is Christ's blood, she told

68

herself, reveling in what she imagined was his sweetness. She had never wanted this before, not ever.

And it did not exhaust him. Quickly his energy began again and they were together in his bed, enjoined, thrashing about, loving, kissing, feeling, smelling, as her orgasms came in recurring crescendos, like a waterfall plunging from terrace to terrace. Later, she lay in the crook of his arm, her hand on his chest, feeling the steady beat of his heart, soaking in his aroma, his aura.

"You have made me a woman," she said, looking upward at the ceiling, groping inadequately for words to explain it. "At first, I thought it is not possible that this could happen, that it was all propaganda, that women's feelings were merely the figment of man's imagination. I thought it was all lies."

"And now?"

"Now I know it is beyond my wildest imagination. Beyond my dreams of it."

"We create the right biological chemistry," he said, laughing.

"It is more than just physical," she began again, knowing that it was impossible to fully explain, only to know. "This. Here and now is my real life. The rest is a sham."

"Nonsense. You have your husband. Your family. Your life." Perhaps he was merely underlining the impermanence of their relationship. The thought quickened her caution. But it was futile. She could savor her vulnerability. Such a truth would be like a bullet in her brain.

"But my real life is here. With you." She lifted herself on her elbow and brushed her lips against his. Then she lay back and looked up at the ceiling again.

"Eduardo," she said. "Explain this to me. What is happening here?"

"We are a man and a woman." He shrugged. She could sense his annoyance.

"You must tell me, Eduardo." She detected a sense of

pleading in her tone. But she really wanted to know. She must know. "You are a man of the world, a man who has experienced life, a man of wisdom. You know, Eduardo. You know better than I. I've been a woman in a harness for years. First, it was my mother. Then Claude. Then the children. But you know, Eduardo."

He patted her shoulder and kissed her hair.

"You exaggerate my wisdom. Once you start to explain, you will talk it all away. We have needs, appetites. They sometimes take over our logic. I understand only that I am a man in limbo, an exile. My esteem probably needs special care. I have lost my country. There is something about you that you carry in yourself that seems to satisfy these needs. That eases the pain."

"And do I give you joy, Eduardo?"

"Of course ..." he paused, then smiled. "How did you say it? Beyond my wildest imagination."

She pinched his ribs playfully.

"I think you are making fun of me."

"Fun? In Spanish it is *reirse de mi.*" I prefer the Spanish. It seems to say more."

"In French it is *tu t'amuse avec moi.*"

She felt a giggle begin in her chest, expelling it, feeling the parameters of time begin to disappear, and with them, all sense of her other life.

"Why can't we just be here, like this, like now, forever?" She looked up at him, watching. He said nothing and she sensed a growing paranoia in herself. The future loomed, filled her mind. A future without him seemed sterile, a living death. Could she cope with it, she wondered.

"What happens now?" she asked, sensing impending panic.

"Now?" He sat up and looked at his wrist watch which lay on the pile of papers on his night table, under the lamp. "Now we get dressed and disappear." He slapped her buttocks and stood up.

70

"So soon?"

"I have things I must do."

"But surely ..." She began checking herself, the outside world, the details of their disparate lives rushing in on them. She watched as he went to the bathroom, heard the rush of water. Then he came out and began to dress. She felt suddenly angry, angry at time, at him, at herself.

"This place is a mess," she said as he brushed his hair. "You must let me tidy it."

"No need," he whispered, hesitating briefly in his response.

"Really, Eduardo. It can be made more liveable."

"It is simply a place to hang one's hat."

"You would be surprised how cozy I can make it." She moved upward on the bed, rested on her knees, and reached out to touch him. "Really, my darling. I can do it for you. Just give me the key. You needn't trouble yourself about it. I can fix it up. Buy you things."

He put the brush down on the dresser, the sound of its impact on the wood a sure signal of his irritation.

"I like it just the way it is," he said.

She saw his annoyance, knew she was causing it, and stood up to placate him, hoping that she might draw him down again. She reached for his crotch. But he moved away.

"I am late," he said, moving toward the door. But he stopped, came back and kissed her hair. "Forgive me. I am testy, already thinking of other problems. Perhaps some other time we will discuss it."

"When can I see you again, Eduardo?"

"I'll call you."

"When? Tomorrow? Next week? What day?"

"It's difficult to make permanent plans. My life is so transitory."

"But my life is tied to yours now. Without you I wander in a maze."

"There is no other way. Not now. Not yet."

71

There seemed a faint glimmer of optimism, a shred of future permanence. It was not enough assurance, she knew. She watched as he started toward the door again.

"I will call you."

"But when?" Was she nagging?

"You mustn't ask." He looked at her for a moment, then turned.

"I love you, Eduardo Allesandro Palmero," she cried after him. But the door had already closed and she was certain he had not heard.

She did not rise from the bed immediately after his departure, but lay there, her eyes resting on the hardened nipples of her breasts. Then she got up and reached for his brush, holding the handle, feeling the lingering warmth of his hand. The sense of loss seemed overwhelming and her eyes filled with tears. She looked at the brush, which suddenly became the focus of her anger. She threw it across the room. It hit the wall with a sharp cracking sound, then fell to the floor. My God, what am I doing? What is happening to me? She dressed quickly and left the apartment.

It was, she thought, an odd coincidence, although she admitted the possibility of cosmic influence. This thing with Eduardo had opened up new dimensions of spirituality. Life was, after all, not only what met the eye. Which is what she felt when Claude informed her that night that they would be at the Chilean Embassy for dinner.

The French ambassador, he had explained, was invited, a small group, sixteen guests, on the following Saturday night. But the ambassador had been called away suddenly and he, as next in command, was designated to take his place. There, she thought, the cosmic influence. She yearned to tell Eduardo. Claude was in good spirits, a fact she resented since she preferred that he would bring home his irritations and thereby give her a greater opportunity for dissimulation. Instead, he was in a particularly good humor, although a little pedantic.

72

"You will like the Chileans," he said. "Lovely people. Very gay. And they are particularly anxious to please. This is all part of their diplomatic offensive."

"They are butchers," she hissed. Instantly, she regretted the outburst.

He looked up at her, fork in mid-air, his frown wrinkling.

"Well, what have we here? A budding expert on political science." Then the fork moved, the wrinkles disappeared. "It is not so simple."

"They have killed many people. And many are in exile." She was trying to remember what Eduardo had told her, but felt her inadequacy. She had merely accepted it and had taken his side for no other reason.

"I would suggest," Claude said, his good spirits fading, his lips tightening, "that you keep that well-informed opinion to yourself when we visit the Chileans. I do not want a diplomatic incident." He paused. "Why not confine your conversation to clothes, hair and children?"

He remained silent throughout the meal. But she was fuming. His attack on her self-esteem seemed to organize her reserves. Now that she had Eduardo, there was no need to be submissive, fearful. She laughed, to herself, of course. I have betrayed you, you pompous ass, she hissed at him silently as he self-indulgently patted his lips with a napkin. I have felt this other man throb inside me. I have kissed and sucked and loved another man's body like I never, could never, will never, love yours. As she said this, wondering if, indeed, an audible whisper had emerged, she was actually helping to clear the dishes.

There was, nevertheless, a message in his criticism. She was ill-informed, particularly on a subject of obsessive interest to Eduardo. Previously, she had had no desire to inform herself on those matters that interested Claude. Perhaps she was resisting subconsciously. But Claude had pointed out her inadequacy in terms of Eduardo. It was odd how her life had changed. There was no subtlety about it. A line had been drawn, quickly, abruptly. She belonged in her mind to Eduardo. For Eduardo she would do anything. Anything!

Spending most of the next day in Cleveland Park Library, she gathered up all the books she could find about Chile. Some she thumbed through in the library. The rest she brought home with her, displaying the books deliberately and pugnaciously on a living-room shelf and on the night table near her bed. Reading about Chile, she felt closer to Eduardo.

Claude lay beside her as she read, the pages of the book illuminated by the small night light. She felt his arm steal around her middle.

"It is late," she said. "Please." She shrugged him away. "I am informing myself."

"That is quite obvious. But you needn't do it with such passion."

What does he know about passion, she thought. Again, his arm stole around her. "Sorry," she snapped. "I never mix business with pleasure." He would not, of course, know which was which.

"I'm sorry, Marie," he whispered, pecking at her ear. "I had no idea you were becoming so sensitive."

"Go to sleep."

"Really, Marie. I am sorry."

"So am I," she said, checking herself. It would be foolish to precipitate an argument. She wondered if she should submit as she might have done in the past. For some reason, she had never refused him directly, only obliquely. She pondered an escape route, finally patted his head.

"You must sleep. Tomorrow is a busy day." She bent over and kissed his forehead. "Only a little while longer. I want to make you proud of me tomorrow."

"But I am proud of you," he said. Somehow he seemed placated and rolled further away from her. She felt relief at her wise strategy. But it frightened her to feel her commitment to Eduardo. She shivered, her eyes going back to the book.

"Do you know why the national character of Chile is one of nervousness and dislocation?" She looked over to Claude. He grunted.

"Earthquakes. Too much fish in the diet. The mountains." She turned to see if there was any reaction. But Claude had already drifted away.

The Chilean Chancellery was a stately old residence located on Massachusetts Avenue in the midst of Embassy Row. The ambassador's wife was lovely, tall and willowy. The ambassador, too, was charming, urbane and distinguished. He was a tall barrel-chested man with well-cut clothes. They were hardly what one might expect Eduardo's enemies to be like. It annoyed Marie to be in this setting. It destroyed her subjectivity, her alliance with Eduardo in all things.

"We are badly maligned," the ambassador was saying and although she did not sit next to him, she listened intently, ignoring her dinner partner, a portly gentleman, the president of some important company that did business in Chile. "It is true we are ruled by a junta. But this is the fate of most South American countries. Otherwise we would be in chaos. We need order first so that we can broaden our economic base and provide our people with a better alternative for communism, which will destroy everything we have built since Bernardo O'Higgins and San Martín freed our country from the Spanish in 1818."

She knew that, she told herself happily. She had even remembered the exact date, April 5, 1818.

"Your April fifth," she blurted out, startling the ambassador as he looked toward her and smiled broadly.

"Yes," he said. "That is exactly right."

"But what about the DINA?" the man on her right whispered. She knew that, too. That was their intelligence agency, their terror troops, as Eduardo had characterized them. They were vicious brutes, he had told her, who reached out to kill enemies of the Junta in every country of the world. The mention of the name made her shiver briefly, for she knew that it was the DINA that Eduardo hated most.

The ambassador heard the reference and did not ignore it. He was obviously defensive, but tolerant. He was a seasoned diplomat.

"You have your CIA. We have our DINA. One must recognize that every country has enemies. In our case, the enemies are so numerous that we must take extra precautions. As for assassinations, they are exaggerated. It is propaganda spread by our enemies." A slight flush on his neck betrayed both his passion and his discipline.

"And what of those who are banished from your country? Or are in your prisons?" She knew it was her voice saying these things, but could not believe it was her mind creating them. How impolitic, she admonished herself, looking at Claude at the other table, pursuing a conversation with his usual intensity. She knew she had made most of the others at her table uncomfortable. But it was too late. The idea of it was in the open and she could see the flush on the ambassador's skin expand upward under his chin.

"Banishment is an old South American tradition," the ambassador began, with an effort at good humor. "That is punishment enough. There is nothing worse for a Chilean, for example, than to lose his country. Nothing worse." He paused, seemed to lapse into introspection. He seemed genuinely sad, helpless in the face of events. It was a familiar diplomatic affliction. In that role, one did not have the luxury to follow one's instincts. "It is all so strange," he continued, clearing his throat. "We are such a small country." How is it possible to hate these people, she thought? Did he know Eduardo? The idea titillated her. Perhaps she would subtly bring out his name after dinner, privately. She lowered her head and played with the food on her plate, noting that he had ignored the question about prisons.

Later, during the after-dinner drinks and coffee in the terrace room off the swimming pool, she insinuated herself near the ambassador, waiting politely for him to finish talking with a plump man who had been at the other table with her husband.

"I hope you didn't think I was being rude," she began when she had caught his eye. The plump man's presence distressed her and she tried to be deliberately vague, hoping that the ambassador would understand.

"Not at all," he said, but she sensed a coolness beneath the surface.

"You see, I am extremely interested in Chile."

"Oh?"

She observed his sudden interest.

"I would like someday to visit Punta Arenas."

"Punta Arenas!" The ambassador laughed. "It is the equivalent of your 'Wild West.'"

"The city on the bottom of the world." She marveled again at her cunning, knowing that she was deliberately ingratiating herself with the ambassador, establishing her credibility. How many people knew that Punta Arenas was the most southern city in the Western Hemisphere?

"It is the political situation that confuses me most," she said, with an air of confession. "Allende was, admittedly, a Marxist. But he was duly elected by the people. All right, he was overthrown by other forces. Why then must there be so much brutality . . . ?" She found herself groping for words.

"You see," the ambassador began, "what Allende tried to do was make a bloodless communist revolution. There is no such thing. Those who have achieved success or are descendants of those who achieved success before them are not ready to give up the fruits of their achievements. Democracy then becomes unworkable. It is our hope that the Junta can keep peace long enough to find new alternatives to give people greater opportunity without wiping out the achievers."

77

"You make it sound so simple." She paused, aimed her dart, then threw it. "I recently met a gentleman at the Roumanian Embassy. He held a different view."

She could feel his alertness. The plump man had drifted away.

"I can't quite recall his name. It began with a 'p'."

"Ah, yes. Palmero. Eduardo."

"You know him?"

"Of course. We are a small country. He is, of course, a political enemy of the regime." A note of sadness crept into his voice. "We were at the University together. Once we were friends. Now he barely talks to me."

"You see him?"

"I know all about him." She could see he was becoming uncomfortable. Perhaps they really are watching him. Eduardo will be proud of me, she thought, anticipating their future meeting, at which she could tell him what she had learned. Perhaps I qualify as a spy, she told herself with some amusement.

By the time Eduardo called on Monday, she was in a terrible state of irritability. At breakfast she snapped at her children, bringing both of them near tears. Claude, thankfully, was distant as he read the morning papers with his coffee. She had been particularly cruel to him. Bitchy would be a better characterization, since she literally had shrunk from his advances as if he were carrying some disease. She might have been less cruel by creating some physical complaint, something feminine. But somehow honor compelled her to make him feel unwanted. I am another man's woman, she wanted to tell him, hoping he would understand even through her silence, by her actions.

"What have I done?" he had pleaded. "Really, Marie, you are acting strangely. I am your husband."

"I just don't feel like it," she protested.

"Are you ill?" He had actually felt her forehead.

"No, I am not ill. I just don't feel like it."

Since it had never happened before in quite that way, it probably loomed larger in his mind than it might have. But in the rejection, she derived satisfaction, like a battle won. I will not submit, she told herself, convinced that "submission" was the correct word. Claude might have used "obedience."

And yet, she was convinced that her relationship with Eduardo bordered on a form of submission. The difference was that she wanted to submit. He would summon her in his own good time and she would come. That was a very romantic idea, she thought, but it was also nerve-racking. The uncertainty sapped her strength and her ability to cope with the details of her other life. There must be some other, more certain way to pursue this, she decided.

When, finally, he did call, her elation was so dominating that she hardly remembered the hurt until after they had made love. She no longer approached him with the fear that somehow it would not be the same. He moved her, beyond what she had thought possible. The moment she would arrive in his arms, her body would react like a crashing wave.

"This is heaven on earth," she whispered, feeling him still inside her, their passion momentarily subsiding, the feel of it like the beached surf sliding back into the turmoil of the sea.

"You are my life now, Eduardo," she told him. "I live only for you. Only to be near you." He was silent, disengaging, lying on his back now, his arm around her, staring upward.

"Is it wrong for me to feel these things?" she asked. "Or to say them?"

"You must not make it a moral question," he said.

"All right then. Why has it happened? Answer me that."

"It is unanswerable."

"No, it must have an answer."

"It is a mystery. Like the concept of God."

"What has God got to do with it?"

He sighed. He seemed on the edge of irritation. She was suddenly anxious.

"And you, Eduardo? Can it be the same for you?" It was a question that had begun to absorb her. What was he feeling? Does he love me? She had tried to resist asking such a question. Suddenly she put a finger on his lips. "Do you love me?" she whispered. "Don't," she said quickly, frightened. "It is not necessary to answer." They were silent for a long time, lying in his bed, staring at the ceiling.

Finally, she told him about her dinner at the Chilean Embassy. His lips grew tight.

"Pallett, that toady!" he hissed.

"But he said he was once your friend."

"He would have me shot as much as look at me!" His anger became palpable. "And he as much as admitted they were watching me. The butchers are watching me. But they will never silence me. Never. I will die first."

She put a hand on his forehead, hoping to quiet him.

"Let me help, Eduardo." The touch of her seemed to cool him. How she longed to be a part of his life. "I can help," she insisted. He looked at her thoughtfully.

"Why?"

"You, Eduardo. What is love without sacrifice?"

"It is too dangerous."

"For you, I will do anything."

"You don't understand, Marie. This is not a game. I am a marked man. They watch me. It is not safe to get involved."

"But I am involved."

He paused, watching her, inspecting. "We shall see," he whispered.

She should have been frightened. That seemed the logical reaction. She should have thought first of her own exposure, the potential breakup of her life with Claude and the children. That had once seemed the real danger. Somehow it had all become reversed. She actually imagined the joy of dying with him. What is life without him now? My God, what am I thinking?

"Love me, Eduardo. Just love me."

She lay on the bed watching him dress. It was part of their rhythm now.

"If only I could be certain that we would meet on a particular day, at a particular time. It is terrible to live with such anxiety. I could cope better with my life if I knew."

"It is impossible."

"Perhaps I could cover over every day at a certain hour. I will clean this place up. I will cook for you. There is so much I want to give."

"I am sorry, Marie," he said, turning to her, his silver-gray eyes calm in the early-afternoon light filtering through the half-opened blinds. "It is impossible." He hesitated, ". . . now." Had she heard him accurately?

The hint of a future with him gave her courage. If he asked, would I give up everything, she wondered. My man. This is my man. Lying there, she knew what decision she would make.

Having made the decision, she drew even further away from Claude and the children. There was, she knew, an element of militancy about it. Even madness. But I am Eduardo's woman was the only reassurance needed and she would repeat it over and over again to herself.

"You must join me for lunch at the State Department today," Claude said the following Monday morning. Again, she had somehow gotten through another week, mostly by maintaining silence and spending her time reading books about Chile. She had decided to begin taking Spanish lessons. The effect on Claude of her sudden turnabout from dutiful spouse to indifferent stranger was profound. He was confused, but had chosen a course of disciplined response. She observed this, but ignored it. What did it matter? Claude was a relationship of the past.

"No. You go without me."

"But the other wives will be there, Marie. And the Secretary of State with his wife." He seemed to be pleading. She noted that pockets of fatigue had begun to show up under his eyes. But the observation carried no feeling with it.

"I simply won't go," she said.

"Really, Marie. What have you got to do that's more important?"

"I'd prefer to stay home. Read my books. And there are household chores."

"Marie!" His body seemed to tighten and stretch as he loomed over her. A fleck of saliva formed at the side of his lips. "I demand that you come with me!"

"Demand?" She snickered, taunting him.

"You are my wife. I demand your compliance."

Compliance, she thought. How ridiculous! One would think I was another country. She did not reply, moving away from him. It was apparently a gesture more infuriating than speech.

"You damned bitch!" he shouted. "Are you trying to ruin me? You have no right. You are killing me. You are destroying my career!"

She had never seen him that angry, and while her mind told her that she should pity him, she found herself actually enjoying the spectacle. She remembered now all the little hurts and humiliations that she had endured at his hands. On numerous occasions, he had publicly insulted her in front of his mother. "If only she was better read, more informed," he had said. "An empty-headed ninny," he had called her. It was his favorite epithet. Not to mention his criticism of her manners, especially after a dinner or cocktail party. "You simply ignored the man sitting beside you," or "You should not have slurped so much wine," or "I saw the way you were eyeing that tall man," or "Couldn't you tell that your brassiere strap was showing?" Recalling this gave her courage. He didn't deserve her pity. He is revolting, she told herself, thinking of Eduardo,

82

remembering the ecstasy she inspired in him. Ecstasy, yes. She felt a warmness suffuse itself inside her, an expectation.

"Listen to me when I talk to you!" Claude was shouting. "I will throw you out on the street." He started to move toward her. Was he getting ready to strike her? She braced herself, prepared to take the blow. If he strikes, she vowed, I will kick him in the groin.

But he stopped short suddenly, standing stiffly, searching for control.

"Have I done something?" he said, his throat constricted, the words hoarsely spoken. "Is there something I have done wrong?"

"Really, Claude. You are making a *'cause célèbre'* over nothing."

"Nothing!" His anger rose again. "You are deliberately hurting me!"

"Because I won't go to your silly luncheon?"

He looked around him helplessly.

"Is this my wife talking?"

"Go to the luncheon yourself. Tell them I'm sick. Tell them anything."

It was beginning to weary her. There could be no resolution now. There could only be his continuing tirade which left her completely unmoved. It is like watching a stage performance, she thought. She heard his voice, repetitive, grating, and tried not to listen. Finally he strode out and angrily closed the door behind him, shaking the glassware and bric-a-brac throughout the house. She was thankful the children had already gone off to school and that the maid had not yet arrived.

Surprised by her calm, she sat on the dining room table and sipped coffee. The focus of her thoughts was on Eduardo, triggering a delicious sense of expectation. As if in reply, the telephone rang. She got up, walked swiftly, felt joyous because she was certain that it was he.

"I will be there, darling," she said into the receiver. There was no question in her mind that it was he. I feel it, she told herself, hearing his response. You see.

"Are you getting psychic?" he asked. She sensed his amusement.

"I feel you," she said.

"About noon?"

"Of course." She heard the click, but kept the phone to her ear, her eyes closed, trying to imagine his closeness.

Again, she did not park the car in the apartment lot, finding a space about a block away. She wore a kerchief and large sunglasses and walked past the desk clerk quickly. The deliberate surreptitiousness made her anxious and she longed for the day when such pretense would not be necessary. She had, she knew, conquered her fear of Claude. His discovery would be just a matter of time. Even that morning she had longed to tell him. "You are not my man." She wanted to shout it at him. "You were never my man." But she had held back. There was, after all, some pragmatism left within her. Her mother had once said and she had remembered: "Don't throw out your dirty water until you are sure you can have clean water."

Before the door had barely closed, she reached out for him, held him, clung to him. Tears spilled out of her eyes. He moved her away from him and looked at her.

"You are crying," he said, kissing the tears, actually licking them with his tongue.

"It's because I am so happy."

He kissed her eyes now, her cheeks, gave her a long lingering kiss on her lips, his tongue darting inward as she sucked it. "You are my life now, my darling," she whispered.

She reached for his hard penis, unzipped his pants, kneeled, caressed, kissed his hardness.

"My beautiful Eduardo," she cried. "My wonderful, beautiful Eduardo." A tremulous shiver began inside her and she knew the waves were beginning to come, delicious wonders happening to her. When finally she drew his hardness into her,

84

she felt herself floating on an endless sea of pleasure and when his own release came, she knew she was on the verge of fainting with the joy of it.

When she became calm, she knew that she had lost track of time, had actually been outside of herself. Each time was better than the time before. How greedy I am for him, she thought.

"Can I possibly go on living without you?" she whispered. She could feel his gaze on her. He was smiling.

"Is it that strong?"

"Beyond all words."

He shrugged. He seemed younger, boyish. She patted his forehead and smoothed his hair. Turning his eyes upward, he stared at the ceiling.

"What are you thinking about?" she whispered.

He was silent for a long time. When he spoke, the words seemed ejaculated, as if they had been accumulating in his brain, pressurized.

"I am thinking about my own futility," he said. "And those bastards who seek to destroy me. But I will fool them. I will cling to life and I will have my revenge. I will taste their blood and it will be like wine. I will drink it. The streets of Santiago will run with it and we will all get drunk on it."

His words frightened her, as she envisioned the literal embodiment of the image he had contrived. What did that matter, she wondered. What did any of it matter as long as they were together. But she remained silent. His inner rage had intimidated her. Whatever he does, I will do with him, she vowed. She wondered if, despite the terror in his heart, he felt the need for her, as she needed him.

Suddenly he sprang from the bed and repeatedly banged a fist into his palm, his lips mumbling indecipherable words.

"What is it, my darling?"

He continued to flay his fist in his palm. His eyes seemed glazed, his lips twisted and tightly fixed. After a while, his anger spent, he relaxed and lay down beside her again. She saw glistening perspiration on his forehead and upper lip, feeling the cooling process as her fingers caressed him.

"It is like fighting Goliath," he said.

"But David won."

"At least he had a weapon, a slingshot, and he knew how to use it." He tapped his forehead. "I have only this." Then he pointed to her. "And you."

"Me? Am I a weapon?"

He smiled. But it seemed a mechanical gesture, not warm.

"Everything I touch becomes a weapon."

"I would die for you, Eduardo."

"Die?" He shook himself. "Who asked you to die?"

He said it gently. She wondered at first what he meant. Then she turned the question inward upon herself and it was unanswerable. Who indeed? She had lived the contented, mostly conventional life of a diplomat's wife. The whole focus of it was to support her husband's ambition and her children's welfare. How irrelevant it all sounded. Yes, she decided. She was quite prepared to make any sacrifice for Eduardo. Even to die.

That night she moved out of the bedroom she shared with Claude and into the spare room. Claude stood against the wall, leaning on it, posturing under a patina of bravado to hide his humiliation. She felt no pity for him.

"I won't stand for this tantrum much longer," he said, searching for his old sense of imperiousness. The threat seemed empty, without conviction, which annoyed her. Then do something, you stupid man. This is just the beginning of your defeat. I will torture you.

"I vow that I will leave you if this persists." She remained silent as she gathered her clothing, emptying her drawers. She wanted him to recognize the finality of it.

"At least you might think of the children," he said flatly. It was, after all, his last refuge. She snickered. He must think his children matter to me.

"I warn you." He pointed a finger at her but she walked right past him, her clothing piled in her arms. He followed her to the guest room. By then, all pretense had disappeared. His eyes had brimmed with tears, which she saw peripherally as she put her clothes in the dresser. She marveled at the lack of pity in her heart, as if he were a total stranger.

"If only I could understand," he said, sniffling, his voice cracked with emotion. She knew he was making a great effort to control himself. "At least, you owe me some explanation."

"There is none," she said finally, tired of his watching her, annoyed at herself for not telling him. Could he be so stupid as not to suspect?

"You realize that you are ending our marriage," he said. "Is that what you want?" His voice was barely audible.

"There is no marriage here."

"But why?" He was pleading now. Was it the moment to tell him, to confess? It was, she knew, not out of regard for his feelings that she held back. Somehow, she reasoned, it would hurt Eduardo. Even Claude, his manhood challenged, might be capable of revenge, of harm. Say nothing, she told herself. Not now.

"This is all pointless, Claude."

"I have a right to an explanation."

"You have no rights. Not any longer." She stared at him, her eyes deliberately fixed on his face, observing his confusion and his pain, unmoved. It must have become unbearable to him. He turned and walked out of the room, slamming the door behind. She felt elation, freedom.

See, Eduardo, she screamed within herself. I have made my commitment. To you. Forever.

V

The game of nations, Dobbs knew, was an exercise of enormous complexity, like playing chess on the deck of a sailboat in a gale. One had to think about the pull of the tide, the whip of the wind, and the subtleties of roll and pitch as the pieces slid in disarray, to be reassembled from memory while the matrix of the original play etched and faded in the mind.

Within minutes of the explosion, agents had obliterated all, hopefully all, of the trail signs. Electronic eyes and ears, fingerprints in his apartment, any telltale signs. The FBI would find nothing. But I know how he died, Dobbs assured himself. And, yet, knowing this was not enough. He had to know why. How, otherwise, could he explain to himself how wrong he had been?

Fingering the files, he opened another. It was a Uruguayan transfer, another stitch of information in the intricate fabric. Latin America was one vast American intelligence pool, he mused, snickering again at all that human rights political talk. This was the real world, he assured himself, tapping a finger

89

on the first page of the report. Two faded photographs lay face up, clipped to the papers. Looking closely, on the top of the picture he saw the faces of two young men smiling back at him.

On the left was Eduardo, about twenty. It was 1956. Beside him was a taller, more assured youth, arrogantly swaggering into the lens, dripping with self-importance. He turned the picture, seeing the name, Raoul Benotti. He had died in that plane crash in Venezuela, the one that had been bombed.

Dobbs knew that Benotti had been marked, fingered for execution. He had followed the trail of the executioner, had watched as Eduardo orchestrated his unique weapons, the women, aiming them with telling accuracy. But how had he set the charge within them? That was what he had to know.

The picture was taken at Punta del Este, just outside Montevideo, where the families of the oligarchs of Chile, Argentina, and Uruguay watered in splendor. It was also the mating ground for these families. They would pile into the hotels and villas overlooking blue waters and incredible white beaches, with retinues of chaperones, servants and assorted retainers, to exhibit their wealth and progeny.

While families frolicked, the Latin male exercised his venery and the ornate bars and beach clubs sported traditional lures, women in search of fleeting affluence among the wealthy princes, married and unmarried. The other picture clipped to the file was of a young woman, Elena Mendoza, then twenty-one. One could see the villainous smirk of the conquistadors, barely softened by the splash of Indian blood which gave a slight slant to her eyes. There was a brief notation that she had died of pneumonia in a Chilean prison six months after the coup, but not until they had extracted what they had required, set before him now, as casual as hors d'oeuvres at an afternoon tea.

Women, always women, Dobbs hissed silently, feeling his own malevolence crying out from somewhere inside his petrified libido, as he forced his concentration on the words.

It was not the first summer that Eduardo had visited Raoul, whose family rented one of the larger villas in the south end. But their boyhood games had graduated from the surf as playground to the nightclubs and bars, where, goaded by the risen sap of their young manhood, they might follow the scent of *chucha,* pussy.

To Eduardo, whose motives had already become obscured by political passions, Raoul, with his smooth good looks and casual self-confidence, was beyond comparison with what Eduardo felt was his own meager portion in that area. Raoul, he was assured by the prince himself, could seduce a stone, and was eager to exhibit his prowess at every opportunity to the audience of his spellbound friend.

He was even, as Eduardo was to witness, skilled in extracting honey from the protected hives of the oligarchs, whose panting princesses could always find ways to dodge their duennas for a few passionate moments with Raoul. Or so it seemed.

"That one," Raoul would say, as they sat idling on beach chairs, ogling the big-titted girls with their trailing duennas, parading before them along the surfline as if they were flesh in a slave auction. "I fucked her in the cabana. Like an Arab. They guarded the entrance while I sneaked under the tent." He howled with joy. "I also fucked her maid and her mother."

"Her mother?"

"See that one there." He pointed to a patio in the distance, where a woman in a gauzy dress stood into the breeze, her body outlined by the wind. "She is the hottest potato in the sack." He laughed again, proud of the pun.

"Somebody will stick a knife in your ribs, Raoul," Eduardo said.

"What is life without danger?" he replied.

"I envy you," Eduardo said sincerely.

"There is an art, a rhythm to this business," Raoul said, prodded by the compliment, lifting a bronzed, muscled arm to wave to a girl heading their way.

91

"That's Anna," he whispered, watching as the graceful figure approached. "Her father is a German, an ex-Nazi." The girl's hair was blonde, her eyes blue, underlining the credibility of his identification. Raoul had a fund of knowledge about these things that was awesome. "A stud must be extra careful," he had lectured. "Jealousy is a double-edged sword. Besides, I wouldn't want to stud my toe." He howled again, the sound trailing off into a suppressed giggle as the girl approached. She kneeled beside him in the sand.

"This is Eduardo," Raoul said, jabbing a thumb in Eduardo's direction as if he were inanimate, which was the way he felt. The girl had eyes only for Raoul. Her gaze pugnaciously washed over his tight bronzed body, resting briefly at the lump in his crotch which, Eduardo knew, Raoul had deliberately accentuated by tightening his buttocks against the canvas seat.

"The sun is strong today," Anna said, insinuating herself into the arc of the umbrella shadow. Raoul reached out and stroked the fine hairs of her arm. She did not pull it away and Eduardo imagined that he could see the hairs rise in response. If he had done it, the girl would have pulled away as if his fingers were charged with electricity.

It was a gesture of propriety, Eduardo knew, a staked claim, since Raoul was hardly interested in conversing with the girl and ignored her attempts at conversation or mumbled bored responses. The girl didn't seem to mind. The great Raoul was touching her and that was all that mattered.

"You will be at the party tonight," Anna said, suddenly anxious. Eduardo watched the tightness form on her lips. It had been the reason for her coming in the first place.

"You didn't forget?" she asked, the anxiety palpable.

"Tonight," Raoul mused. He smiled. "I must check with my friend."

"You can bring him, of course," the girl said quickly.

"I go where he goes. He is my guest." Raoul said, knowing he was torturing the girl, increasing the tension.

"Eduardo will be very welcome. There will be lots of pretty girls." She had turned her blue eyes toward Eduardo, penetrating in their entreaty, since Eduardo now held the key to the invitation.

"I go where Raoul goes," Eduardo said, feeling his own malice. Raoul winked at him. "Very good," his wink said. "Play with her." But Eduardo could not sustain his cruelty. "Why not," he said.

"There is your answer," Raoul said, suddenly tightening his hand around Anna's slim wrist, acknowledging her presence in a more direct way. He swung his legs in an arc, spreading them slightly as he flattened his feet in the sand, placing himself before the squatting Anna so that she was crotch high. He could see her eyes dart to the bulge at his crotch, grown larger now, as the stud had fixed on his target.

The girl seemed to sense the attention, perhaps feeling the fledgling anxieties of impending forbidden pleasures. Raoul bent over and stroked her bare shoulders. This time the girl moved, tore herself away, for appearances' sake. Raoul was a blatant exhibitionist and enjoyed the perpetual gaze the women lavished on his person.

"Let's swim," he said to the girl, reaching for her hand. The invitation offered more than the obvious and Raoul turned and winked to Eduardo.

"You, too, Eduardo. Come on, it's hot as hell here." He looked at the girl. "And getting hotter."

Eduardo joined them, following them into the water. He watched them dash ahead into the surf, Raoul's sinuous bronzed body arrogantly assured, literally dragging the girl along as she giggled with expectation and anxiety. The surf was calm now. Little rivulets of waves, miniatures of an angrier sea, spent themselves impotently, darkening the edges of the white sand.

They were out chest high quickly, snuggling together like flotsam logs, entangled in each other's limbs. Eduardo approached them hesitantly, diving like a porpoise, the intensity of his own activity designed to mask his interest. Raoul had lowered the girl's shoulder straps and was nuzzling his bare chest against hers. The waters hid what was going on below, but they were blue and crystal clear and Eduardo swam close underwater to get a better view. Raoul had freed his erection from the sides of his swimsuit and had directed it into the crotch of the girl, who was obviously savoring it through whatever sensations could find their way upward through her one-piece bathing suit.

Eduardo surfaced in confusion and embarrassment, annoyed at his compulsion to be a voyeur, which he felt was somehow demeaning, unworthy. He had surfaced quietly behind the girl's back. Raoul winked at him, smiled broadly, enjoying his own performance. He raised one finger, a signal to remain attentive, looked down at the girl, then swung her around to face Eduardo, his hands cupped on her breasts.

"Look at the latest in bathing tops," he cried. The girl struggled to free herself, but Raoul had her wedged against his body, his erection, the startled Eduardo surmised, lying now in the furrow of her buttocks.

"Please, Raoul," the girl protested, facing Eduardo, her eyes rolling in exasperation. Eduardo tried to look away from the tan hands wrapped snugly around the white melons on her chest.

"You like the style, Eduardo?" Raoul shouted.

"I'll scream," the girl pleaded.

"One scream and I will take the top back to the store," Raoul said teasingly as he stuck his tongue in her ear. She stopped struggling. Eduardo felt her humiliation and dipped his head in the water to cool his burning cheeks.

"You shouldn't be upset," Raoul said soothingly now that the girl had quieted. "He is my friend. A friend of a friend is a friend. Tell him that you are also his friend."

The girl hesitated.

"Tell him ... or ..." Eduardo sensed the first hint of malevolence. Surely the girl had also felt it.

94

"All right. All right." She turned her head toward Eduardo. "You are also my friend."

"A good friend." Raoul coached.

"A good friend," the girl repeated. Raoul's hands were kneading her breasts now.

Eduardo wanted to leave. You are being cruel, he admonished Raoul, but would not voice the sentiment. He was not quite certain whether the girl was being pained or pleasured, a reluctant or willing participant. Raoul continued to smile, kissing her ear and cheek and winking at him.

"And there is something I would like to show the friend of my friend," Raoul said.

"No. Please, Raoul," the girl said quickly, squirming.

"A friend is a friend."

Her eyes looked skyward in exasperation.

"A friend is a friend." She shrugged. Was it resignation?

"And here are the somethings." Raoul's hands dropped below her breasts, holding her viselike over her rib cage. "Dadaaa!" Raoul mocked a fanfare and the girls breasts, nipples stiff in a ring of goosebumps, glistened pugnaciously.

He had shifted her body so that she would not be visible from the beach. Eduardo stood transfixed, but only momentarily, then dived and swam toward shore, looking backward only after he had gained the beach. They were still locked together. He was curious at the reaction of the girl, wondering if his pity was wasted. His answer was not long in coming as he watched them walk out of the surf hand in hand.

"She is something, eh, Eduardo?" Raoul said. Eduardo had closed his eyes, letting the sun dry him as he lay in the beach chair. He squinted upward, saw the girl's smiling face, her hands playfully jabbing at Raoul's forearm.

"You'll be at the party tonight," she said.

"And Eduardo?"

"And Eduardo."

Then she was gone and he could feel Raoul settle beside him on his beach chair.

95

"If it was me," Eduardo said, "I would have kicked you in the balls."

"Then she would have hurt her own hand," Raoul said. He paused, slapping Eduardo on his stomach. "Someday I will teach you about women."

"Teach me," Eduardo responded. "I have been surrounded by them." But he knew that Raoul was right.

The patio of Anna's parents' home was decorated with long strings of Japanese lanterns and a three-piece band scratching out American dance music. A light breeze rustled the lanterns and the paper tablecloth under the punch bowl and the hors d'oeuvres that stretched across a long table. White was the dominant hue. The girls wore flowing white dresses and the boys white linen suits. The guests were, as always in Punta del Este, the sons and daughters of the oligarchs, a tight-knit group, more than welcome in the home of this ex-Nazi who had squirreled a fortune into the boot of the hemisphere, investing lavishly in the one commodity that gave him instant status, land.

Raoul, looking luminescent in his glistening white linen suit, a blue silk handkerchief spilling out of his jacket pocket, surveyed the group, knowing that the female eyes were watching him.

"Delicious," he said.

"What is?" Eduardo asked.

"The scent of cunt."

"You're unbelievable, Raoul. Your whole life is wrapped up in your crotch."

"Is there anything else?"

His lectures were an exercise in futility, since, largely, they were given in his own head. You are looking at the dry rot of the twentieth century, he had wanted to say. It is hopeless, he decided. Besides, he adored Raoul. Even his blatant envy, in which Eduardo reveled, could not dim his adoration, and he loved to bask in Raoul's aura, knowing that proximity to Raoul enhanced his own importance.

"How does it feel to be in the home of a butcher?" Raoul said suddenly. He would do this on occasion, reveal a tiny morsel of morality when one least expected it.

"And here again is the butcher's daughter."

Anna came toward them, radiant in white chiffon, her blonde hair bouncing, as she carried her smile forward, reaching out to touch Raoul's hand, acknowledging Eduardo's presence with a brief nod. She glided into Raoul's arms and he moved onto the dance floor, merging with her, a mass of white with four pairs of extremities. She rested her head against his cheek, her eyes closed, as Raoul undulated slowly to the music's rhythm, exhibiting his superior magnetism to the group.

Eduardo pressed into the shadows, his shyness transformed to observation as he contemplated his peers. Within himself, he could not quite subdue his emotions with his intellect. It had been his principal exercise of late, but it was giving him increasing difficulty. The disparate affluence of his family had begun to enrage him. We have so much. They have so little. "They" were the vast underpriviledged, a nation within a nation. He had begun reading Marx, listening to the growing sounds of unrest that slipped into his consciousness through the press and his occasional contacts with servants and radicals on the campus. Observing the display of arrogant superiority fed his disgust and allowed him to play the role of poseur and snob in this gathering, where he had actually begun to feel alienated.

The alienation was more than political. It was social. His relationship with girls was a trial and an agony. Near them, except for his mother and sisters, he felt awkward, clumsy, self-conscious. Could it be that he could not resolve his romantic view of love with the physical reality of sex? He could react, sometimes with embarrassing effects. Once he had actually had an orgasm while dancing with a girl and he had been reluctant to dance ever since. The moments before he fell asleep were an agony of physical hunger for him as his body craved sexual surfeit. Sometimes the image of Isabella and his father intruded. Even the sense of revulsion had reshaped itself and emerged as erotica and this, too, had filled him with guilt. But he had never confided that to anyone, certainly not Raoul, who would have ridiculed it. He had also not told Raoul that he was a virgin. Raoul would have been dumbfounded.

"Eduardo," Raoul whispered as he swung Anna into the shadows. "Come pick yourself a cherry." Eduardo watched as he buried his tongue into her ear. She shivered lightly and giggled. "We will have to leave unless Eduardo finds himself a friend," Raoul warned. Anna, obviously frightened, crossed the patio and returned with a tall flat-chested girl who, like Eduardo, seemed either shy or intimidated by some inner alienation.

"This is Estacita," Anna said with mocking sweetness. The tall girl reluctantly held out her hand, and Eduardo took it, feeling the nervous moisture of both of them.

Raoul beckoned and drifted further into the shadows in the direction of the sea wall. In the distance, the surf pounded the beaches.

Raoul removed a silver flask from his back pocket and took a long sip, passed it around to the group. Anna hesitantly followed, sipping freely. Eduardo lifted the flask but plugged the opening with the tip of his tongue, and Estacita refused. Anna melted into Raoul's arms again and they danced to the musical sounds, although only their pelvises moved in languorous circular motions. Estacita, giggling nervously, turned her eyes away, concentrating on the barely distinguishable surf in the distance. Eduardo continued to observe his friend and soon they were oblivious to him. Estacita moved back to the crowd, filling him with a vague sense of loneliness. He walked to the table, helped himself to some punch and faded again into the shadows, watching the couples, paired off in some mysterious mating game from which he felt brutally excluded. Contempt was no substitute for loneliness.

Later, he roamed to the sea wall, looking for Raoul. He and Anna had disappeared. A muted curse hissed from somewhere on the beach below and he peered over the shallow wall following the sound. He could make out vague thrashings in the darkness, the sounds of struggle.

"Raoul," he called, his voice lost in the shudder of the surf's sound. The thrashings persisted. "Damn you," he heard. Then the sharp sound of slapped flesh. He lifted himself over the sea wall and struggled forward, his shoes filling in the soft dunes. Again he heard the slap and could see movement in white, like sheets flapping in the wind. Hurrying closer, he reached the figures. Raoul had Anna pinioned against the wall and she was resisting energetically as Raoul struggled to keep her still. He could see his friend's bare buttocks glowing like odd globes in the faint light.

"Raoul," Eduardo hissed. The sound froze them and Raoul's face turned toward him, twisted with anger.

"Mind your own business," he mumbled. His voice was heavy, his speech slurred.

"He is hurting me," Anna pleaded. "Help me, Eduardo."

"Goddamned tease," Raoul hissed, groping beneath her dress.

The girl struggled furiously, whimpering finally as her energy failed. Eduardo gripped Raoul by the shoulders and pulled him away. They both fell into the sand. Anna slumped against the wall, rearranging her clothes. Eduardo was no match for Raoul, who quickly subdued him, straddling his body and pinioning his arms. He could smell the alcohol on his breath.

"You must stop this," Anna called, rushing to them now, an

edge of panic in her voice. Eduardo looked upward into Raoul's face, watching the contortion settle, the familiar look return.

"You should have minded your own business," he said, smiling suddenly and shaking his head. He released Eduardo, who stood up and smoothed his clothes while Raoul, unruffled, calmly hitched up his trousers and redid his belt.

"You'd think I was about to murder you, you bitch," Raoul said.

"You know why?" Anna pouted. Eduardo was confused, as his eyes wandered from Anna's face to that of his friend. Raoul turned to Eduardo, seeking judgment.

"I am a bareback rider," he said.

"And I don't like playing Russian roulette." Anna whispered.

"Screw yourself," Raoul said with disgust, grabbing Eduardo under the arm and hurrying forward.

"Where are you going?" Anna cried.

"The hell away from here."

"But the party . . ."

"Fuck the party."

They did not look back, moving as swiftly as possible through the small dunes, parallel to the sea wall beyond which the music blared. They reached a path of wooden slats and walked swiftly toward the crescent road which fronted the beach, stopping only to empty their shoes of sand. In the distance, the lights of the hotels flickered. Eduardo followed silently behind Raoul.

Had he mistaken the incident, Eduardo wondered, humiliated that he might have really intruded on some odd game. They went into the bar of the Mirador Hotel. Raoul squinted into the darkness and, nodding at the bartender, squeezed into the crowd at a spot to which the bartender had beckoned them.

"Ricardo," Raoul said, acknowledging, as always, his proprietary interest. The bartender smiled and put a double Scotch in front of Raoul.

"Give him ginger ale," his friend mocked, as if Eduardo's lack of interest in alcohol somehow denigrated his manhood. Eduardo caught the message of bemusement in his friend's tone.

"I thought you were raping her," he said, the words, he knew, a confession of his ignorance. Raoul lifted his glass, drained it, replaced it on the bar, and laughed.

"Raping her." He pounded his chest. "Me?"

"It actually sounded like you were murdering her."

"She loved it." He paused. "We were merely having a little dispute on some of the more technical aspects."

"Technical aspects?"

Raoul signaled the alert bartender for another drink.

"Eduardo. You are truly the stupidest man I have ever met when it comes to women."

"I'll grant you that," Eduardo said morosely.

The bartender came over and leaned on the bar, pointing with his eyes to a dark corner of the lounge where a woman sat by herself. She wore sunglasses and an odd snarl on her lips, but was attractive, in her early twenties. Raoul slid toward the bartender.

"She must raise the fare back to Santiago. And her lover has also stuck her for the price of the hotel," the bartender whispered. Raoul patted the bartender's arms and looked at Eduardo.

"He is the cleverest bird dog in Punta del Este," Raoul said, watching the bartender bask in his sense of achievement. He stood up and, beckoning Eduardo to follow, moved through the crowded lounge to the woman. She did not look up as Raoul slid into the seat beside her.

"Ricardo says you might welcome company." The woman looked to the bartender, who nodded a protective assent. She looked toward them and, with difficulty, let the snarl fade from

101

her lips, managing a thin smile. But she did not remove her sunglasses and was, therefore, difficult to observe. Eduardo surveyed her. The sunglasses also created the illusion that she could not see him. Her skin seemed milk-white in the sparsely lighted room, her hair soft, but jet black, done in a pompadour. Because she was sitting it was difficult to see whether she was short or tall. The rise above the table showed large full breasts, features not lost on Raoul, who eyed them with unabashed interest.

"I am Raoul and this is Eduardo. We are also Chilean."

The woman nodded. She had acknowledged their presence with little interest. Raoul looked at Eduardo, winked and prodded him with his elbow.

"Ricardo says you have a bit of a problem."

The woman nodded, displaying nothing of her internal self. She was, despite her predicament, quite lovely, Eduardo decided.

"It is purely financial," she said.

"I understand," Raoul said, winking again to Eduardo. "And I am prepared to be your benefactor."

"I will need *bastante pleata,*" the woman said. "Cash."

Raoul confidentially dipped into his pocket and pulled out a wad of bills. It was another familiar characteristic, the display of cash, always folded neatly and pinched with a heavy silver money clip. With a flourish he counted out the bills on the table, almost depleting his roll.

Eduardo could not tell whether the woman had watched the process. Beyond the dark glasses he could see nothing.

"And I am also the benefactor of my friend."

"That will require an extra sum," the woman said. Obviously she had watched the counting process with eagerness. Raoul's head fell back as he laughed, signaling the waiter to bring more drinks. They came quickly.

After Raoul had polished his off, he said, "The price is outrageous to begin with." His speech had become slurred. He called for another double Scotch.

Eduardo, admitting his lust for this woman, was suddenly fearful that Raoul was merely toying with her. He felt the charge of his own excitement.

"I can offer some ..." he hesitated ... "benefactions." He nearly swallowed the words.

"You are my guest," snapped Raoul. "Besides, I am the negotiator." Another drink came. Raoul drank and ordered another. Raoul was being irritable and ornery again, Eduardo observed. The woman shrugged, took the bills from the table, and stood up. She was quite tall. They followed her through the crowd, into the lobby of the hotel, pressing into the small elevator. A bored operator brought them to her floor.

Eduardo felt his heart beat heavily. The woman was thin-hipped, with firm buttocks that swung in a tight arc, suggesting promise and power. He felt the fear rise in him. Raoul staggered beside him. The woman stopped to open the door of her room. Her lover had apparently been initially lavish. The room seemed one of the best in the hotel, with a wide view of the ocean through a large bay window that opened onto a small balcony.

Inside, the woman for the first time removed her glasses. Her eyes were puffy. She had obviously been crying. But her age was more readable. Eduardo imagined she was just a year or two older than they. Raoul poured himself a drink from an opened bottle on the cocktail table. Eduardo's eyes met the woman's. Let him, she seemed to say. Without her glasses she was less self-assured. He imagined he noted an element of disgust in her demeanor. She was also less arrogant. She sat on the large double bed, hesitating. Eduardo felt awkward, shifting his weight from one foot to the other.

"Well," the woman said, reaching behind her to unfasten the clasp of her dress. Material fell off her shoulder, revealing a pink brassiere strap. She unpinned her pompadour and her hair collapsed to her shoulders.

"Why don't you look at the stars?" she said gently to Eduardo.

103

"Yesh, the shtars," Raoul said, staggering toward the bottle again, his face clenched with drunken concentration. The woman shrugged, darting him a look of bemused resignation. For the first time she smiled broadly, genuinely, he imagined. He went out on the balcony, stretching on a divan and looking up at the canopy of stars. The night was warm, the sound of the surf gentle now as the tide had moved further out to sea. In the distance he could hear faint music, probably from Anna's outdoor party.

The woman's scent preceded her presence, the light smell of gardenias. Her voice was soft. He suddenly remembered Isabella, which only served to frighten him further as the image of that night outside his father's study flashed through his mind.

"Your friend is beyond immediate hope," the woman said gently. "He is obviously ignorant of his body. Liquor is not an aphrodisiac."

She seemed so knowledgeable, strong, confident. He felt intimidation now, although she seemed softer somehow than the hard arrogant woman at the bar. She moved her body closer toward him. The gardenia scent grew stronger.

"It is amazing how ignorant men are about women," she said. He wondered whether she felt his presence, since she did not wait for a response. "He could not bear the fact that he could not move me."

"Who?" he whispered, his throat tight.

"Juan." She sighed. "I did admire him greatly. Of course, I told him that I loved him, which was a lie. I could have lied about the other. But he did not move me, and I finally told him that and he left. Just like that. I was at the beach today and he simply upped and left."

"He was your lover?"

"In a manner of speaking. But he could not bear the truth." She paused. "And yet it was not his fault. He was not the first. No man has moved me, not one, and, believe me, I have had many lovers."

"You seem so young." He was finding his courage now, the implication clear.

"I am twenty-two." She turned toward him and smiled. "My name is Elena, Elena Mendoza." She put out her hand and giggled like a girl much younger.

"I am Eduardo Palmero."

"I am not a prostitute in the traditional sense," she said. "But when one is desperate and there are fools..." She paused. "He is a fool, you know." She jerked a thumb toward the room. "He is quite taken with himself, too much with himself to ever really move a woman."

"They seem to go mad for him."

"There is more than what meets the eye," she sighed, looking up into the sky. "What a lovely night." Her hand reached down and covered his as if the need to touch a stranger's flesh seemed important. The feel of her made him shiver and he felt his loins react, the blood surging.

"I doubt if I will ever find a man who moves me," she said, squeezing his hand. "Perhaps it is me. Sometimes I am convinced it is me."

"You are lovely," he said, his throat constricting. He felt the heat of a deep flush.

"You are very kind to say that, especially since there is really no need."

"I mean it."

She squeezed his hand.

"I know," she said.

"It is not easy to be a woman in this society," she said. Apparently she had given the matter a great deal of thought. He caught the spark of her intelligence, the political implication, and felt himself drawing closer to her.

"It comes from generations of thinking of us as chattel, as a commodity for their instant gratification." She chuckled. "I hate men. Yet, I forgive them. Can you understand that?"

"Yes," he lied, admitting his confusion to himself. He had only a partial understanding.

"This thing with Juan. It is not the first time it has happened."

"Perhaps you're too honest."

"Perhaps."

"And what will happen when you find a man that moves you?" He was feeling courage now. The soft gardenia, salt-tinged scent of the night air, the faint rhythm of the surf, the nearness of her flesh goaded his manhood. He felt the throbbing of a compelling erection. He looked at her. Her kimono had opened and he could see the nipples on the white globes of her breasts. His breath seemed to catch and the enunciation of words became difficult.

"I will follow him everywhere. To hell and back," she said firmly. "I will have need for only one man then."

"And if he betrays you?"

"Well then . . ." she hesitated, searching in her mind. "Then I will kill him . . ."

He shivered, feeling the strength of her conviction. She pressed his hand.

"There is nothing on earth I would not do for a man that moves me. But he must be only my man. I would be faithful to him until death. I do not seek the embrace of a Casanova. He must be mine, and mine alone . . ." Her voice drifted into silence. "I am talking nonsense," she said.

"You would do anything for him. Anything?" He was confused, since he had not yet tasted the power of it.

"Of course," she said, responding again.

"And would the same be true of a man? If a woman moved him?"

"I cannot say. I'm only a woman." But the thought must have lingered in her mind. "I would be perfectly willing to direct a docile slave. Perfectly willing. Unfortunately it has not happened." She turned to him and smiled. "And you. Would you take advantage of such power?"

He shrugged. "Why not?" It was so far from the realm of his .

106

experience, he could afford to be cavalier. After a pause he said, "But how do I find it?"

"Search for it," she said turning toward him, opening her kimono further. He looked downward to the thatch of dark hair between her legs. She watched his eyes.

"Fish the waters," she said. "Someone will bite the hook." He felt the awkwardness of his innocence. "And you, my benefactor. Let us see who moves who." A hardness had begun to seep back into her, which he noted indifferently. His desire was overwhelming him.

"I've never been with a woman before," he blurted, feeling his helplessness. Somehow he trusted her with this secret. She moved a hand down to his crotch, caressing his erection.

"Well, there doesn't seem to be a physical problem," she said, unzipping his pants and holding the hard flesh in her hand.

"Do you think I can move you?" he gasped, his breath shortening. He felt an exquisite lightness as her fingers touched him, then a consuming sense of urgency as concentrated pleasure engulfed him and a sound gurgled in his throat.

"I am ashamed," he said, after he had recovered himself. She cradled his head in her arms and moved his mouth to her breast.

"Never be ashamed of your pleasure," she said. "It is a gift. I envy you."

"But I have failed ... "

"Shh." She caressed his head and he sucked her nipple in some vague memory of his infancy. He felt the security of it, the warmth of her flesh, the odd comfort of her caress.

"You are beautiful," he whispered.

"You are also beautiful," she said, stretching out on the divan, helping him remove his clothes. He felt the flood of his manhood begin again.

"You see. Life is renewable."

He felt tears run down his cheeks, the scent of her filling him with a joy he had never known. Then her hand was guiding him and he was enveloped by her. It is paradise, he thought, as all the hurts of his life were suddenly being sucked out of him. Her body moved under him, tantalizing.

"I love you," he said, feeling his body overflow again, the delicious, mounting, unbearable pleasure, the release of all that had ever pained him. "I love you," he said again, hoping that he might hear her respond. But her breath barely moved against his cheek and he knew that he had not moved her.

"And if I had moved you," he asked later as they sat quietly on the divan looking into the blackness of the sea.

"Then I would follow you forever, even to the edges of hell."

Dobbs put down the file and shook himself, as if the physical act might loosen his momentary fixation on Elena Mendoza. So they had really wanted to know this man, Eduardo Allesandro Palmero, to crawl inside his soul. It was something he knew that he, Dobbs, also wanted. And it annoyed him. Somehow it seemed unprofessional. The soul, after all, should be a private place, hidden, buried from all prying eyes. Even his.

VI

Frederika Millspaugh unwrapped the plastic covering of her tuna fish sandwich, unlocking the strong, pungent fishy odor. The Amtrak New York to Washington train had just left the Philadelphia station and was gaining momentum, heading southward toward Wilmington when she remembered the sandwich, which she had thrust into her handbag on her way out of Harold's apartment. It was nearly ten o'clock at night, and while she had made the snack as a hedge against her later hunger, the condition arrived earlier than expected.

The odor made her feel conspicuous, slightly foolish, even a little greedy. She knew that the man sitting next to her reading a book in the Spanish language surely must be smelling it, offended but politely ignoring it. Seeing him, as he had filed behind her into the train, she had a vague premonition that she had somehow engaged his interest. But he had settled in as the train left New York, opened the book and had moved little, apparently absorbed by what he was reading, proving again her faulty perception. She had paid little attention to

109

him up till then, but now felt uncomfortable as she looked at the white bread and the badly made sandwich. The lettuce had been wilted to begin with and the sojourn in her warm pocketbook had increased its disintegration. But the observation did not turn off her hunger. She actually felt her stomach yearn for it, making embarrassing noises, which the man surely must have heard. After all, you can't not smell or not listen, she thought.

"Would you like a half a tuna fish sandwich?" she asked him. He turned slowly from the book, his silvery gray eyes briefly moving over her face like a spotlight, then darting to the sandwich. He smiled, showing white teeth.

"You might as well share in the feast."

He slapped the book shut, seemed to look at her with some interest, which secretly flattered her. His eyes had, from the first moment, already captured her interest.

"Why not?" he said. She could detect the carefully practiced English pronunciation that masked his obviously Latino background.

She handed him one half of the sandwich, which he took between long, delicate, tapering fingers. He had well-cared-for hands, she noted, conscious of her own cracked nails.

"The train is a little boring at night," she said. "All I see when I look out the window is my own face."

"Even in the daylight the view is not inspiring." His language was precise, unquestionably studied. "I mean the landscape, not the face." There was an air of courtliness about him, she thought. A phony, she decided, in her habit of deprecation. She was quick to label people by the amount of sincerity she imagined them to have.

"You seem to be greatly absorbed in that book," she said perfunctorily, hiding her distrust. It was an annoying defense mechanism, this compulsive putdown. But she had learned it was safer that way. Better to be surprised by people's goodness.

"Yes. It is absorbing. Written by Pablo Neruda, the great Chilean author."

110

Chile, she thought, remembering. Allende. A few years ago it might have prompted a passionate reaction, perhaps even violence. But that was another Frederika, the revolutionary Frederika. She could barely remember that other person.

"You're a Chilean," she said, vaguely interested. That was another aspect of her latest incarnation. She could be only vaguely interested. Her juices, like the tides, had ebbed. It was the way Harold had put it, and despite her protestations, he was exactly right.

"Nothing seems to turn you on any more, Frederika," Harold had told her over drinks in that kitschy little place on Sixty-eighth Street around the corner from his apartment. She sipped a beer, watching the singles rat race taking place around the bar with mild contempt.

"Maybe I've felt it all. Maybe there is nothing left to feel."

All weekend she had wallowed in self-pity, but even that condition lacked any real engagement.

"Accept, Frederika. Accept."

She watched Harold's face, the once straggly beard scraped clean along the cheeks and chin, although the thick mustache was still there, well trimmed, with only the hint of a droop at either end. He wore wire-rimmed goggles now. The little grannies were discarded, and the hair, once down to the shoulders, was clipped neatly with the ear lobes showing. He wore one of those tapered imitation leather shirts, split down to mid chest, with a big shiny gold medallion hanging from his neck. He was acting Playboy macho and it was more amusing than sad.

He even fucked differently, she had thought, with a kind of practiced cerebral technique, which was also amusing, but offered little in the way of sensual delights. But that was another matter. Even getting laid had become a bore, which was one reason she rarely dated anymore. Actually, after the curiosity had passed, it had always been a bore, a kind of heatless submission.

111

"I'm a burnt-out case," she said with mock cheerfulness.

"At twenty-eight?"

"Twenty-nine."

He was an editor at H. K. Books now and they had attended a cocktail party at the apartment of another editor, which was the excuse for the weekend in the first place. Everyone seemed very into money and "things," although they were the first to admit, almost apologetically, she thought, that most of what they published was "pure shit" but that was what the public wanted.

"It's over, Frederika," Harold said. He put a hand over hers and squeezed it.

"Over?"

"The way we were."

"Christ, Harold. That's the title of a movie."

"Jeez, you're right." He felt embarrassed, shrugged and tossed off his neat Chivas, about which he had made such a fuss with the waiter.

"If only you can stop being the voice of my conscience," he said. He had been the most radical of them all. She had met him briefly at Berkeley, then later when they went with Mailer to the Pentagon. She smiled, remembering that she had once been his "woman" and they had spent most of their time in crash pads and sleeping bags. Who were those people, she wondered. Last night, lying next to him, not sleeping, she had smelled the real Harold. Apparently the musk had worn off and the pores of his body had cleared and the smell of the old Harold had come again into her nostrils, masculine-sweaty, and the memory of it had made her eyes mist with sadness. Gone. It was all gone.

"I'm sorry," she told him.

He ordered another round.

"It's over," he said again. He looked at her and she could see his hazel eyes behind the glasses, a bit frightened, but clear, with that unmistakable quick intelligence which people recognized as

112

a sign of leadership. "The moving finger writes. Hell, we changed the fucking world, Frederika."

"Big deal."

"They're starting to write books about us. We're becoming legendary romantic figures. We did it and it's over." His cheeks began to flush. Little red circles like dabs of rouge appeared on his cheekbones. "For everything there is a season."

"My God, Harold."

"There's truth in it, Frederika."

"First a movie title. Then the Bible."

"Well, we're no longer a subculture."

"Mainliners, eh?"

"Yes. As a matter of fact. We're getting into leadership positions. We're going to run the whole goddamned country."

"No shit." She was being deliberately deprecating again, resuming her pose. He put his hands up and shook his head.

"You can't leave it alone. You can't forget it. Still got to live like it was in the sixties. Come on, Freddie." He hadn't called her that for years. "Phase out. You got to come down off the mountain."

He was, of course, absolutely right. But she was caught in limbo now, treading water. She had tried, really tried. The magic word had been relevance then, and even when she entered Georgetown Law School it had seemed, at first, like a new beginning. Most of her classmates were still part of it, or so it seemed. But whatever it was that had moved her then had disappeared and she had dropped out.

Even now, waiting on tables in Clyde's Omelet Room, where the tips were pretty good, she would see some of her old Georgetown classmates. They were lawyers now. Into money, as they told her, or so she imagined that they told her. They seemed like shadows, apparitions now, barely perceptible as people. Like her mother and father living in that fancy condominium in San Diego, hustling to fill up their leisure, somehow getting through the day with tennis and shopping

113

and gossip, then rushing to make the scene at the happy hour in the private condominium club.

"Maybe you should see a shrink?"

"I've been there, Harold," she said tossing off her beer. Her stomach felt bloated. "I've been everywhere," she sighed.

"Oh, come off that tired-of-it-all shit, Freddie. You're even beginning to look the part." He must have known that his words had bit deep. Despite all, her vanity had not been crushed. By some fluke, she had maintained her looks without even trying. None of the previous abuse had shattered them. The bad food, the pot, the occasional pills, uppers, downers, speed, LSD. The lack of sleep. The sleeping around. Recently she had caught herself trying to remember all the men she had gone to bed with. She could barely remember their faces, although she could recollect some odd shaped penises.

"You're still beautiful, Freddie," he said gently. "I don't mean it that way."

He hadn't. She knew that. When she had taken off her plaid shirt and faded jeans, she had stood before him for a moment, displaying her nakedness. It seemed the best moment of the weekend and it had happened when she had just arrived, like giving her a ticket of admission.

"Jeez, Freddie. You still look like a young kid."

Actually she hadn't been laid for nearly six months and had barely paid attention to her body. She liked what he had said, had enjoyed that first touching, as if it were the harbinger of more to come. But it was all illusion and it had quickly gone sour. She consciously manipulated his body to make him come quickly. Which he did. She felt nothing, wondering if he had really felt pleasure. The image fled quickly, dissolved by the voice of the man beside her.

"I am a Chilean," the voice said. He turned toward her and bit into the sandwich. Then he put up one finger as he waited for the dryness to dissolve.

"It's a bit dry," she said. "We should have something to

114

drink with it. Feel like a cup of coffee?"

He stood up. He was tall, and waiting for her to move into the aisle, he let her pass and they walked in the direction of the snack bar. She felt him watching her. Then he quickly stepped ahead of her to open the door between the cars. At that range she could smell his breath, slightly fishy. His hand had looked strong as it gripped the door handle. At that moment the train lurched slightly and she touched his arm, feeling the hardness of his taut muscle. At the snack bar, he ordered two coffees, which were served in styrofoam cups. They leaned against a little counter opposite the snack bar. She could see his face now, although it seemed slightly hidden behind the mist of steam from the hot coffee.

"You're a long way from home," she said, oddly observing her own curiosity.

"Five thousand miles, to be exact."

"That's further than it is to Europe."

"And to some parts of Asia."

"What the hell are you doing so far from home?"

He smiled, not joyously. There was a hint of deprecation.

"I'm not here by choice."

"I see," she said. Sipping his coffee, he seemed to be withdrawing from her. She barely read the newspapers these days and Chile was remote.

"Were you in prison?" She had remembered something about Chilean prisons, torture, juntas. Perhaps she had seen references on the cover of some magazine. Politics were anathema now. A bore, she had told herself. Earlier in her life she had been too greedy, and her taste buds had become jaded, beyond sensation.

"Yes. As a matter of fact." The answer startled her, drawing her interest. He finished his coffee and she followed him back to their seats. He stood aside politely to let her through to the window side. She continued to hold the coffee container. When he sat down he opened his book.

"Were they cruel?" Did she really care, she wondered.

He closed the book.

"Cruel?" He watched her now, his eyes roaming over her face, searching her.

"They tortured you?"

He grimaced, lines spreading in a frown across his forehead.

"I try not to think about it."

"Is that possible?" She knew it was. Hadn't she blotted out whole chunks of years from her memory, willed them out of her thoughts whenever they tried to emerge?

"Not really," he said and she saw now that she had broken the ice. He put the book beside him near the arm rest, a sign of his engagement. She felt herself flush and knew that the pores had begun to open in her armpits, as if her body had begun to thaw.

"I really don't know a damned thing about Chilean politics," she said. Nor do I care, she wanted to add, but she liked the sound of his voice, the way he inflected his speech with that preposterous precision.

"Few Americans do," he responded. There was an air of pedantry about him. Despite that, she wanted to hear more.

"So you were in prison?" She knew she had taken a lucky shot, had inspired his interest. He nodded.

"I was in jail once," she said. "Overnight. We all sang songs until our throats burned out."

"Where I was, there were no songs." He was dipping deep into himself. She imagined his tongue was touching some exposed nerve in his mouth.

"That bad?"

"It builds character." There was a brief sarcasm. He was bottled up, she decided, on the verge of uncorking. She wondered how it was to feel such anger and envied him for it.

"I'm sorry," she said. Was she genuinely compassionate?

"It is far from over," he whispered. He glanced behind him furtively. "The game has not been fully played."

She felt the sense of danger, suddenly excited, waiting for more.

116

"I don't understand." She did, of course, and knew she was goading him.

"I am a voice. They will not be happy until all the voices of opposition are stilled. I am their gadfly and that is the only way they can stop me."

"I had no idea." She had not calculated her reaction; she was genuinely startled by his outburst.

"They are beasts. They are there merely to protect the *status quo,* the wealth of the few who own most of the land. And the investments of American business, while they let them rape our land. Our copper. The Chilean people are in chains."

"Jeez, I didn't expect a speech." She was immediately sorry for the sarcasm.

"I apologize. I hadn't expected to give one."

"No. Don't apologize. It's me. Not you."

He talked quietly, calmly, even when he had made his little speech. His words were not unlike words she had heard before. Once she had responded to them by raising a clenched fist, marching in protest. There had been causes then. Inspiration. It had all happened in the time when she was alive. Once she had thrown a firebomb into the branch of the Bank of America in San Luis Obispo. She had actually taken instruction in methods of violence and had on occasion helped make bombs, later used in their combat when they were "the army of the revolution." He remained silent. She wondered if her flirtiness put him off.

"I'm not much into causes these days," she said. "I've had it with them."

"It is necessary to believe in something," he said.

"It is the same bullshit. Same types. Different faces. All in it to manipulate other people." She paused. "Am I offending you?"

"Of course," he said, showing a flash of incredibly white teeth.

"I'm a burnt out case," she mocked, stretching. She closed her eyes, remembering again the life of the other Frederika.

117

"You don't really believe your group will be back in power?"

"I not only believe it. It's all I live for."

"Well, that's something."

"What do you live for?"

"Omelets," she said, then explained the remark.

"Are you a Marxist?" she asked. It had been so long since that label had any meaning for her, when the sound of the word was a call to arms. She had been politicized once, had seen the world through the telescope of the political lens, and although she had somehow resisted the uniformity of thought, she had participated in all of the discipline, all of the feeling.

His voice drifted back into her consciousness. "I am a Chilean and our party was under a Marxist oriented philosophy. But we were unique to Chile. Our movement was for Chile."

She had seen that look before, a gaze turned inward, seeing nothing up close, only the dream inside. A single-mindedness. She felt oddly moved, faintly rekindled. Without realizing it, she gripped his forearm and held it tightly. He made no move to disengage her.

The train had slid into Union Station and they stood up. He removed a large leather foreign-looking valise from the baggage rack. Opening it, to repack the book, she noted soiled clothing and piles of files among its contents. He saw her watching and quickly shut the case.

"I meet in New York with friends from time to time," he said, as if some explanation was required. They walked together to the front of the station. It was cold and she found herself shivering in her light clothes.

"Can I drop you somewhere?" he asked.

"I live on Wisconsin Avenue, above Georgetown."

The truth was that she didn't want him to leave her now, to lose him. "Tell you what. You come to my place. I'll whip up a real snack."

He stood facing her in the street. She had to look up to see his eyes, the silver lost in the shadows. He was a well groomed man, she noted, not like the men she had been with in those relevant days. Before he consented she knew that he would. Perhaps he, too, had found something, she wondered hopefully, feeling sensations in her body that she thought had disappeared.

While she laid out the bacon strips on her frying pan, she watched him sitting in the single overstuffed easy chair of her small efficiency apartment. His feet were propped up on the ottoman and he had lit a cigarette from which the smoke curled upward through the shade of the reading lamp. The bacon crackled and curled, releasing its lovely aroma, and she called to him.

"How do you like your eggs?"

"Scrambled."

She scrambled the eggs and put in some toast as the bacon soaked out its grease on a brown paper bag. There was something odd about his sitting there quietly in the easy chair, something foreign, a kind of formality. An American might have stood over her as she worked, making small talk. Again the idea of courtliness popped into her mind, an image gathered somewhere about Latin men of the upper classes who put a high premium on politeness and courtesy. Was that it? Or was she simply rationalizing? There goes Frederika again, she thought joyously. The old Frederika. The one with the analytical nose.

He still wore his jacket and tie, another oddity for her, and when she came into the room with the steaming platters he seemed lost in thought, his long fingers touching each other in the delicate attitude of prayer.

"Coffee's coming," she said, placing the platters on a cocktail table near the couch, then patting the seat pillows. "Come here. You'll be more comfortable." She felt her aggressiveness and when he stirred in obedience she felt again her old strength. "And, for crying out loud, take your jacket off. Make yourself at home."

He took off his jacket.

119

"And the tie." He removed his tie and sat down beside her, placing his napkin on his legs.

"In my next life I'm going to be a chicken," he said. "My whole presence on earth revolves around eggs. My veins must be choked with cholesterol."

She got up, poured the coffee and came back. She sensed that he was loosening up, becoming less of a walking polemic, which pleased her.

"Can I call you Eddie?" she said suddenly. She had been watching him, noting how long and dark his lashes were, the strength of his chin, his lips' sensuality. She was being stirred, she knew.

"Of course." She wondered if there was any interest in her on his part.

Perhaps I am taking too much for granted, she told herself. "You mean that?"

He turned toward her. "Do I sound insincere?"

Raw nerves, she thought. He is touchy. "You see my friends always called me Freddie. I assume that friends make up names, or shorten them. There's a kind of intimacy about that, don't you think?"

"Of course."

He seemed to be slipping away. She decided to be silent and they sipped their coffee quietly. She could hear the faulty faucet dripping water rhythmically into the sink. Watching him, she saw his eyelids droop momentarily.

"Tired?"

"Tired. Yes." He straightened. It had been an unguarded comment, she realized.

"No. Lean back," she said. "I know what tired means."

"I think I had better be going," he said, but without conviction.

"Where do you live?"

"Not far."

"Alone?"

120

"Yes."

There seemed a secret comfort in that. Alone! She certainly knew what that meant. She wanted to touch him, but she held back.

"Just stretch out," she said, getting up, clearing the plates from the cocktail table and clicking off the reading lamp. Without looking back, she went into the kitchen and began to wash the dishes. After a while she stole a glance into the room, noting that he had, indeed, stretched out the length of the couch. Shutting the water tap, she went into the room, tiptoeing to the closet, removing a blanket from the top shelf. She covered him gently, hoping that the weight of the cover would not wake him. He didn't stir.

Dumb Freddie, she told herself. You've given a strange man the only bed in the joint. But she was happy. She had been afraid that the suggestion of opening the couch to its studio bed would put him off. From the closet, she brought out her coat, wrapped it around her and slumped in the easy chair, her legs on the ottoman, cuddling her chin into the wool collar.

She didn't sleep, waiting instead for her eyes to become accustomed to the dark. She wanted to see him, to watch the movement of his breathing. To imagine things about him. He was an "exile," he had told her. She could understand what that meant. Wasn't she, too, an exile? Only he was still in the battle, while she was a fallen soldier. Dear brave Eduardo, Eddie. Perhaps she simply hadn't had the courage to continue. But now. Now she could continue the fight through him, with him. She remembered what it was like to fling that firebomb into the plate glass window of that bank in San Luis Obispo.

"Let me do it," she had insisted. They had met in a wooded area of a state campground and had talked for hours about symbolic acts, the necessity to keep alive the battle with little symbolic acts. There were about ten of them and on the table of the camper which they could see through the open door was

121

the carefully constructed Molotov cocktail, incongruous. They had used an empty bottle of Pouilly Fuissé wine which they had fished out of a garbage can with the label still intact. They were sitting around Indian style, legs crossed beneath them, passing around a joint which barely lasted one time around the group and, even now, she could remember how happy she felt, the kind of high that seemed never to come again.

She had been perched on the back of Lenny's bike, her thighs wrapped around his tight hips, her crotch jammed up against his buttocks, stirring her, for her hand clutched his penis, feeling its hardness as Lenny gunned the bike in the direction of the bank. Nothing before or since had ever come up to that moment, when the bike sped toward its destination and the high wind created by its speed whipped against her cheeks and hair.

He had decelerated when they moved up the quiet street, and turned onto the sidewalk, idling in front of the plate glass window. Calmly Lenny had taken a pickaxe and broken the glass while she lit the firebomb and threw it through the opening, watching it explode as it hit the floor. Then she jumped onto the back of the bike again and they moved into the night, winding along the quiet streets, into the woods, following the trail they had mapped out in advance, to the place where he had parked the pickup truck.

She had helped him put the bike in the back of the truck, covering it with tarpaulin. Lenny had driven the truck to high ground and they could see the fire that they had created lighting up the sky. It was beautiful, she remembered, even now, without a shred of remorse. Lights off, Lenny drove the truck through the hills, heading west along secondary roads to the prearranged rendezvous with others in an abandoned barn about one hundred miles away. They stopped only once along a dark stretch after about an hour's drive and made love along the side of the road. The ground was soft under her bare skin and she imagined that she was tuned into the natural rhythm of life as she felt him inside her, another symbolic act, she had decided, which embellished the meaning of what they had done.

Was that the high point of it all, she wondered. Now, as she sat in the chair watching Eddie, the memory came back, bringing with it all the old wonder. Even the later image of Lenny tending bar in the St. Francis Hotel couldn't dull what she now felt.

But then the scream crowded into her thoughts, which must have become dreams, as she quickly found her sense of place. Awake, now, she saw him screaming on her couch. He was apparently still asleep, although he moved restlessly, as if writhing in pain. It was genuine pain, she knew, despite its happening only in his mind. She watched him suffer until it became unbearable to her and slipped beside him, holding him in her arms. He stirred, mumbled something, then breathed a long deep sigh and was still. She continued to hold him, feeling in him the sense of her comfort.

She observed time passing by the growing whiteness behind the slats of the blinds. In the gray light she watched his face, the breathing quiet, and she felt an overwhelming urge to kiss his lips, slightly puffed and open to expel his breath, which seemed sweet and clear. Resisting, she continued to watch, and finally he was responding to her gaze through gradually opening eyes.

"You were having a nightmare," she whispered.

"I don't remember."

"You seemed to be suffering and you screamed as if you were being tortured."

He was silent a long time, but his eyes were open.

"It stays in your soul." he said.

"What?"

"The pain of it. Actually, they did it to me only once in the first days, but it was enough to make me fear it forever."

"What?"

123

"You don't want to hear about it."

"Yes. You must."

"They put these wires and pinched them on to my genitals. I told myself that I would have courage through it all. And I did. I had planned to tell them something, to give them raw meat. But until I had been through the pain, they would not have believed me, so I told them a tiny bit of what they wanted to know. It was that ... or—" He coughed to cover his inability to continue. "It wasn't much really," he said after a while.

"It's inhuman," she said with disgust.

"On the contrary. Very human."

"You're crazy."

"There is a relationship between the torturer and the tortured."

"And that's human?"

"Yes."

"Here is something also very human."

"What?"

"Me. Feel me."

She cradled his head in her arms, against her breasts. His hands reached for them, squeezing and fondling. Opening her blouse, she let him touch them with his lips, stroking the back of his head. She felt an uncommon stirring inside of her. The old Freddie is coming back, she told herself.

He kissed and suckled her breasts for a long time, like a child gaining sustenance. And she felt as if milk were actually flowing from them. After a while, she reached down and opened his pants, caressing his hardness, her fingers gentle, seeking, it seemed, the hurt place. The need to kiss the hurt place was overwhelming and finally it became an irresistible longing and she moved downward and did it, feeling the soft moving flesh, as if it were not attached to him, a hurt animal.

She heard him moan and knew that she had succeeded in making him forget the pain and she felt the pleasure of giving

124

pleasure, a sensation barely remembered, but now returning to her in full strength. Through her lips, she felt the tightening, the throbbing, and then the release as he felt the moment of his greatest joy, this magic gift that she had proffered. I am me again, she told herself. Giving again. And, for the first time, sharing, taking.

For a moment there had been a confused sensation, as if her body had burst into flames, a pleasure-pain exploding somewhere inside her. Again the image of the fire-bomb flashed in her mind, the heat a targeted flume, aimed at her essence. It had never happened that way, ever.

"Why you?" she whispered. "Why now?"

He looked at her, saying nothing.

"Chemical or psychic?" she asked. When he did not respond, she said, "There are only questions. Right?"

Again, he said nothing, studying her.

They had coffee together, watching the gray Washington morning. It had begun to rain, a steady downpour that put a sheen on the streets and the cars, making her apartment seem like a refuge. She had opened the studio couch and they had repeatedly made love there and then he had begun to dress.

"I wish you could stay." she said. "I don't have to go to work until later in the day."

"Unfortunately, I must go."

"Where?" She waited, but there was no answer. Questions again.

"Are you going to be one of these mystery men?"

"No."

"Who are you really? What do you do, really? Did it mean anything to you, really?"

"Really," he whispered, smiling.

When she had first moved into her apartment and invited men to stay with her she couldn't wait for them to leave. Some she had actually chased out the door without regard to their feelings. Now she felt a sense of impending loss, but hesitated

125

to make it known. She wanted to ask, "When will I see you again? When will we love again?" Instead she said, "You will always be welcome, Eddie. Anytime. Really. Anytime. There are no other men in my life."

"I'm being watched." he said, buttoning his shirt. "It may not be very healthy to be around me."

"You think I'm afraid of them."

He explored her face. "No. I don't think you're afraid. But you should know that I'm being watched. Perhaps hunted."

"I've been there myself. And I don't give a damn."

He put on his jacket and stood over her as she sat now on the hassock near the easy chair, her terrycloth robe drawn tightly around her body. Unlike the passionate younger men of those other days, with long hair and little glasses, straggly beards, blue jeans and scuffed boots, he looked thoroughly conventional, an establishment figure. Except for the gray, silver-flecked eyes. There was something beyond them that she could not fathom. They seemed to operate on their own energy, with a power to command.

"I'll call you," he said. She wondered about his sincerity. Others had said it in precisely the same way. She did not get up to let him out, but listened to his walk as he moved down the corridor.

Because she had been so long with her indifference, she distrusted this renewed interest, even her strange wonderful new sensations. But when she found herself going through the motions of her day and nightly work serving tables in Clyde's Omelet Room, with thoughts of Eddie dominating her mind, she felt reassured. She had not slipped back into her mental and emotional grave.

Even the other waitresses noticed some difference in her. One of them, a slim redhead named Marcia with whom she had developed a kind of "at work" relationship, expressed the collective insight.

126

"You seem to be pretty perky, Frederika."

Does it show, she wondered. Like her, Marcia had been through the various stages of the "greening" as they jokingly referred to it, the drugs, the politicalization, the easy exchange of flesh, the crash pads, the rock turn-on, the euphoria of protest and rebellion, now gone stale. There was nothing left to feel, they had decided, since they had felt everything. And since their indifference was shared, Marcia could be depended upon to notice subtle changes.

"I'm not sure yet," Frederika told her.

"What does that mean?"

"I met a man."

"Really." There seemed an element of sarcasm in her response.

"But I'm not sure yet."

Toward the end of the week, she was sure. She could not find his name in the telephone book and he hadn't told her where he lived or anything beyond his cause. When he had not called by then, she began to feel anxieties. Would she ever see him again? Perhaps he was merely an aberration, a strange illusive interlude. She was conscious of Marcia watching her all week.

"Want to come over to my place for a drink after work?" she had asked repeatedly.

"Can't."

"That man still working."

"Still working." It was the kind of feeling she wanted to keep to herself.

By Friday evening, she had decided that maybe it was better to feel nothing. Certainly it was safer. But she did not give up, and when he finally appeared near closing time on Friday her hope was vindicated. She had not seen him come in and find a seat in the corner near the window, and the sudden shock of recognition made her knees shake and she had nearly dropped a plate of omelets.

127

"Eddie." She moved to his table. "You came."

"Of course." His eyes burned into her, telling her what she wanted to know. "I was getting worried." She had lowered her voice, as if in response to what she imagined was his furtiveness. Marcia was standing near the omelet bar watching her. She mustn't let on, she decided. She mustn't identify "the man." As if he were an ordinary customer, she handed him a menu.

"I made better eggs at home," she whispered, pencil in hand.

"I know," he said.

"I'll bring you some wine."

She went to the bar, ordered a goblet of wine, then returned.

"Will that be all, sir?" she said raising her voice for Marcia to hear.

"Yes."

"Will you meet me later?" There were, after all, logistical arrangements to be decided.

"Of course."

"When I bring you your change, I'll give you my key."

He smiled. Why was she being so conspiratorial, he wondered. But it obviously pleased him. It was the way he apparently wanted it to happen. I will let him keep my key, she decided. When she had carried out the secret operation and seen him palm the key in his hand, she drew a deep contented breath.

"No more than a half hour," she said.

"Was that him?" Marcia said when he had gone.

"Who?" Had she been that transparent?

"That dark man. The one in the corner."

"Him?"

"I guess not." Marcia shrugged, but Frederika had no illusions. She had sensed something.

He answered her ring swiftly, and she observed with pleasure that he had lent another dimension to the space of her apartment, an aura, the lingering smoke of his cigarette which still smoldered in the tray, the odor of his presence. His coat lay on the cocktail table and he had removed his tie and laid it across the back of the couch. To her it seemed like he belonged there. Then she was in his arms, breathing in the essence of him, nuzzling his neck, holding his head between her hands, kissing his face, his eyes, his nose, his cheek. He moved her away with a strong tight gesture and looked at her.

"You're very beautiful, you know," he said.

"I feel that way."

"And I wanted to come sooner."

She had wanted to inquire further, but held back, feeling a growing understanding between them. In time, she thought, he will trust me.

"Can I get you something?" she asked. But he was unbuttoning her blouse and reaching for her breasts.

"I know what I want." She felt his eyes watching her, caressing her breasts, the nipples hardening. She was proud of her body now as she arched forward, enjoying his pleasure in her bosom, happy that it was large, full, well formed. She was aroused by his growing passion, reaching for him, then kneeling to squeeze his erection around her breasts, which he kneaded, and she felt the pulsating of his heartbeat against her own, drawing his buttocks toward her, feeling his warmth, his closeness.

"I want you to want me," she said, looking up at him. Then she moved toward the couch, opened it, revealing her double bed, and they undressed fully, moved toward each other, filling the chill between the sheets with their warmth. She drew him inside of her now, felt her body billow like a sail to a fresh wind, as he moved slowly with a languor that told her he did not wish their lovemaking to end. Not ever, she told herself.

"I wish I could say what you mean to me," she said, hoping that he, too, might be discovering this same wonder, the sense of rebirth. She marveled at the calm, unhurried progression of

129

their mutual response, the relentless sputtering of the fuse on a stick of dynamite, then the explosion, powerful, absorbing; the pulsating stillness of heated tungsten, long burning and bright, the climax of a burst of light lingering hotly. It was strange to her, this sensation of joy non-ending and she whispered her gratitude at the power of him, the long hardness.

They dozed and when she stirred again he was still in her, only soft now, sleeping. Gently, she disengaged, then held him in her arms until she grew drowsy. Again, in the darkness, they awakened, held each other, long, endlessly until the light filtered through the drawn blinds. When their passion ground down, the explosions ended, she propped pillows behind them and they half reclined while he smoked a cigarette. What she wanted now, most of all, was to know him. Details were vague, incomplete. Was he nontrusting? He had told her that he had a wife in Santiago and a son and that he had studied at the University of Santiago. He was born in Santiago, grew up there, in the shadow of the Cordillera. He had believed in Allende, had followed him, was appointed in his goverment, had been imprisoned and finally exiled. The story was fleshed out, of course, but the dominant detail was the passion for return, revenge.

"Will they ever let you come back?" she asked. He seemed to be watching her during her questioning, although her eyes were deliberately closed, fearful, perhaps, that they would reveal the fierceness of the attachment growing inside her.

"They? Never. Besides, they have eliminated me from the rolls of the citizenry. I am a man without a country." He hissed the words.

"Will you become an American citizen?"

"Of course not. I am a Chilean."

"Then what will you do?"

"I will come home again."

She knew what he meant. He had lit another cigarette and

in the quiet of the room she could hear the tobacco burning as he puffed, and the light changed as the glow reddened.

"Is there a movement?"

He was silent, puffed again, but this time she pressed, sensing that it was the right moment.

"Is there a viable exile movement?" She sat up. "Eddie, I want a piece of your life. Don't shut me out."

"It is not as simple as it sounds."

"I thrive on it." She told him then about her early life, the politics and the violence, and she told him about the fire bombing. The words came out in a rush as if they had been pressed against her brain for too long and needed this release. She knew now that she had been waiting for this moment to tell somebody.

"You've given me life again, Eddie. I'm ready to be a soldier again."

"Were you ever caught, ever questioned by the authorities?"

"No."

"They knew," he said. "They had their people infiltrated into every group. They were watching you all the time."

"If they were, they would have pulled us in. We did damage. We violated laws. Even in that last gasp. The May Day thing. I was not arrested. I always managed to escape." She remembered then how much she hated the thought of being jailed, although she had enjoyed that one time with the others.

"You were never fingerprinted?"

"No." She had remembered how they had always been frightened of being fingerprinted.

"And you are certain there were no informers?"

"How could I ever be certain of that?"

She was conscious now of a sudden irritation. Was she telling him everything? They had actually been making Molotov cocktails in the basement of that house in Haight and

131

were taking instruction in preparing plastic explosives and learning how to construct crude timing devices. The instructor was called José but it was obviously not his real name. They did not use real names. Her name had been Bunny, because once, during that summer before she had entered Berkeley, she had lied about her age and worked as a Playboy bunny and someone had seen a picture of her in costume hanging in her room before she had taken it down out of shame. There had been that explosion that destroyed half the house, killing José, and someone had said they had combed the place for fingerprints. She wondered if she should tell him that?

"They burrow in. They all work hand in glove on an international scale."

"Who?"

"Their intelligence. In Chile the butchers have the DINA. They were trained by the CIA and have full access to CIA files, computers, devices. They are now in the process of liquidating their old enemies all over the world. Our people. They are effective."

She felt again the excitement of the old danger.

"We were never afraid of them."

"If they wanted to they could have snuffed you out like a candle."

"We laughed at them."

"You weren't a threat."

He said it quietly, but he must have sensed that he was being cruel. "I don't mean that as an insult. There were restraints. In our case it is an international war. Soldiers fall every day."

She felt now that he was reaching the outer limits of his warning and that he was about to break new ground. Her heart beat wildly and she reached out to caress him.

"What can I do, Eddie?" she whispered.

"I have no right to involve you."

"You don't need a right. It's my commitment." To you, she

132

wanted to say, but held off again. She wondered if the the old passion for justice had returned. She did not love one man then. She loved them all, the idea of their courage had moved her. She had loved to be part of them. Now she wanted to be part of this one man, only him.

"There are others. It is not so simple."

"I know."

Again they made love and slept finally until bright sunlight was coming through the slats. She drew the blinds and the clear winter light blazed through the room. He showered, dressed swiftly, and without waiting for coffee, kissed her on the lips and let himself out. When he had gone, she lay down again on the crumpled sheets and slept until late afternoon.

It was a week later when he reappeared. She had thought of him, without anxiety this time. She knew he would reach her again and, perhaps it was her own rationalization, she felt reasonably secure. It was a question of trust, she told herself. He was being deliberately secretive for reasons that he hinted at. She missed him, of course, and it was all she could do to keep herself alert, especially during work. Marcia noticed her lack of attention.

"My God, Frederika. That customer has been sitting at your table for ten minutes without a menu."

"Damn. Where is my head?"

"Probably on that man."

"What man?" she said defensively. Too quickly.

"That one," Marcia said, putting a finger to Frederika's temple.

"I don't think I feel well," she said suddenly, but it seemed a pallid, halfhearted excuse.

"They'll get you every time."

It began to rain when she got off from work. She had brought an umbrella and was walking up Wisconsin Avenue to her apartment house, shielded from the rain. Suddenly he grabbed the umbrella's handle.

133

"Eddie." She put her hand on his upper arm, the muscle hard and taut as he moved silently up the nearly deserted street, past the darkened storefronts.

"Did I frighten you?" he asked.

"I don't frighten easily," she said with mock bravado. Actually, she had been momentarily panicked, but it had happened so fast she did not have time to react. "You'll have to do better than that to scare the hell out of me." He laughed. They embraced in the elevator of her apartment house.

"I missed you," he whispered when they closed the door to her apartment.

"Really?"

"Really."

He seemed less tight, almost playful, as if he had just gotten some good news. Standing together in the center of the room, he watched her, his face in transition, the humor in it fading as he reached for her and began kneading her breasts. Feeling the beginning pressure of his fingers triggered her own response and she felt again the sensual joy of his nearness. How can I tell him, she sobbed inside of herself, wanting to voice her gratitude for what he had given her, even the pain of it.

Later, when they had reached that first plateau of satiation, she lay thinking about him, and her reactions to him. The door of her subconscious seemed to have suddenly opened and she sensed she was observing for the first time the odd contents. He had closed his eyes, was dozing, and she lay propped against the side of his chest, her head rising and falling to the rhythm of his breathing.

I will do anything for this man, she told herself, feeling a special joy in this new rebellion. But it was not enough to merely think it. She decided she must tell him, tell him now.

Her hands began to move gently over his skin, where they paused to play with the curly hair of his chest, downward over his belly. She felt the change in his heartbeat, a swiftness as she reached down for his penis, felt him stir and knew that he had

134

opened his eyes and was watching her. Under her touch, his penis stiffened, the response giving her great satisfaction, almost as a child might view the final phase of constructing a sandcastle.

"You must let me be part of your life, Eddie," she said.

"You are part of my life."

"It's not enough. Not enough for me. I want more." In the context of her present activity, the idea of it seemed silly. He may have caught the humor. His erection was large and powerful, throbbing now, a marvelous, miraculous physical wonder, she decided. It was, in fact, larger than most in her experience.

"I couldn't ask for anything more than that," she said, caressing the tip of it with her tongue. But the emerging thought had not faded, and she moved upward, keeping her fingers on the hardness.

"I want participation," she said. "If you don't let me into your life, then what is it?" She wondered if he would feel that she was pretending an ultimatum. She let it lie for a moment, watching his reaction. "I love you, Eddie. You've changed my life. I want to give, to be giving. I will do anything for you." Then she looked down at his erection again. "And I want that. You." She lifted herself, moved her body over him and directed his hard penis into her, feeling its fullness, moving her body as if she were seeking the core of herself. She felt it occurring, a wrenching, soul-engulfing, overwhelming immediate explosion of pleasure, fulfillment. Why, she wondered, seeing bursts of color in her mind, even as she watched his face. He was observing her as well and, although she felt the beginning of his release, his silvery gray eyes seemed calm with intelligence, as if he were deciding something, probing some imponderable. She continued to watch him as the tension in his body subsided. Then she slackened her upper torso over him and held him tightly until she felt his body soften and relax.

135

"If only the completeness of it was lasting enough," she said. "But when you're gone the longing begins again." Her arms tightened about him. "I am a part of you. It is my need to prove it to you."

"I don't need further proof," he said. "It is not necessary."

"It is to me."

He became silent now, tapping her buttocks to signal his wish for disengagement, and she rolled over to his side again. Had she gone too far, she wondered. He had not professed any special love to her. Had not said the words. But what I spoke, I had to say, she told herself.

"I don't know where you live. I don't know how you spend your day. I feel deprived."

He stood up, lit a cigarette, and opening a slat in the blinds, looked out into the early morning grayness. She watched him, his long slender body graceful in his nakedness, as he puffed heavily and let the smoke billow out of his nose and mouth. Then he moved away and began to dress. She felt suddenly panicked by his actions, forcing her own restraint. Surely, I went too far, she told herself. It is over now. He doesn't need some hysterical lovesick ninny hanging on to him, burdening him. Closing her eyes, she felt the gathering moisture behind the lids, and then the tears rolling coolly down the sides of her face. Her nose filled, but she deliberately held back her sniffles. He must not see my crying. She could tell by the change of sounds that he was dressed now. Then his movement stopped and she could feel his eyes penetrating the grayness, watching her, deciding. Her heart and breathing stopped, and her mind seemed caught in limbo on the burrs of his indecision. Please, she begged, but the sound of his footsteps moving toward the door spoke his answer. The door opened and closed and the sound of his movement quickly faded, leaving the room in its own special silence.

She could cry now, she thought, the sound of her sobbing and sniffling drowning the silence. Soon she was gasping for

136

breath, knowing that she was giving in to self-pity and loneliness, helpless in the shame of it.

Lying in bed, she seemed to will herself into a state of paralysis, hating herself for yielding to the pain of it, but not wishing it to end. She watched the light change in the room, wondering if she could ever summon up, or want to, the urge to move again. There seemed no point to it anymore. Maybe I have died, she told herself, or I am wishing it to happen.

Then, when the room was brighter, and the sounds in the streets below indicated that the city was fully awakened, the sound of the telephone burst into the air. Him, she knew, as her body moved suddenly, the energy recoiling. She picked up the receiver.

"Eddie?"

"Yes." There was an echo. He was obviously in a booth, the sound muffled.

"All right," he said. She could not summon a response. The tears rolled in a stream again.

"It's all right" he said again. "I will call you in a few days."

Then the phone clicked. She continued to hold the phone until the buzz began.

VII

Who is being investigated here, Dobbs wondered, angrily. His mind had wandered. He was thinking about himself, his lost insight. Perhaps I have been at this game too long, he decided. I have grown as dry as a leftover leaf in winter. Was he really looking for a motive behind the Palmero hit or something in himself. Or both.

Furtively, like a self-conscious bird, he looked up from the files on his desk, glancing in either direction and behind him, a visual sweep to be sure no one was there to observe him. He had given strict orders that he was not to be disturbed. And he had double-locked the door. Then why had he suddenly searched the room with his eyes, he asked himself, knowing that the answer was his own fear. He shivered at his faulty logic, fingering the files again, forcing his concentration.

But again he looked up, turned from side to side and behind him. The table was jammed tight against the wall, stark, pictureless, a secured space. Someone was here, he was certain, in the room with him, watching him, sensing things inside of him, sensors crawling under his skin like maggots in a dead carcass. Eduardo, he whispered. The audibility shocked him, because the word had slid out of his mouth. He had not willed it to be said.

Opening another file, he noted his fingers shook. Eduardo, he said, this time in full control, deliberately louder as if to ridicule what had happened previously. Stop bugging me, he said in a conversational tone, as if Eduardo were within earshot.

It took a long time for the meaning of the words in the report to penetrate his mind. Finally his interest was magnetized again and he felt the pull of Eduardo's as yet unfathomable world.

The wife! Miranda Ferrara Palmero. An excellent Polaroid color shot showed her clearly; graceful, slender, with high cheekbones, creamy skin and longish dark hair almost to her shoulders, parted in the middle, giving her face a Madonna-like air. Another Polaroid showed her again with a young child, a boy, clinging to her shyly. By any standard, the woman was a beauty. She seemed strong, proud, aristocratic in bearing, oddly symbolic of Chile's emancipated female.

The writer of the report was quick in confirmation. Miranda Palmero was, indeed, something special even in Chilean eyes, much accustomed to beautiful women. The Ferraras could trace their huge land holdings to Bernardo O'Higgins himself, the Irish-Indian bastard who liberated Chile from the Spaniards and then gave away much of the land to those who had helped him.

Ferraras were both oligarchs and intellectuals, poets, doctors, politicians, businessmen, and the activities of their offspring were grist for the newspaper mill. In a Manila envelope was a pile of clippings. Miranda with her father at the opening of the races. Miranda riding. Miranda at tennis. Miranda sailing. Miranda in a night club. Miranda at her wedding. There was

140

Eduardo, handsome, even glowing in his winged collar and tails, standing beside the radiant beauty. The couple on top of the wedding cake! One clipping described the event as the ultimate merger, the inevitable melding of the old with the new, good genes coming together, the ceremonial crossing of the great bloodlines of Chile. Who could have foretold how it would turn out?

The report was long. Miranda was voluble, excessive, and the interrogation was obviously a catharsis, a long tirade of self-justification. There was deep guilt here. The woman had harangued, raged, boiled with emotion as she spilled her life into the recorder. With uncommon detail, the writer had even described the setting for the interrogation. A huge, ornate room, in the Ferrara compound in the foothills above Santiago, pre-Columbian art abounding, a dominant oil of O'Higgins, surrounded by family mementos, shrines to the Ferraras. It had started on a bright sunny morning and gone on until well beyond midnight.

"So it was fashionable to be compassionate," she had raged. One could almost hear her well-bred voice modulate in emphasis as it seethed with anger over this enormous intrusion. "We are all compassionate. We have eyes. We see suffering. We see poverty. We see injustice. We bleed. We pray for them. We are not stone hearted." Perhaps she had paused, lit a cigarette, which dangled from ringed tapered fingers.

"With Eduardo Palmero it was not enough merely to be compassionate. With Eduardo he had to bleed with them. He had to cut his wrists with them. There was no middle ground. I had to conspire with his family to preserve his inheritance for my child. As it was, he had given much of it away to finance them." "Them" spat out of the page as an expectoration.

"Who are 'they'?" the interrogator had asked. Obviously, it was the root motivation of the interview. Dobbs checked the dates. Eduardo was in prison at the time, and they were putting electrodes to his testicles to get out of him what she would have given freely, if she knew.

"They would crawl over the house like lice, all these so-called saviors. I detested their presence. They revolted me. They stunk. It was the bone of contention from the beginning. He and his friends would have handed us over to the Russians on a silver platter. And that pig Allende. He was a bumbling idiot, a foil for their manipulations. In a few more years there would be nothing left. We would be on refugee boats heading north, begging our big brothers to throw us the crumbs of their hospitality."

"Did you fight about this?" the interrogator had asked slyly.

"Fight?" There might have been a long hesitation, a deep tug on the cigarette, two great streams of smoke flaring out of her nostrils. "Fight implies a relationship. We had none."

"Not even in the beginning."

"Not even then. I loathed him."

"So why the marriage?"

There was a long pause. She might have shivered. They were reaching the raw nerves.

"He was a Palmero. I was a Ferrara. Marriages are not made in heaven. His father was clever. He pursued the marriage like a fox. My father could not resist."

"And the child?"

"It was my duty to create one." The pronoun seemed odd.

"It was my duty," she repeated calmly, showing her contempt of the interrogator's ignorance, a flash of aristocratic arrogance.

"And he was the father?" She would be containing her rage now, at the point of exasperation.

"Ferraras are not given to whoredom," she had said, speaking for the gallant line of her predecessors. "We are also quite fertile. Our conceptions are quick." Dobbs could sense the intimidation in the male interrogator, who seemed confused.

Humanity is a weakness in this business, Dobbs was thinking. It had been his refuge. But it was gone now. A sense of humanity might have saved this case. What, after all, did he know of the love of women?

"There was no love between you?" the interrogator asked.

"Love?" She might have looked at him coldly. But the interrogator needed more.

"If you say it was over from the beginning, then how could you ... ?"

"I could," she must have said quickly. "It is quite possible."

"But you said you loathed him?"

"With my soul."

"And you loathe him now?"

"More than ever."

"And did you loathe him at the time of your conception?"

"Especially then."

"And how did he feel about you?"

"I would have hated me," she would have cried. "He should have hated me. From his vantage point, I would have detested me. Everything he wanted me to be, I was not, could not be. If I were him, I would have put a knife in my heart."

"Then he loved you."

"If that is the word."

"And you could not love him?"

"No. I told you. I loathed him."

"Why?"

"I don't know."

"Was it his politics?"

"Maybe."

"You are not sure."

"No. Why are you asking me this?"

"I am doing the questioning."

"It is enough that I loathe him. I denounce him. I disassociate myself and my child from everything he stands for."

143

"And do you care what happens to him?"

"No."

"Even if he was executed?"

"Even then."

"You have no compassion for him?"

"No."

"Did he treat you abominably?"

"No."

"Then why?"

Hesitation again. The interrogator seemed to have gained the upper hand.

"I cannot answer that question. I don't understand it at all. I'm sorry. Don't talk to me of love. What does love have to do with it?"

Dobbs could imagine the long pause, the tension in the air, the terror of some old memory.

"If it is true that love is an illogical emotion, then so is loathing." The woman had whispered, her throat barely able to support the ejaculation of the word.

"Then why did you marry him?"

"I told you."

"You were forced by duty?"

"In a manner of speaking."

"That is why you loathed him?"

"Not at all. The marriage was logical. It was an excellent match from our family's point of view. His father saw me as the force to change the direction of Eduardo's life. He was a man who could get what he wanted."

"It would have been better if you loved him."

"Of course."

"Did you try?"

"Try to love? Can one?"

We are getting nowhere, the interrogator must have said.

Dobbs understood, imagining Eduardo's father trying to manipulate fate. Hadn't he tried as well, and failed?

144

* * *

Eduardo knew his father had been watching his face, but the distraction of the tennis ball as it collided with the racket had interfered with his concentration.

"Are you listening?" his father said sternly. The veranda overlooking the tennis courts of the club glowed violet in the late afternoon sun. The air was dry, light; the scent of eucalyptus, which came in like the tide at night, was already settling sweetly over them. His father had chosen the tennis club for this talk so he would not miss his late afternoon game. He always kills two birds with one stone, Eduardo thought. At moments like this the image of Isabella always intruded and he could not find the old respect.

"The firm must continue to have a Palmero," his father said. He had announced by letter to his father that he would not attend law school.

"It has you," Eduardo said quietly, respectfully.

"Now," his father replied wistfully. "But in ten years ..." His voice trailed off. He put a hand on his son's arm, haired along the ridges under his knuckles.

"I would not be happy at it," Eduardo said, sipping the golden sherry in the tapered glass.

"But, my God, Eduardo. You are the only son." There was a brief air of pleading as he glimpsed the shattered dream in his father's eyes. They displayed the beginnings of his impending old age.

"We are different, Father," Eduardo said. It was then that his father had begun to talk quickly, his voice velvet, with the lawyer's art of persuasion. But the sound of the tennis ball intruded. His mind had been filled with the arguments for his own case, his lack of interest in law, the absurdity of endlessly accumulating property, the lack of justice in it. We cannot always be taking without giving something back, he had wanted to argue, but what was the point? His father would think of it as youthful stupidity. A ball cracked, sharper than

145

the others, like a gunshot. He had seen the racket swing swiftly in the girl's arm. It was only then that he noticed the girl.

"It is your duty," his father droned on. "I cannot leave this to your mother or your sisters and certainly not their husbands." His views on his daughters' choice of mates were well-known. But then he had always shown contempt for the females of his household. With good reason, Eduardo agreed, seeing the disgust surface on his father's face as if any thought of his wife and daughters could fill him with nausea.

Eduardo's mind was absorbing his father's information, but his senses were alert to the girl on the court, long legged, the short whites tightly wrapping a fullness in her breasts and buttocks, long hair tight in a pony tail as she glided over the court, humiliating her male partner with her grace and skill. He felt a stirring in his crotch and crossed his legs, sipping again from the glass. But he did not turn his eyes away from the girl and finally his father noticed.

"Miranda Ferrara," he said, "lovely to watch."

"Excellent player." Remembering Isabella, Eduardo determined not to show interest. He had seen her before, of course, always with detachment since she seemed beyond his aspirations, an intimidating figure with her arrogance and confidence.

"And quite beautiful," his father said, still watching him, the challenge implicit. Had his father known he was outside of his study, watching? He tore his eyes away and looked into his father's face.

"I know I'm a disappointment to you, Father," Eduardo said, surprised at his wavering voice. Their discussion seemed remote from his real interest now as he imagined the girl on the tennis court behind him. He watched as his father shrugged and dipped his head into his drink.

"I wish I could be what you want me to be," he whispered. But his father's face had quickly changed, the mask of ingratiation forming as he looked beyond Eduardo, who turned as the

146

girl came toward him, his heartbeat accelerating. A deep flush seemed to wash over his entire body. His father stood up and Eduardo obeyed the impulse of politeness. It was odd how much he aped his father's sense of politeness.

"Miss Ferrara," his father said, adding quickly, "this is my son, Eduardo."

She held out a limp hand and touched Eduardo's, the flesh of his palm perspiring as he looked into her dark eyes, flickering briefly as if he were a piece of stone in her line of sight. On the surface it was all so formal, so ritualistic, while beneath he surged, sputtered. When she reached for his father's hand, anger erupted, barely contained as he remembered Isabella. I will not let this happen again, he thought, the rage boiling, making his tongue thick. Then she passed on, a regal figure moving through an aisle of admiring subjects.

He would remember the moment, of course. His mind would try to unravel the mystery of the sudden attraction, like a hook shoved into his body, as if he were merely a carcass to be hung on a rack.

Later, agitated, he had gone back to his own apartment in Santiago brooding over his inaction in not explaining himself to his father, annoyed that he had been deflected. Could he know then that the distraction would last a lifetime?

He had, by then, already allied himself with the political left, who had eagerly welcomed a son of the oligarch. He had joined with the FRAP forces against Frie, had met Allende, and was already composing unsigned articles for the party journal. His father deliberately avoided the subject, a wise man. "You are plotting the destruction of your own family," he might have said. Which, in a way, was curiously true.

So politics had been merely an undercurrent. The meeting had accomplished little between father and son. Only the sudden attraction for Miranda had made the meeting memorable for Eduardo. He could not get her out of his mind, nor out of his body. It was as if she had, like some invisible substance, seeped into his pores and spread through his cells, commanding his attraction. The brief memory of her flesh touching him could send him into a paroxysm of autistic passion with visible, very physical reactions.

He began to haunt the places she was known to frequent. It was relatively easy to find out where they were since she was of great interest to the press, the beautiful, vivacious, wealthy, untouchable princess of the Ferraras. Occasionally at a dance or a night club, or at a party, he would nod her way, receiving in turn her cool acknowledgment, devoid, he was certain, of any interest on her part.

He began to save her clippings and paste them on the inside of his closet door, hidden from the eyes of his occasional visitors, a gallery for his private pleasures or guilt. It was annoying to be so helplessly obsessed, he knew. Nor did it help his self-esteem, since personal discipline was an important factor in his make-up, up till then a source of pride.

His father, a man of infinite subtlety, continued his pressure, perhaps sensing his son's vulnerability. Did he know? Eduardo wondered, a curiosity that filled him with dread, since the idea of it could summon up the early pain of Isabella.

One day his father arrived at his apartment unannounced. Eduardo had just come home from a party meeting, drained from exhortations since he'd had to whip himself into participation, an added strain that certainly had diminished his effectiveness. He was morose and had barely taken off his jacket when his father arrived. The older man was fresh from the exhilaration of some negotiation, although it was odd that he would arrive without the courtesy of a call in advance which would have put Eduardo on his guard.

"You look terrible, Eduardo," he said, surveying his son with that stifling sense of proprietorship. Knowing it was true, Eduardo ignored the observation. He wanted his father to leave. He was an intrusion. Alone, he could contemplate Miranda, summon up his private image of her, the sensual, supple beauty. Sometimes he could almost reach out and feel her hair, its softness caressing his fingers.

"I have been working hard," he said finally, to shift his father's concentration on him, or, at least, interrupt his visual surveillance. There was, obviously, something special on the older man's mind. He hoped it would not be the law thing.

"I worry over you, Eduardo," his father said suddenly. He was not going to be circuitous tonight, hardly subtle. Eduardo braced for a frontal assault. He knows, Eduardo thought, thinking of Miranda. He felt his face flush.

"Would you like a drink, Father?" Eduardo asked half rising in his chair. His father waved away the idea as if he were brushing away a stubborn fly. It seemed serious business.

"They are using you, Eduardo."

So it was political, Eduardo thought, relieved. Sooner or later it would have to come to that. A rebellious son might be a political tradition, but it was supposed to phase out early, like a disease that had run its course. Someone had sent him, Eduardo suspected.

"I have never tried to interfere, Eduardo."

"That is true." It was true only on the surface, perhaps to his father's perception. Actually, from Eduardo's point of view, the intrusion had been massive.

"As an intellectual exercise it was amusing," his father said. "Compassion is a noble emotion, but the reality requires far more pragmatism. Your Allende and his group are trying to destroy us."

"Not destroy. Redistribute."

"Euphemism. Take from us. Give to them." A slight flush mantled his father's cheekbones, showing the anger beneath. "Property belongs to him who can hold it."

"It is a shortsighted view," Eduardo said. "You know that, Father. You cannot continue to take. It is pointless to simply amass, while others starve."

"Well, then we must feed them."

149

"They are also looking for dignity."

He was careful not to appear scolding. He could not find the courage to confront his father, the patron.

"It could get nasty," his father said. "Chile, as we know it, would go down. Your people are agitating too much. Allende is a fool, a stupid dreamer. He cannot change human nature."

"We must have a counterbalance for excessive greed."

The barb found its mark and his father stood up. He was a tall man and his full height was always an intimidation, since Eduardo was still shorter by a head. He felt the old fear again, the power of his father.

"You must stop this, Eduardo," his father commanded. Is it simply a personal embarrassment or are they beginning to feel the pinch, Eduardo wondered, sensing his own elation and guilt.

"I am committed," Eduardo said respectfully.

"Committed? Do you really know what your commitment is?" He knew the question was rhetorical. "You are committed, my son, to your family's destruction. Without property we are nothing. This is the ultimate reality. To be landless in Chile, without wealth or property, is to be nothing. I have not worked this hard for my family to be nothing." His father's rage was like a descending storm brewing in a dark cloud.

"I insist that you stop this," his father said. It was a command that even his father knew would not be obeyed. It was merely the throwing down of the gauntlet, the test. Already he was sure a far subtler plan was at work. My father knows his son, Eduardo sensed, girding himself for other methods of persuasion.

"I am sorry, Father," he said. The older man straightened his jacket. He was fastidious in his dress. Do I love him? Eduardo asked himself. Affection had never been demonstrative in the family, although he believed that his father truly loved him, perhaps as he loved all his possessions. Yet he had destested all the females in the household.

150

"You are his favorite," his mother had insisted. It was a point on which he needed great reassurance, especially after Isabella. "You are the future. Your sisters are nothing to him." She paused and tears had filled her eyes. "And me, as well."

"Try to understand," Eduardo said, as his father moved to the door. The older man paused, put out a hand and gently stroked Eduardo's cheek. Eduardo wanted to touch his hand, but held back.

"You will understand only when you have your own son," his father said gently, turning and letting himself out of the door without another word. He will not give up so easily, Eduardo thought, wondering what the next onslaught would be.

Thoughts of Miranda eased all pain, except the pain of longing for her.

Occasionally, he would go home for the weekend, more out of obligation and guilt than desire. Sometimes all efforts at persuasion failed to lure him back. His mother, in an effort to recapture her self-esteem, had taken to throwing huge parties, mostly to display her wealth and to assure the world that the Palmeros were, indeed, one of the great united loving families of Chile. Eduardo would avoid these despite his mother's entreaties. They were lavish events, huge buffets, formal dress, dancing to the continuous music of rotating orchestras, a flaunting of wealth and affluence that disgusted him. Perhaps, from his mother's point of view, it was necessary to create these events merely to get his father home, since it would be unthinkable, and his mother knew it, for his father not to appear.

"You must come," his mother had insisted one day a few weeks after his father's unexpected visit.

"I'm sorry, Mother."

"I insist."

"Really, Mother. I am only an embarrassment." It was a tack he had decided to take as his political role had increased.

"The radical son has no place there. It stands for everything I am against." He could sense the wheels of persuasion grinding in her mind.

"Everyone will be there. Simply everyone." He might have ignored the entreaty, but something tugged at the back of his mind.

"Who?" It was a question he would rarely ask.

"Lots of young people. Raoul."

They had gone different ways by then. Raoul had entered the military.

"The uniform, you ass. Women go mad for uniforms." He remembered his amusement at that remark, although he still, in his heart, adored and admired Raoul, while hating his arrogance. His associations were more political now. Raoul represented everything that he was against, like his family.

"And beautiful young girls," his mother said, almost lasciviously. Although it was rarely mentioned, Eduardo could feel the pressure of his family's matchmaking. She rattled a long list of names from the best families of Chile. "... Miranda Ferrara." She had thrown the dart at the mark. Miranda. In his house. His hand began to shake as it held the phone. He let her continue her persuasion, but he knew what his decision would be.

It was incredible, even to him, that he could sustain such passion for a woman who had barely muttered a phrase of greeting his way. It was not natural, he decided, adding to his own anxieties. Was he doomed always to love from afar? Of course, it was love, he admitted, although it was not the sanitized version of love in books and movies. It was visceral, passionate, erotic. He could masturbate and excite himself to shuddering orgasms by simply imaging her body beneath its tight tennis things or conceiving that it was her hand caressing, stroking, inducing his joy. Miranda. There was no way to drive her image from his mind.

What would he give up for her? It was a new twist to his

152

obsessions and it began to haunt him now. And yet, sometimes he could feel a deep backwash of humiliation over his own weakness and inability to expunge her. She was, after all, the epitome of what he could easily believe was the dry rot of the Chilean oligarchy, living a life of ease and leisure with not an iota of social consciousness. Of course, he could be wrong about that. He had never conversed with her, could not even find the courage to confront her in the mildest of social forms, knowing that what he feared most of all was outright rejection. It was a finality that he could not, would not bear.

The large house where he had spent his childhood was festooned and geegawed for his mother's party, a lavish display of decoration, food and liquor. Servants were everywhere, putting the finishing touches on the vast display of wealth. They were still polishing the huge rock crystal chandelier that hung from the three-story ceiling into the center of the large foyer, a huge imposing and intimidating symbol of arrogant prosperity.

Dutifully, he visited his mother in her room, kissing her cheeks and filling himself with the familiar scent of her. It was the smell of her that bridged the gap between babyhood and maturity and it wasn't until he finally breathed it that he knew he was home. Then he went to his old room, which was kept as usual, as if he would soon return from boarding school. The objects on the wall, his soccer awards, his old red striped soccer jersey, pictures of a Mexican actress who had once captivated him, all seemed meaningless as if the boy he once was had never existed.

He lay on his old bed, looking at the ceiling, thinking of Miranda, listening to the sounds of preparation in the house, the voices of the servants. He must have dozed. Then the ceiling was descending on him and he felt his helplessness as it lowered, stopping suddenly, touching both his nose and upright toes. In his panic, no logic existed and he felt his pores open and the sweat begin to cascade down his back and sides.

153

Stuck here, he could sense his own rot beginning while all the old fears lost their meaning. Still, even on the ledge of impending death, Miranda retained her luminosity and became his single regret. He was certain that the idea of her staved off the final descent of the ceiling and he remembered the power of its protection when he awoke with a start, bathed in sweat and still shaking.

The music had begun and it might have been the first chords that had released him from his dream. Getting up, he went to the adjoining bathroom, showered in steaming water and began to dress in the formal attire that the maids had laid out.

Without knocking, Raoul walked in, resplendent in the uniform of a captain of the Chilean air force. He is beautiful, Eduardo thought, intimidating in his wonderful physique, sculpted into his dress uniform. His features had sharpened, the bone structure more defined now that some of the baby fat of youth had disappeared. Eduardo was fussing with his studs.

"So the proletarian is putting on his uniform."

"You look like a toy soldier."

They embraced in a *gran abrazo*, the surge of affection between them still strong despite their different paths. But there was an awkwardness now and Eduardo sensed that they would take refuge in deprecating humor and wisecracks.

"The house is literally dripping with fresh pussy," Raoul said, lighting a cigarette and pushing the smoke out through both nostrils.

"Same Raoul."

"I think your mother's trying to marry you off." He paused. "In your case it might not be such a bad idea. Keep you out of trouble."

"I'm not in trouble."

"That's what you think."

"No politics, Raoul."

Raoul shrugged, chasing a brief frown that had wrinkled his

154

forehead. "Doesn't matter anyway. If you go too far, we will simply cut off your balls."

"There are worse fates."

"Name one."

Downstairs the party was in full swing. Eduardo's parents stood in a receiving line greeting an endless procession of guests. One by one his sisters came over and greeted him, wiping off their lipstick from his cheeks. His father looked at him, nodded and smiled thinly. Raoul had already cut one of the beauties from the crowd and had begun to dance, undulating in half rythm, concentrating on his prey. Voices swirling around him, Eduardo searched for Miranda. Walking halfway up the stairs again to gain a better view of the crowd, he felt the agony of loss. Perhaps she had not, would not come. When he could not find her, he proceeded to the bar and downed a double Scotch, coughing as the liquid passed his gullet. He was not used to it. Then he had another. And a third.

People greeted him. Old schoolmates. The daughters of his mother's friends. He nodded politely, waiting for the liquor to anesthetize him as he wandered through the crowd, searching every female face for Miranda.

By the time she arrived, he was already slightly dizzy and his vision was distorted. He was not used to alcohol. Leaning against the wall, he watched her, surrounded by young men, giggling, dividing her attention coquettishly, cool, arrogant, beautiful. He felt his face flush and his stomach knot. It was only when Raoul joined the circle that he found the strength to unlock his knees and amble forward.

" . . . and here is the son and heir," Raoul said. "Arch traitor to his class. You know Eduardo, Miranda." His easy intimacy with her galled him.

"Yes, we've met," she said, flashing a clear white smile his way, then turning to Raoul.

"I saw you play tennis," he said, his tongue thick, although he imagined that he had covered it well.

155

She turned to him again. "I'd rather play tennis than anything," she said, winking at Raoul.

"Than anything?" Raoul, as usual, was lascivious. Eduardo's gorge rose.

"My game is soccer," he said, stupidly.

"Wonderful," Miranda said without interest, turning again to Raoul. The other men had drifted away.

"Did you enjoy the Riviera?" Raoul asked. Eduardo resented the intrusion of a subject foreign to him. He had never been to the Riviera.

"I've never been," he said. But she had ignored him.

"Cannes was wonderful." Then they began to play "do you know" while he stood around awkwardly, shut out of the conversation, determined to find his courage.

"Can I get you a drink?" Eduardo asked. She paused, putting a finger on her chin in an attitude of indecision.

"Champagne?" Raoul suggested.

"Yes, that would be nice."

"Make it two, Eduardo," Raoul said. Angrily, Eduardo turned and moved through the crowd to the bar. The arrogant sonofabitch, he thought, the old boyhood awe congealing into hatred. He downed another double Scotch, took two glasses of champagne and renegotiated the crowd to where they had been standing. But they had gone. He saw them on the dance floor, their bodies close. Raoul was whispering in her ear. Unsteady hands made some of the champagne spill, dripping over his fingers. An image of Miranda in Raoul's arms, naked, intruded. He wanted to fling both glasses at him. Never had he felt such hatred. Moving through the dancers, he reached them. Raoul looked at him strangely and shook his head, his meaning clear. When Eduardo continued to stay with them, Raoul said, "Not now, Eduardo."

Miranda's eyes were closed, her cheek resting against Raoul's, her body mashed against him. His mother and father danced nearby, watching him.

"You are being ridiculous, Eduardo," Raoul said.

"I am ridiculous," he mumbled, his stomach churning.

"Are you drunk?" Raoul asked. Miranda opened her eyes and looked at him with contempt. His father moved closer to them, perhaps sensing something going wrong. More champagne slopped over Eduardo's fingers.

"Why don't you sit down, Eduardo?" Raoul said. "You are embarrassing yourself."

"I want to dance," Eduardo mumbled, his tongue thickening, his cheeks hot.

Raoul turned, releasing Miranda, and faced Eduardo, whose legs seemed like jelly.

" . . . for Godsakes, Eduardo . . ." Raoul began, caught in mid-sentence by two splashes of champagne in his face. The high cheekboned face paled, the eyes blazed, the lips curled, as he gathered his dignity. Luckily, most of the liquid had spilled and what was left was like a brief drizzle. Eduardo could see his father's face, the jaw suddenly slack. But it was Miranda's look of disgust that shattered him, and even through his drunkenness he felt his shame as he turned and pushed his way through the startled dancers.

Upstairs in his room again, he lay on his bed and, remembering his dream, watched the ceiling, hoping it would descend and crash, snuffing out his miserable life.

"I can't believe it," his father said softly beside him. "It is not like you, Eduardo. Are you all right?" He felt his father's cool hand on his forehead, caressing him, pushing a shock of hair upward. He could not recall how long it had been since he had felt such a caress. Eduardo nodded, although he felt tears slide out of his eyes, over his cheeks.

"Did Raoul insult you?"

He shook his head. He could feel his father watching him, sensing the love the older man felt, knowing his own. He wanted his father to embrace him.

"I'll be all right," he whispered, knowing that it would never be true.

"Is it the girl?" his father asked gently. He did know.

Eduardo did not answer.

"So . . ." his father began, swallowing what was to come. So they had found his vulnerability, he told himself, feeling his head clear momentarily. It was the time to offer a denial. But none came. And he knew that he was ready to sell his soul for Miranda.

VIII

Being near the big old Georgetown Public Library had hardly been a consideration in Jack and Penny Anne McCarthy's purchase of the Van Lovell place on R Street. Even the historical aspects of the place were less a consideration from an aesthetic point of view. What they were buying, they both knew, was the social values that the place suggested, the idea that they could purchase a spot in the social hierarchy of Washington by simply buying the historical significance their new home suggested.

It was quite typical of Washington's transient social whirlpool, where image counted for everything. Van Lovell had been Secretary of the Navy back in the 1880's and he had built this house—once the glittering center of Washington's party life—and with it, of course, came political ferment. The house passed on to a series of Cabinet ministers from the administrations of Teddy Roosevelt to Woodrow Wilson. Then old Joe Kennedy had rented it briefly during the Roosevelt administration. That counted for huge brownie points in the image-making process. The fact that he had only lived in it for three months hardly counted against it. Later, Mrs. Carter Howell had owned it and she had become a legendary social arbiter. Presidents had dined there, and kings, and it had been written up constantly in the local press. Once *House Beautiful* had done a picture layout, which the real-estate broker had mentioned umpteen times, not without a stimulating effect. And, after all, since Jack McCarthy was going to be an Assistant Secretary of the Treasury, it would make one hell of a springboard. A New York financial practice was all right. But Washington. There was a big stage for you and what good was it without a proper backdrop, especially if you had the money?

So they had purchased it and Penny and Jack McCarthy had become, in those first Nixon years, the fun social couple of Washington, and the big house was once again written up, and coincidentally, had been done again by *House Beautiful.* Penny had posed with François, her little miniature poodle, suitably groomed and coiffured, although a bit nervous. There they were in front of the mantel, over which hung the huge Chagall that had come down through Jack's Aunt Martha, who had had all those wealthy husbands and to whom they were deeply indebted for the windfall of her inheritance.

But Jack had this thing about being too conspicuously ambitious. The accent, of course, was on "conspicuous" because it was his ambition and the disappointments about it that finally killed him. All that Watergate business had left his psyche in shambles, not that he had been involved. They had shut him off early in the game. That was frustrating enough. But when the old crowd and his old lawyer buddy from Wall Street, John Mitchell, got it, that was the end for Jack McCarthy.

Penny McCarthy had been granted two years to muse about her twenty years with Jack. Two babies had come and gone, both married and living in Portland, Oregon, of all places.

160

That was about as far away as chickens could possibly stray from the coop and still be within the continental limits of the United States. Perhaps it had all been her fault, although the doctors had assured her that Jack had died from a heart attack and that he had had a history of rheumatic heart, which was what had kept him out of the military service.

She had not, of course, told them about his drinking habits, a fifth of vodka as a daily ritual, the last inch of the bottle always taken before bedtime to make him sleep. Pass out, rather than face another confrontation with his impotence. That was one part of it that she was glad was over. Especially since she was convinced that his impotence was caused by her frigidity. We are both unfeeling stones, she had decided, although she could never quite find the courage to tell him it was really her fault. She had tried everything to engender some response. Perhaps it was the trying too hard, the contrivance of it, that finally killed desire. Not that there was ever much to begin with, even at the beginning. She had pondered that point while he was alive and it had underpinned the rationalization for her own unfaithfulness. After all, she was entitled to find some reason for being a woman. Which was another nightmare! She had only confirmed what she knew. She was colder than ice, if that was possible. And while all this was going on, it seemed a miracle that they could maintain that great facade and attract such interesting people to their home. They went everywhere, and even at the very end, Jack could still be impressive. That, she had decided, was his principal quality. He was impressive, forever the harbinger, always the potential, never the realized.

Sometimes in the emptiness of the big house, which she clung to, she could still hear his voice, sweet and deep, the voice always clearing before the mind honed the inner articulation. He could always talk so beautifully. But it was only she who really knew how thin the crust was. Finally, in the end, she had actually begun to love him again, and when he had

161

gone she felt she had lost a lover. If he had not gone so swiftly, she might have confessed to him her infidelities and could envision a deathbed scene, heavy with expiation. But he could not grant her even that satisfaction and simply expired in his sleep. She had not heard his last gasp, nor had she discovered that he had died until late in the afternoon when she had returned from a luncheon.

Jack's death, of course, changed her life, gave the final knell to the brittle ring of her social life, the constant comings and goings of people needed to fill the void. Now, the void could not be filled with people. Conversation actually seemed to become extinct in her mind. That, too, was a signal that something had changed radically in her chemistry, and sometimes she felt her conscious self drifting further from what had once seemed reality.

It was the discovery of the Georgetown Public Library that redirected the drifting and, she was certain, saved her sanity. The library had, of course, been there all along, but she had never been inside it until after Jack had died. Now it became her life, a ritual, to spend her days in the quiet reading room, amid the compelling essence of the dreams and fantasies of others. It was, after all, safer that way. No danger.

By then, too, friends had ceased to call. Those that did received curt acknowledgments and sometimes stony indifference. Invitations dwindled. She could imagine them all saying, "We give up on Penny. She's never gotten over Jack's death." Or, "Let's leave Penny alone. She's wallowing in self-pity these days. Let her wallow."

She dealt in projects, tackling authors one at a time. I am searching for wisdom, she had convinced herself, and she had undertaken the investigation with both diligence and discipline. By that day in February, with the leaves long gone from the dying ginkgo trees, she had already worked her way through Shakespeare, Dickens, Tolstoy, Dostoevski, Thackeray, and was pursuing Balzac when she first spotted him reading at a corner table, the light from the high windows crawling along the polished surface as he quietly took notes, his head rarely moving, revealing a remarkable concentration. Occasionally when she was deeply absorbed, she felt his gaze wash over her, but when she looked up, he had turned back to his work. It was an odd sensation, deflecting her concentration. Sometimes she tried to catch him in the act. But he was too quick.

Some mornings they were the only two people in the reading room. And the only sounds were their own stirrings and the occasional whispered conversations of the librarians. At first, she was annoyed by his presence and the little game they seemed to be playing. She wondered if it were merely her imagination, a psychic pull from an odd magnetic field. Finally she came to expect him, to want him there, although neither showed any covert signs of the other's presence.

He never stayed the entire day. Sometimes he would leave the room quickly. At other times, he would spend the hours reading, scribbling notes, then carefully replacing the books he had pulled out. She was determined not to feed her own curiosity. Nothing must deflect her attention. Her peace of mind depended on it, she was convinced. That, and keeping the big house neat, well maintained.

She did all the chores herself, including cutting the grass and trimming the shrubbery, keeping the silver and glassware shined and the house well dusted, tasks which kept her busy until she went to bed, resisting all errant thoughts, concentrating on complete emptiness of mind, a discipline she had actually begun to master.

In the mornings, before she walked to the library, she spent an hour in strenuous exercises, while Bach wafted through the house stereo system, which Jack had installed himself with such care. The exercises had been difficult at first, but now she was hard and stretched and could contort her body to the full extent called for by the exercises. She had cut her hair as short as possible and had pared her wardrobe to gray slacks and white blouses and serviceable cotton underthings which she changed daily. She had deliberately installed, it seemed, a clock in her mind. Not a moment was allowed to be unfilled, but not with trivial deflections or contrived escapes. She took no newspapers, had her television set removed, and had installed a telephone answering device to take her calls. The message she transcribed on the tape was, she knew, impolite, but hadn't she, after all, taken the call? She never returned them.

Even her children had apparently given up on her, although they took to writing her long letters which she read with mild interest. One of her fears was that they would disrupt her life with some sudden emergency, to which, she knew, she would have to respond. She never went to a store to make a purchase. Food was delivered and her meals rarely varied. Oatmeal for breakfast. A cheese sandwich for lunch. Meat and a green vegetable for dinner. She didn't drink liquor or coffee, had given up cigarettes and sugar.

If there were any lapses in her rigid schedule, they were either inadvertent or subconscious. Occasionally, she had dreams. Most times, she could will herself to forget them. In a way, her life was tranquil and she had structured it to suit her new self, to cope. Most important, she had, with deliberate and skillful mental discipline, emptied herself. And her most conspicuous achievement was that she was not lonely in the sense that she could define it. Nor did she miss not having Jack around anymore. She missed no one.

Her most recent delight was discovering that Balzac had written how many books in the *Comédie Humaine* series and she estimated that there was a good six months of Balzac's world ahead of her. She began to hope that the man would complete his project quickly and leave the reading room of the library to her. She could have, of course, changed her seat, but that would mean disruption and she had learned that disruptions required adjustments and adjustments required concentration and the act of achieving concentration meant a form of compromise. So she stayed put, trying to will the man's presence out of her consciousness.

One night, just as she had closed her eyes, an image of him appeared in her mind. Despite every effort of her will, it persisted, would not disintegrate. It was focused in remarkable clarity, the long lashes which shaded the gray eyes, the white teeth, the dark tanned look. As the sun's brightness had moved across the polished table, it had illuminated his hands and she saw again the tapered graceful fingers tapping lightly on the table.

The image did not last long at first, but when it came back the next night and then popped into her head during her exercises, she began to realize she would have to find some wellspring of special energy to will it away. But the harder she tried, the stronger his recalled image became. Then one morning as she approached the library, she saw him leaning against a stone pillar at the foot of the brick staircase leading to the library's entrance. He was smoking a cigarette, holding it delicately between his long fingers, expelling the smoke in thick gusts from his nose and mouth. The day was clear, remarkably pristine, with a delicious but icy nip in the air. A breeze crackled the dry leaves, still on the ground, lifting some on its eddy. Seeing him gave her an unaccustomed sense of danger. She ignored him and sprang up the stairs, reached for the brass handles of the double doors, and, pulling, felt the resistance. She knew he was watching her.

"It's locked," he said.

She paid no attention to him, banging on the door with the heel of her fist.

"I've done that," he said.

She did not feel embarrassed by the obdurate door or even the futility of the exercise. It was simply something that had never happened before and that was quite enough to challenge her courage. Her rigid new life had not prepared her for sudden changes.

"The librarian is probably late," he volunteered politely. "It happens sometimes," he said.

She stood on the upper landing, feeling foolish. She wondered if she should turn and walk home, but that, too, would be a break in her routine, something to fear.

"I see you here all the time," the man said as she continued to face the door. "You're doing some research, I suppose." She resisted the urge to nod her head, hoping he would go away. Once she had made it a point to avoid doing what was deliberately rude. That, too, had been thrown away with her old life. But the man was not to be put off.

"It's strange that such a beautiful library would have so little use by others," he said. "But perhaps at night. In any event, I'm glad I found it. It's a perfect place to work, don't you think?"

His voice seemed soft, velvety in the crisp air. She hoped the librarian would come soon.

"It's not really as complete as I would like," he continued. "The college libraries are far better and, of course, there is the Library of Congress. But I like the solitude here. Don't you agree?"

Holding her arms stiff against her sides, she balled her fists tightly and stubbornly now, persisting in facing down the door. It was a manufactured tension, she knew. She wanted to respond to him and was summoning all of her courage now.

"What a lovely day. Don't you think? It reminds me of Santiago."

Santiago, she thought. Was it in Spain?

"In any case, winter is better than summer in Washington."

Then he was silent and she continued to stare at the door. But her ears were alert now, waiting. She had wanted his silence and now he was obliging. Finally, she turned. He had moved downward a few steps and was lighting another cigarette. The match flared, but she could barely see the flame in the brightness. Then the smoke curled thickly from his mouth and nostrils. As he puffed, he looked up, his eyes set off by a brief spark, a glint, accentuated by a teariness from the smoke's irritant. She found herself looking at him directly now.

166

"This hasn't happened before," she said, as if her lips were moving without her control. He shrugged, then smiled. She noticed that his mustache was neatly clipped. She had never studied a face in such detail before, wondering suddenly if her reading had conditioned her to notice details with greater concentration. He did not appear to be looking at her face with the same interest. A flash of the old insecurity began. She had an urge to pat her hair, but resisted.

"I'm wondering how long we should wait."

She resented the "we," then realized that she was secretly pleased. Down the street, she could see her house. There is still time to escape, she told herself. Still time. But now it was her legs that were resisting.

"Maybe it's a holiday?" he suggested. "What is today?"

References to time seemed an intrusion. She did not know what day it was.

"I don't know," she mumbled.

"Damn!" he said suddenly. "Of course, it's Washington's Birthday, or at least a day designated as Washington's Birthday. I read somewhere that it's a legal holiday." He laughed. "We are two fools," he said tossing his cigarette on the pavement and stamping it out with his heel. It was, of course, what she dreaded most, the twist of fate, the odd happening, the surprise. Sweat beads had broken out on her back, chilling her.

"Well, since the day is spoiled, how about a cup of coffee?"

"I don't drink coffee," she said quickly.

"Tea then," he joked. Was he mocking her, she wondered. He watched her. She knew now that he was noticing, contemplating. She became frightened now and remained silent. Finally he shrugged.

"Well, then," he said. His body seemed to move slightly in a courtly bow as he turned and started down the street toward Wisconsin Avenue. She watched him walk, his back straight, his step light and graceful.

167

"Wait!" she called. Her arm had left her side, a gesture to draw him back, as if it did not belong to the rest of her body. He turned, walked back part of the way. Her hand reached for her hair, an old gesture.

"I live just up the block." She pointed to her house, the windows glistening in the morning sun. "Over there. And I think we might find some tea." She doubted that and watched his hesitation with fear. Perhaps he can tell I am lying, she wondered, sure of her fear now. He looked at his wrist watch. Observing, she knew it was an empty gesture. It was a sign of her old way of thinking. I know what he is saying and doing, but what is he really thinking, what is his motive? She was back in the world of the old hypocrisies.

"Why not?" he said. Quickly, she regretted his decision. He could have saved her, she thought. He could have declined. She heard his footsteps clicking along behind her as she gained momentum, fighting the urge to break into a run.

As always, the door was unlocked. When Jack was alive the doors were always double-locked with a security system of electronic tripwiring hooked into the nearby police station. She had had all that taken out and discovered, in her new life, that she did not have a single moment of fear.

Until now! She felt a hollowness in her stomach as she heard his footsteps entering the house, a new sound. She felt the floors creak in this new odd way.

"Quite an interesting place," he said. "I have passed this house many times."

"I'll see if I can find some tea."

She left him in the big high-ceilinged parlor, but she stole a look at him from the kitchen, fidgeting in front of the fireplace, looking about the room. She knew there would be no tea, but she did feel compelled to bring something. Opening the refrigerator, she took out a carton of milk and poured out two glasses, laughing at herself, remembering how silly it would have been in the old days. Then, she would have rushed to

168

bring ice as well. Liquor had always been available, regardless of the hour.

"Hair of the dog?" It was Jack's voice returning, a voice that had been silent in her mind for so long.

When she returned to the front parlor, she noticed that he had taken a seat in the old wing chair. Jack had hated it, preferring the overstuffed leather chair at the other end of the room.

"No tea," she said. The smile of her recollection had remained on her face. She put a glass of milk beside him on the table and took a seat on the couch opposite him.

"So," the man said. "You have lived in this lovely place for a long time?"

"Yes." Time again. Her mind was not used to calculating. "Perhaps ten years," she said tentatively.

"My name is Eduardo Palmero."

"Spanish?"

"Chilean."

"Chilean." Another surprise, she thought. Her mind had insisted on his Spanish antecedents.

"Actually, my father's people were originally Italians. But it is a common mistake."

There was a long silence. He reached over and brought the milk to his lips, sipped, then conscious of having put a rim of white on his upper lip and mustache, he reached for his handkerchief and patted. It was then that she realized how much she wanted to touch his face.

"And you?" he asked.

"Me?"

"A name. Your name." He appeared boyish. A nest of wrinkles covered his forehead in a frown.

"McCarthy," she whispered. But he had caught it.

"Ah, Irish. We had a great leader named O'Higgins who helped free us from the conquistadors. There are monuments to him all over Chile. We love the Irish."

169

She wanted to tell him her first name. Penelope. Penny. Even the idea that the name belonged to her had been a measure of her will. She had simply rejected it, obliterated it from her consciousness, except as a practical matter.

"Anne." It was her middle name. By giving him that she thought she might continute to retain her distance from the other Penny.

"Anne," he repeated, contemplating her now as she sat bunched up on the couch facing him. She tried to see herself through his eyes. A woman, almost fifty. Brittle as dry tinder, a body without softness, like a ripcord from her exercises. Cut-off hair. Thin skin, wrinkling. And menopausal. It embarrassed her to think it. But he was not simply observing casually now. He was inspecting and she felt an odd excitement begin.

"You live alone in this big house?" he asked.

"Yes." She looked down at her hands. She wore no rings. "My husband died." His inquiry should have been resented, but she was oddly pleased. She felt the urge to find a mirror and rush up to it and view herself, fix herself. There was inside of her this desire to be attractive, to attract him. She noted physical signs in herself. The nipples on her small breasts had hardened. What is happening?

"And you go to the library every day?"

"Yes." Again, she could not resist. "I am now reading Balzac."

"From end to end?" He smiled.

"From end to end."

"How marvelous!"

She felt her growing delight. "You think so?"

"In school I read Père Goriot and Eugènie Grandet. I remember them well. How wonderful it must be to find the time to see that world. Paris in the 1800's."

"Yes." So, he could understand, she thought. And what of him, she wondered, feeling a sense of sharing intrude, this thing she had shut out of her life. It was the moment, she

170

believed now. She could move forward into a new ground, thin ice, full of uncertainty, vulnerability, terrible risks. Or backward to the tight, structured calm she had worked to achieve. She felt frightened, disgusted with herself for her lapse of discipline, knowing that it would be wrong to move forward, to reach for forbidden fruit. But her will had been eroded. She felt her nostrils flare. It was an extraordinary observation of herself, she decided. Perhaps her body was making a decision despite her mind. But hadn't she erased her femininity?

"And you?" she asked quietly, digging her fingers into her thighs. She was offering herself now, she knew, was moving forward, frightened.

"Actually, I am writing a pamphlet."

"And the subject?"

"Human freedom." She could feel his energy surge. "Human rights. They are disintegrating everywhere. Chile is merely one example. Without freedom there will be nothing. You see . . ." He cleared his throat. She half-listened as he told her about Chile, Allende, his government service, the fall, his imprisonment. She tried to absorb it, but it hardly mattered. He could have been reciting the alphabet. "We were trying to create something in Chile that would be a model for the world. Marxism with freedom. We were not simply going to reorder ownership. We were going to create a free society without greed and acquisitiveness, with sharing." He was standing in the center of the room, a fist clenched, banging into his palm. She could sense his own belief in his inner nobility, although she listened to his words as an abstraction. He moved to the couch and sat down beside her.

"Sometimes I forget myself," he apologized. "I become too absorbed in the dream, in the pain." She felt his presence, his closeness. He lifted an arm and looked at his watch. Moving her arm, she touched the back of his hand lightly. Then her fingers opened and she held it. Her mind was growing blank as she held tightly and watched him. He was silent, contemplating her. She felt the terror of her own uncertainty now, the lack of confidence in her womanliness. He will reject me now, she decided, disengaging her hand from his. But he reached out and grasped it again.

"You are a fine looking woman, Anne," he said quietly, watching her. She imagined he was penetrating her face with his eyes. He is talking to someone else, she thought. He is really imagining that I am someone else.

"Really, Mr. Palmero." She felt her coquettishness. This is silly, absurd, she thought. But he was stirring her. Something was happening.

"Classic," he said. "A quiet maturity."

"Yes. Maturity." She agreed. She did not want to guard herself and looked downward. To her surprise, she found herself looking at his crotch, imagining his nakedness. Will I faint, she wondered, feeling her heartbeat accelerate. She wanted to turn back, felt her will disintegrate. Then he suddenly reached for her breasts. Her response was now without mystery, blatant and aggressive. She felt a churning somewhere in the middle of her and she knew she was on the verge of release from herself. She knew he was sensing it, responding to it. Her mind was conscious of his sudden activity as he reached for the buttons of her slacks. Vaguely, she heard the sound of ripped material as he removed them and with them the cotton pants as her legs spread, the whole center of herself crying out for completeness. Her eyes were closed, but she wanted to see him, only it was too late because he was inside of her now and her body was without mind, a thing running on a power beyond her control.

She felt herself moving on the edge of a windstorm, pushed, helpless, and the wind was passing through her, billowing her body, filling it taut, moving it with a crashing hurricane force, beyond control. Then a sound came. Was it the savage force of wind or her own scream? Since she had forgotten how to conceptualize time, she knew only that what she had experi-

172

enced was ending slowly, the wind dissipating, like dead leaves gliding to the ground. His weight on her was delicious, warm, powerful, and his flesh against her bare torso soft and sweet. Then a hardness began inside of her again and what had occurred was repeated, then ended slowly again. Somehow, when she was alert to her sense of place again, the light had changed in the room, the morning brightness gone.

He had gotten up and somewhere she heard water rushing. She lay still, unmoving, her legs still spread, as if now this would be her primal position, forever open to him, waiting. Finally she got up, gathering her clothes, and went to the upstairs bathroom where she washed, then went to her room for a fresh change of panties and slacks. Leaving the room, she paused, saw herself in the mirror, looked closely, inspecting her face. The skin was taut, not nearly as wrinkled as she had imagined, and her hazel eyes were turned green now in the new light. Her cheeks, drawn tight over her cheekbones, were flushed, her lips puffed. She smiled at herself, noting her own satisfaction. Was she beautiful? For a moment, her fingers were caressing the skin of her face. Then she heard movement below and she hurried down the stairs.

"You are an exciting woman," he said. He was sitting again on the wing chair, watching her come toward him. Under his gaze, she felt different, transformed. She stood over him, holding his hand.

"Eduardo," she said, kissing his fingers.

"I must say," he said, "I hardly expected this."

"No," she said, putting a finger to his lips, "no talk." They remained silent for a while, she standing above him, watching his eyes. Soon, he said, "I really must be going."

She hadn't expected that; the sense of loss became magnified. There was a touch of panic. She continued to hold his fingers.

"Really, Anne." He whispered the strange name. Who is Anne, she wondered. "Really, Anne, I must go."

"But where?"

He laughed, watching her.

"There are things that I must do. There is a whole life out there."

"What do you do?" She had the right to ask that now, she told herself. There was this sense of possession now. He looked at her, contemplating her again, stroking his chin.

"I have my work," he said.

"Work?" It seemed somehow an intrusion. He shook his head, laughed, slapped his thigh with his one free hand and stood up.

"My principal business is the freeing of Chile." She felt the pressure of his hand and let it slide out of hers.

"Of course," she said.

"And yours is the reliving of Balzac." She had forgotten.

"Of course." But she was wondering now if that would be enough. That was the old life. Now, it was Anne's world. But she had not learned to live with Anne yet, which was why she had remained silent when he had finally let himself out. Nor did she rush out after him with some admonition on her lips like: "But when will you come again?" Instead, she sat in the wing chair, where he had sat, a space that she had never occupied before, wondering how she would be able to get back to the safe routine of her previous life. Then she cried. She could not remember the last time she had done that.

Getting through the rest of the day and the night required all the willpower she could muster. She prolonged her evening meal by eating more than usual. The unaccustomed intake left her crampy and uncomfortable and she tossed and turned in her bed until the sun rose. The Bach was grating and she finally shut it off. Then she couldn't concentrate on her exercises, alternating between cursing him and loving him in her mind. Who is Anne? she asked herself repeatedly, but the answer was an echo of silence.

She returned to the library, nodded at the librarian, assum-

174

ing the same thin disinterested smile that she had practiced so many times before. Her heart was pumping with agitation, and her knees had, oddly, lost their smooth motor reflexes. He was not there. Searching amid the stacks, she peeked around corners until she was certain he was not there. Then she went to the Balzac shelf and pulled down one of the books at random. She didn't look at the title, but took her accustomed place, patting the spine of the book on the table to assure that it would stay open.

Alert to every sound, her ears discovered the noise of the place. Once so silent, the library was now a cacophony of disjointed sounds, among which she tried to identify his movement, his footsteps. She heard the ticking of the big clock on the far wall and the breathing of the librarian, even the swirl of her dress, a strong "wooshing" sound. It was maddening, a terrible intrusion on her concentration. Nineteenth century Paris was remote in the opened pages of Balzac. Finally, after an hour had passed, she stood up and approached the librarian.

"Why is it so noisy here?" she asked. Her voice seemed a roar as it emerged from her lips.

The librarian looked at her, tipping her head in an attitude of disbelief.

"Noisy?"

"Yes, there is far too much noise."

There was still enough logic in her to feel embarrassment, and without looking at the librarian again, she went out into the street and stood in front of the building, looking both ways. Perhaps if she walked toward Wisconsin Avenue, she might see him. She started down the street with swift strides. But she could not see him there either. Then she returned to the library, hoping that, perhaps, he had arrived from the opposite direction. He wasn't there.

Again, she tried to concentrate on the opened book, but the words swam meaninglessly before her eyes. Standing up, she went to the stacks and took another one, then tried again to concentrate. If he doesn't come, I shall have to scream, she told herself, and then, miraculously, he was there, poking around in the familiar stacks, gathering his material, placing his note pad at his usual place at the table.

"You're late," she said, feeling the sense of possession again. He looked at her, said nothing, and smiled. Thank God, she told herself, feeling the new sensations begin again.

"Will you come to see me later?" she asked, hoping he would not detect the urgency in her voice. He watched her face, his gaze lingering, the long lashes shading the gray silver-flecked eyes.

"Perhaps," he said. "If I can finish the task I've set for myself today. I am behind schedule."

The tentativeness frightened her. She wanted to insist. Again, she sat down and attempted to read her book, watching him as he worked, swiftly, with deep absorption. Seeing him calmed her, and although she could not regain any concentration, she was content to sit there near him.

Normally, she would have returned home for lunch, but now she refused to move, feeling him beside her, watching the clock, which she had hardly noticed before. Time had captured her again and she found herself watching the pendulum swing and the barely perceptible movement of the clock's hands. Once, he lifted his head and smiled briefly, then returned to writing furiously on his note pad. Finally, at three o'clock, which must have been the hour he had set for himself, he stood up, returned the books to the stacks, stuffed the papers in his brief case, and turned toward the door. She rose and followed, remembering her sweater, but leaving the books on the table, something she had never done before.

"You were working very hard," she said when they were in the street. The weather had turned colder, which produced a glazed mist in his eyes.

"I am hurrying to finish," he said, standing there, his weight moving from one foot to the other.

"Would you like to come to the house?" she said, her eyes shifting in embarrassment. He looked at his watch and she felt the panic of an impending rejection. Then, summoning unaccustomed coquetry and masking her anxiety, she said, "I make a terrific glass of milk." He laughed, suddenly engaged.

"Ah, yes," he said. Then he looked at his watch again. "But I can't stay too long."

They walked toward the house and she put her arm in his, squeezing the upper part, feeling the heavy muscle. She had not seen his arms naked and now she tried to imagine what they looked like.

"For a while there, I thought you weren't going to come."

"I had other business earlier. But I'm determined to finish this pamphlet before the week is up."

A week, she thought. Three days actually. It was Tuesday.

"And then?"

"There is a great deal to be done," he sighed.

The sense of time was now oppressing her. Inside the house, he put his brief case down and started toward the wing chair, but she held him back.

"Let me show you the house," she said. Perhaps if he filled the house, stamped his presence on it, he might be tempted to change the schedule he had created for himself. It was possible to ignore time, she had learned. Holding his hand, she moved through the house, the study, the kitchen, the maid's quarters, now vacant, another parlor, then up the back stairs.

"These old houses are quite mysterious," she said, feeling like a young girl, remembering vaguely having done this in some big house in another life. On the second floor, she showed him the sleeping rooms, all neatly kept, fresh sheets on every bed. Despite the fact that no one slept in the beds, she had changed the sheets weekly and carefully dusted and polished.

177

Each room smelled sweet. Finally she came to her own bedroom, with its high canopied bed with crinoline edging. Jack had always despised it. No wonder, considering his affliction.

"This is mine," she told him, turning toward him, her body moving tightly against his. It seemed instinctive on her part, deliberately, aggressively suggestive. I must have him now, in this bed, she told herself, feeling her body's sudden craving as her hands reached for him, caressing. His nature responded and she could feel him hardening and soon he was kissing her, filling her mouth with his tongue.

"Let me undress you," she whispered, removing his jacket, then his tie, unbuttoning his shirt, slipping his T-shirt over his head, then unbelting him, unzipping, rolling down his shorts, watching, caressing, touching the smooth hardness of his erection. He stood there, an object to be observed, and she was acutely aware of his enjoyment of her attention. He has a right to be proud, she told herself.

"Now you," he said, as he began to help her undress while she wondered if he would be as pleased as she. She continued to stroke his erection. Then, when she was naked, she stepped back, catching a glimpse of herself in the mirror. Her body was firm and slender, her stomach flat, her buttocks tight, her breasts small but still upturned.

"You have the body of a young girl," he said, reaching for her.

Then they were in her bed, and the joy of him being there with her was overwhelming. Before he could enter her, her body responded with a kind of massive seizure of pleasure, an orgasm that drew its essence from the pit of her being, a gale wind now repeating itself when finally he had entered. She wrapped her arms and legs around him, knowing that she was discovering herself, a new self, Anne!

Later, she watched him. His eyes appeared to be seeing something at the top of the canopy, but she sensed that he was looking inside of himself. The reality of time was fully existent in her mind now.

"Do you really see me as a young girl?" she asked.

His concentration was deflected and he looked at her and smiled.

"You are a young girl."

"I'm forty-nine."

"Now, you are talking chronology. I'm talking about what my eyes see and my flesh touches." He gently put the flat of his hand on her stomach.

"And inside?"

"Very young and very beautiful."

"Would you please say that again?"

"Very young and very beautiful."

"Thank you." She kissed his cheek. A tear rolled out of her eye. "Do you mean that?"

He hesitated, then ignored the question.

"I'm forty-two," he said suddenly. There was an air of regret in his manner. "Age is an enigma."

"An enigma?"

"I feel young and old at the same time." He hesitated and looked at her, on the verge of revelation, she thought.

"Once, forty seemed old," he sighed. "Chronology has lost its meaning. I have found more strength in myself than ever before in my life." He was not talking directly to her. There was a distance, a barrier. What does he mean? she thought. "Maybe it is anger, the search for vindication, revenge, that gives me this odd energy."

"Revenge?" Still, she had not engaged him.

"Or maybe it is the sense of impending death."

At the mention of death, she swallowed hard, gasped. He must have felt the shiver run through her.

"I have a great deal to do...." He was guarding himself now. He closed his eyes and she watched his eyelids flutter for some time, kissing them, as if the act might still them.

179

"Stay with me, Eduardo," she said suddenly. She felt panic, that terrible repetitive sense of impending loss. Her voice startled him and he rose in the bed. She could sense his preparation to take leave.

"You have to go?" She said it for him. How can I keep him here forever, near me forever, she asked herself.

"Yes." He kissed her forehead and bounded out of bed. She watched his strong back move, the buttocks beautifully rounded. As he turned to pick up his clothes, his genitals swayed. To her, it was an odd, beautiful sight. She lay back observing him.

"Can you feel that this is your home, Eduardo?" she asked.

"You mustn't think in those terms, Anne."

"It is not thinking. It is simply a fact of life."

He shrugged, ignoring her, tightening his tie.

"I am yours now, Eduardo. There is nothing I won't do for you." She stood up and walked to him, her face close to his now, watching him in the mirror. "There is nothing that I have, that I own, that is not yours." The saying of it was exhilarating, important. Anne could do things like that. Not Penny.

When his tie was straight, he turned toward her, kissed her on the lips.

"You are talking nonsense."

"Like a young girl?"

"A very young girl."

She paused, watching him. He looked clean, hard, sure of what he was.

"You will be at the library tomorrow?"

"Yes. All week."

"And after, will you be with me?"

He hesitated.

"Perhaps," he said. Then he was gone. She listened for the sound of his movements down the stairs, opening the door.

Running to the window, she watched him walk swiftly toward Wisconsin Avenue. She wanted to cry again, but this time the tears would not come.

That week he did come every day, and by the end of it, her life had completely metamorphosed. She no longer did her exercises and she could not concentrate on her reading, sitting instead at the library table, seeing him through the pores of her body, resisting the temptation to look at him, fearful of creating a distraction for him. The sense of time had fully returned. Even her eating habits had changed and she had stocked her refrigerator with foods from her other life. Gourmet foods, caviar, exotic cheeses, a crown roast. She had found a recipe for chocolate mousse and had stayed up half the night creating it.

While she had not asked him, she had assumed that he would stay for dinner on Friday night and she had prepared an elaborate feast, setting the table in the dining room, which had not been done for years. Her best china, the Waterford glasses, the golden candleholders were laid out, even a beautiful display of flowers from the florist had been delivered. She had searched her closets for one of her old gowns, an Adolpho, once the rage, and she spent a great deal of time that morning reworking it to fit the leaner body of her new self, of Anne. He had seen the set table when he came in the house on Friday afternoon.

"You are expecting guests?"

"Yes, later." She enjoyed the humor of it.

"Your table is exquisite," he said.

"It is for you, Eduardo."

"For me?"

He did not pursue the point. They went up to her bedroom. For the first time, he appeared distracted in his lovemaking, although her own intensity was undiminished, and when she had calmed down, her mind groped for a strategy to prolong

181

his presence. To her, the relationship was permanent. It must never end, she decided. It would be like death.

"Stay with me, Eduardo," she said. It was a litany now.

"I live alone. My work makes it impossible to share. It is too dangerous."

"Look, Eduardo"—she moved her hand in a sweeping gesture—"I have this." She walked to a corner of the bedroom and opened a breakfront with a small key. That morning she had carefully gathered all her papers, the bankbooks, a statement from her accountant. She put it in front of him.

"I am worth three million dollars, at least," she said calmly.

He fingered the books, but said nothing.

"I am saying, Eduardo," she said slowly, touching his face gently, "that everything I have is yours." He laughed and shook his head in disbelief. Was he laughing at her? He must have sensed what was on her mind, reaching out and drawing her close to him.

"Am I that valuable?" he asked, perhaps mocking himself.

"You are to me," she responded quickly.

He shook his head. There was an air of disbelief in the way his expression changed, as if he were searching for some logic to her act. He thinks I am mad, she decided.

"It is what I want, Eduardo," she said, watching him, hoping that he would finally understand.

"Why?" He emitted the word as a barely audible whisper.

It was important now, she realized, to say exactly the right words, to bridge the gap between the ridiculous and the sublime. Only Anne could do that. Penny would have thought it ludicrous.

"You are my life," she began, hesitating. He would not want to feel owned. "You have given me . . ." She hesitated again. "I love you," she said at last. It seemed the most innocuous phrase she could think of. I am reborn because of you, she wanted to say. I am alive at last. I would die for you.

182

He reached out and patted her cheek. She caressed his hand. "Incredible," he said. But she did not understand.

Later, they ate the meal she had prepared. She watched him eat, experiencing, for the first time in her life, the essence of happiness. He must never leave me, she decided.

IX

When Marie LaFarge moved out of her husband's bedroom, she had fully expected the outward props of her life to disintegrate. She was living in limbo now, she told herself, waiting for the moment when Eduardo would send for her and she would never return to the cage of her present existence.

In her mind, she had escaped from the cage, had spread her wings and moved from beyond the bars, only to find herself perched uncertainly on a shaky limb. It was cold out on that limb and the sun shone only when she was with Eduardo. But Eduardo was elusive, and when they met he insisted on the secrecy of their relationship. He would call her once a week, perhaps twice, and she would go to him.

"You must not tell him," he had warned when she had told him that she had moved out of Claude's bed.

"But why? I want the world to know."

"Not yet." The sense of expectancy reinforced her optimism.

"When?"

"Please, Marie. You must not endanger yourself."

185

"I want my life to be your life. I don't care about danger."

And when it was time for her to go, she always held back, lingering. If he had gone, leaving her in the bed, she would wrap herself in the sheets like a mummy and imagine that she could be part of the room, always there, until she would become jealous of the inanimate objects that were fortunate to share his presence. Sometimes he would insist that she leave first.

"You must go. I have work to do."

"What sort of work?"

"I am writing a document."

"What sort of document?"

"A manifesto, the fundamental words of our movement."

"Please, Eduardo. Let me stay. Let me watch you. I will not disturb you."

"Please, Marie."

After those times with Eduardo, she dreaded coming home. It seemed an alien place now, although she went through the motions of devoted motherhood. Claude had reacted with his usual calculated methods, designed to maintain appearances at all cost. Nothing, after all, must stand in the way of his career. And since she had not actually left the house, appearances could still be preserved for the outside world. It is only temporary, she told herself.

"How long is this madness to go on?" Claude asked her one evening at dinner, after the children had gone off to watch television. She knew he had, up till then, been deliberately proper. But she also knew his discipline and surmised that he had swallowed great draughts of bitter bile to maintain his control. She had, after all, challenged his manhood, a very precious commodity, especially to a Frenchman. She wished he would have had the guts to respond to his true emotions and throw her out of the house. But nothing she could do or say had been enough to cause Claude to explode. His career was, as it had always been, the main priority of his life.

"It isn't madness, Claude."

"Then what is it?"

"Loathing."

She could see his upper lip tremble and his eyes blink with abnormal speed as he sought control. What she wanted most was a confrontation about "another man." If he accused her, she would admit it, she decided. She longed to admit it. Only fear held her back.

"You are trying to ruin me," Claude said, after a long pause, when he seemed certain that his voice would be strong, controlled.

"That is absurd," she said with contempt. Actually, she pitied him. In comparison to Eduardo, he seemed so inconsequential.

"Perhaps if you saw a psychiatrist," he said. She wondered if she sensed an edge of sarcasm.

"A psychiatrist?"

"Surely what you're doing is not normal. The mother of two beautiful children. The wife of a successful and rising diplomat. I wouldn't consider what you have done as rational." He tapped his forehead. "Something is going on up there that bears some scrutiny."

"Save your money," she said, getting up from the table. She feared that if the conversation kept on, the confrontation would be inevitable. She picked up the dessert dishes and coffee cups and brought them into the kitchen. She could hear his footsteps behind her.

"Marie," he pleaded, on the verge of losing control again. He put his hands on her shoulders. Briefly, she saw his eyes, the pain that lay there. "You are torturing me." She shrugged his hands away and averted his gaze. It is easy to be cruel, she observed, hating herself.

"There is nothing here for me anymore," she said quietly. "Why can't you understand that?"

"But the children."

187

She wanted to say, "The hell with the children," but that might confirm her madness to him. Besides, she could not understand why she no longer loved her children. Perhaps, she thought, it was because they were not Eduardo's children. Maybe I do need a psychiatrist, she told herself.

"It will pass," Claude whispered. "I will be patient."

"Never," she said. It had not been meant to be said.

Because there was no regularity to her meetings with Eduardo, she lived in a constant state of tension. Sometimes he would call her on Monday. Sometimes Tuesday or Wednesday. It seemed a kind of unwritten understanding that she would never see him on weekends. She had thought about it, but since it was part of the rhythm of their lives, she did not let her mind dwell on it. Occasionally, though, after they had made love and she imagined that they had achieved their most intense closeness, her courage would rise above her caution.

"When you are not with me, Eduardo," she asked, "where are you?" He did not stir, as if the words had not been spoken. But she persisted. "What is your life like when you are not with me?" He continued to remain silent. "Mine is a nightmare. I walk through a dream. I live only for you to call me. I live only for this." She caressed his body.

"It is better that you don't know," was all he would say.

Despite her longing, when she was not with him, she could still feel a residue of passion, an afterglow. At night, though, when she would slip between the sheets of her bed, she would make a conscious effort to empty her mind of him. Most of the time, she was not successful. Beside her, on the night table, were piles of books on Chile which she would read for hours, sometimes until the first gray signs of morning. Occasionally, she would hear Claude's footsteps along the corridor. They would reach her door, hesitate. Thankfully, they would begin again and move away toward their old bedroom. Even when she slept, there seemed no respite, and when she awoke the sheets were badly wrinkled and the blankets on the floor.

Once, odd sounds seemed to come to her as part of a restless dream and she opened her eyes to find Claude in her bed, fighting to pry apart her legs. He had been drinking and the smell of whiskey, as his mouth searched for hers, sickened her. Freeing one arm, which he had pinned behind her, she flailed at his groin until he desisted.

"You lousy bitch!" he hissed, his lips twisted, his eyes blazing with hatred. But she felt no pity. Why doesn't he ask me? she thought. I will tell him now. But he did not ask. Without looking at her again, he limped from the room, slamming the door behind him.

The incident had left her frightened and restless and the next day she bought a strong chain and attached it to her door. At dinner the following night, he apologized.

"I'm sorry, Marie." He was feigning contrition, she knew, but she determined to accept it.

"It was foolish."

"I had been drinking."

"Yes, I noticed."

He played with his spoon.

"What would be the harm if you saw a psychiatrist?" he asked. He was not being sarcastic now. It was obviously a sincere conclusion. She looked at him and laughed. It seemed to come in a long rolling sound, uncontrollable and rippling, as if in response to a hilarious joke. The ridicule was, she knew, pure malevolence on her part.

"You are a bitch, you know," he said, his face suddenly pale. He threw down his napkin and rushed angrily from the table.

A few days later, when she told Eduardo about the incident, he was shocked. Then she informed him that she had moved out of Claude's bedroom. The knowledge agitated him further. His reaction confused her. He should be happy, she thought. I have made a commitment to him. I am faithful. He paced the floor of his apartment in his bare feet, puffing deeply and frequently on a cigarette.

189

"I had no idea," he said.

"You think I can sleep with another man?" she said angrily. "My skin crawls at his touch."

"And you have not told him about us?" he asked suddenly.

"No."

"Does he think there is another man?"

"No. He is blind. He is an idiot."

He smashed out his cigarette in an ash tray and lit another one.

"It could be a disaster for him to know," he said finally.

"He will know sooner or later. I can't go on like this."

"You must."

"Must?"

He sighed, came toward her and sat beside the bed, stroking her arm gently. "I had no right to involve you."

"Involve me, Eduardo? You did nothing. Why explain it? You have given me a new life. No. You have given me life."

"I have endangered you," he said. "I am deeply involved in dangerous work. A complication with your husband would be a disaster. It could destroy everything we are working for."

"We?"

"The Chilean people."

"But, darling. You must understand. There is no life without you." Was she going to lose him? She shuddered. "How can I do anything that will hurt you?" she said.

"Then you must make it up with Claude."

"I don't understand."

"You must not make Claude suspicious. It could not only hurt me ... and you, but endanger the lives of many innocent people."

"If only you would confide in me, my darling." She balled her fists, feeling the full force of her frustration. "But you tell me nothing. I am simply a woman in love." She paused waiting for some response, frightened. "Tell me how to act so that I will not do foolish things to hurt you or your friends.

Tell me. I will do whatever you ask." He continued to stroke her arms, then leaned over and kissed her deeply.

After, he stood up, paced the floor again. Then he was suddenly back with her, and from his expression she knew he had reached a decision.

"I have something to ask of you, Marie," he whispered.

"Anything, darling."

"It is simple. But it could be dangerous."

"Why can't I persuade you that nothing I can do for you can frighten me. I will do anything." She kissed him again, and she felt tears brim over her eyes. "I am capable of killing for you, Eduardo." It was an odd thought. Could she really do that, she wondered.

"Hardly that dramatic," he said, shaking his head with amusement. He moved to the closet, brought out a box, and took something out of it. Returning to the bedside,·he held out his palm, on which rested a small, shiny object. She looked at it and touched it. It felt cold.

"It is an electronic device." Lifting it, he held it between his thumb and index finger.

"What does it do?"

"It listens."

"I see." She was concentrating now. It was important. He was making her a part of his work and she was grateful.

"I want you to put it somewhere."

"Where?"

"You must be very clever." He paused. "I want you to put it in the study of the Chilean ambassador. In his residence. His private study."

"But how ..."

He put a finger on her lips. "You must be very clever. You must get an invitation and it must be in a large group so that they will not be suspicious. They are very shrewd." She was trying to absorb the information and what it meant. Since she had moved out of Claude's bedroom, she had refused all

191

invitations. She knew Claude was telling them that his wife was ill. Eduardo brought over a brief case which lay against the wall. Opening it, he took out a large envelope and withdrew from it a package of large photographs, which he spread before her on the bed.

"These are pictures of the study. I have marked all the possible points where the device can be placed."

She followed his graceful white fingers as they traced the area in the pictures, feeling the special joy of the complicity.

"There are so many possible choices that it would be difficult to make a mistake."

"But where is the best place?" she asked. She looked at the pictures.

"Here." He pointed at a bookshelf.

"I could slip it under a dust jacket." She looked up proudly, touching his fingers.

"An excellent place. But everything will depend on the question of time. Ideally, you should be invited into the study by the ambassador, and when his attention is deflected you could do the job."

He gathered up the pictures on the bed, replaced them in the envelope, and put them on the floor on top of the brief case.

"I would suggest you study them carefully again," he said. But her mind had already snapped a clear picture of the study, and her thoughts were already alerted to strategies. Surely, she could persuade Claude to solicit an invitation on the basis of her sudden interest in Chile. It was then that the idea of physical proximity to Claude intruded, and she felt a wave of revulsion wash over her. If only she could find a way to do it without that. Perhaps she might befriend the Chilean ambassador's wife, a lovely lady, easy to meet and talk with.

"Above all, you must not arouse suspicion," Eduardo said suddenly, with emphasis, as if reading her thoughts. He held up the device again, his fingers on the rim, then placed it on top of the envelope.

He stood over her now, his fingers running through her hair. She rested her head against his body, caressing him again, holding him tightly.

"I will not fail you, my darling."

"I am sure," he said.

"Thank you, Eduardo," she said hoarsely, kissing the flesh of his belly. Before she left, he wrapped the device in tissue paper and put it in her hand. She held it tightly for a long time before she finally put it in her purse. "I will show him how clever I am," she vowed.

That night in her own bed, she did not feel the same tug of emptiness. Now there was a sense of mission, participation. Claude, of course, must be manipulated to be her instrument of entry into the Chilean Embassy. Anything is possible for Eduardo, she assured herself.

"Good morning, Claude," she said pleasantly as he arrived at the breakfast table. It was the first time in weeks that she had actually taken any notice of him. He seemed to have bloated slightly and there were dark circles under his eyes. The children had already been packed off to school and she had taken great care with her morning toilette. Not a hair was misplaced and she had dabbed herself with the scent Claude had liked and which she had deliberately abandoned. She had, up till then, rejected anything that gave Claude pleasure.

His face suddenly brightened, although she could tell he had quickly rallied his defenses. It had never been Claude's way to be taken in easily. He was naturally cautious. He would test her first.

"You look very charming this morning, Marie."

"Thank you, Claude."

The smell of freshly perked coffee was heavy in the room. Coincidentally, the sun was shining and the day clear, a fitting background for the illusion of harmony that she wished to convey.

"Lovely," Claude said as he sat down, the folded newspaper beside him on the table. She sat down in her usual place, feeling his gaze. He is confused, she thought. After a while, he withdrew his hand and sipped his coffee. Enough for now, she thought, feeling the excitement of her deception.

"You seem quite different today, Marie," he said. She could sense his subtle sarcasm. It was, after all, safer for him to be cautious.

"Perhaps it is because of the wonderful morning," she said, her eyes deliberately averted, as she lifted the coffee cup to her lips. He continued to observe her, the newspaper ignored.

"Is there something you would like to say, Marie?"

"Perhaps later," she said pleasantly, turning to him now, offering the faint hint of a smile. Slowly, she warned herself. You are such a pompous ass, she mused as she looked at him, wondering if she were wearing a proper expression.

"I would like that, Marie," he said, his hand sliding near hers across the table. With an effort, she kept it still.

"I suppose we have lots to talk about."

"Yes."

His hand touched hers and again she resisted the desire to move it away. Then the full weight of his hand was on hers and he was squeezing it. Although her indifference was absolute, she could feel his emotion. The fool, she thought. After a while, he withdrew his hand and sipped his coffee. Enough for now, she thought, standing up and moving toward the kitchen.

"Marie," he called. She stopped and turned, conscious of improving her posture. She felt her breasts strain against her brassiere and knew she was deliberately emphasizing their fullness.

"Yes, Claude."

"We will talk later."

"Yes."

Getting through the day required an enormous effort of will. If only Eduardo would call, she thought, feeling the need for reassurance. Make it up with Claude, he had told her. And then? But she had not dared to ask that question. She was now

194

part of Eduardo's life, of his work, and that was a step forward, perhaps a tiny step from the present limbo.

That evening Claude came home with a great bouquet of yellow roses and a bottle of champagne. There seemed to be some sentimental currency in it and she remembered that it was one of the elements of his courtship, yellow roses and champagne. How ridiculously contrived, she thought. At dinner, she kept the scene deliberately cheerful. The children talked of their day with great enthusiasm and she forced herself to listen, feeling Claude's eyes on her, watching for any signs of retrogression. Without his realizing, she deliberately delayed the children's departure for bed. It was Claude who intervened finally. When they were alone, he opened the champagne.

Please help me, Eduardo, she pleaded to herself as Claude handed her the champagne, clinking the glass with his.

"To better days ahead, my darling," he said, sipping the champagne and watching her with a silly, glazed, fawning look. She tossed off the champagne in a single gulp, hardly tasting it. He quickly poured her another glass. The expected lightheadedness seemed slow in coming.

"Is it over, Marie?" he asked tentatively, touching her arm, caressing it, still fearful of rejection.

"I'm not sure, Claude," she said. Better to be tentative as well, she had decided.

"These last weeks have been the worst of my life, Marie. The worst."

She wondered why she could not summon pity. Only contempt. Holding out her glass, she let him pour her more champagne. He did it eagerly and she knew that he, too, was being calculating, deliberately plying her. I will do this for Eduardo, she thought. By the time the lightheadedness began, he had moved toward her and summoned the courage to hold her in his arms.

"Perhaps I have been too self-centered," he said. "I will

195

change, Marie. You'll see. I have been thinking it over these last few weeks. It is all my fault. I promise I will change."

She endured his fondling, and the fear of showing indifference forced her to increase her outward response. The objective, she told herself, was to get through this as quickly as possible.

"It will be beautiful again, my darling," Claude said. She could feel his mounting excitement, encouraging its acceleration by caressing his genitals. The touch disgusted her, but she did not falter. She listened for the quickness of his breath, the swift pounding of his heart. His hands groped into her body. She imagined that he was interpreting his own ardor as spontaneity and she fed the fantasy by increasing the strength of her endearments.

"Can we?" he asked.

"Yes."

She had wanted to say later, but it had passed beyond that point and she did not want to arouse his suspicions. Removing her pantyhose, she lay on the couch. Closing her eyes, she let her mind wander while she mechanically drew him inside of her. She was thinking of her girlhood and suddenly she missed that part of her life, before Claude, her father's strong hand in hers, walking on the *Champs Elysées,* the smell of flowers in the Tuileries, the view of Paris from the top of the Eiffel Tower. She had been safe then, beyond abuse, beyond this. She might have lost herself in these memories if Claude had not hurt her. She was dry and tight, like a virgin. It was detestable, revolting. Thankfully, he did not last long, falling on her in a heap. She waited. His breath became regular again and his heart slowed, she observed with clinical objectivity. She made no move to crawl from under him, waiting for him to act.

"It will be different," he said.

"Of course," she responded, wondering if he could sense her revulsion.

She moved out of the spare room and back into their

bedroom, finding that it was possible to endure anything for the sake of one's objective, Eduardo's objective. I am playacting, she told herself, an idea which sustained her. Claude's sexual appetite seemed insatiable, and she endured it with a strange sense of pride. His deprivation had been total, and he had not, out of spite, she was certain, allowed himself the relief of another woman. That would be typical of Claude to deliberately savor his suffering, to increase his self-immolation. If only he could know of her noninvolvement. Someday she would tell him. How deliciously castrating it would be.

"I feel like I've been raped by an army of barbarians," she told Eduardo a few days later when they were together again in his apartment. He put a finger on her lips.

"You mustn't talk about it," he said.

"Not talk about it," she protested, feeling anger even as she caressed him. "It is loathsome. I can barely live through it. I feel violated."

"He is your husband."

She looked up at him. "He is nothing to me."

"Then perhaps we had better forget about it." He was pouting now, and she contained her rage.

"You're not jealous?"

"If it is too much to endure . . ." His voice trailed off. But the implied threat struck home.

"If the roles were reversed, I would kill you for it."

"Kill?"

A shadow passed over her face, triggering her own fear. "I could not bear the thought of you with another woman."

"Another woman?" He seemed surprised. Was she being too intense? Was she going too far?

"I am jealous of every moment you spend without me." The new idea appeared to break the tension. "I will endure it only until I have done what you have asked," she said quickly.

His face brightened. He put out his hand, smiling. She took it, squeezed it, like two people sealing a business deal.

"Agreed," he said. She felt her anger subside. But somehow the deal seemed incomplete.

"And after?" she asked quietly.

"After what?"

"After I have done it."

She watched him, frightened again. He was, she knew, trying to formulate an answer, but she dared not hear it.

"Please, Eduardo. I am sorry. It's not necessary to answer that." He seemed relieved. "I cannot bear being away from you."

But the idea of their future together would not go away. The more she endured Claude, the more it plagued her. I can't live like this, she told herself. Yet, she took solace from a new thought. If she proved herself, if she showed Eduardo how clever she was, how cunning, he would overcome his own caution. He is afraid for me, she decided. But when he sees how efficient I am, how fearless, he will not resist our being together always. Let Claude take the children. Nothing mattered now. Only Eduardo.

It did not take her long to persuade Claude to work at securing an invitation from the Chileans. They had begun to do the party circuit again and she had sought out the Chilean ambassador at these events, ingratiating herself with coquetry and what he must have observed as a surprising knowledge of his country.

"It is my great ambition to visit your country," she told him.

"You will fit in nicely," he said. He was a tall man, barrel-chested, with well cut clothes and an obvious interest in women. When she discovered this, she became boldly flirtatious. "The women of Chile are the most beautiful in the world."

"It is the men that make them so." What a perfect retort she had contrived, she thought.

He seemed to puff himself up like a proud bird, and she

pressed her advantage. She suddenly yearned for Eduardo to stand beside her invisibly and see her in action.

"We used to believe it was the climate," he said.

"There is a lot more to the environment than the weather."

He caught her drift, obviously a man experienced in such byplay. She was amused by his naïveté. Can't he tell I am playing with him?

"Only a country where men appreciate women can gain such a reputation," she pressed. "And, of course, the women must feel the truth of it to allow it to perpetuate."

"I will accept that for our hemisphere." He winked and bent over, whispering in her ear, "If you'll allow that the women of France reign in your hemisphere."

"We do have a reputation of sorts."

"So I have heard. Is it deserved?"

"I hope so." She hesitated and looked into his eyes. "At least, I do my part." She could see a slight flush begin near his jowls, and she marveled at her own forwardness. This will be easier than I imagined, she decided.

But when the Chilean invitation came a week later, the victory was merely pyrrhic. Eduardo had not called and she was helpless with anxiety, almost to the point of revealing the full force of her irritability to Claude, who seemed to be watching her microscopically for any sign of relapse. His attentions were stultifying, smothering. On the morning that the invitation arrived, she dashed out of the house after the children had gone to school and drove the car to the parking lot of Eduardo's apartment building.

She waited for three hours, watching the entrance, feeling foolish and conspicuous. Suppose he has been killed? Or kidnapped? He had described his danger and had warned her to stay away from him except when he told her to come. She sat there in the car, sick with worry. Then, unable to endure the anxiety, she got out and walked quickly to the apartment house, averting her eyes from the desk man and rushing

199

toward the elevator bank. A couple came in behind her in the elevator and she rode to the top of the building before coming down again to his floor.

In front of his apartment she knocked quietly, pressing her ear to the door. There were no sounds from within. She knocked again. Still no stirring within. Then she rang the buzzer and still no answer came. A woman passed through the corridor. When she was out of sight, she dipped into her pocketbook and, finding a blank envelope, scribbled a note on it, slipping it under the door. "I have news," she had written, wanting to say more.

It was not until she returned home that the full impact of the panic seized her. How can I stand this, she asked herself, pacing the floor. Where is Eduardo? That evening they went to a reception at the State Department honoring those who had given gifts to the Adams room on the top floor. She was listless and withdrawn, barely spoke to people, hoping that she looked attentive despite her indifference.

"Are you well, darling?" Claude asked as she prepared for bed.

"I think I am getting the flu," she answered.

"Is there something I can do?" Claude asked. He was being unctuous and she dared not look at him for fear he would see her loathing.

She awoke the next day exhausted, and her image in the mirror frightened her. There were heavy dark pouches under her eyes and her skin was pale and unhealthy looking. When Claude and the children left, she went back to bed and lay there staring at the ceiling. It was only when the telephone rang that she realized she had dozed. Hearing Eduardo's voice, she was instantly alert.

"You shouldn't have done it," he said. His voice was low, muffled. "They watch. They listen."

"I had to. I can't stand it, Eduardo."

"It is too dangerous."

200

"I don't care."

"And the news?"

"I will be there on Friday night, at the Chilean Embassy."

"Good."

"Will I see you today?" she asked, wanting to press the issue. There was a brief silence on the line.

"Not until it is done," he said. "That is why I have not called. I think they are watching me closely now."

"I must see you, Eduardo," she said. An idea had occurred to her. Once again the line was silent, but this time it was her voice that filled the void. "The pictures. I want to be sure where it can be put."

"You don't remember?"

"I want to be sure."

She could feel him sigh into the phone.

"I want to be sure," she repeated. His hesitation reassured her, and although she was deliberately lying, she knew that she had found a way to manipulate him.

"I am not afraid," she said. "If I have you, I am not afraid."

"All right."

"Today."

"Yes. Come at noon."

She jumped out of bed, took a long lingering bath, perfumed herself, feeling her body's signals of longing, and when she arrived at his apartment she groped toward him like an animal in heat. The touch of his flesh enervated her and her body lurched with pleasure and abandon.

"You must love me forever," she cried, feeling the pleasure come in deep waves again. "I want you in me always, always." She must have been making loud noises, as he put a hand over her mouth. "I can't help it," she said, when she realized what she had done. "I must shout my joy. You are my life."

After a while her body relaxed and her mind cleared. When she opened her eyes, he was watching her.

"I need you so much, Eduardo."

He kissed her forehead and the tip of her nose.

"I had to be near you."

"And the pictures?"

"I'm sorry, Eduardo. I lied." She knew it would be impossible to lie to him directly.

There was a flash of anger. "I told you it was dangerous."

"I don't care."

"But there are others," he said. "Other lives are at stake. They are ruthless killers." His arms tightened and he banged a fist into his palm. "Your assignment is of the utmost importance, Marie."

She remembered her conversation with the barrel-chested ambassador.

"He seems so harmless, almost naive."

"That's what he would like you to think. Believe me, he is a key man for them here, and what we learn from him could be most crucial, most crucial."

"He fancies himself a ladies' man."

"He is and I'm sure he finds you irresistible."

"Well," she said gaily, "I must admit he does respond to my blandishments."

"That is certainly not hard to comprehend." She felt secretly pleased, although she would have preferred him to be jealous.

"It will be no problem, no problem at all for me to get him to show me his study."

"I'm sure of that."

She laughed. The anxiety of the previous days had dissipated.

"What you do to me, Eduardo." She bent over and kissed his flaccid penis, caressing its shaft with her tongue. He lay quiet for some time, but he did not grow hard.

"I'm sorry," he said. "My mind seems to be on other things. And I am anxious about your safety. You had better leave."

"Must I, Eduardo?"

"Please, Marie. Your safety is essential."

She searched her mind for some excuse to stay.

"Can I see the pictures again?" she asked, proud of her cunning. He looked at her archly.

"But I thought . . ."

"One more time. It would be better to be sure."

He bent under the bed, found his brief case, and pulled out the envelope and pictures, handing them to her. She spread them over the bed and studied them for some time. She felt his breath on her bare shoulder.

"Well?" he asked.

"I want to be sure that I have explored all the alternatives." She stroked her chin, feigning absorption. But it was his nearness that held her attention. Finally she turned toward him and her lips sought his, her body pressing against him.

"You are my life, Eduardo. There is nothing else in my life anymore but you."

Although she hadn't intended it, the words seemed like a warning. When she released him, he gathered up the pictures and replaced them in the envelope, then returned them to the brief case.

"Everything else in my life is pointless," she said, unafraid now, caution gone. He must know, she told herself. "I will do anything you ask of me. Anything."

"Please, Marie," he said. "You must go. I fear for your life."

"And what of yours, Eduardo?"

His eyes averted hers.

"I am fully prepared to die."

"If you die, I die."

"You mustn't talk like that. It is my cause."

"And now mine."

He was silent for a while. She sensed that he was choosing his words. If only she knew what he was thinking.

"Are you sure about the room now?"

"Yes."

"And you have the device?"

"It is perfectly safe." She had put it in her jewelry box.

"The Chilean people will be grateful."

"That is ridiculous." She was suddenly angry. I am not doing this for the Chilean people, she wanted to tell him. "It is for you, Eduardo, for you." She drew him toward her, caressing him, feeling again the fury of her sexuality and the joy of discovering his response again. He grew hard. She felt a sense of victory. "I love you. That is all that matters to me. There is nothing else." She drew him inside of her and she felt her happiness again, her fullness as a woman, and nothing else truly mattered.

She arrived at the Chilean Embassy in a low-cut gown, designed to display as much of her upper flesh as was appropriate for a diplomatic event. Taking great pains with her toilette, she began early in the day, fussing with her eyes and skin as she never had before.

"Still at it?" Claude called from the living room. Previously, before Eduardo, his impatience would have been close to rage and he would have railed and cursed, his anger resounding through the house. And she would have been suitably obedient and deferential. Not now. She was contemptuous of the absurdity of his blandness and she deliberately stalled the final touches to her hair.

"Please, Marie. It's growing late."

She wanted to make a grand entrance, which was not diplomatic etiquette but, for her purposes, a necessary gesture to draw attention to herself. It would take some doing to get the ambassador to take her to his study, and despite her previous optimism, she was not without trepidation and had spent the last few days mulling over the possibilities that might defeat her purpose. I cannot fail, she told herself, removing the device from the jewelry box and placing it in a little pouch that she had constructed within her dress, dead center, where the slope of her dress reached its lowest point. She could simply slip out the device by reaching between her breasts and placing it in one of the alternative places shown in the pictures.

"Hurry, Marie. Please," Claude pleaded. She looked at the clock. She was already a half hour late. He was at the foot of the stairs as she moved down, tightening an earring, her purse held under her arm.

"You look exquisite, Marie," Claude said, kissing her lightly on the cheek. She was pleased, only because he had validated her own assessment. A beautiful woman was an enormous asset in the diplomatic world, she knew, stimulating courtliness and a display of manners and quaint archness which passed for communication in the ritual of diplomatic socializing.

"I have never seen you looking so radiant," Claude said as they drove to the Chilean Embassy on Massachusetts Avenue.

"Thank you," she said confidently.

"And I love you," he whispered, the words meaningless. She deliberately did not acknowledge them.

When they arrived at the embassy, the guests were still having cocktails in the front drawing room. With a quick sweep of her eye, she noted that there were approximately sixty guests, noting on the posted seating list that there would be six tables of ten. She looked at the six wheels. She had, as she had surmised and hoped, been seated next to Ambassador Pallett, at his left, as protocol required that a guest ambassador's wife be seated at the host ambassador's right.

In the foyer, the ambassador and his wife greeted her and Claude with kisses and compliments. She squeezed the ambassador's hand to heighten whatever effect she might be having.

"You are exquisite," he whispered, his lips lingering on her cheek a shade longer than might be appropriate. Then he led them into the front drawing room, where black-tied waiters passed silver trays of drinks. She felt the ambassador's eyes washing over her even as he passed through the crowds, playing the affable host. She watched him peripherally, circling the room, and occasionally when she turned full face, she would deliberately lock her eyes with his, encouraging his attentions. She knew that he was heading for her, merely performing the expected social rituals.

Eduardo had explained that the ambassador's study was on the same floor as the reception rooms, behind the double staircases that rose on either side of a large chandelier. It had seemed a simple process to find the study and plant the device, but suddenly confronted with the imminence of the plan, she began to question its simplicity. She felt conspicuous and was beginning to regret her deliberate attempt to call attention to herself. Perhaps it was the wrong strategy, she wondered, wishing that she could somehow will herself to be invisible.

"Your scent is positively divine." It was the ambassador's voice. She turned quickly, felt the intensity of his gaze as his eyes searched blatantly downward into her décolletage. If only he knew, she thought, feeling her attack of anxiety vanish.

"You're very flattering," she said, moving closer to give him a better vantage for his obvious interest. "And your home is always so breathtakingly beautiful."

"Yes, I agree. We Chileans have an eye for beautiful things." His meaning was unmistakable.

"I would love a grand tour," she requested quietly.

"It would be a pleasure to show you around."

"I'd love to see where you live and work."

"Well, actually, we have our main offices a few blocks away. Mostly, this is a residence." Another of the guests had come up to join them and his voice had become considerably more formal.

"You do not perform any official functions here?" It was an insipid question. As a knowledgeable diplomatic wife, she knew the answer. But she was determined to plant in his mind the idea of the study. He exchanged a few words with the other guest, a silver-haired man who looked vaguely familiar. The ambassador grabbed him under the elbow and they moved away to join another group, but she knew he was merely depositing him in another place.

"So you will give me the grand tour?" she asked when he had returned.

"I look forward to it."

"And you will be the only tour leader?" It was a bold probe, but his reaction reassured her. His voice seemed to take on a new intimacy.

"I wouldn't think of sharing the experience," he whispered.

"Nor I," she said, feeling ridiculous as she watched the man puff up again like a bird. He looked at his watch, excused himself with a conspiratorial wink, then announced to the guests that dinner was to be served, and the group entered the adjoining dining room.

"You've made quite a hit with the ambassador," Claude whispered as he brought her into the dining room. "And see where he has placed you." He could not conceal his pride in her.

"He's rather a pleasant fellow," she said.

"Lucky, I'd say." He bent over and kissed her cheek. "To have you for the evening." Claude's fawning added to her contempt. He had never expressed jealousy if she had been flirtatious with men of greater rank and importance. Claude seated her and went off to another table.

Before she had lifted her fork, she felt the ambassador's leg against hers, stroking it as he talked animatedly with the woman at his right. Deliberately she held her leg inert until the main dish was served and she deemed it appropriate to return the pressure. His face glowed with pleasure as he turned toward her.

"I'm afraid I've been neglecting you," he said. He had, she knew, overcompensated by giving the ambassador's wife more than her fair share of attention.

"I don't feel neglected." The reference was pointed and she increased her pressure on his leg, which he eagerly returned.

207

"I am, you know, tremendously interested in Chile."

"Ah," he said warmly. "I'm delighted."

"Frankly, I don't quite understand what's happening there. It is all so confusing."

"Yes," he said. "We are having our troubles. We had not expected things to come to this. We are a beautiful country, a beautiful people."

She thought of Eduardo, his passion, his fear. It annoyed her to see Eduardo's enemy so vulnerable.

"You Americans do not understand us. We are an example of the failure of civilian government. It is, thankfully for you, beyond your comprehension." His leg continued to rest against hers; then it began to move in a steady rhythm. She could feel his anticipation. Yet she wanted suddenly to talk about terror, thinking of Eduardo and his anxieties.

"We read all sorts of things about your intelligence services."

He stopped the movement against her leg. His eyes opened in surprise and she wondered if she had gone too far. Then the stroking began again, and she returned the pressure to reassure him.

"The activities of our intelligence services are much exaggerated. We must protect ourselves as you do. The French, the Americans, the Israelis are amazingly efficient. And the CIA is everywhere. Why should a country like Chile be singled out? We have been given few alternatives."

She retreated into the familiar cliché of trivial femininity.

"I don't understand such things. I only know what I have read in the American press."

"We live in a dangerous world, Madame LaFarge."

"Marie," she added quickly.

"Marie," he seemed to savor the name as if he were tasting the first sip of a rare wine. Then she felt his hand touch her thigh. Even he must have realized that he had gone too far. He dropped his napkin, then quickly bent to retrieve it, watching the faces around him. But no one noticed, and he quickly moved to converse with the ambassador's wife on his right, his leg not leaving hers. He seemed to have increased the pressure, an accurate gauge, she thought, of his excitement.

She touched the spot between her breasts where she had placed the device, then began to talk to a little man on her left, who appeared to be hard of hearing. He smiled benignly. She knew he had not heard a word she uttered.

After the dessert, which she ate with unaccustomed eagerness, more out of nervousness than desire, the ambassador clinked his glass and stood up. He cleared his throat and, watching her, began what seemed like an elaborate toast to his guests, who were all characterized as distinguished, the ladies portrayed as elegant and beautiful. He looked toward her pointedly as he made this reference and she felt Claude's eyes resting on her, his pride certainly unbounded as if he were receiving a compliment for a pet orchid that he had grown himself. It was all so brittle and insincere, without any meaning for her, irrelevant to her new life. This is absurd, she thought. Yet she knew her face was beaming up at him, hopefully glowing with admiration.

When he sat down, his leg immediately took up its accustomed place and she bent over and whispered to him, "You were quite marvelous." But his reaction was deterred by another man who rose to make a countertoast, also complimenting the beauty of the ladies, but his eyes were on the wife of the Chilean ambassador, who certainly deserved the accolade.

Finally the guests rose and the men and women were separated in the old tradition, the women off to the front drawing room for coffee and the men to a back parlor to enjoy brandy, coffee and cigars.

"I know it's all very archaic," the ambassador said, "but we follow the tradition. Sometimes we get complaints, but after all, diplomats may be allowed some leeway in following the amenities."

209

She shrugged. He was obviously embarrassed now that the moment of truth had arrived, stealing a glance at his wife among the group of departing ladies.

"I hope it is the appropriate time for me to collect my special good fortune." She wondered if she had inadvertently winked, for he immediately blushed and led her quickly to the foyer.

"The house was built with perfect symmetry," the ambassador said. "The two drawing rooms are identical, as you can see, although the colors and furnishings are deliberately different." He seemed to have assumed a formal approach and she wondered if he were actually frightened that his private tour might be misconstrued by an observant guest. It was only after he had passed through the drawing room, out of sight of the others, that he began to loosen up.

"And this is the library," he said, taking her arm, squeezing it, then in a quick motion sliding the door shut. With his back to the high doors, she could see his arm move behind him and turn the lock. Quickly, she looked toward the end of the large library to what Eduardo had explained was the entrance to the study. But before she could turn her head back to face him, he was pressed up against her, his lips searching for hers. She let him kiss her, felt her lips pried open and his tongue shoot into her mouth. A hand slid itself down into her bodice and caressed a nipple.

"I'm wild for you, Marie," he whispered.

"Please. Not now. Your guests."

Gently, she moved him away. His face had flushed a deep scarlet.

"And what's in there?" she asked, feigning breathlessness and patting her hair. At first, he seemed puzzled by the question.

"In there?" She wondered if he would understand the implication of her inquiry. Where it's safer, you ass. Must I say it? He came toward her again and put his arms around her, kissing her neck.

210

"It can't be safe here," she said.

"I've locked the door."

"Still ..." He kissed her again and she let her hand fall limp, feeling his hardness against the backs of her fingers. "Please. I am afraid."

Again, she managed to release herself and moved toward the door of the study. He pursued her and as he kissed her again, she turned the handle. The door was locked. She felt a sudden burst of anger and pushed him away.

"Not here."

"I want you," he said.

"Not here," she replied firmly. She could see the bulge in his pants and, looking up at his face, noted his confusion. Reaching into his pocket, he drew out a key chain and quickly opened the study door. Eduardo would be proud of her cunning, she thought. Had he known that the door would be locked? She moved into the study, searching for signs of familiarity as she converted the pictures in her memory to the reality of the room. The ambassador shut the door behind him and clicked the lock with some flourish, designed to alleviate her fears. She moved quickly to the bookcases behind the antique desk. He did not lose a second in pursuit, gathering her into his arms again, pressing his lips tightly against her own, his body pressing against hers as she searched for a place to put the device. His hand groped at her buttocks and she could feel the relentlessness of his erection now. There was no escape, she knew, as she spotted a place for the device inside the jacket of one of the books. She managed to turn in his arms and place her back against him. His arms came around her, feeling for her breasts, and she reached backward for his erection.

"This is madness," she said, turning her head toward him, but still facing the bookcases.

"I must have you," he murmured. "I must."

She bent over and lifted her gown, gathering it around her waist and leaning forward. With one hand she gripped the

211

edge of a bookcase. Anticipating the situation, she had worn no encumbering underthings. She heard the sound of his zipper and then he was groping for her, plunging his erection in the general direction of her parts. She was dry, but reaching for him, she managed to insert him. She bit her lip to prevent herself from crying out in pain. I must endure this, she told herself repetitively as she reached into her bodice for the device. Then, finding it, she slipped it quickly under the dust jacket of a book. Behind her, his body moved like a piston. This must end. Please! Fortunately he reached a climax quickly, and he stepped away, releasing her.

She turned and let her dress fall, smoothing it. His face was beet red and he was sweating profusely.

"I can't tell you how much pleasure . . ."

"Quickly," she said, taking his hand and leading him out of the room. She noted that he still retained enough presence of mind to relock the study door. He passed through the library, unfastened the latch, and they moved back into the foyer.

To her relief, the powder room in the foyer was empty and she stepped in. Her knees were shaking and she was seized with a sudden fit of nausea. The recently eaten dessert seemed to turn sour in her stomach and she gagged, disgorging the half-digested mess into the toilet. When she recovered herself, she cleaned herself up, repaired her makeup, and went back to join the guests. In the foyer mirror she noted that all her rouge could not hide the unaccustomed whiteness, the pallor. Had Eduardo expected this, she wondered as she forced a smile and entered the drawing room to join the ladies.

X

As she sat in the carpeted waiting area in the Pan American section of the Miami airport, Frederika Millspaugh felt like someone outside of herself, a different person. She was wearing a pink jumpsuit, a blonde wig, large round-framed sunglasses, and a white scarf around her neck. Beside her on the floor lay an elegant Louis Vuitton brief case. It was all totally out of character, someone completely different from the person inside.

As she waited, she tried to amuse herself by imagining that she was the person that she was depicting, this someone else. On the plane down from Washington, she had actually answered the hostess in a southern accent.

"Ah would indeed lak some coffee," she had said, bringing her voice to a higher pitch. That was, of course, the only thing she did say on the journey, although the man next to her tried to engage her in conversation. But Eduardo had warned her about that. "Talk to no one. No one," he had emphasized. Trying on the clothes he had brought her, she had actually made him laugh with her posing and gestures. She had even made him try on the blonde wig. With his mustache and dark face, he looked ridiculous.

"The perfect picture of the Chilean transvestite," she had said.

That had set him off and he doubled up in a spasm of laughter and she imagined what he might have been like as a young boy. For a moment, the burden inside him seemed lifted and he was unguarded.

"What was Santiago like when you were a boy?"

"Beautiful." His eyes seemed to probe backward in time. "We played soccer in the green fields framed by the snow-capped Andes. We wore white uniforms with red numbers, and red and white striped socks." He must be seeing it all in color, she thought, watching his face. "The field was actually on a high plateau and we could see the waves breaking in the distance along the white beaches."

"It sounds a lovely setting for a school."

"Yes." He paused. "Sometimes . . ." he seemed reluctant to continue, as if he might reveal too much. "I can hear the sounds of the boys. Eduardo! Eduardo! Kick this way. This way." He imitated the voices in a high falsetto. "I was good, always in the center of the action. And sometimes, when I was very good, the boys would carry me on their shoulders. Nothing since has ever given me the same exhilaration, the same sense of achievement."

She tried to envision him as he saw himself, a heroic figure, his young hard body, muscles tight under a marble-smooth skin, white teeth shining in the sunlight. My God, I can see him, she thought, feeling his sadness. How far from home he is. Then the image seemed to fade inside him and no amount of questioning would restore it and his past slipped away from her. Sometimes, after they had made love, her own floodgates would open and she would talk endlessly about her childhood, wondering if he could imagine her.

"Braids," she began once. She could see herself so clearly as

214

a child of twelve. "My entire childhood seemed built around braids. My hair was down to here then, and my father adored it and would not allow Mother to cut it. So she braided it, day after day, hour after hour. She would stand behind me braiding my hair and rolling the braids around my head. Sometimes the braids were allowed to hang down, but once some kids put the ends of the braids into an inkwell. We were in art class, and it wasn't until I got home that I saw what they had done." She paused, wondering if he was listening.

Finally he said, "Was that the end of the braids?"

"No." He is listening, accepting the gift of my life. It seemed a presumption on her part to think so mythically, but it was important to her sense of giving to tell him.

"The braids did not go until I was fifteen. I had a boyfriend named Lenny. And he was just like the Lenny with the rabbits, big and stupid, but beautiful to look at and touch. He didn't like my braids. So one day I let him cut them off."

"Why?"

"I wanted to prove my love," she said. Perhaps it had not been exactly like that, but it was the kind of romantic idea that heightened the meaning of her life for her.

"Will we have to cut off your braids now?" Eduardo teased.

Then she had tried on the entire disguise, complete to the white scarf and the Louis Vuitton brief case. She felt silly, but he inspected it with great care.

"Good," he concluded. "A typical middle-class glamour girl on her way to fun in the sun."

"You don't think it's too conspicuous?"

"Conspicuous, yes, but not to the people who watch. Definitely outside the realm of their profile for a conspirator, a terrorist."

"Is that what I am?"

"In a way," he mused.

A shiver of fear ran through her. He had warned her of danger.

215

"Are you sure?"

"I'm sure."

"This is not a game. It is quite dangerous."

"It is your game, Eddie. That's what is important. Will it be of help to you?"

"Of enormous help."

"Then that is what I want."

It was, indeed. She was part of him now, drawn in. And she made him repeat the assignment over and over again, as if she hadn't remembered every detail.

"You will simply take a flight to Miami. You will arrive at noon. Go directly to the Pan American waiting room. You will sit in the waiting room, in the row facing the counters. You will place the brief case next to you on your left side. And you will be reading a magazine. *Vogue.* That's all there is to it."

"And then?"

"Just sit there. Someone will sit beside you. A woman. She will be there only briefly. Then she will get up and leave."

"And switch the brief case."

"Yes. Then you go into the ladies' room, change into the clothes in the brief case, replacing them with the clothes you will be wearing. Then you will take the plane home." He paused. She could feel his reluctance to explain further. But she pressed him.

"And what's in this brief case?"

"It's better that you don't know."

"Why?"

"Then you can't be responsible."

"But I want to be responsible, Eddie. That's the point."

"I'm sorry, Frederika."

She unzipped the brief case and took out a flat package, holding it in the palm of her hand.

"Can I guess?" He took it out of her hand and replaced it in the brief case.

"Really, Frederika. You mustn't take this lightly."

216

"I don't, Eddie. It just seems that if I am carrying out an important assignment, then I should know what I am doing."

"I promise I will tell you. But not now. I prefer to spare you the danger of knowing too much. Perhaps if we can achieve this without complications, then the next time."

She understood. There was to be more. She felt relieved. So now I am almost a part of it, she thought with pride. Defined purpose was what had motivated her before. There was a cause, and although the ultimate objective was unclear, she could understand the purpose and she could believe in the idea of it. The people! When Eddie said it, the old feeling welled up again and she felt that same sense of defined purpose.

"We do this for the people," he had said.

"The people of Chile?"

"Yes. But that is only the beginning. It must start on the mainland in Chile and then it will swallow up the rest of South America."

Yes, of course. But she could not decide whether her compassion was real or merely manufactured out of her love for Eddie, her willingness to sacrifice for him. Perhaps, she thought, it was best that she did not know what was in the package. Not yet. Not now.

She turned the pages of the magazine without comprehension. Her peripheral vision remained alert and her ears listened for every sound. She felt someone sit down beside her and she forced her head to remain motionless. It was a woman, as Eddie had said. The scent of her was distinctive. Then she was gone. Frederika waited the appropriate time. Eddie had said ten minutes. Then she rose, picking up the exchanged brief case. It was light. Walking across the airport lounge, she went into the ladies' room and opened the case. In it she found an outfit of blue jeans and sandals, into which she quickly changed, stuffing the jumpsuit and scarf and shoes into the brief case, along with the blonde wig and sunglasses. When she came out again, she felt more like herself.

217

It was late afternoon when she returned to her apartment, expecting that he would be there, waiting. He was not. She found it odd. She had assumed he would be there to share her experience. Besides, she was proud of herself. Finally she dismissed his absence, knowing, surely, that he had good reasons. Instead, she tuned her ear to the telephone, expecting his call, the ring shattering the silence. He knew when she would be arriving. Certainly, he also knew how necessary it was for her to tell him that she had succeeded, succeeded for him, for his cause. Yes, he would call soon and she put any sense of anxiety out of her mind. But when he had not called in the next hour, she felt the onset of doubt. Still, it was not enough to upset her and she decided, as he had instructed, to go to work.

She put on her waitress uniform, threw a light coat over her shoulders, and went out. In the elevator she imagined she had heard a phone ring, punched the next floor and ran up the stairs listening at her door. Silence confirmed, she went to the elevator again.

She had hoped that the night's work would be a distraction. Nothing seemed to help and she spent most of the evening looking through the window, wondering if he had chosen to meet her at work.

"That's the third time you misstated an order tonight," the omelet maker reprimanded.

"I'm sorry."

She went through three days of it. The anxiety became unbearable. Something has happened, she was convinced. Allowing herself that possibility somehow eased the pain, for it implied a third force was at work, beyond his control. She dared not think that there was another reason for his absence. Such a thought was too cruel for her to bear. Finally, she was afraid to leave her apartment, fearing that she would miss the phone's ring. She called in sick, spending her days and nights in bed listening. A number of times she dozed off and awoke hysterical, barely able to get her bearings, the thread of some forgotten nightmare clinging to her consciousness. He was being tortured and she was watching him. His screams filled the air and they were slicing away at his genitals with a knife and fork. My God, she cried when she had recovered her sense of place and time. Where is Eddie?

It had not seemed odd that he had never told her specifically where he lived. He has his reasons, she persisted. And she accepted his only explanation. It had been part of her earlier conditioning not to question.

"It is better that you don't know," he had told her. But was it?

Was she right in her acceptance? Or simply naive? What did danger matter now? She was committed.

When finally the phone did ring, she was so numb with anxiety that she could not believe the sound and did not answer until the fifth ring.

"Frederika." At the sound of his voice, she felt her chest heave and she could not respond.

"Please, Frederika. Are you all right?" He repeated himself until she felt herself quieting.

"Yes."

"I will explain," he said.

"I was out of my mind with worry."

"There was no other way. I had to be sure you were not followed."

"No, I wasn't. I am sure of it."

"I had to be sure." There was a long pause. "I will be there shortly."

"Please, Eddie."

"Yes. I am not far away. I will be there." The phone clicked dead.

She got out of bed, her head pounding, trying to recover a sense of balance. He was coming. That was all that mattered. For the first time in days, she looked at the apartment, which was a mess. Sniffing the air, she caught a staleness, some of which came from her own body. She dashed to the shower, cleaned herself quickly, tidied the apartment, and was just tightening her robe when she heard his key in the door.

He had barely set foot in the apartment when she reached for him, pressed him to her, clung to him, her lips tight on his, her tongue groping.

"My Eddie! My Eddie!" she cried, gasping for breath.

"I wanted to come, but I was afraid for you. I had to be sure you were not followed."

"Who cares?" she cried, opening her robe and putting his hand on her breast. Why did this man do this to her? she wondered, forgetting the pain. She began to undress him. As she removed his jacket, a flat package fell to the floor.

"Another?"

"Yes."

Again, she felt the joy of sharing his life and the idea of it made the touch of his flesh sweeter. When he was naked she began to kiss him, determined not to let a square inch of his body escape her lips. Then she crouched before him and pressed her breasts against his erection."

"My beautiful Eddie. My beautiful Eddie."

"You must understand," he said softly. She felt her pleasure coming from deep inside of her, sensing his urgency as he moved his body in swift jerking motions.

"I need you," she cried, feeling her orgasm begin, washing over her with the heat of an explosive force. She saw his eyes watching her and the joy of it was beyond even the experience of the other times with him. Am I just a bitch in heat? she wondered.

Later, they lay in her bed and she still clung to him.

"I'll never let you go. Never." Then she kissed him again from his head to his toes. "Every piece of you is mine." Soon she felt herself relaxing, a sensation of floating, and her eyelids grew heavy.

There was another voice in the room, accelerating her sense of wakefulness. He was still beside her and she was suddenly aware of a tension in him. The radio was on, and an announcer was reading the news. Rising on one elbow, she looked in the direction of the sound, noting the time on the clock radio. It was three A.M.

"I must have slept for hours," she said.

"Quite a long time."

"I was exhausted." He was alert, but not to her, she realized. "What is it?"

He put a finger on his lips, emphasizing his concentration. Then a commercial came on and he relaxed for a moment.

"What is it?" she repeated.

"It is done," he sighed, swallowing hard. His eyes had misted and there was a strange sadness in him.

"What?"

"We have eliminated Benotti." He paused. "Raoul," he whispered, turning toward her, hugging her.

"It had to be done," he said.

"I don't understand."

The man's voice on the radio began again. She felt his body tense.

"Listen."

"Still no further information on that crash of a DC-9 in Venezuela. Sixteen Americans were on board. More than one hundred people are said to have perished. Initial reports indicate that there were no survivors. . . ."

He sat up quickly.

"It was the only way." He tapped his finger on the edge of the night table. "We are fighting back now. It was the only way we could get him."

"Who?"

"Benotti. Raoul Benotti. He was the head of DINA." He cleared his throat. "He had become something other than what he once was."

"Did you know him?"

He looked at her strangely.

"Yes."

She sensed that he wanted to say more. He must have checked himself. Instead, there was a long silence.

"He was on that plane."

He turned to her and nestled her head in the crook of his arm. After a long pause, in which he seemed to have gathered strength, he said, "You are a genuine heroine. An authentic Chilean heroine. He was the worst of the lot, the most blood-thirsty. Don't think there won't be reprisals. We welcome that. The real war has begun again." He kissed her hair. But something had begun to intrude. What had she done? The monotonous radio voice blared on, and again she could feel his concentration drift toward the voice. When there was no repetition of the story, he switched off the radio and continued to stroke her hair.

"They thought we were scattered and defeated," he said, his inflection revealing the hard edge of stubbornness and deter-mination. "This is the opening shot of our return. We will show them our courage, our resourcefulness. We can play their game."

She remembered the voices she had once heard in the hills around San Luis Obispo before she had thrown the bomb into the bank's window. In that act, she could detect the same singularity, the hard-as-flint tenacity, the reaffirmation of cour-age. She could have walked through a hailstorm of bullets. Throwing the firebomb seemed simple, hardly dangerous. But something nagged at her, spoiling the moment. She knew it was there, but it would not rise to the surface of her con-sciousness.

"I can see them meeting now at the palace, worried about their own skins," he was saying. "They will shake the trees to dislodge what they think is the rotten fruit. They will think that their own people are disloyal. That is always their first

222

consideration. There will be shakeups, chaos, revenge. It will get all mixed up." Then he turned toward her.

"And, yes, some of our people will die. Maybe me. Maybe now, you."

She could find no fear in herself. Only the sharing of it with him mattered, she told herself.

"I told you, Eddie, I'm not afraid."

He was silent, gathering his own thoughts, and once again she felt a tugging of some errant disturbance, faint, like the tracks of a tiny bird.

"What I did . . ." she began. Perhaps she was seeking more tribute for herself, more reaffirmation to make her participation of some special importance. "Did it matter?"

"Matter?"

She knew he could see her clearly in the dark and he looked at her for a long time. She watched him. The lines of his face were softer in the darkness and he looked younger, more mysterious, strong, powerful.

"You provided the proof, the absolute validation of the essential information. What plane? What time? The route of the journey. He was traveling under a pseudonym and was using three different airlines. He was to meet with the American CIA people on the coast of Louisiana."

"You knew all that?"

"It was on the tapes."

"Tapes?"

"That's what was in the brief case."

"I see." Her role was considerably expanded, even in her own mind.

"In this kind of work, the proof, the validation, is essential. And the delivery of the information must be carefully planned. One cannot trust the airwaves, the mails, the telephones. Information is transmitted hand to hand. A chain. You were an important link in a chain."

"You are mine," she whispered, her teeth poised like the

223

jaws of a shark around the flesh of his earlobe. She bit hard, with just enough reserve not to break the skin. And then she joined him on the summit of pleasure.

He left sometime before the sun came up. He had given her another flat box, which, she knew now, contained additional tapes. Tomorrow afternoon she would go to the Miami airport again and repeat the action of the previous time.

"Exactly the same."

"Exactly."

She thought of the wig and the jumpsuit in her closet and wondered if she would experience the same exhilaration now that she knew the specifics of her role. It seemed so simple, so unheroic and pedestrian, although she enjoyed the idea of stepping outside of herself, living a role. After he had gone, it occurred to her that she had not asked him where he could be reached. How could she possibly endure an ordeal similar to what she had gone through in the last few days? Suppose he was killed, or kidnapped, or simply had to go underground. She vowed to confront him with these things. It was too painful not to know more.

The second trip to Miami was even less eventful than the first. The plane was half empty and no one sat beside her. Again, she affected a southern accent in reply to the stewardess' question about having a cocktail.

"Ah don't reckon ah would lak one now," she said, and the stewardess passed on.

The Miami airport was routinely familiar now and she immediately walked to the Pan American area, bought a copy of *Vogue*, and sat down in the waiting room. Even the *Vogue* pictures were familiar. It was the same issue. The pages blurred and she lifted her head to watch the people passing through the waiting room. A plane had just arrived and she could see the anxious faces of the people searching the crowd of arrivals as they came through the security area. A young mother held her baby. An old man, bent and gnarled, watched myopically through thick lenses. A tanned couple in bright costumes stood on tiptoes for a better view of the oncoming crowd. An aged woman embraced a young man as he eagerly passed through the gate.

She shivered now, feeling for the first time the enormity of her act. The tug expanded now and the guilt emerged from under its protective layers. And, although she recognized it and felt the pain of it, she found the acceptance of it in herself galling. Like a suicidal urge, its power gripped her and she knew it was wrong, evil, to be doing this thing. Yet, she pressed relentlessly on. For Eddie, she told herself, her nerve ends alert now to the emergence of a dark-haired woman with heavy makeup, studiously well dressed and carrying a Louis Vuitton brief case. She did not look directly at the woman but could see her clearly through the dark glasses which masked her eyes' sideward glance. The woman moved with a purposeful stride, heading toward where Frederika was sitting. Behind her, near the entrance, two men watched with transparent indifference. Then, for the first time, Frederika felt a sense of personal danger. It washed over her, accelerating her heartbeat. Her fingers shook and she felt a lightheadedness. Actually, she knew, she was exhilarated and the danger gave her courage which had waned in the face of the onrush of guilt.

The woman sat down beside her, crossed her legs, began to light a cigarette, then punched it out in the ash tray at her elbow. She sprang up as if she had forgotten something, and in that split second made the brief case switch. Frederika closed her eyes, waiting for the two men to descend on her. I understand, Eddie, she screamed inside herself, absorbing the fugitive feeling of alienation and fear, savoring it, welcoming it, because it was bringing her closer to the core of her man.

But when she opened her eyes, the men had disappeared and she was sitting alone on the row of seats. She must have sat there blankly for longer than she imagined; for when she recovered her sense of time, her plane's departure was imminent and she had to run down the long corridor to catch it. Only when she had already boarded, did she remember that she had not changed her disguise and the stewardess was the same one she'd seen on the plane that brought her to Miami less than an hour ago.

"I'll bet you enjoyed your Florida stay," the stewardess said, smiling mechanically.

"I don't understand ..." Frederika mumbled, turning her head away with obvious annoyance. The stewardess moved away with practiced delicacy. I've trapped myself, Frederika thought, by my own silly weakness. Turning, she looked about the cabin, which was crowded now, wondering which of the men or women might be working for the enemy.

During the entire trip, which was uncomfortable and bumpy, she remained in a state of nervous tension, and when finally the plane landed at National Airport and taxied to the gate, she could barely find the strength to stand. Had she betrayed him by her stupidity, she wondered, deliberately waiting while the other passengers filed out of the plane.

"Sorry," the stewardess said, coming toward her, still smiling, "we don't go back until tomorrow." Frederika ignored the reference as if she hadn't heard and moved out of the plane. By the time she reached the street outside, she had convinced herself that she was, indeed, being followed. Yet she could not bring herself to test the suspicion. Her fear was not for herself, she protested, but for Eddie. Dashing toward the outer circle of the stream of cars, she put herself in the path of an empty taxi and let herself in the door when the cab had stopped.

"You can get killed like that, lady," the driver said.

"Statler-Hilton." The idea had come to her from a road sign as she looked through the back window, wondering which of the following cars contained the enemy. Before the taxi pulled

226

up to the hotel entrance, she had paid the driver and opened the door.

"What's the rush, lady?"

Ignoring him, she ran into the lobby, then up the stairs to the mezzanine, which contained the public rooms and the women's lavatory. In a toilet stall, she quickly changed her clothes. Then, when the room had emptied, she rummaged in the waste bin for something to cover the brief case. She found a newspaper, inserted the brief case between the pages, and sure of its concealment, strolled casually into the corridor, then down the back stairs to the street, where she hailed another taxi and gave the driver her own address. It was paranoia, she knew, but if her stupidity betrayed him ... She could not bring herself to complete the thought.

Once she was in her own apartment, she was certain the insecurity would dissipate. It is an anxiety fit, she observed about herself. There had been other occasions in her life when something like this had occurred and she had searched for some reason for its happening. Now, she stood in the quickening darkness of her apartment, her hearing alert, her heart pumping, unable to assuage her fears. After a while, she found the courage to move to the window. The blinds had been drawn and she picked up a single slat and looked downward into the street. Traffic moved thickly, south and north on Wisconsin Avenue.

She was looking for something, she knew. A stationary figure, relentlessly patient, like an unused chess piece in a swift game. A number of people on the street below seemed to fit that category. A man, brief case in hand, slumped against a hydrant. There was another figure, a woman—it was the way she held herself, stiff, straight, with an air of determination, her eyes fastened on the front of the building, that prompted Frederika's suspicion. Perhaps that woman was watching her at this moment, although only a tiny portion of Frederika's eye was exposed through the thin opening in the blinds. If she was being followed, if there was someone out there waiting, it would have to be that woman, she decided. Then she admonished herself for such lack of control, glad that her rationality was taking over again, her anxieties dissipating. Looking around her apartment, she discovered that nothing had changed. She flipped on the lights and started to change her clothes, preparing to leave for work.

But something prompted her to periodically peek through the blinds. The woman was still there, tenacious in her stiffness, a sentinel. She is waiting for someone, Frederika decided, preparing to leave the apartment. We shall see, she told herself, as she went down the elevator. Her courage was returning now.

She deliberately crossed the street at the corner so as to get a close view of the woman, Tall, middle-aged, with straight features in a bony face, she wore a cloth coat over gray slacks, and her concentration on the facade of the apartment building was so intense that her eyes did not seem to flicker as Frederika passed. Relieved, she hurried on to work, searching the faces in the crowd, as she always did, looking for Eddie.

Having lived through the ordeal in the aftermath of her last mission, she knew what to expect, although this knowledge was not enough to give her tranquility. She had, she suspected, bungled the assignment and endangered Eddie, as well as the others involved with him. If any harm came to him or the others, she would never forgive herself. Forgive? Could the relatives and friends who died in the plane crash ever forgive her? She shivered, stepped up her pace as if greater speed would put distance between herself and her guilt.

When she thought in these terms, she would force herself to imagine terrible atrocities committed at Benotti's behest—tortures, killings, brutalities beyond even her ability to conceive. But Eddie hadn't told her what they were.

228

She was thankful that Clyde's was crowded. It helped her keep worrisome thoughts out of her mind.

When she returned to her apartment after work, the old chain of disturbing thoughts began again. She lay in bed, wide awake, unable to assuage her physical fatigue while her mind spun like a top. Then she remembered the woman across the street. She had not noticed her when she entered the building. This is ridiculous, she told herself, as she sprang out of bed and padded across the cold floor to the window. Opening the blind a crack, she looked out. The woman was still there, watching, alert, as consumed as ever. Couldn't be, she decided, and when she looked again after an hour or two of additional tossing, the woman was gone. Relieved at last, she felt her body relax, grow drowsy. The last thing that passed through her mind was a picture of Eddie, coming toward her, his arms outstretched. It was only an image, an apparition.

She managed to get through the next day by expending enormous energy cleaning her apartment. She scoured the kitchen, crept around on her hands and knees and scrubbed the floors. Then she washed down the walls and polished the wood furniture to a bright sheen. When she got to the windows, she pulled the blinds and sprayed the glass with cleaning fluid. It was only then that the memory of the woman came back, and looking downward into the street again, she saw her. It was cold, and vapor came out of the woman's mouth, but she seemed alert, watchful, driven. The sudden opening of the blinds seemed to have caught her attention. She looked upward briefly, then turned her eyes away.

When Frederika went to work in the early evening, the woman was still there. Later, preparing for bed, Frederika again glanced through the blinds. The woman persisted in her vigil. Perhaps she is mad, Frederika thought. But the idea quickly left her consciousness. It was Eddie that rose again to dominate her mind. No. She was not quite the disciplined soldier she was expected to be.

She must have dozed off. The telephone rang, shrill, demanding. Eddie. She reached for the phone.

"I have wonderful news."

"Oh, Eddie!" Hearing his voice left her speechless with emotion.

"I will be there shortly." He hung up and Frederika felt renewed again, on the verge of happiness, the sense of expectation delicious. Her body began to focus on her lover.

He must have been close by. Hearing his key in the door, she bounded out of bed and switched on the lights. He was there, his skin chilly against hers as she held him in her arms, reveling again in the taste of him. Kissing her deeply, he lingered, then moved her away as he began pacing in agitation.

"Carlos Lantissa in London." He made a motion with his hand, slicing it sideways across his throat. "Another beast struck down in the jungle."

"London!"

He stopped pacing and slapped his thigh.

"We got him in a restaurant. Poison. It was magnificent. The information was letter perfect."

"Anyone else?" she asked, feeling her chest constrict.

"I don't understand."

"It was not like the plane crash?"

He moved toward her and held her in his arms, patting her hair.

"One other." He paused. "We had to be certain. It was necessary. In a war, innocents are exposed."

"I know." She did not want him to see her courage falter.

"Besides, they killed many of us in their prisons. After torture. Three of our people were gunned down in Caracas yesterday."

She wondered if they were the men she'd seen at the airport, but she dared not say that she had observed them. Only that he was here with her now—that was all that mattered. The rest was part of some bad dream. She debated telling him about her mistake, her forgetfulness, but she held off. Not now. She drew him toward the bed, watched him as he undressed, and soon she was locked in his arms, pinned to him, shuddering with the joy of his nearness, knowing that what she was doing was worth the effort ... for this.

"I love you, I love you," she whispered, endlessly repetitive, like a mantra. Then later she told him about her mistake. He listened quietly, without emotion.

"I was sick with apprehension."

"You must steel yourself," he said as he lay back looking into the ceiling. "We must assume the worst."

"I already did that."

"It is a game of great tensions, great dangers. Sometimes one wonders if they know all the time what is happening."

"Who?"

"The CIA. Perhaps the DINA."

"And they simply let it happen?"

"It might serve their sense of expediency."

"Then what is the point?"

"I don't think about anything beyond the destruction. The objective is to kill as many of the butchers as possible, as quickly and efficiently as possible."

She shivered. He is bloodthirsty, she thought. She looked at him. And beautiful. Being with him reassured her, although his objectives were sometimes murky, at least to her.

"The problem is to sustain one's alertness," he said suddenly. "It is very tiring. Paranoia is a double-edged sword."

She held his face in her hands and kissed him. As she had learned, paranoia could be painful. Then she remembered the woman in front of her building.

"There is one thing." She pictured the woman outside, the relentless vigil. "An odd detail. Perhaps it is purely my

231

imagination. There are two hundred tenants in this building."

She could feel his sudden alertness, a reflex.

"There is a woman watching this building," she said.

He jumped out of bed, moved toward the blinds, and lifting a slat, his eyes searched the street.

"Where?"

Frederika got up and stood behind him, pointing to the spot where the woman had stood.

"She is gone now. She does not usually stay this late." She looked at the radio with its luminescent clock. It was four A.M.

"Usually? Then it has been a regular routine?"

"Why, yes." She hesitated. "You might say that."

"What does she look like?"

"Tall, thin. A rather bony face. Middle-aged. You might call her ... " She searched for the right word. " ... patrician. She was dressed rather mannishly, in a trench coat and pants."

She watched his face, observing the gathering concern, the beginnings of agitation.

"Do you think she was out there when I arrived?"

"I don't know." Then she checked herself quickly. "She was there earlier. She would have been there at that time. Yes." He looked into the street again, narrowing the blinds. Touching his bare shoulder, she felt his tension.

"What is it, my darling?" she asked gently. He remained silent for a long time, although the tightness of his shoulder muscles indicated that he was reacting. "What is it?" she repeated.

"How was her hair cut?" he asked, his voice clipped, businesslike.

"Short, like a man."

"And the color?"

"Graying."

"And the color of the trench coat?"

"Navy." She was surprised that she had absorbed so much detail.

He turned, let the slat fall, and began pacing the room. The apartment was chilled and she slipped back into bed, watching him as he walked about.

"What is it?"

He didn't answer.

"It is my fault," she said, feeling the whole facade of this new life crumbling.

"What have I done, Eddie?" He stopped briefly, looked at her, his face drawn, his lips tight. "Please, Eddie." Then he turned away.

In his look, she read her own fate. I can't bear it, she told herself.

"I'll do anything, Eddie. Anything. I'm such a fool."

But he continued to ignore her, his mind elsewhere. Occasionally, he would peek through the slats again.

"Is she one of them, the enemy? I should have warned you."

He stopped his pacing and began searching for his clothes, saying nothing, his anger controlled, although she felt it in the room, the heaviness palpable, overwhelming.

"Eddie, please." She ran out of bed and grasped him in her arms, holding him tightly, kissing his face, the tears beginning. He made some halfhearted efforts at placation, but his response was cold. She felt his indifference and saw whatever emotion he might have felt suddenly lost, squandered by her absent-mindedness.

"It's my fault, Eddie. My stupidity."

"No." She sensed his bitterness.

"I can correct it, Eddie. You'll see. I'll do whatever you tell me has to be done." She released him and he continued to dress. "Don't hate me, Eddie. I'll make it up, you'll see, Eddie." She swallowed hard, the bile boiling in her throat.

"It has nothing to do with you," he said.

"No. You're trying to humor me. I've endangered everything, right, Eddie? She is the enemy. She has found out. I've bungled it." She jammed a fist into her palm. "Please, Eddie.

233

Give me the chance. I'll make it right. I can do it. I have the courage to do it." A panic was gripping her. I must not lose him, she told herself. I cannot lose him.

"It's not what you think," he said gently.

The thought confused her.

"You mustn't lie to me, Eddie. I know what I have to do. I can do it. I know I can do it." He had finished dressing. He turned to her.

"Do nothing," he said. "Nothing." His eyes narrowed. She imagined she could see his contempt for her. "Please, Frederika. Do nothing."

"And you? What will you do?"

"I'll be back," he said, moving toward the door.

"No!" she said. "You won't! You are leaving me! You are going away!" She was losing control now, feeling the weight of hysteria. "I'll kill her!" she cried.

His slap hit her sharply across her cheek, the sound almost as painful as the blow. Then he was gone.

XI

Dobbs pushed away the file, first extracting the color Polaroid photograph of Miranda Ferrara Palmero, holding it out between his thumb and middle finger. He slanted it in the direction of the window light, as if the natural, now fading light might offer more insight than the yellowish lamplight that arched over the table.

Perhaps he was missing something, he asked himself, although the question had become the essence of his enigma. He was a fish in strange waters. The truth of that undermined all of his previous self-praise about his professionalism, his thoroughness. His superiors had cited him again and again for what they believed was his instinctive understanding of human frailty, human motivation, human psychology. And he had accepted these honors, believing them. This Palmero case only reinforced what he had secretly begun to believe about himself—his own ignorance, his incompetence. It was, he knew, a strong condemnation. But no one was bugging his brain and he could afford to be honest with himself. No textbook could provide more than surface answers to human passions.

Miranda's picture revealed nothing, a flat image, devoid of humanity, and he did not have the imagination to superimpose it with life. Not like Eduardo! He could feel himself reaching out to Eduardo, barely touching. Perhaps it was Miranda's hatred that had brought them closer.

"But when you first married him, did you love him?" the interrogator had pressed.

"I told you. I detested him even then."

There seemed a special delicacy in the next question, as if the interrogator was aware of the rituals of the oligarchy.

"An arrangement?"

"There was more to consider than the mere emotions of the principals." She had spat out the words with contempt. "The merger of two great fortunes took precedence over the merger of people." The interrogator had noted a long silence. "I loathed him."

"Why?"

"Perhaps because he was forced upon me."

"And his feelings?"

She had put out a cigarette, stood up, paced the large room, looking upward as if imploring God. When she finally returned to within earshot of the interrogator, she had fixed her eyes on him, glaring, two burnt coals glowing.

"I could have told him to jump off the highest mountain in Chile and he would have done so. I could have told him to slit his throat with a knife and he would have done so. I could have told him to put a bullet in his brain and he would have done so. He was beyond logic, obsessed with me."

"So the marriage was more than an arrangement."

"All right, I'll tell you. I was the ransom, his father's bribe to him to keep him out of politics, to be a good little boy. I was the candy." She mocked, imitating a child, "I will give you this candy if you will only play like a good little boy and not get into mischief. I pleaded with my own father not to allow this."

"Why did he?"

236

"Money. Property. Greed. He was an old-fashioned man and I was an only daughter, the spoiled beauty. For him, the marriage was the moment of truth. He demanded continuity from me. And Eduardo's father was a subtle one, sly. He bid quite high. He presented an offer that could not be refused. And my father demanded my consent." She had dabbed her eyes. "A woman's tears mean nothing. And I adored my father. I worshipped him."

"And your mother?"

"She had been pampered beyond endurance and had long ago succumbed to my father's disciplines. She was nothing." The flashing eyes moved away from the interrogator's face. The full lips barely moved as the voice continued.

"It was the most lavish wedding in Santiago. Five hundred guests and the two fathers puffed up like peacocks at the stew they had cooked up for us. We were the darlings of Chile, the envy of the world. The virgin princess led to the slaughter."

The interrogator must have offered a confused expression and Miranda had cackled nervously.

"Hard to believe? Yes, I know. I had often wondered who would believe me when the time came to tell it." She had held out her arms in a pantomime of display of her physical assets. "I am still fine to look at. My body is good. It was perfection then. See my teeth? Still white. And the purple eyes. Little bags beginning, but more than the hint of what they were." She picked at her skin, pinching a cheek, stretching the wafer of flesh, which bounced back to the skull. "The skin still good. There." She pointed to a picture, a painting in an ornate gold-leafed frame. "That was me then. I had what is the stuff of men's dreams. To Eduardo, I had come down from heaven." There was another long silence, more pacing of the large room.

"Then why was the bargain not kept?" the interrogator asked finally. It was, after all, the heart of the exercise. "In less than a year he was back in politics. They had sent him to put out their party organ in Valdivia. He betrayed you."

"Yes," she snapped. "He betrayed me."

"Why?"

"He would not accept what he had bought. He had assumed he was getting fire. He got ice instead."

Eduardo would always remember the sound of the sea beating against the jagged rocks two hundred feet below and the pounding of the wind against the window of their bedroom. The gale had come up suddenly and soon the thunder rolled above them with explosive force, shaking the ground on which the house perched precariously at the edge of the mountain.

Her father had given her the house, his vacation retreat on the coast sixty miles above Santiago. Miranda had gone there as a child, but lately her father had used it to entertain his various mistresses and it was one of the gifts proffered in the bargain struck between the heads of the two families. Isolated, built of granite and marble from the nearby quarries, it seemed—in her father's mind, at least—the perfect spot for a woman to find the love of a man. Obviously it had worked for him many times, and her father must have sensed that it was, in his daughter's case, the badly needed medicine to smooth her passage to womanhood.

If there had been protests to the marriage on her part, Eduardo had blocked them from his mind. Certainly Miranda did not, in their six month courtship, give any hint of defiance. If she was quiet, aloof, he imagined it was her way, although he certainly knew that she did not love him.

"In time," his father had assured him. Nor did he inquire as to the details of the bargain. Beyond having her, everything else was of little consequence to him. Every ounce of his being cried out for her, overcoming his doubts. She was something worth living for, he told himself. Nothing else could possibly matter. He had not, in those six months, done anything more than caress her fingers, the touch of them sending shivers through his body, creating palpitations and swellings in his loins. The mere sight of her could stir him, and sometimes his desire for her grew so powerful that he dared not face her without first relieving himself of the burden of his own sexuality.

And if she knew she was the object of his obsessive fantasies, she hardly spoke of it, revealing, actually, nothing of her true feelings.

If she was not affectionate, she was polite, and although he was not yet tortured by her indifference, he pushed these anxieties from his mind. There was nothing he would not do to possess her. Politics paled. If necessary, he was prepared to go to law school and step into the role of patron of the family under his father's tutelage. Up till then, he had no regrets, only fears that we would not ultimately please her.

As the moment of truth approached, he waited in the drawing room, watching the turbulent sea, listening to the wind and the exploding thunder, wondering if it stirred her desire to be protected by him. I will never let harm come to you, he vowed silently, his eyes searching the ominous maelstrom beyond the thick glass panes. The servants had prepared a lavish dinner and they had sipped champagne. He had even toasted her, silently, since his throat was too tight to speak coherently and his mind and heart too overflowing with the ecstasy of having won her. She is mine now, became a repetitive phrase in his brain as he watched her, the golden princess of his dreams. What did it matter how he had won her?

When he had waited an appropriate length of time, he climbed the wide staircase to the master bedroom suite, knocking politely at the door, his legs like jelly. There was no reply and he opened the ornate door into the darkened room, revealed suddenly by the flash from a bolt of lightning. She was already in the bed, although he could not see her face, only that her hair had been let down and lay spread along the pillow.

"Darling," he whispered. Still no answer came. He came

toward the edge of the bed. Her eyes were closed, her breathing quiet. Bending over her, he put his lips on hers, feeling instantly his desire surge. Her lips did not respond. He shook her lightly, heard a brief gurgle as a breath caught in her throat. Perhaps it was the champagne, he thought, still trusting. He moved away from the bed and into the large adjoining bathroom. Her makeup case was open. She had obviously done her nightly ablutions. Her toothbrush hanging beside his in the rack was damp.

It was only when he saw the little opened vial of pills that his curiosity deepened. He lifted the vial to his nostrils, smelled them. They were odorless. Then he looked at the label. "Take two before retiring." Sleeping pills. A brief panic seized him, but then he overturned the vial into his palm. There were many still left. It was hardly an overdose.

He ran to the bed again.

"Miranda," he called, his voice rising as he said her name. She did not stir. He felt a sob grow in him as he reached over and took her in his arms, kissing her cheeks, her eyes, her hair. Her eyelids fluttered at his touch. He imagined they opened briefly, then, leaden, they closed again. She was in a dead sleep.

Undressing, he crept in beside her. She was naked. Her flesh felt cool, and despite his anger, his anxiety and humiliation, his penis remained hard. He slipped an arm under her and drew her toward him, whispering her name in her ear, tears welling over his eyelids, falling to her cheek. He could not tell how long he held her in this position, his body stirring, although his anger grew as the night wore on, excited by the sounds of the storm roaring outside. Perhaps the storm had frightened her, he wondered. But what she had done had extinguished the luminosity of the moment, his moment. And he had determined that he would not, could not disappoint her. Had she forgotten and simply took the pills as part of her nightly routine? The idea softened his anger, but only for the moment. Love me, he cried into the night, holding her, feeling her soft flesh next to his own. You must love me.

Later, as he lay there, still holding her, listening to the storm's abatement, he began to curse his own vulnerability. Why had he consented to this idea? He had let it happen, had let his father manipulate the event. He cursed what he had become, although he could still feel some pride in the possession of her. But she is mine. It is her duty, he railed, getting out of bed and pacing the floor. Finally, he threw the covers off her, watching her nakedness, feeling the force of his anger and sexuality. Then he moved over her, spreading her legs roughly, placing his penis up against the dark thatch where her legs met. He wanted to cry, scream out his anguish. You are mine, he pleaded, conscious of his own self-loathing as he checked himself from moving his body further. Instead, he continued to hold her, kissing her. She did not stir. Love me, he pleaded as he felt desire roar through him and the joy begin somewhere deep in his brain, the storm lashing out again inside of him, the sea angry again, the wind shuddering, the thunder explosive. He felt ashamed of his pleasure, rolling over her to his side of the bed. She had wanted that, he decided, his logic suddenly clear. I did not give her that satisfaction. He was convinced of his insight, also of his love for her. He lay awake the rest of the night, watching the dawn come, then the morning.

The sky had cleared into a deep blue. The sun had risen high when she finally stirred beside him. He watched her come out of the deep narcotic slumber, insisting that his face be the first object she would see.

"Why?" he asked, when her eyes finally squinted into the sun. It was already late afternoon and he had not slept. He knew she was gathering her senses, trying to surmise whether the act had been done. The realization dawned. She was still virginal.

"Are you disappointed?" he asked.

"I'm sorry, Eduardo," she said. "I could not face it."

241

"Am I so repugnant?" It was a question that gnawed at his pride. He wished he did not have to ask it. She closed her eyes again.

"I could not face it," she said. He reached out and touched her cheek, feeling the coldness. His penis rose instantly. He could not will his desire into submission.

"If only you knew how much I love you," he said. Her lips curled. It seemed to him to be contempt. Not even a smile for his weakness.

"I know, Eduardo. I am truly sorry."

He began to caress her again. Surely there was some way to reach her. He knew he could forgive her.

"I can't help myself," he said.

"Nor can I, Eduardo."

"In time . . ." His words trailed off. He remembered how his father had said it, with such confidence, such wisdom. But he had trusted him once before. The image of Isabella was branded into his mind. Again, I am cheated, he thought, feeling the backwash of self-pity.

He moved her body close to his again, kissing her lips, feeling again her coldness.

"I love you," he said again. And when she did not move, a lump of clay in his arms, he said, "It is a curse."

"I suppose," she said. He could feel her indifference. Then she added quickly, "But I will do my duty." He wanted to block out the sense of the words. He squeezed her breasts, his tongue rolling over her nipples. Still, there was no reaction. He reached down and caressed her clitoris. She did not stir.

"Are you frightened?" he whispered.

"No," she said. She lay there without emotion, her eyes open, her lips pursed. "It would have been all right last night," she said.

"I suppose you would have preferred it that way."

She looked at him and nodded.

"But I am a man!" he said, the anger rising again, the humiliation palpable.

"Do it then!" It seemed a taunt. Then she threw the covers off and spread her legs. His eyes washed over her womanhood, the beauty of it. He had dreamed about it, seen it in his mind, desired it. Now he was intimidated by it.

"Do it!" she hissed. "For God's sake, let's get it over with."

He wanted to protest, but she reached out for him and pulled him over her.

"Do it!" she said, guiding him roughly. He felt her physical irritation, her dryness.

"Not like this." He tried holding back, but she urged him forward. He felt her body's pain, although he could not confirm it in her face. She strained forward, plunging his penis into her. He felt her tightness close over him, vise-like.

"There!" she said, her breath gasping. "I have done my duty."

He felt his helplessness as his body again quickly gave way to its own pleasure, and although he was consciously ashamed of it, he let it sweep over him again in a delicious fury. His body shuddered. She lay there, still a lump of flesh, accepting her duty.

"I love you," he whispered. She said nothing, waiting. Finally, he fell backward on the bed, his own exhaustion reaching through his humiliation. He closed his eyes and heard her go into the bathroom and slam the door. Before he fell asleep, he wondered why he could not bring himself to hate her.

To the outside world, their parents, her friends, they could pass as a reasonably loving but reticent couple. To themselves, they were an arrangement and their life together an exercise in politeness. It was his cross to bear, he decided, since he was the loving one. She was true to the bargain, obedient and dutiful. And he kept his end of the bargain. His father had bought for them a large house in Santiago, giving them additional property and shares in a variety of companies. From a business point of view, the merger was a spectacular deal. But the financial aspects held little interest for him and it was she who took command of the records and finances when he entered law school.

He was older than the rest of the students and he kept mostly to himself, especially avoiding his old political friends, who soon grew tired of his aloofness. Naturally, they did not take his defection lightly. A scion of one of the first families of the oligarchy was always a visible prize for the left, but even an attempt by Allende to bring him back to the fold failed. It was, he knew, against the grain, and glimpsing ahead, he could see his life spread out like a lush carpet—money and the power it gave, and the endless manipulations to preserve it, a life of ease, servants, and, in the end, a perpetuation of the privilege in his children. The prospect disgusted him, although he knew it was the kind of life that Miranda had been bred for. So had he. What had gone wrong?

Beneath the surface of what seemed like a truce or, worse, a suspension of life, he was in a perpetual state of mental torture. Its root was Miranda. The more she became indifferent, if that was possible, the more he became inflamed. He began to watch her, study her, observing every movement and expression as if he were studying a complex cell under a microscope.

"What is it, Eduardo?" she would ask when his inspection became an irritation.

"Nothing."

"Why are you staring?"

It became, on her part, a litany. He was not conscious of it, as if she were a magnet and his eyes a metallic substance. Perhaps he was subconsciously trying to will her to love him and this fixation was an attempt at hypnotism. Why doesn't she love me? he would cry within himself, never daring to confront her with the question.

In his arms, at the beginning, she would lay motionless, accepting his ministrations mutely, doing her duty. Her indifference gnawed at him. The contrast to himself, his own sense of ecstasy when he touched her, when he felt her, when his body

244

merged with hers, seemed bizarre, somehow inhuman. He was alternately gentle and insistent. She refused him nothing and gave him nothing. And yet, in terms of pure physical pleasure, the wonder of her exasperated him. She was his gift and curse. He had, he knew, bargained with the devil. Nothing could move her.

"What do you think about when I do that?" he asked once, when the pain had become unbearable. Her eyes were closed and he lay over her, supported by his elbow, watching her closed eyelids flutter.

"Nothing," she responded.

"Just your duty?"

"I am your wife."

"Surely there is some feeling?" The way the question was posed frightened him and he was grateful for her silence.

"How long do you think I can endure this?"

She opened her eyes and looked at him, as he searched her face.

"A lifetime," she said. "There is no question about that." She paused. "We have obligations."

"To whom?" He was being sarcastic. The question needed no answer. But it was the key to her life and she persisted.

"To our blood." She had paused. "And our children."

"Children?"

"Of course. It is our duty to conceive children."

"Like this?"

"It is the way it is done." She was mocking now. But she had inadvertently given him a weapon.

If she was to continue her indifference, he determined to hold off, to whip his desire. He no longer submitted himself to his own passion, and although it steamed and churned within him, he would not go near her. If she noticed, she said nothing, certainly relieved and, perhaps, hopeful that a conception might already have taken place. It hadn't.

Miranda's life changed little since their marriage. She had

her friends, her tennis, her parties. She was still the center of interest everywhere she went, and if she had little joy to give him, her smile warmed everyone else she touched. He followed her obediently for the first six months, hoping that his father's admonition of "in time" might suddenly become operative. It didn't. They drifted, speaking little, always polite. He imagined he was trying to wipe away, destroy his love for her somehow, but it was impossible. Its intensity continued to burn, fueled, it seemed, by the depth of her indifference.

He knew there would be a limit to his endurance. Despite his love for her and his pain, his intelligence had long ago rejected all of her values—perpetuation of wealth for its own sake, a clear contempt for the have-nots. She had an absolute belief in the aristocracy of power through family and heritage. The rights of privilege were everything. It was his own family's dictum as well. He began to look upon his life as an exercise in futility.

It was when the idea of killing himself popped into his mind that he realized how far afield he had gone. He was surprised, too, at the seriousness with which he entertained the idea, contemplating in detail the method he would use. He had rejected the grand gesture, a bullet in the brain, a knife in the heart, throwing himself in front of a train or truck, hanging himself. Such a dramatic gesture might have meaning if he had sought martyrdom, a permanent impression for political motives, for example. His was to be the death of failure, a simple exit of a wayward soul.

He began to dwell on the method of the overdose as an appropriate poetic gesture. Only Miranda would understand the irony and, after all, that was just, since it was only Miranda's reaction that would matter. Would it make the slightest impression on her, he wondered. He would stare at the little vial of her pills on the ledge of the medicine chest, wondering when he would find the courage to use their contents. It would be so simple. A handful of pills down the gullet, a passage into slumber and then a swift painless demise.

He might have done it, too, if the matter of his death had not become an object of concern. It was as if the idea had permeated the air, seeped into her brain, a supernatural transference.

"I have prepared our wills," she said one evening on the rare occasion of their dining together. She moved an envelope across the polished granite table.

"That's ridiculous," he said. Had she actually read his mind?

"Actually, it was your father's suggestion. His firm drew it up."

"But who will benefit?"

"If you die, I will. If I die, you will. Then when there are children . . ." She shrugged and slid the envelope further across the table in his direction.

"There will be no children," he said emphatically, watching her face.

"That's absurd," she said.

"Is it?" He continued to explore her face. It betrayed nothing of what he was thinking. God, how he loved her, he thought. At least, she will need me for that. The idea of it made his loins churn.

"Never," he whispered.

"Just look it over. Then sign them. It is quite necessary."

"The hell with it!"

"Don't be a fool!" she admonished, her eyes narrowing in anger. So she is human, after all, he thought happily, knowing that the idea of his suicide was losing its allure.

The next day he quit law school and presented himself at party headquarters, where his return was compared with that of the prodigal son. He asked for an assignment outside of Santiago and was quickly assigned to Valdivia, a northern city, where he was to supervise the editing of the party newspaper and participate in expanding the party base. It would not be an easy task. The city was dominated by citizens of German origin who were extremely conservative.

247

"How will you explain it to your father?" Miranda asked. It was her only reaction. There was no question of her going with him.

"I'm going without you," he told her.

"Of course."

He tried to write a long letter to his father, justifying his action, but the words kept congealing on the paper. Could he explain his own sense of warped maturity, his hopeless one-sided love for a frigid wife, his flirting seriously with suicide? How could such information be conveyed to someone outside yourself? Especially to someone who, he knew, loved him.

Although his political instincts seemed crystal clear at times, he wondered about the sincerity of his commitment. It occurred to him that perhaps he was merely acting to destroy a system of life that had made him unhappy. Sometimes he could feel passionately what he espoused. But distrust of emotion was conditioning him. Emotion was the enemy, he decided. Surely, there was some way to overcome it, perhaps to use it, but never to allow it to dominate or control.

Above all, he envied Miranda, her coldness, even though it tortured him. Every nuance of indifference was a dagger in his heart. Yet he admired her uninvolvement. His intelligence could be in revolt, but nothing—logic, objective reasoning, ridicule—could erase what he felt for her. He had seen her on the tennis courts, a perfectly innocent pastime, and it had become an obsession, a monster. He had betrayed his political instincts. He had betrayed his father. He had betrayed himself.

In the end, he could explain nothing to his father. As for Miranda, she would endure the temporary embarrassment, providing, she insisted, that appearances were kept up. It was becoming trendy now to have a radical husband. The party of Allende was, as a matter of fact, taking on an air of respectability in some circles. Conditions in Chile were in decline even for the wealthy. Ominous signs were on the horizon. She might live with that. Divorce, of course, was out of the question.

There was the religious issue but, more important, there was the financial problem. She was not going to deprive her unborn children of the fruits of the Ferrara-Palmero merger.

He was quite proud of the fact that he had prepared his mind for his departure. That was why he had been so baffled by what occurred. He was fully packed. His bags were actually piled in the foyer ready for the morning journey. It was near midnight. He had poured himself a cognac and stood by the windows watching the flickering lights of Santiago which lay like a luminescent carpet at his feet. It was his habit now to take a cognac before he got into bed. It made him drowsy. Sometimes he would take two or three or more, depending on his mood and the state of his agitation. Miranda, he knew, would induce her sleep with sleeping pills. It was a fact of their lives together. She anesthetized herself to endure him. He anesthetized himself to hold himself back. There was, he knew, spite in both their motives.

"May I join you?" He was startled by her voice. Turning, she appeared in a soft yellow dressing gown that he had never seen before. Over it, her brushed hair seemed to glow as it fell in sharp contrast. Beneath the dressing gown, he could see her full, lush body.

He poured out a drink and, handing her a snifter, watched her tapered, ringed fingers delicately caress the glass. If only it were me, he thought. She stood beside him, watching the lights outside, sipping the cognac. He felt her magnetism, heard the softness of her steady breathing. His heart began to beat wildly.

"I know it's my fault," she said. The words came in a velvet whisper. Distrust it, his mind told him. He said nothing in response.

"I'm sorry," she said.

"You can't bake bread without flour," he said stupidly, censoring the original crudity.

"We are simply different," she said. He felt her glance move

249

over him, a rare feeling. He had never even felt that she had noticed he was alive. I will resist her as always, he pledged to himself. Her onslaught was too obvious, surely a ploy.

"Everyone has a cross to bear," he said, sensing the power of his self-pity.

"I have given you nothing," she said.

"That is true." He had tried to disguise his bitterness.

"You have every right to be . . ." She seemed to have lost the word.

"Humiliated. Hurt. Unhappy. Foolish. Choose it."

"I know," she sighed.

He moved away from her, poured himself another cognac, and sat down on the chair. She continued to look out the window, her back toward him. He could not draw his eyes away from the delicious curve of her body, the straight back reaching downward into the curve of her tight buttocks. His hardened penis quivered in expectation. It is unbearable, he told himself.

When she turned to face him, he knew how fragile was the extent of his resolve.

"I can't remake myself," she said, lowering her head. A single lamp lit the room. She moved and it was behind her, the light passing through the flimsy dressing gown.

"It is cruel," he said. But she seemed to be perplexed by his meaning, hesitant in her answer.

"I suppose," she said. She seemed to be holding herself in a pose, ever the narcissist. Despite his resolve, he could not contain the onrush of pleasure, the sharp tingling down his spine. Logic receded. His energy seemed concentrated in his manhood. He was taut, ready to burst. He undid his robe. His hard, quivering penis stuck out of the fly of his pajamas. He looked at it, stupidly, his face flushing.

"You see."

He wanted to cry. His body shook as he stifled a sob. I hate myself, he shouted inside. He knew she could not bear it,

250

watching as her eyes looked away. Yet she came toward him. You mustn't, he told himself, his will gone now, reaching out for her, touching her, lifting her dressing gown, feeling her flesh, kissing the soft thatch of hair at the edge of her flat belly. His tongue lapped at her, like a dog. His head pounded.

"Feel something, dammit!" he shouted, moving her body over his, plunging his hardness inside of her, feeling immediately the surging wonder of his body's pleasure, a suffusion from his head downward, from his toes upward, as if his entire body had reached into her womanness, devouring, begging for her mercy as he gorged himself on her.

Even after, his hardness would not dissipate and he carried her into the bedroom and moved inside of her again, holding her tightly, engulfing her with his legs and arms, his lips pressed against hers until they hurt, his nostrils breathing in the scent of her, his eyelashes fluttering against her cheeks. His mind seemed vacated, his intelligence gone. Only his oneness with her mattered. Later, when some rational sense returned, he realized that she held him clutched between her legs, her arms locked over his back. Was it happening, he wondered, daring not to delude himself. It was the only sign of response, the holding.

He would remember this moment as the high point of his life and the high tide of his self-delusion. He did not leave the next morning. They made love throughout the day. She brought him food on a tray and they talked little since he was afraid that what was happening would disappear in words. It was too fragile to disturb, and each time he moved over her and she held him, it was balm to a weathered soul, an elixir to still his self-pity. He was ready to forgive her anything, to reverse his own betrayal of what had seemed a perverse bargain up till then.

"I love you," he told her again and again. She said nothing. He refused to be clinical. Had he moved her? He dared not ask. When he was not loving her, he was watching her, a feast

251

for his eyes, her face, her hair, the upward curve of her full breasts, the gentle sweep of her hips, the tight flesh of her stomach. He kissed her navel, the beginning of her, moving downward and upward, hungry for every part of her. It was dangerous to know such happiness.

Is it happening to her? It was the one question for which he might have given his life for an affirmation.

Toward evening of the next day, he saw her pass into sleep, the fading light inhibiting his view of her. He got up to light a lamp that sat on a table across the room. Pulling the chain, he saw the puddle of yellow light illumine a book, somehow oddly placed. Later he would wonder why his eye had caught it, some preordained, demon-inspired movement. It was actually the Bible, and it made little sense being where it was. Miranda was, he knew, a devoted Catholic, but she had never brought the Bible into their bedroom. Or he simply had not noticed. Picking it up, a paper slipped from its pages, a kind of chart. It fluttered to the floor and he stooped to pick it up, putting it into the puddle of light to read it.

On it was a graph, neatly drawn, with little number notations on intersecting lines. Some of the numbers were consecutive, others changing, providing a rising, steady curve upward as the lines intersected the rising points. His heart lurched. She was recording her temperature levels, the present date coinciding with the beginning of the rise in the curve. He felt the blood rush to his head as he moved quickly to the bedside, shaking her awake. Her eyes opened in fear. When she saw the paper in his hand, her fear vanished, giving way to the old recognized contempt.

"You bitch!" he said, waving the paper in front of her. Then he crumpled it and threw it across the room. He felt victimized, unclean, betrayed. "I was a fool!"

She shrugged, remaining silent, turning her eyes away. She had sat up. Now she reclined, watching him.

"You felt nothing." It was not a question. His anger had quieted and his sense of futility seized him again.

"I am what I am," she said, gently now. "It is not in me." Then she smiled, an odd, owlish grin, as if the entire episode had been an amusement, an entertainment.

"Hopefully, some good will come of it," she said. "The temperature was at its highest."

"But it meant nothing!" he sputtered, reaching for words that would not come.

"It doesn't have to."

"I thought, perhaps . . ." he began. His words trailed off. He did not want to reveal his humiliation any further.

"You didn't seem to mind," she said. She had, after all, witnessed his one-sided ecstasy.

"You are like ice," he said, a salve to himself, since he had not stirred her, and could not.

He dressed silently, quickly, thinking only of how fast he must get out of this room, away from her. He did not wash. Perhaps it was deliberate, he thought, an unconscious desire to carry away the smell of her.

"If we have a child, you will have to love a piece of me," he said, a tiny note of triumph seeping into his tone. He did not look back. Nor did she respond.

XII

There had been one other time in her life when Anne had been afraid to admit her happiness to herself, afraid that the admission would make it disappear. She was seventeen and it was summer. Her parents had that big old place in Camden, Maine, overlooking the postcard harbor. They had come there each summer since she could remember and her days had been filled with sailing her tiny sloop around the harbor, haunting the wonderful public library on the edge of town, and trying to understand the changes that were happening in her body and mind.

It was no mystery to her that, of all the summers she had spent in Camden, the one that had burned itself into her memory was the brief four weeks she had spent with Biff Maloney.

It was a preposterous name. He was a preposterous person, the son of a local yacht mechanic. Muscled, tan, tall, he had blond curly hair and deep dimples which framed a big white toothy smile. There was, of course, a deep class distinction between the locals and the summer people. It was not uncommon. The locals scratched out a living from the summer folks, resented them, but relied on their coming to replenish the coffers for the lean winters. It was the rhythm of life in Camden. Everyone accepted it. And when the line was breached, there were always those who rallied round before the breach had scandalized the community.

She had never noticed him before, although she had passed the boatyard hundreds of times, tacking around the harbor. An errant gust of wind had bounced her tiny sailboat against the hull of a cabin cruiser at the end of the boatyard dock, where Biff was hanging from a harness over the stern painstakingly painting the letters of the boat's name. She was called *Paradise Found*, which struck Anne as silly and pretentious. To make it worse, Biff had transposed the last two letters in the word "Paradise" so that it read "Paradies." He had looked down at her from his vantage in the harness, shaking his head with feigned contempt as she struggled to find the wind again. He stuck a finger in his mouth, held it up to find the breeze, then pointed in the wind's direction. She knew, of course, where it was, but she was stuck in the lee of the *Paradise Found*'s bulk.

"The tiller to starboard," he called, smiling now, since she had lost all control and was bobbing helplessly.

"I didn't ask you," she cried, annoyed at what she perceived as his arrogance. She squinted up at him. His vacuous grin was broad and his dimples deepened. She noticed the dimples immediately. Simpleton, she thought. Embedded in the class distinction was the unspoken belief in the genetic decay of the locals. They were simply born dumb, her father had once told her, and she had believed him.

"Get a motor," he hooted. Looking up in exasperation, she discovered the spelling error and felt the onrushing joy of impending revenge.

"Get a brain," she cried, watching his confused expression. He looked up at the sky. " 'Brain', you idiot, not 'rain,' " she murmured inaudibly. He shrugged and cocked an ear. He thinks I'm the dumb one, she thought.

She pointed to the letters on the hull and finally he saw what she was referring to, although it made little difference in his understanding.

Finally she had to spell it out for him and he pulled on the rope so that the harness could ascend to the deck. He was lost from sight for a moment. Then she saw his head over the rim of the rail.

"Darn right," he called, showing her a note pad on which the words were spelled right. Dropping a rope ladder, he descended. She watched him climb downward, holding the rope ladder to keep the boat from drifting. His tanned legs were lightly haired and he wore tight shorts which packed in his well developed buttocks. Above his waist he was bare, tan, muscles rippling under golden skin. In the harness he had been hardly formidable, merely dumb. Now as he got closer he was awesome, big and beautiful. It was her first jolt of awakening sexuality, the beginning of womanhood, and she could reckon the moment exactly.

"They woulda give me unshirted," he said. "I ain't no good at spellin'."

Her heart was pounding. He let himself ease into the sailboat. She could smell the musk of him now. This must be the way a man smells, she thought. His bare arm brushed against her shoulder. Sliding across the seat, he completely enveloped her, his hard bicep pressed against her back as he jiggled the tiller. She felt paralyzed. She would never know whether it was from fear or from pleasure, but she sat rooted as he stretched one leg over the rail and pushed the hull of the cabin cruiser. The little sailboat shot free and into the wind.

"There," he said, not bragging, genuinely helpful, even humble. "You done me good. I didn' mean you were a lousy sailor."

257

The boat moved swiftly now and, as if in deference to her seamanship, he gave her the tiller and the rope.

Her hands were barely able to keep their grip as his huge arm still buttressed her. He was not shy. Natural. That was the way she would always see him in her mind.

"I'm Biff Maloney," he said.

"I'm Penny McCarthy." Anne had not yet found her identity.

"Penny!" He slapped his thigh. Had her name struck him as funny? She looked at him now, trying to be analytical despite his overwhelming physical presence. She had a difficult time keeping her eyes from the tight pouch of his crotch. She had never seen a male organ except in anatomy books in a doctor's office, and, somehow, the curiosity had always seemed unclean and she'd been able to subdue it.

"Better get me back to work. They'll can me," he said, showing no anxiety. In three tacks she got him back near the rope ladder. He grabbed it, then stood for a moment, looking up and squinting at his error.

"I'm no darn speller," he said, smiling. He is beautiful, she decided. Dumb, but beautiful.

Thinking about him made her happy. She was not immune to the idea of class distinction programmed into her from infancy. And she knew he was stupid. But that didn't stop her from wanting to see him again.

She had all the leisure in the world and could easily conform to his nonworking hours. After that first day, she took to sailing close to the boatyard docks as part of her regular course. He would wave to her and she would wave back. She was, of course, deliberately calculating, contriving to meet him at every opportunity. On his part, he was so thickheaded and easily manipulated that he was soon sailing with her every day after he got off from work. She preferred that. On the water, they could easily escape the notice of people by heading into one of the many coves that lined the shore.

Biff didn't talk much, but he was gentle, and she found it gave her pleasure to touch him. They'd stretch out, pulling in the sail and letting the boat drift, watching the changing colors of the sun as it dipped slowly in the west.

"You are one big teddy bear," she told him.

"Yeah."

"You like being with me, Biff?"

"Yeah."

She did learn some rudimentary facts about him. He was born in Camden. His mother had died. He had only gone to school till the fifth grade. She was surprised to learn that he was sixteen, a year younger than she, but that hardly mattered. The image of the teddy bear that had popped into her mind was very close to the truth.

"Where do you go every day?" her mother would ask.

"Sailing."

"All day? You come home so late. I worry sometimes."

Perhaps because Biff was inarticulate and there was little conversation between them, she found herself actually withdrawing in communicating with others, especially her parents.

"You okay, Penny?" her father said to her one night.

"Yes."

"You look strange."

"I'm okay."

She sensed that they had begun to watch her with increasing interest, although she did not pay them much attention. Biff was her life now. He absorbed her completely. When she was not with him, she thought about him. Was she secretly wishing that her mind might become as simple as his? He was never unhappy. He could stare for hours at the sky and never say a word. She felt like his mother. I can make him do anything, she mused.

"What are you thinking about, Biff?" she asked him one evening on the boat.

"Nuthin."

259

"Do you like watching the sunset?"

"Yeah."

She knew that when she touched him, she gave him pleasure. Sometimes she scratched his back and arms. He seemed to purr like a kitten.

"You like that, Biff?"

"Yeah."

As for her own pleasure, she knew that something profound was happening in her body, but she could not define it. Those were days of sexual ignorance. No one talked about it, and there was not a single book in the Camden Public Library that referred, even clinically, to sexuality.

Sometimes they would pull the boat to the shore and lie on the grass, holding each other, not saying a word. She nestled in his arms like a baby. She loved to smell him and feel his tight, smooth flesh. When they had known each other two weeks, she lay against him with bare breasts, feeling the ends of her nipples tingle. There is an instinct about these things and soon he was sucking them and she was loving it. She wanted more to happen, but she wasn't sure exactly what.

An only child, she had always been introspective, living within herself, fantasizing. And even though she knew that Biff had little mental capacity, she believed that there was something mysterious blocking his intelligence and that she could find the key to unlock his mind.

When she was away from him, she missed him. He was never out of her thoughts. She wrote him little poems and read them to him, although she knew that they made no impression.

She knew he was reacting physically. She had felt his hardness against her body, but had not had the courage to touch him there. It was not fear of him. Rather, fear for herself. She had a rudimentary knowledge of how pregnancy occurred.

But, beyond that fear, another anxiety began to plague her. Her parents' curiosity was getting more blatant. They pressed her for answers.

"There is something you're not telling me, Penny," her mother would say.

"No."

"Where do you go? What do you do?"

"Nothing. I go sailing."

"Where?"

"Around the harbor."

But she was arriving home later and later. She began to miss dinner and her parents' suspicions became an obsession. Finally, her father found one of her unfinished poems.

"What is this?"

"A poem."

"It's a love poem."

She had blushed. "It's a secret poem."

Her father would not confront the subject further, but sent her mother instead.

"Is there a boy?"

"No," she lied.

"Are you telling me the truth?"

"Yes."

"Are you sure?"

"Yes."

"Can you explain the poem?"

"I write poems."

Still, the suspicion was not strong enough to interfere with her relationship with Biff. In the few weeks that she had known him, the weather had been perfect and she had been able to sail every day. Then one day it rained.

"Where are you going?" her mother asked.

"Sailing."

"In the rain?"

"Yes."

She was no longer thinking in logical terms. Her world was Biff now. Nothing else mattered. She was happy, but did not tell herself that, for fear it would go away.

They did sail that day, but moved quickly to a nearby cove, pulled the boat ashore, and used the sail to make a shelter for them. They lay together on the grass. It was damp, but the warmth of their bodies dispelled the chill.

"I love you, Biff," she whispered, pressing his hand to her bare breast. "If only . . ." She paused and looked at him, his expression, as always, sunny and vague, his smile glistening in the soft light filtering through the white sail over their heads.

"Yeah," he said.

"Do I make you feel good?"

"I always feel good with you, Penny," he said.

"We'll always be together, won't we, Biff?"

"Yeah."

"Do you like to touch me here?" She cupped her small breasts

"Yeah."

"And would you like to see me naked?"

"Yeah."

She unbuttoned her slacks and rolled her panties down. His eyes watched her nakedness. Lifting his hand, she brought it to her belly and downward to the patch between her legs. Her body lurched. What is happening?

She asked, "Am I beautiful?"

"Yeah."

He is mine, she thought. I can make him do anything. She started to unbutton his pants.

"That's bad," he said, but he did not stop her. She wondered where she found the courage, and when the long, hard piece of flesh flopped free, she gasped. Biff also looked confused as he watched its throbbing, glistening head. At first she turned her eyes away. But there was something in its strangeness that magnetized her. Finally she touched it. Biff gasped, his eyes half-closed, as the thing seemed to lurch and a white substance came out. Something terrible has happened, she thought, turning away.

262

"Are you all right, Biff?"

"Yeah."

"What was that?"

He didn't answer, and when she turned to him again he was dressed. She put her clothes back on.

"I didn't hurt you?"

"Na."

"I love you. I would never hurt you."

"Yeah."

She lay down next to him again and hugged him close.

But the death knell of parting was already ringing in her ears. She lay in his arms a long time that afternoon. When she came home, her parents were waiting. They wore anxious expressions, as if someone had died.

"We know," her mother said.

"What?" She looked at her parents with the same blankness that she had learned from Biff.

"We followed you in the skiff. We saw you sail into the cove," her father said.

"We know about Biff Maloney," her mother said.

She swallowed hard and lowered her eyes.

"He's retarded," her mother said. "Did you know that?"

"I suppose so." I will not cry, she told herself.

"Has anything happened?" her mother asked gently. She could only vaguely sense her meaning. A great deal had happened. How could she bear to lose him? He was the only thing in her world worth loving.

She moved her head from side to side, that sure of her answer.

"Well, that's a relief."

"Tomorrow you're going to your grandmother's house in the Adirondacks," her father said. She felt trapped, the sense of loss overwhelming.

"Thank God, the other people don't know," he sighed.

"What people?"

263

"Our friends," her mother replied. "You would be the laughing stock."

He's beautiful, she wanted to say, and natural, and I love him. She would never, ever, love anyone again.

The next day she went away. She did not cry, but the loss was to plague her for most of her life. Nor did she ever go to Camden again. What she felt for Biff was buried deep inside her. She hadn't felt it for years, not until now.

Perhaps it was the fear of acknowledging that same happiness that made her want to fully possess Eduardo Palmero. She could not bear for him to leave her. Where did he go? What did he do? She wanted to ask, but always fell short of finding the courage. She wondered, too, if it was the money she had offered that made the essential difference in their relationship, but she had wanted to show him how much he meant to her. If necessary, she would have gladly given him her life.

Although she had offered him the use of the money, he had said little about it. He would sometimes disappear for days, causing her deep anxiety. She no longer went to the library, no longer exercised, no longer ate sparingly. She began to neglect the house and would spend hours in front of the window, waiting for him to come. Always when he arrived, she was reborn.

"I can't bear it when you are gone," she said. It was the sense of parting that had triggered the memory of Biff Maloney. Could Eduardo know what kind of suffering that could bring? Parting was not sweet sorrow, she thought. It was agony. When he came to her after a few days' absence, she would devour him with a hunger which she could not have believed she was capable of. She wondered if he was merely submitting. Although he was physically effective, she had the feeling that his mind was elsewhere.

"What is it?" she asked. He must have felt her observation, acknowledging his thoughts.

"We are on the verge of great things, Anne," he said softly.

"Great things?" She seemed puzzled by the reference, then

264

remembered what he was working on in the library. "The manifesto."

"That and other things. We are starting to fight back." She felt the pressure of his hand quicken on her head. "It will not be easy, but we will do it."

It was confusing to her, still unclear. His presence was all that mattered. She moved her hand along his thigh, felt the lump between his legs, then the stirring in him and her own beginnings. She was Lazarus arising, she told herself, feeling the passion smolder and begin inside her, awakening her to all of life's possibilities and sensations, a rebirth of her womanness. Deftly, she undid his pants and watched his erection, a staff of power and strength, the sight of which gave her courage.

"You're beautiful, my darling. Beautiful." She bent over him, kissing the long hardness, feeling the full delight of it and his reactions. I am a woman, she told herself, repeating it. "You have made me a woman, Eduardo, and brought me back to life again." She looked up at him, saw into his eyes, the circles of gray and the speckled silver, a flash of his internal sunlight. Remembering Biff, she wanted to see the mystery of it again. She brought his hand to her breast and he caressed the nipple while her body began to pulse. Caressing him rhythmically, she watched as his sexual energy gathered, gained momentum, shuddered, and his seed overflowed deliciously in front of her eyes and she erupted

"How beautiful, Eduardo. My Eduardo. How beautiful."

He said nothing, and it was his silence that interested her, since she wanted to know what he was thinking. She held him, peaceful now.

"Everything is in place," Eduardo said suddenly. It seemed like an interruption between them. But she listened carefully. Somewhere he had this other life, she knew.

"It has taken us months of planning." He lifted an index finger, as if he might be a professor making a point. "They will see how efficient we can be. You see, the main point has al-

265

ways been our inefficiency," he sneered. "The Allende people are inefficient. They are dreamers. Well, we will show them."

"Of course, darling." She listened, but with little comprehension.

She turned toward him and kissed him deeply. "Why can't we be together always?"

He did not answer.

"But why?" she pressed.

"Later," he said, after a long pause. She was confused, but did not push for clarification.

Yet there was the hint of promise in his words, or was it only in her reception of them? I must not press too hard, she vowed. In the end, I will possess him, she assured herself.

"I understand, Eduardo. I truly understand." She did not, of course. She watched him looking upward, his eyes glazed, as if they were searching elsewhere.

"Would you really, Anne?" he asked quietly.

"Really what?"

"The money."

"Money?"

"What you said the other day?"

She hesitated, groping for the right answer. Did he have any doubts? She reined her elation. So money could be the key, after all. She had once been ashamed of her money, wondering how it continued to amass in odd places all over the world. She only guessed that she had three million, since she hadn't looked at the statements from her investment counselor for years.

"Did you really mean it, Anne?"

"Did you have any doubts?"

"It seemed incredible," he said quickly. "Incredible. At first, it seemed like an insult. My pride . . ."

"Eduardo"—she moved the palm of her hand over his bare chest—"it is the point of the exercise." Could he believe that she could settle for anything less than total commitment of

266

herself, of her life, of her fortune? What price can one put on one's life, she wondered.

"I thought about it for a long time, Anne," he said. "I could not understand. I try to analyze myself." For the first time since she had seen him in the library, he looked different, as if she were viewing him through a gauze lens. His features had softened and he seemed like a boy. He lifted himself on one elbow and looked into her eyes. "What is it you see? I don't understand. Am I so different?"

She had been trying to assemble her thoughts, gathering the bits and pieces of meaning to herself, hoping she might find some way to articulate the answer. She could sense that he wanted words now, that words were important.

"I am forty-nine years old, Eduardo. Nothing." No, I must amend that, she thought. What I say must be pristine, in perfect pitch. "Little has ever moved me. I have had children. I have had a husband. I have seen my parents die. My husband die. I have had the best of wordly goods. But I have not felt a sense of life until I met you."

"But you seemed content."

"Controlled. I was under control. I had found a way to survive."

"But why me?" He seemed troubled now. His eyes moved downward over his body. "What is so special about me?"

It was the edge of the abyss, beyond words.

"It is primarily . . ." He paused.

"That! And everything." They were the only words she could muster. She had never, although she admitted this to herself for the first time, wanted men. Not after Biff. She had welcomed Jack's impotence. Even her affairs had had little physical meaning, except, perhaps, for her own peace of mind in trying to prove her womanness, her desirability. But that, too, had been hollow, without substance. It is all so mysterious, she thought. Then she could see his features changing again, as if the lenses of her camera eye had been replaced.

267

"And you would give me money?" he asked.

"I would give you anything. Anything." she said, feeling a surge of happiness. "Anything," she repeated, her hand caressing his genitals now. "You are beautiful," she said.

"Beautiful?" he paused. "You are seeing something I do not comprehend."

"You don't understand?"

"No."

And me? she wanted to ask. How do you see me? An aging woman. What is more undesirable than an aging woman?

"You think I'm a silly love-struck fool?" She was sorry to have said it.

"No." Again she wanted to ask him. Do you love me? How do you see me? But she held back, her courage faltering.

"I mean it, Eduardo. I will give you anything within my power to give you." It was the sound of an old fairy tale, and she was the queen . . . or the witch.

"Then I must ask you."

She continued to caress him, feeling his eyes on her, watchful. She waited. His sexuality lay dormant as his mind reacted.

"This thing cannot be done without money. It is essential. It must be funded from a private source. In that way, our bargaining power increases."

Gently, he put his hands on hers to freeze the caress. "You see. If we take the money from the Cubans, our bargaining power decreases. We lose essential control. Above all, we must not lose control. And this is the essential difference. We are not interested in the brotherhood of socialism. What we do must be indigenous to Chile. It must be completely Chilean. That is the essential difference." He was becoming agitated. "They, the Americans, think of this thing of Chile's as some worldwide conspiracy, based on the export of the Soviets and their urge for hegemony, the domination of the world, with Chile being the first phase of the domination of the South American continent. What we want is for Chile alone. Only Chile. You see.

268

That is the point of the manifesto. Things will follow in their natural course. Just as in Chile. Indigenous."

She listened, but absorbed little.

"How much do you need?"

"A quarter of a million."

Perhaps I should be hesitant in my answer, she told herself, feeling suddenly an odd sense of power. Power over him. Like Biff. She savored the discovered moment, time suspended, a new and greater sense of herself than she had ever felt before.

"In gold Krugers," he said.

"Gold Krugers?"

"Coins. Each Kruger an ounce. A better exchange than money."

"When do you want it?" She felt his anxiety now. The frozen caress thawed. He removed his hand and she put her lips on his face, letting them roam over his eyes, his nose, finding his lips, then after a long kiss, his ear.

"Anything, my darling. Anything."

"I can't believe it," he whispered.

"Whatever is mine is yours, darling Eduardo."

"You see, Miranda," he said suddenly. The words were clear.

"What?"

He sighed.

"It is nothing." He moved over her. She wanted to ask him to explain, but she said nothing.

XIII

It was shame. Dobbs recognized the emotion, the same secretive guiltridden feeling that he had when he reached behind the bookcase in his own home to bring out that pornographic magazine he had once purchased in a Washington bookstore. For days, he had worried that he had been spotted by them, the watchers of the watchers, as they referred slyly to CIA internal control. He had even fretted over whether or not he had erred in locking the magazine in the trunk of his car. And when he got it into his house, slipped between the pages of the evening paper, he had racked his mind for a good place to hide it.

The bookcase in his study was, he was sure, an excellent place, although he lived in fear that in a frenzy of inspired housecleaning his wife would find it. Sometimes he hoped she would, evidence of his guilty secret, the symbol of his vulnerability. It would prove his lack of impotence. It would show her that there was still the old craving. How then could he better tell her how she had killed it in him by her disinterest?

Eduardo, you sly bastard, he whispered, sure now of his presence in the room. How I envy you your passion? That was the question which described the nub of his shame, his personal shame.

His professional shame was that he could not have foreseen what was emerging between Eduardo and the three women. Never mind that it had aborted his carefully planned surveillance. He had been betrayed by himself. That was why he was searching through these papers, the random words that strung together to describe a life which he could not touch with his understanding. It haunted him now. And he knew it would obsess him throughout the rest of his dry, barren life. Why? Why had he been unable to foresee?

He reached for a file marked "Palmero-Valdivia." He had seen it once, glanced over it with little interest or comprehension. Now he opened its pages and began to study the transcript.

"Translated from the Araucanian dialect," the line above the text read and under it was a brief history of the Araucanian Indians. No matter how many of them were butchered by the conquistadors and by later "liberators," they had never surrendered. They were the only Indian tribe in the Americas that had never surrendered, the writer had pointed out with, it seemed to Dobbs, unprofessional pride.

"And you first saw Palermo when he came to write a story about your village?"

The old man had nodded. He was small and wizened, the interrogator had pointed out. There apparently was an interpreter present, and the interview seemed choppy.

"It was for the party magazine," the interrogator added. "And your daughter first saw him then?"

The old man had nodded again. His face registered no expression.

"She was working for the mission," he said, pointing to the

mission wall, beyond which rose the ancient steeple of an old Spanish church. "She was fourteen and somehow she had remained pure, a virgin."

"How did you know this?"

"We knew."

"And she simply disappeared with him?"

"He said he wanted her." The old man turned his eyes away, looking into the ground with guilt.

"What did he give you?"

The old man shrugged.

"How much?"

"Two hundred. It was more money than I had ever seen at one time in all of my life."

"And he took her away?"

"Yes."

"And then?"

"She came back."

"And where is she now?"

The old man shrugged.

"I have money," the interrogator said. The old man began to talk again.

Eduardo had expected his anger at Miranda, at himself, to abate in Valdivia. Instead, it intensified, and although he threw himself into his work with vigor and zealousness, he could not wipe it out. Perhaps it was the anger that added the fire to his speeches to the dock workers, the farmers, and factory hands and gave more bite to the articles he wrote for the party paper. Allende and the other party functionaries sent him long letters of commendation. He worked tirelessly, more out of fear that, if he should slow down, he would be tormented by his memories of Miranda. He saw her face everywhere, imagined her body, even as he copulated with the whores of Valdivia.

Since he had not the constitution to drink heavily, he found

273

his escape only in women. Somehow it was the only way he could escape the torment, as if he could lose himself in the imagined womb of Miranda.

"Say nothing," he would tell them. "I will pay you double if you do not speak." They looked at him with thickly made-up, startled eyes.

He had rented a small house in a decaying neighborhood not far from the city's center and just a few blocks from the party headquarters. Because it was so close, it became another meeting place for the party workers, who swarmed over the house as if it were their own. Sometimes, if offered drinks or food, they would stay long into the night. He hated to be alone. Yet he was deliberately aloof, except when it came to party matters. Luckily, the level of intensity among the party workers was high and their absorption in these matters could sustain their interest.

Because he was wealthier than the others, he was treated with exaggerated respect and he was able to deflect any attempts at intimacy, especially by the women, many of them young students who formed the bulwark of the party's support, after the workers.

It was not that he didn't want them. With all women now, he could feel a sense of Miranda in them, but the prospect of intimacy, communication, thwarted him. He preferred the whores. He could pay them to be silent, to offer nothing but their bodies.

His father, he discovered from others who came to the city on business, was so upset with him, his pride so offended, that one could not mention Eduardo's name in his presence. He had even forbidden his mother and sisters to communicate with him. This he had expected. Eduardo's betrayal had been deep, and he was certain that Miranda, who played the role of abandoned wife with great aplomb, had not helped the situation.

What did it matter, he told himself. Their lives were fantasy-ridden, dissolute with greed. The curtain was swiftly coming down on their way of life. It was tragic that they could not see it happening or, fearing its demise, did nothing to stop it. In his mind, he could wipe out much of his previous life. All except Miranda!

It was worse, surely far worse, than a physical affliction to ache for her, to want her. And yet she would do her "duty." To contemplate it made him ashamed of his manhood, his inability to control the focus of his desire. It was with Uno that he discovered the depths of his damnation.

He had seen her first in the mission, a child-woman not much older than her wards, emaciated children who played in a dust bowl at the far end of the mission wall. The old padre was showing him around the mission, his myopic eyes squinting into the sun-drenched courtyard. Eduardo had come to the village, a tiny hamlet wedged into the edge of the Cordillera about fifty miles north of Valdivia, armed with a writing tablet and his camera and bent on using the plight of the Araucanians as a symbol of the ultimate dehumanization of the Chilean ruling class. The government had declared the Araucanians a kind of protected endangered species, but that had done little to relieve their extreme poverty.

"They are children," the old padre sighed as his bent body labored to make the long hegira around the littered courtyard. It was the fashionable epithet of the Church, whose power had always been on the side of the oligarchs. Eduardo outwardly expressed sympathy with the old man's opinions. The objective, of course, was to portray the opposite view. He was beginning to learn the power of charm, dissembling to achieve a specific goal.

"The best they can look forward to is the kingdom of heaven," the old man said. As he approached the spot where the children were playing, they suddenly stopped and stood at attention. When he passed before them, they each bowed and kissed his ring, while he blessed them with the sign of the cross.

Uno stood a few feet away, watching the spectacle approvingly. It gave Eduardo a chance to view her, a doll-like creature, barefoot, her skin the color of cocoa, hardly more than four and a half feet, but well proportioned. Her eyes watched him briefly, then turned quickly away as he concentrated his gaze on her. The ceremony over, she shepherded the children back to the dustbowl, where she seemed to be administering some kind of game with sticks and stones.

He continued to watch her as she moved. Considering her shabby gray smock, tied at the waist, there was an odd grace to her walk, and when she turned in a swift motion, her hair rustling as if a breeze had caught it, he knew why he had observed her with such interest. She seemed a tiny, dark replica of Miranda, a primitive doll carved from the petrified wood found beyond the last timber-line of the Cordillera.

The old man had moved away, and it was only when he called to Eduardo that he interrupted his concentration.

"I was curious about the game," Eduardo said, to cover his embarrassment. But his thoughts were with the small child-woman.

"A simple game," the old padre said. "They play it all their lives. They are the meek." he whispered. "The Son of God has put them in our care."

Eduardo checked his temptation to enlighten. Nothing had changed in this village for centuries.

"And do they still practice the old tribal customs?" he asked gently.

The old man shrugged. It was a question he deigned not to answer. A bell rang in the steeple and the children stopped their play and straggled into the church. Again he had an opportunity to watch the girl as she led the motley group toward them.

"May I take their picture?" Eduardo asked.

The old padre motioned to the girl, who came forward, her head bowed. He spoke to her in an odd-sounding dialect. She

276

responded with a whispered word and lined the children against the sun-drenched wall, then stepped away.

"And her, too," Eduardo said. He motioned to her while the old man spoke to her.

He began to take their pictures, stepping closer as he snapped, finally capturing her alone in the lens as he moved forward. She seemed frightened, her lips tight, her eyes lowered.

"What is her name?"

The old padre mumbled her name. It sounded like Uno, but he knew that was not correct. It will be Uno then, he told himself.

"Tell her to smile," Eduardo requested, wondering how far he could go with the old man.

"She does not know what that means."

"Then tell her something funny that will make her laugh."

"They do not laugh," the old man said, his contempt showing now. Eduardo did not press the point, but snapped his pictures, then put his camera back in its case. The old man waved the children away and they continued their ragged march through a stone door, from which came the smell of food.

"Why don't they laugh?" Eduardo asked, wondering if the question would end his interview. The old man looked at him through his myopic eyes.

"Would you laugh if you were them?" It seemed an incongruous answer. He had expected something like, "It is God's will." The walk had wearied the old man and he sat down on the steps at the entrance of the broken-down stone church. He had hoped that the old padre would be his interpreter. He wanted to visit in the village, to take pictures. He had already shaped the story in his mind. There was enough squalor to portray their plight.

"Is there someone in the village who also speaks Spanish?" he asked the old man, who was beginning to drowse, oblivious to the flies that swirled about his nose.

277

"Terrano," the padre said, pausing. "The girl's father."

"Where is he?" He felt his palms begin to sweat.

The padre pointed in the direction of the village, a vague gesture. The old man, he could tell, was growing bored with him.

He started to go. Then, hesitating, he halted, watching the old man, the eyelids heavy with fatigue, the gray hairs sprouting on his face. The image of the girl hung in his mind. Uno! Although he had long been an atheist, he felt the sense of blasphemy in his thoughts about the girl, a corruption in himself. It is Miranda, he assured himself. Part of her curse.

"Could you ask the girl to show me to her father?" he said. He had already dipped his hand in his pocket and when the old man opened his eyes he saw the money.

"And this contribution," Eduardo said, "for your trouble." His hypocrisy was an obscenity.

The sight of the money revitalized the old man, confirming Eduardo's cynicism. The padre clapped his hands a number of times in quick succession. The girl appeared and the padre spoke to her in the strange language. Without looking at him, the girl nodded and began to move away toward the courtyard entrance.

"He is an old fox," the padre said to Eduardo. "Keep an eye on your pockets." Then the aged eyes closed again, and looking back as he reached the courtyard entrance, he saw the ancient head reposing on the old man's chest.

Outside the mission, Eduardo followed the girl closely, watching her swift, graceful movements, the easy swing of her girl-woman hips, noting how well formed her legs were, tapered at the ankles, her feet not yet swollen like those of the other Indian women. They came into a clearing, a clutter of litter and rusting junk. The stink was abominable. A small, dark, muscular man sat in the entrance of a makeshift shack with a corrugated tin roof. From the interior of the shack came the cackling of women's voices in the strange dialect. Barefoot children roamed about the clearing with scrawny dogs. When they saw the girl, they clustered around her skirts, but she waved them away.

The dark man, his small body like rip cord except for a slightly distended belly, watched the oncoming man without interest. His daughter spoke to him and he looked up desultorily. The girl moved away and squatted some distance from them. Eduardo's eyes followed her. It was only then that he noted the man's engaging interest.

"You speak Spanish?" Eduardo asked. He did not use the same tone of deference he had used with the padre.

"Why?" the old man asked in Spanish. His teeth were rotted and his lips snarled as he spoke.

"I—" Eduardo hesitated, feeling the girl's father's eyes searching him. Is he reading my mind? Eduardo wondered. There seemed an edge of cruelty about the man's fierceness. "I am interested in telling the story of your village," Eduardo said. The words seemed hollow. He looked briefly at the girl, who turned her eyes to the ground. He tore his gaze away.

"What story?" the man said. He picked up a tin can from the hard ground and drank from it. It seemed a kind of beer, a greenish liquid that dripped from both sides of his chin. He did not bother to wipe it away, letting the droplets linger until they fell to his chest

"The Araucanians," Eduardo said stupidly. The man drank again. Eduardo felt Uno's eyes watching him.

The man's eyes narrowed. He emptied the can and threw it at one of the dogs. He was obviously drunk. The barefoot children had vanished into the air, along with the scrawny dogs. Eduardo took his camera out of its case and pointed it at the man, who put both his hands in front of his face. He had imagined that the man was ignorant of cameras. An old fox, he thought. The padre is right.

"I have money."

Eduardo felt his shame, looking briefly at the girl, who again

279

turned her eyes to the ground. He fanned the bills in his hands.

At the sight of the cash, the man's eyes opened wide. "A story, you said," the man mumbled. It was obvious that he did not comprehend.

"For a newspaper."

The man looked at him blankly, but held out his hand. Eduardo gave him two bills. The girl's father looked at them closely, folded them, and put them in the band of his pants. Then Eduardo lifted the camera and began taking pictures of the hut, the rusting debris. Turning, he captured the girl in his lens again.

"You want to fuck my daughter," the man said, his face a blank. He looked at the girl and spat into the ground.

"You filthy bastard," Eduardo said. He was not sure the man had understood. His features registered no reaction.

"She has had no man."

"No thanks to you." He was still not sure that the man understood him. He had put the money back into his pocket and began to move toward the girl. Her father stood up and followed him. Standing over the girl, he lifted her to her feet. Her face, like her father's, was mute. Or he did not know how to read their signs?

"The padre keeps the men away," the man said. "I am her father. I can give her to you." He spoke to the girl in the strange language. The girl merely lowered her eyes. He could not determine what he loathed more, his own temptation, or the man's callousness.

"I will tell the padre," Eduardo said. The man ignored him. He moved the girl in front of him and squeezed her breasts.

"Good," he said.

Eduardo grabbed him roughly by the shoulders and pushed him away. But the man kept his balance and snarled at Eduardo.

"She is only a woman."

"And you are an animal."

280

"But I can see that you want her." He had lowered his voice. His eyes blazed like coals. "And you have money."

Eduardo wavered. He looked at the girl, felt his own desire, and his own compelling need to understand what was driving him. Yet, he could tell himself that she was in need of protection from this vapid life on which she was impaled. There are good instincts in that, he assured himself. Who is the greater monster, he wondered, watching the man who eyed him now.

Eduardo thrust his hand in his pocket and threw all the bills on the ground, scattering them. The man groped for them like a bird pecking at a handful of scattered feed. Eduardo watched him with contempt, waiting until he had gathered all of the bills in his hand.

"Tell her," he commanded, his voice harsh.

The man looked at his daughter and spoke to her. She looked at Eduardo, but her face told him nothing.

"I will be good to you," he said gently, knowing that she could only understand his tone, not his words. Despite his disgust with himself, he felt special joy in the knowledge that he could possess her.

"And that." The man pointed to the camera, which Eduardo unhitched from his shoulder and gave to him.

"You bastard," he said again, unable to look at his face, moving away, but first making sure that Uno was following. He heard her soft padding walk behind him as he followed the path in the direction of the mission. At the edge of its wall he retraced his steps down the burro path he had ascended earlier. Balancing himself on the jutting rocks that lay on the trail, he turned back occasionally to observe her following him. She was watching him now, he knew, and her eyes no longer looked downward when he looked directly at her.

In two hours, they reached his car, parked along the dirt road that led to the main highway, ten miles to the west. She sat beside him in the front seat, watching the roadway. He was certain she had not been in a car before.

It was, he knew, the most bizarre act of his life. It offended every moral bone in his body. In many ways, it was an offense against himself.

"I will not hurt you," he said. She showed no emotion, her eyes steadily watching the roadway as night fell slowly over the Cordillera where she had spent the whole of her previous life.

"I will be good to you," he pleaded, not looking at her. "I need someone to love." It seemed a cry from the depths of himself and, for a moment, he felt the power of his confession. He was certain that she did not comprehend.

The car slowed in traffic along the two-lane highway as they moved closer down the coast to Valdivia and he did not arrive at his house until nearly dawn. She had dozed fitfully, but in an erect position, and was instantly alert when the car had stopped.

"This is my home," he told her. "Your home."

He had not touched her up till then. Now he took her hand, surprised at its smallness, and led her into the house. She showed no fear, her face reflecting the same even expression, as if she lived behind a veil that screened out emotion.

He felt stiff and exhausted, his energy sapped. Because he was not sure of her and was genuinely frightened that she might run away, he brought her to his own bedroom. He could not bear to let her sleep on the couch, like some dog. He pointed to the bed and she walked toward it. Then she dropped to the floor and stretched out at its foot.

"No, not there," he cried, bending over and lifting her onto the bed. She lay there, flat, her arms folded like a corpse. He smiled down at her gently, bent over and kissed her on the forehead. Then he locked her in and stretched out on the couch. Luckily he was exhausted, his mind drained of intelligence. Plunging into a vacuum, he felt his body slip into a deep, dreamless sleep.

When he awoke he felt the panic of strangeness and it took him a few moments to regain his sense of place. Remembering Uno, he felt the pores of his body open. What had he done?

282

He felt the enormity of the crime against himself, against her. He had bought her as if she were a commodity to be traded or bartered against her will. Was it his own selfishness? The need to replicate Miranda? Or was he subconsciously delivering her from the life of drudgery and despair, the futile charade before she would enter the kingdom of heaven. If that was the truth of his motivations, he could live with that.

And, after all, he had not touched the girl, not invaded either her body or her soul. It was a cleansing thought. Enough to provide the courage to open the door of his bedroom.

She was still there on the bed where he had left her, looking darker against the sheets than he remembered her yesterday. Her eyes were open and, as before, expressionless.

"Good morning, Uno," he said pleasantly. At the sound of his voice, she got off the bed and stood before him, a small, perfectly proportioned doll. He observed her closely, seeking to discover what in her had reminded him of Miranda.

"Come here," he said gently, moving his hands in pantomime. She drew closer to him, barely inches away, and he could smell her odor, like that of an animal. Then it occurred to him that she had not relieved herself. He took her arm and guided her toward the bathroom, realizing that she had never seen a plumbing appliance. Even the priest had used the outdoors, as the animals did. Taking her arm, he led her gently to his overgrown garden, a miniature forest. She understood and squatted behind a bush, and discreetly he turned his eyes away.

It was Sunday and, for the first time, his consciousness absorbed the sounds of the bells clanging around the city. She heard them, too, hesitating as she came toward him again, her ear cocked in attention.

"They are calling the slaves for their shot of subjugation," he said. Guiding her to a chair at the kitchen table, he searched the cupboards for food. He found bread, cheese and fruit and made some tea. She did not begin to eat until he sat down at

283

the table. He watched her and she reminded him of a squirrel, nibbling away with her front teeth, looking blankly ahead of her.

"Later, I will take you back to the village," he said. "I can't imagine what possessed me." He drank his tea and watched her.

"If only you could be Miranda," he said, the idea inflating him. "My little dark, ebony Miranda." He paused. "Why is it such a complexity?" He reached out and patted her head. She continued to eat. "I shall tell you all about my private hell. Then I will take you back to the village, where you will live yours."

When she had finished everything on her plate, she looked down, contemplating its emptiness. The smell of her filled the room, running out of her pores, a gaseous presence. Leaving her there at the table, he got up, went to the bathroom, and filled the ancient tub with warm water. At least, I will send her back clean, he thought, but the idea of her small naked body in the tub had begun to move his sensuality. He felt his penis begin to harden.

When the tub was filled, he brought the girl to the bathroom and undressed her. At the sight of her perfectly formed body, his penis rose to fullness. Her breasts were small, but high, the nipples protruding from large, dark puddles. He felt them, kissed them, watched them harden. He deliberately averted his eyes from her face, wondering if she felt anything.

"Are you frightened?" he asked. She had worn nothing under her gray smock, and although the scent of her disgusted him, it also excited him. She had a tiny thatch of hair at the base of her motte and he could not resist kissing that as well. Lifting her, he put her in the tub and, soaping his hands, moved them over her body until her skin slickened. His fingers gently probed and cleaned every part of her body. He could not understand his passion to suddenly cleanse her. Perhaps it was his own heart, his mind, or his soul that he wanted to cleanse. What am I trying to wash away? he wondered. The

284

girl was docile under his touch. He wondered again what she felt.

"What do you feel?" he asked, remembering Miranda. Was it this lack of response that reminded him of Miranda? He washed her hair, soaped her again, titillated the tight, small crevice between her legs, massaged her nipples until they stood.

"So there is something inside," he thought joyously, lifting her from the tub. She was light, hardly an effort, and he wrapped her in a towel and patted her, watching her eyes now. They looked at him blankly.

"You are my little doll," he said, drawing him to her, enveloping her in his arms, wondering if she had ever received such love, such warmth.

"You must feel that I love you," he said, hating his ridiculousness. "Will you be Miranda?" he asked, as a supplicant.

Carrying her to the bed, he unwrapped the towel and put her on it. The old smell of her was still on the sheets and soon her body was immersed in it again. Undressing, he stood before the edge of the bed. Her eyes watched his erect penis.

"So here is something," he said, sensing the madness of it. He looked about the room. Was someone watching? He walked to the window and pulled the blinds. The light in the room was muted.

Standing beside her again, he lifted a fragile hand and put it on his penis, making it stroke him.

"This is my manhood," he said. "It has a life of its own, mindless ... like you." He wondered if she was really mindless.

Then he disengaged her hand and spread her legs, putting his tongue in the little crevice. He could not distinguish whether she was wet from him or herself.

"Does it move you?" he asked suddenly, watching her.

"Would you feel anything if I cut your heart out?" he said. He squeezed one of her erected nipples. Her expression did not change.

"You don't feel pain either?" he asked.

He lifted her to a sitting position and put his hard penis between her breasts, pressing them around it. He moved her arms around him so that her hands held his buttocks, and leaned her head against his belly, caressing her hair.

"Do you love me, Miranda?" he asked the silent room. He could feel the coolness of her breath against his skin.

"You must love me forever," he said. "I insist on that. You must not let me love alone." Then he made her lie flat on the bed, as he kneeled over her, directing his swollen penis against the tiny pink gash.

"Surely you have seen this before," he said suddenly, oddly clinical, absorbed in the process. "Sooner or later it all comes to this," he said, feeling a sob gather in his throat. He moved forward, feeling her small opening part, wondering why she did not cry out.

"You must love me," he cried, feeling a sob gather deep inside him. "Miranda," he cried, moving forward, the weight of his body plunging the hard penis forward, slowly penetrating, feeling the pain of it.

"Feel something," he shouted. "Anything, pain, pleasure, disgust!" He continued to move forward, her tissue yielding, beginning to lubricate the passage. He felt her heartbeat's speed, the pumping of her blood. Or was it his own. Then her body began to twitch, her lips parted slightly as she gasped for breath. She was fully penetrated now, her body opened like a flower, moving on its own power. Her eyes had closed. He could not tell if it was pleasure or pain, or both. Was he feeling the power of her race now, he wondered, the brutality of the unconquered, dominating by their submission. He moved his body ruthlessly, feeling her squirm beneath him.

He felt his pleasure begin, a suffusion of energy at the base of his spine, focusing its center in his loins, his hard piston moving without mercy in the fragile form below him, vanquishing, self-contained in its awesome power. Then she screamed, a long wail of anger, like an animal being quartered

286

while still alive. It was impossible to believe the sound could come from such a tiny figure, but it continued, both frightening and exciting him, urging his energy. Then he felt the pleasure come, an ejaculation that shook him as if his blood had become a gusher, pumping through his veins with an intensity that he had never felt before. Only then did her screams stop and he lay on top of her, his pores dripping with the liquids of himself, their odors mingling.

He could not tell how long he lay over her, still penetrated. When he opened his eyes, she was watching him. Was the mindlessness gone? Did he detect some communication? He disengaged himself and lay flat beside her, staring at the ceiling. He could feel her eyes watching him, but he did not turn toward her.

"Did I rape your soul as well, Miranda?" he said. "And you, Uno, what did it matter who opened your womanhood? It would have been done sooner or later. Genetic programming, some inchoate force that sustains the race of humanity, the mysterious push of life. Do you know what I'm talking about? Do I know? What is self-perpetuation?" He paused, moved his hand to feel her flesh.

"Who am I, you ask?"

"I am Eduardo searching for the missing part of himself. We are all searching for the missing part of ourselves."

"And have I found it?"

"I thought it was Miranda. It is a delusion. As you know. You are not Miranda. You are a primitive. One step above an animal. And if I have given you my seed, we will propagate a strange race. Whose genes will dominate? What does it matter?"

"Have I been unjust to you? Exploited you for my own pleasure?"

"Yes, I admit that. I am just as vulnerable as the next man."

"Did I enjoy the manipulation."

"Yes, I took pleasure in it."

"And did I move you?"

"We shall see."

He got up, gave her her smock. She dressed and they drove north again. He did not talk to her and she sat, as she had sat yesterday, watching the road, her eyes expressionless. He no longer wondered about his motives. He wanted her away from him. She had somehow become the focus of an evil in himself, a terrible vulnerability. He wondered what she might tell the old padre.

Darkness came. He moved the car off the highway and onto the dirt road, bumping along, headlights ablaze to light the way. He drove cautiously. Occasionally an animal would find itself trapped in the circle of the headlight's illumination. There was a full moon, which helped his vision. When he felt he was close enough to the trail that led upward to the Cordillera, he opened the car door and signaled for her to leave. Obediently, she stepped out of the car, and for a moment, like a trapped animal, she appeared in the circle of light. As he backed the car away, the beam moved and Uno disappeared. The car headed back toward the highway.

He arrived back at his house as the sun poked its way above the peaks of the Cordillera. Exhausted, he threw himself on his bed. The smell of her was still pervasive, and although it triggered the memory of her, he fell into a deep sleep.

Three days later he found her squatting in his doorway, a fragile lump of flesh. Her feet were raw and bleeding, and he carried her into the house, washed and bandaged them. It was different now, he knew. Somehow what he had done to her had exorcised him, and although he felt a sense of shame, he no longer felt any desire for her. Something had come over him, he decided, and until he saw her in his doorway, he had almost begun to believe that it had all been part of a dream.

He had thrown himself with renewed vigor into the party's work, and Miranda seemed less of an obsession than she had

288

been. Until now, he had actually imagined that he was free of her.

He let her sleep on the couch, fed her, and allowed her to stay in the house when he was off at party headquarters. During the next few days, he kept his co-workers away and did not answer any phone calls. He did not talk to her as he had before, and when her feet had healed, he again drove her to where the trail began. It was daylight then, and when he let her out at the foot of the trail, he motioned with his arms for her to leave.

"You must go back," he cried. She stood immobile, her dark face a mask. In the way the sun angled over her face, he could see the harbinger of her future face, wrinkled, prunelike, lined and dry like burnt cork. He motioned furiously with his arms.

"Go back."

Finally he got into the car and angrily reversed it, moving it over the road. The wheels had kicked up a huge cloud of dust and he could no longer see her in the rear-view mirror. Stopping the car, he let the dust settle, waiting to see if she had gone. In the thinning cloud, he saw her, squatting now, a speck beside the road, immobile, waiting. Another curse, he thought, as he put the car in forward and slowly approached the girl. She watched him come, stood up and waited, while he got out of the car and slammed the door, hearing the echo in the hidden canyons.

Looking up, he squinted into the peaks of the Cordillera, the snow-capped wonders glowing like platinum swords stabbing into the sky. He felt his own smallness, his inability to control his own destiny. Annoyed with himself, he started up the trail. She moved with him now, a few feet behind, her legs surer than his on the rocky trail. If there was pain in her newly healed feet, she showed no visible signs. After three hours, he reached the village, saw the steeple of the ancient mission in the dusk and retraced his steps to her father's shack.

The father squatted near the glow of a fire, outside of the

shanty, the flames playing a shadowy dance on his face. As before, Uno squatted a few feet off, watching them, showing no expression in her face, although the reflection of the fire made her eyes glow like embers.

"I've brought her back," Eduardo said. Her father looked up at him. Only his head moved, the sinews of his neck etched by the firelight. He shrugged.

"And I want you to keep her here."

Her father looked at the girl.

"She did not suit you. You should beat her."

"I'm not a savage."

The father shrugged. "Then I shall tell the padre to keep her. The padre knows."

"Knows what?"

"That she has become your woman."

"She is not my woman."

The father looked at her, rattled some words in a foreign tongue.

"She is your woman," he said.

"I have no woman," Eduardo answered, looking at the girl, her primitive foreignness disgusting him. "Is it money you want?"

The father nodded.

"And you must keep her here. She is not to follow me like you made her do last time."

He looked at the girl, then at Eduardo, who could tell from the man's apparent confusion that the long hike to Valdivia was her own idea.

He reached into his pocket and pulled out a neatly folded pile of bills. Squatting beside the man, he showed him the money, which he divided in half.

"You will get this now," Eduardo said. "And the other if she does not return."

The man nodded. Eduardo looked briefly into Uno's face. It told him nothing.

"In three months. Remember, if she comes, you will get nothing."

He did not look back, walking swiftly away, groping through the brush to the downward trail, lit only by the light of the moon. It was after he had been walking for nearly an hour that he heard the scream. He told himself it might be a beast in the throes of a deep pain. But he knew better.

In three months, he sent one of the young men among the party workers into the village with the other half of the money. When the young man returned, he confirmed the delivery. If he wondered why it was done, he said nothing. As for Uno, Eduardo blocked her from his mind, although sometimes in his dreams he would hear the scream again and would awake in a cold sweat.

XIV

In the gray light of the early morning, Anne watched his face. The tiny hairs of his beard had begun to sprout like the first shoots of a spring garden and she wondered, with delight, if she could count them, including all the hairs of his mustache. After all, wasn't that, too, the measure of her knowing him? His breath was easy and the flutter in his eyelids told her that he was dreaming. She was suddenly jealous of this private world of his. If only she could scoop him up and lock him into a cage forever.

Perhaps her staring had awakened him. His eyes opened quickly, not in gradual stages, as she imagined his awakening might come. He was instantly alert, alive. And it triggered something deep inside of her. She threw the covers aside and looked at his naked body, the member erect, ready, as if she had willed it that way. She discovered, too, that she was ready and she straddled him, feeling every sensation of the descent into her and the instant eruption that had been caused. What occurred was quick, a sudden gust, a new assault on her senses. Her body shook for a long time and her heart pounded.

"You see," she said after a while. "Is that answer enough?"

"I wonder," he said, and she contemplated the extent of his own pleasure in her.

"I will do it today," she said, feeling the need to prove that what he had asked was on the very top of her consciousness.

"What must be done?"

"I have to call my investment counselor."

"All you need do is transfer funds. He will probably have to do some liquidation, and surely he will try to talk you out of it."

"Then I will threaten to remove my account. See, I am not totally ignorant of business matters."

He seemed pleased by her response. She had even forgotten her investment counselor's name. She hadn't talked to him in at least a year.

"Then you must consult a gold broker and provide your own vault space to which the Krugers will be delivered. I estimate that we will get nearly seventeen hundred Krugers, depending on the price of gold at the moment. It will probably weigh about one hundred pounds."

The concentration on technical details amused her as she watched his excitement mount, feeling pleasure in it. He sat up and folded his hands together.

"I'll get two leather bags. That should do it. Yes," he said, as if the thought were complete now. "In two days would be ideal. Ideal." He seemed relaxed and she wondered if she had truly begun the process of keeping him with her always.

To her delight, he stayed with her throughout the day and the next night, and they moved about the house together like an old couple grown used to each other. She called her investment counselor in New York. She had looked up his name in her papers, a Mr. Handelman. She was proud of herself, hoping he would admire her decisiveness as he listened to her talking.

"I don't care about the future of the gold market, Mr. Handelman. Just effect the transfer and arrange the details of the transaction." She smiled and held the phone upward so he could hear Mr. Handelman's agitated voice.

"Please, Mr. Handelman, just carry out the transaction and arrange the vaulting at Riggs' Dupont branch." She had just remembered her safe-deposit boxes lying there in the big vaults, the clutter of her life and possessions, jewelry, deeds to property, birth certificates. Meaningless geegaws, she told herself, watching Eduardo. "Now there is value," she whispered, pointing to him.

"What?" He hadn't understood.

"I was studying comparative values."

When she hung up, they called the stores for food to restock her kitchen and when it arrived they both packed her cabinets. Then she cooked steaks and they ate ravenously in the dining room.

"What lovely china," he said.

"Just things."

Toward the end of the day, she could feel his restlessness begin and she steeled herself for what she knew was his coming departure. She detested the idea of it, but quieted her greed for him. We had better move in slow steps, she assured herself, remembering his reaction of last week. After all, he will have to come back for the gold.

"I just want you to know, Anne," he said as he faced her near the door, holding her shoulders, looking into her eyes. "You cannot know how grateful ... " His sudden inarticulateness surprised her as he stumbled forward. "Someday the people of Chile must know what you are doing ... the people. They must know."

He enveloped her in his arms and she felt him kissing her hair, and then he was gone and she was alone in the house. She watched him walk down the quiet street to Wisconsin Avenue.

When he was out of sight, she turned up the stereo, the Bach tape sending its sinuous sounds throughout the house as she moved her body to the complex rhythms. She literally felt that her bones creaked as she struggled to bring her dormant muscles back to life. The idea, she knew, was to physically evade her longing for him, exhaust herself so that her mind might stop imagining, questioning where his was. Aside from his cause, that obsession, what else was there in his life? Finally she was too tired to continue and she fell exhausted on the couch. Perhaps she would be lucky and sleep until he came again.

Which he did, of course. She had grappled with the details of getting the gold into her vaults, which meant she had to take an unaccustomed taxi drive to the Riggs branch on Dupont Circle. The Krugers came in carefully wrapped rolls, and after the guard moved them into a cubicle, she transferred them into two large steel safety-deposit boxes. When she came home, she sank into a chair in the front parlor and watched the light fade. Then the phone rang.

"Is it done?"

"Yes."

"Then tomorrow we will do it."

"Yes."

She sensed his hesitation.

"I need you now, Eduardo."

"We must be careful ... " he began, then, whispering, "The telephone is not safe."

"Please, Eduardo."

He seemed to contemplate his response. She could hear his hurried breathing. The hollowness of the sound indicated that he was in a telephone booth.

"Someone is following me."

What was he saying? What is this mystery?

"Then come when it's dark. I'll leave the door open."

"All right." The word was curt, final. The telephone went dead abruptly.

Sensing her power over him, she felt somehow corrupt. Perhaps if she had made the sum smaller and doled it out like food, he could be sustained by it indefinitely. She wondered what her possessions were really worth and dialed Mr. Handelman's number.

"I was just going out, Mrs. McCarthy," he said. His voice was distant, cold. He must have concluded I've lost my mind, she thought.

"What are my holdings worth, Mr. Handelman?"

"Nearly five million." He answered instantly, as if he had just calculated the amount. "We have been very fortunate." He paused and added with a touch of sarcasm. "But if you continue to be headstrong . . . Gold is a ridiculous purchase at this time."

"Five million, you say." She ignored his brief lecture. This did not count the jewels. Another half a million, she calculated, remembering the heirlooms that had come down from Jack's family and her own. I will tell Eduardo when he comes, she decided, putting down the phone after a courteous dismissal.

She had not contemplated her wealth for years. In her hostess days, she had spent lavishly, but not without a firm hand on the pocketbook. Nothing in her life, she knew, had ever been pursued without obstinate single-mindedness. Poor Eduardo, she thought, half in jest, fearing that if he could read her thoughts, he might think it the beginning of his diminishment and suspect her of some form of castration. She was amused at the idea. Power did have its compensations.

That night she watched him enter her house, leather bags on either shoulder. He unhitched them and put them on a chair. Then she clung to him, felt his arms guiding her to the couch. She sat beside him, touching him, unable to keep her hands from his flesh. His mind, she saw, was agitated, concentrating on other matters.

"It is all settled. The wheels are in motion," he said. "Are you certain that there will be no problem with the gold?"

"I can't imagine any."

"Nothing you can think of. The gold is in the boxes at the Riggs branch?"

"Yes."

"And there will be no problem about gaining access?"

"Eduardo. It is mine. It is my property."

He put his head back against the back of the couch and closed his eyes. Beneath the lids, his eyeballs twitched.

"This is a tense business," he said. She put her hand on his forehead. It felt warm and she wondered if her touch soothed him.

"It will be fine," she said, kissing his cheek. He put his arm around her and squeezed her shoulder.

"I am very grateful, Anne. Truly grateful."

Gratitude seemed a thin reward and, for a moment, she felt a stab of anxiety. Why doesn't he speak of love? she wondered, but she let that pass.

"Come to bed," she whispered. It seemed like a command and she watched his hesitation. "Come to bed," she said again, her hand unbuttoning his shirt and groping for the flesh of his chest. "Now." It was power. She reveled in it.

Holding his hand, she led him up the stairs. And then they were naked in bed. She could not get enough of him.

"Do you forgive me my greed, Eduardo?" she said as she watched him fight drowsiness.

"Of course," he said and soon he was asleep and all she could hope for was a place in his dreams.

Moving the gold from the safe-deposit boxes was, as she had predicted, quite simple. They had taken a taxi to the Dupont branch, ordered it to wait, and she walked into the bank with Eduardo at her side, signing the admittance slip to the vaults without incident.

"This is my husband," she felt compelled to tell the guard as he opened the heavy door and led her to the boxes. When she had turned the key in tandem with the guard's master key, Eduardo helped her remove the boxes to the cubicle, where they emptied the Krugers into the two leather bags, which he rehitched over both shoulders.

"It is a beautiful heaviness," he said as they walked through the bank outside into the bright sunlight. The taxi waited and they both got in. It moved slowly through the traffic, heading toward Georgetown. He looked outside through the rear window.

"What is it, Eduardo?"

"One can never be certain." She followed his gaze, seeing only the stream of traffic. It seemed so far from the reality of her situation. But she did not have time to explore the thought further, for Eduardo tapped the driver on the shoulder as the cab moved through the thickening traffic in Georgetown.

"Pull over, driver. Let me off here."

The taxi swerved to the curb and Eduardo kissed her on the cheek.

"I will call," he said.

"I don't understand," she began, with genuine bemusement. It had not occurred to her that what was happening was possible. Why was he leaving her?

"I will call," he repeated, opening the taxi door, slamming it shut, then heading toward Wisconsin Avenue. The taxi moved forward, and soon he was lost in the crowd.

Within moments the panic began. "Please stop," she said, tapping the driver's shoulder.

"But I thought ... " the driver began. She put a twenty-dollar bill in his hand.

"Keep it," she said. He stopped the cab and she got out, hurrying in the direction that Eduardo had taken. Moving swiftly, she turned up Wisconsin Avenue, focusing her eyes for distance, surveying the moving crowd ahead.

Her panic grew as she walked. The crowds moved slowly. Eduardo! She wanted to cry out, to shout his name. She walked up Wisconsin Avenue to Calvert Street, then crossing the street, went south again to M Street. Eduardo had melted, disappeared.

"I will call," he had said, and she clung to this as her

talisman. Of course, he will call, she convinced herself at last, refusing to yield to her panic. I have conquered it, she told herself proudly as she finally headed toward her own house.

But the victory was too tentative to sustain itself, and before darkness came again she was starting to waver, questioning her own grip on herself. She remembered his question. Why me? And she could not explain it. As long as she lived, she was certain she would not be able to explain it. Only that it had happened. That it was there. The need for him was palpable, overpowering, embodying not only sexuality, which was part of it, but the entire force of the man. Why me? She suddenly cried out aloud, feeling excruciating pain, a hurt without specificity.

He did not call for two days, most of which she spent in bed, searching for sleep. But she was determined not to slide into the old abyss, and each moment conquered gave her the courage to hold back the forces of despair.

The sound of his voice effected a magical cure. She sensed his ebullience. "We have done it," he said.

"Done ... ?" She paused, pondering his meaning. "How wonderful."

"Thanks to you."

"When are you coming, Eduardo?"

"Tomorrow," he said. "I will come tomorrow." There was a long silence as neither of them spoke. "Early."

"But why not now?" she said.

"I will come early," he repeated. Then the click came and the buzz of the disengaged line began.

She awoke after a deep sleep, savoring the delights of expectation, feeling the juices in her body flow, a raging river frantically searching for the sea. She was also beginning to take pride in her own sense of discipline and courage, getting through the moments without him without panic. She jumped out of bed, switched on the Bach, and began a series of

300

strenuous exercises, doing them in double time, enjoying the swift movements, the strength of them, an affirmation of her body's control.

By the time he arrived, she was showered and dressed and had prepared a breakfast of toast and butter and camomile tea, with eggs standing ready for him to choose the kind he wished. In the sharp morning light, he looked tired.

"My God, I missed you, Eduardo." She pressed her face against his.

"Careful. I will scratch you."

She felt the bristles along her cheek and pressed closer, as if it were important to deliberately force the irritation.

"We have begun," he said. "The counterattack has begun. I cannot tell you how much you have helped our cause."

"Yes you can." She felt playful, an odd sensation for her. He looked at her with a puzzled expression. She was determined to capture his mind, to make him empty all other thoughts, to think only of her.

"You think I'm a crazy woman." She started to kiss his face again, his forehead, his eyes, his cheeks, his ears, the nape of his neck. She put one of his hands on her small breast. Her breath came faster, her heartbeat stronger, urgent.

"You move me, Eduardo," she whispered quickly. "I cannot help myself. Something is urging me on." She reached for his penis, felt it slowly harden through his pants as she solicited his response with greediness. What is the limit to my need, she wondered as she quickly stepped out of her slacks and helped him undress. She was standing on her toes, her pelvis tilted to take him, then moving downward, gyrating, feeling the suffusion of him and his response, shuddering but less demonstrative than hers, so that she wondered if he felt the same degree of sensation. But it could not be possible. Then she cried out in pleasure again, wanting to scream out an obscenity. Is this me? Who am I?

301

Later, after she had made him breakfast, she sat on the closed toilet seat and watched him shave with Jack's old razor. She had helped him shower, laving his body with soap and working the faucets as she might have with her own child.

"Too hot?"

"No. Just perfect."

She dried him with a big bath towel, then wrapped him in her terrycloth robe. "It is too small," he said.

"Then we will get you one that fits ... Stay with me, Eduardo," she whispered, watching the razor pass smoothly over his skin. She admired his grace of movement, the fingers tapered, acting with a life of their own. He did not stop his movements, as if he had heard nothing.

"Stay with me," she repeated. She wanted to add, "And let me worship you." But the old fear of overstepping made her reticent. Finally she said, "Where do you live? Where do you go? What is your life away from me?" He continued his stroking of the blade.

Finally he answered her. "If I tell you, then I make you part of it. It is better this way."

"I am part of it, Eduardo."

"Only peripherally."

"But I am part of you."

He finished shaving and scooped up hot water in his palms, dipping his face into it. He toweled his face dry and turned toward her. His skin glowed now, the tired lines faded, and he seemed younger.

"You must accept the reality of my life," he said. The whiteness of the tile set off the silver flecks in his gray eyes.

"Reality," she repeated. "What is that?"

He lifted her and put an arm around her shoulders, drawing her with him through the hall to her bedroom. Then he propped the pillows of her bed and lay down. He was relaxed now, comfortable. She could feel his sense of well-being and rejoiced in it. He belongs here, she told herself, to me. Sitting beside him on the bed, she touched his chest, felt the beat of his heart.

"I am engaged in momentous work. It is dangerous. There is no way I can settle down. It is a gypsy life. I am a hunted man. There is simply no peace for me." He closed his eyes. Did he feel peace now?

"Is it that important?" She could not understand anything surpassing the importance of this, of their being together. What was worth more than that?

"What will it bring you, Eduardo?" she said.

He opened his eyes. "It is not for me," he said. "There are things that we must do that are beyond ourselves."

"There is nothing beyond ourselves," she said, marveling at her own measure of selfishness. "There seems to be no point in anything else." He stroked her hair and looked up at her, saying nothing.

"And will this other thing ever end?" she asked quietly, feeling the tears mist her eyes. "Or is this the way it must be always?" I will never accept this she told herself. Never!

"Really, Anne. There is no knowing."

"Then it will always be one day at a time. Nothing ever beyond the day, the minute, the hour."

"It is a conversation that can only end in infinity."

She was fearful now, holding back. This is just not enough, she told herself, looking beyond the present to the long days and nights of absence.

"And when will you need more gold?" She wondered if he could sense the implicit bribe. His eyelids flickered.

"You are not a Chilean," he said suddenly. "You have no right to squander your fortune."

"It is not squandering."

"And I have no right to accept it."

"You have every right. What I have is yours, Eduardo." She bent down and held him in her arms. If you asked, I would give you my life, she told herself.

"The needs are without bottom," he said. "An enterprise like ours demands more and more. Besides, you don't know what we do with it."

"I don't care."

"How can you not care?" he seemed troubled, agitated. She felt his breathing quiet as she held him.

They slept, and sometime in the middle of the night, she heard him stir and slip from her side. She feigned sleep, watching him dress swiftly, then come toward her and kiss her forehead.

"I will call soon."

Soon! She wondered what that meant, looking forward again to the aimless days and nights. "When?"

Mumbling a response, he moved away and she heard the sound of him on the stairs, then the closing click of the door. It was the snap of the lock, the finality of it, that triggered her actions. She dressed quickly and, throwing on her old trench coat, ran into the street. He was already turning onto Wisconsin Avenue. She ran toward it, watched him walking swiftly, two blocks away. Clinging to the storefronts, she followed him, alert to his movements, anticipating when he might look back. She knew his caution and, perhaps by instinct, would stop suddenly, jumping into the shadows. At times her anticipation was accurate and he would turn, assure his security, and move on. At Calvert Street he slowed and crossed, starting north again. Then he was gone. By the time she reached the corner of Calvert and Wisconsin, she had lost all trace of him. He was here, somewhere in this area. On the west corner a large apartment building loomed. She watched its facade for a long time until the chill made her shiver. Then she walked to a row of nearby townhouses, the windows dark, the occupants obviously asleep.

She berated her lack of efficiency, although she considered the frustration a fitting reward for her guilt. It was, after all, a revolting thing to do, a compulsion born of anxiety, that

304

horrible crushing sense of impending loss that could drive her into the depths of depression.

Helplessly, she stood rooted to the corner, the vapor pouring from her mouth, her hands thrust into the pockets of her trench coat. She had not dressed properly, another punishment. Finally the cold defeated her and she began to walk south on Wisconsin Avenue, occasionally looking backward, searching for a sign of him.

Back in her house, she crawled into bed again, filling the place where he had slept with her own body, seeking warmth, extracting it partly from the memory of him and the smell of him that still lingered on the sheets and pillows. She tossed and turned, unable to escape into sleep.

More than anything, it was the foreboding of impending loss that prompted her search, her vigil, as she thought of it. One cannot fully possess without knowing, she told herself, daring not to believe that he had another life without her, refusing to acknowledge anything in herself more than curiosity. But when he had not called by mid-afternoon, the old panic exploded inside her and she dressed, warmly this time, with thermal underwear and old woolen gloves she had found around the house. Then, as darkness descended, she walked north again to Wisconsin and Calvert and stood in the shadows of a storefront near the bus stop. It was important, she decided, to take a position that might not be suspect. Somewhere in this area was Eduardo. She searched the faces of the people that passed in front of her, as if somehow the likeness of Eduardo could be found there. Above her loomed the facade of the apartment building, clusters of lights, as people lived their lives in their circumscribed allocation of space. From her vantage point, she had a view of the four corners, the Holiday Inn on the northeast side, a cluster of small shops on the southern ends of the intersection, and at the northwestern side, the large apartment house, where, logic told her, was the most obvious place for Eduardo to have gone. She bemoaned her lack of cunning the other evening. She might have watched the windows of the apartment building to see which had lit up and that might have been a clue. Now, standing stiffly at her post, like a sentry, she felt her own alertness, certain she would know, would find out, if only she had the courage to stick it out.

The streets were nearly deserted when she felt fatigue and knew she must leave, rest, try again another time, tomorrow night. She had already decided that a daytime vigil would be too risky, too conspicuous. But when he did call a few days later, he sounded furtive, distant. Did he know that she was following him?

"I must talk quickly. I think I am being watched."

Was it she that he had sensed?

"I need you, Eduardo."

"Two more days. Please."

"It is an agony, Eduardo. Where are you? Can I come to you?"

"No. It is very sensitive. Very sensitive." He paused, then lowered his voice. "We need more gold."

The thought cheered her. It was the umbilical cord. The panic subsided, although she still felt its outer edges.

"How much?"

"The same."

"When?"

"Can it be ready in two days?"

"Of course."

"Good. You are wonderful, Anne."

"But I need you now, Eduardo."

"It is too dangerous. I must be careful."

She felt the temptation to say that she would hold back the gold, but she feared such a move just yet.

"I will have it ready," she said, thinking suddenly of his danger. "Could you die, Eduardo?"

"We will all die someday."

He hung up, leaving her with the lingering thought. My

306

God, how will I live without him? The idea of his death prompted a renewed energy of compulsion and she dressed again for her nightly routine. It had become a ritual, and she felt part of the environment of this particular spot in Georgetown.

She had become attuned to every sound, every sight. Even the cars passed with an element of predictability and the faces that she peered into seemed to nod in greeting, although she acknowledged no recognition on her part. There was, however, something different happening. She sensed it, waiting patiently, watching the streets in every direction as the night progressed and the crowds thinned.

The streets were almost deserted when she heard his familiar walk, the cadence unmistakable. She moved back into the shadow of a building as he moved across the street and walked toward the apartment house. The facade was almost completely dark and she concentrated on watching the windows, waiting for a telltale sign. At first, she was tempted to chase after him, to call his name. My Eduardo! The environment seemed so foreign to him as he strode purposefully, quickly, with a sense of mission. Holding back, she waited. The lobby doors closed and she watched the building facade, feeling the minutes tick off in her brain.

Then, four floors up, she saw a flicke· of light. It lingered briefly, and she was able to see a shadow move behind half-drawn blinds, certain it was he. She waited, daring not to breathe, knowing that she had discovered what she had sought, although the victory of it gave her little pleasure. Did he live there, she wondered? Then another shadow passed and Anne's body seemed to freeze, confronted with a terror that she had put out of her mind, had refused to accept. A woman!

The pain of her fists clenching restored movement again and she felt the beat of her heart, a pounding sensation, like an earthquake beginning inside her. The effort to calm herself came instinctively, sharpening her cunning as she moved back into the recess of a storefront, outside the range of visibility of the apartment. Through the window of the storefront, she watched, huddling her chin deep into the collar of her trench coat, calculating the exact location of the apartment, burning it into her memory.

Not that the idea of Eduardo and another woman was an absurdity. She felt a sudden lack of cleanliness, a vileness inside her, and knew that her heart was toying with hate for him. Perhaps there is another explanation, she decided, the violence subsiding. It is a co-worker, a co-conspirator, a colleague. She had not gotten a clear view of the woman, who was still faceless, ageless. She regretted now her reticence in not probing deeper into his past. A man in his forties surely would have a wife, children, other women, relationships, all the things she had dared not ask about. But nothing outside of him had had any meaning for her.

Suddenly the window of the apartment grew dark again and she felt the full measure of her own loneliness, knowing despite her attempt at rationalization, that he was sharing something up there, something beyond her, with someone else. She leaned her forehead against the store's door and saw the shadowy objects inside lit by a tiny lamp in the rear. It was an antique store, and the old bits and pieces took on odd shapes in the oblique light, leaving the details of their configuration to her imagination. Mute objects, she thought, like her. Survivors. The idea seemed to buttress her courage and she determined to stand there, all night if necessary, ignoring the chill, even if her body petrified. She would wait, lurk. She had to know. She looked up again and watched the darkened window, understanding that the focus of her obsession had shifted.

XV

Frederika, rubbing the hurt place on her cheek, looked through the slats of the blinds, waiting for Eddie to appear on the street below. The spot where the woman had stood before was empty and, except for the passing of an occasional car, the street was deserted. Then he appeared, walking swiftly.

A flash of movement caught her attention. It was the woman, crossing the street with the sure step of a cat in the jungle. Rushing back from the window, she ran to her bed and slipped under the blanket. She is coming now, she knew, feeling her vulnerability, her nakedness.

Earlier she had been brave, talking of killing. Now her courage had passed out of her like liquid from an overturned bottle and she lay in the bed, sure of doom, welcoming the possibility as her only alternative to Eddie. She waited, listening, knowing in her soul that the woman would soon be here, in this room. But her mind still could not grasp the woman's motive. She is a relative of someone killed in the plane wreck. The idea calmed her momentarily. That was a motive she could understand. Punishment was on its way, deserved, avenging. But the calm was brief. Whoever she was, she was the enemy, the enemy of Eduardo, her Eddie. He had struck her. It should have been a knife in her heart.

She buried her face in the pillows, screamed into it with all her strength, felt the muffled sound bounce back into her head.

Despite the inevitability of the woman's impending presence, the buzzer startled her. Coming first in short bursts, it changed quickly to an unending wail. Finally she rose from the bed. Opening the door, she stood aside as the woman came into the room.

Like a filmed dance in slow motion, the woman emerged in Frederika's consciousness, half-developed, an unfinished photograph. In the gray light, her face appeared dead white, with eyes like pinpoints of light, like a pumpkin head, backlit by a candle. The odd imagery solidified Frederika's fear and paralyzed her sense of motion. The woman focused on her, as if the gaze could strip her flesh from her bones, and she huddled deeper in the blanket she had wrapped around herself. Then she saw the pinpoints of light deflect, leave her face, and dart around her apartment, inquiring. The woman's hands were thrust deep in the pockets of her coat, and as she turned back toward her, Frederika could see the sneering, tightly pressed lips, the uplifted nose suggesting an imperial opinion, as if, she, Frederika, were a piece of obscene garbage floating on the scum of some stagnant backwater.

"He was here," the woman said. It came as a hiss, like the sound of a trapped rattlesnake. They stood facing each other. The woman's voice seemed almost comforting in the charged air, suggesting a humanness that belied the image in Frederika's mind.

"He was here," the woman repeated. The ends of her nostrils quivered. Had she actually caught Eddie's scent? She looked at the coverless bed, the wrinkled sheets, the indented pillows, the obvious evidence of passion. The strange woman

310

was taller than Frederika, her hair clipped short like a boy's. Her fear diminishing, Frederika could study her now. She was, after all, only a woman.

"Who are you?" she asked, ashamed of her previous fear, sensing the beginnings of indignation. She shivered and tightened the blanket around herself. The tall woman seemed tentative, vulnerable, as if she had walked into a den of lions and could not quite decide how to cope with the situation.

"I demand to know why he was here," the woman said. Her tight lips still sneered, but the thinning darkness was swiftly chasing her mystique. Frederika watched her. She stood stiffly, holding her body as if it was incapable of any other configuration, devoid of suppleness.

"Who are you talking about?" Frederika demanded.

"You know." It was as if an obscenity hung on her tongue, and she had not the courage to utter it. Frederika remained deliberately silent, her mind reacting now, observing. This is not what it seems, at all, she thought.

"Eduardo Allesandro Palmero," the woman said. The name was spoken with odd formality. It reached her as the name of a stranger. Not her Eddie. She could deny the knowledge of his existence, she thought. It was her first reaction. But the sound of his name seemed to place him in a new dimension, sparking her curiosity now. There is another woman searching for Eddie. It came to her as if she had been suddenly doused with icy water. There was another woman. It was her turn to hate now. She wanted to be cruel.

"He has just left my bed," she said, watching the words, like bullets, find their mark. The woman's lips quivered and her eyelids fluttered. A nerve palpitated in her cheek. She was losing control. Was she his wife? Frederika turned from her with contempt and moved toward the bed. She flung the blanket from her body, flaunting her nakedness, turning briefly to show her the fullness of her body, its richly turned curves, her womannesss. She felt an odd sense of pride and victory as

311

she propped up the pillows and slid slowly into the bed, her arms crossed behind her head, her jaw pointed upward. She could now feel the woman's helplessness.

"And who the hell are you?" she asked, feeling the venom pass through the air. Again she knew that the tall woman felt the impact, although she could sense the gathering of her pride. Watching her, Frederika was goaded to muster more cruelty. This woman must suffer, she decided.

"He is my lover," she said, superior now, watching the tall woman lose her ominous aura. The woman's hands fluttered behind her for a moment, as if seeking support. Finally, she groped toward a chair and sat down. The light, thickening between the slats of the blinds, etched the lines of exhaustion on the woman's face. Her shoulders hunched forward as if she hadn't the strength to hold them up.

"Are you his wife?" Frederika asked. She was surprised at her lack of compassion. This pitiful woman is nothing to me, she told herself. She would not have been worth the killing, Frederika decided.

The woman shook her head and turned, averting Frederika's eyes. She is feeling my cruelty, she thought proudly, wanting to hurt more, to strike harder blows.

"You are absurd," Frederika said, enjoying her malevolence.

"I know," the woman said. Is she part of Eddie's operation, Frederika wondered. She was hardly the vaunted enemy, this laughable creature. Perhaps she is an unrequited lover, Frederika thought, feeling a first brief tug of pity. Smiling thinly, she recalled how Eddie's powerful sexuality could move her, and she felt puffed up with the full breath of her superiority as a woman. The person before her was hardly female, a man almost, and older by far than herself. She was a hag. Frederika resisted the temptation to throw off the covers and spread her legs in front of the woman. Let me show you where Eduardo Allesandro Palmero has been. She giggled silently, reveling in the sudden image of his hard erection inserted in her.

"What are you?" Frederika asked, the contempt blatant. She had wanted to say "who," but felt better implying a less than human designation. "You've got one fucking nerve," she cried. The woman was staring at her with a fixed glazed look, and it suddenly occurred to Frederika that she might be unbalanced. She remembered her vigil, the preposterous obsessive idea of it, and she cursed herself for feeling the least iota of fear. Then why had Eddie suddenly become upset?

"Come on. Let's have it?" Frederika said, goading the woman. "Eduardo Palmero is my lover, my confidant, my friend." She became suddenly cautious. Surely, this was not a rival. But the idea, now loosed, disturbed her.

"What is he to you?" she asked, clicking her tongue.

"I can understand your arrogance," the woman said quietly. The words were subdued and controlled. She was recovering her poise. Frederika felt a certain alertness, an anticipation of something unknown, unwanted. She had been expecting the woman to burst into tears, an acknowledgment of total surrender, defeat.

"What does that mean?" she croaked. Her voice had caught, indicating the return of terror, a new fear. She wondered if the woman had sensed it. Confirmation was quick. The woman stiffened again.

"We seem to be sharing the same commodity," the woman said softly. What does she mean? Frederika thought. She rose in the bed and sat up, pulling the blanket around the upper part of her body.

"You really must be sick, you know," Frederika said. She shook her head and looked at the woman. "And I'll bet you really believe it."

"Did you think you were the only one?" the woman asked. Her voice was clear now, decisive. She had regained her poise.

"Frankly, I don't think it's any of your business," Frederika said. Did she really want to hear more? He had not told her that much about himself. But was it necessary? Considering what had passed between them? What she felt she knew about him? The mental barricades were falling now, all the careful efforts at self-protection. But surely not this woman. She was older, old. Weird. No, she decided. She is making it up, imagining it.

"Tell me," the tall woman said, her lips firm now, the edges moving upward in the direction of a smile. "What have you done for him?"

"Done?"

"What has he made you do?"

"I do nothing against my will." The words had spilled out and she knew that she had left herself vulnerable. "You are quite sad, you know," Frederika said, attempting to retrieve her advantage, but it felt hollow, and she knew that the strange woman had sensed it.

"I would do anything for him. Anything he asked." Frederika was surprised at her own militancy. And her defensiveness.

"Anything?"

"Why are you asking these things?" Frederika asked, feigning indignance.

"What is he to you?"

Silence hung in the room. Frederika felt the tension between them now, the odd sharing, and the commonality. It was hate, palpable, material, a thing that could be touched. She had never felt such an emotion, not with the same intensity that engulfed her now. The woman is physically repulsive, she decided, comparing herself, the knowledge of her own youth, to the faded woman sitting before her. She could detect the beginning of the wizening process, the body's accumulated wreckage. But she was embarrassed, because she felt Eddie slipping from her, the image of him changing rapidly, even as she sat here. She did not want to hear the woman's response. It was better that she left, that it was ended between them. We share nothing, she decided. I am having a nightmare.

314

"Everything," the woman answered at last, her voice strong, emphatic. "Eduardo is everything. He is my life." The words came without emotion, controlled.

"That is impossible," Frederika said. "A woman senses things about her lover." She looked at the woman again, as if to confirm her previous thoughts about her. "No, it is impossible. You are doing this purposely. It's a goddamned lie."

The tall woman shrugged. She conceded no victory and Frederika's own sense of superior knowledge was quickly draining from her, the stopper removed, water running from an unclogged sink.

"I'm just as confused as you are," the woman said.

Frederika watched her. "I could kill you," she said suddenly, the hatred filling her, overflowing. "I could kill you and it wouldn't affect me one bit. Last week I helped kill a planeload of people and it ate my heart out. But I could stick a knife in your belly right now, and it wouldn't mean a damned thing to me, not a damned thing."

It was an admission and she knew it. The thought of Eddie sharing his body with this woman disgusted her. "And what did he make *you* do?" she said bitterly.

"He made me do nothing," the woman said. Then hesitantly, but proudly, she said, "I gave him money."

Of course, Frederika thought. How else could she have had him? She had to pay for him. "That is obvious."

"Just as obvious as you." The woman's strength had returned now. She stood up again, rising to her full height, less stiff now but still imperious. Perhaps it was the fact of her standing over Frederika that reinforced the impression. Frederika was looking up, annoyed at the circumstances.

"He used you," Frederika said malignantly. "You should not have taken him seriously. If you gave him money, it is because he needed it for his work, his cause. If you took it seriously I feel sorry for you."

"I feel sorry for both of us," the woman said quietly.

315

"You needn't waste your pity on me. I am his woman."

"We are both his women."

"You?"

"Yes."

"That is absurd." It is absurd, she told herself again, but she could feel the tentativeness of her self-assurance. Who is Eddie? Are we really talking about the same man? A glimmer of hope rose, then faded as quickly as it came.

"What do you know about Eduardo?" the woman asked.

"I know what I want to know."

"Yes, I understand," the woman said. "The question is: Is it important to know? I thought so. And look where that has brought us."

Frederika imagined she could feel the woman shifting gears, searching for a new path through this underbrush of confusion. She is seeking sisterhood with me, she thought, resisting it. I will not be part of it, she vowed. She wants to use me to share him. The insight bemused her. Never!

"It has brought us nowhere," Frederika said. "It is all in your head. Perhaps you have been used. But then, Eddie is involved in dangerous work. It is important work." She hesitated, aiming the barb. She wanted it to stick deeply into the woman's flesh. "You had no right to go beyond." Beyond what? Her mind filled with a grotesque image of Eddie and this woman in copulation, a quivering greedy woman with hanging, aging skin, and Eddie, eyes tight, pressed against her ugliness, offering his beautiful body on the altar of sacrifice. But the image lacked integrity. The woman before her was thin, the skin on her face tight, her movements lithe. Her hands bespoke a certain elegance, long graceful fingers gloved in incredibly white alabaster skin. Her neck was not crenellated. The age was around the eyes, sad with wisdom.

"You had no right," Frederika repeated. Despite her revulsion, she felt the beginnings of being drawn toward the woman. It is not possible, she told herself again, her anger

316

mounting to a new threshold, then sputtering. She felt a wave of nausea roll over her. Then her body began to shake with chills. She huddled in the blanket.

"I think he has betrayed us both," the tall woman said. Was she gaining an advantage over her? He was using her, Frederika insisted to herself. It could not be the same with her. It could not be.

"You're a goddamned liar!" Frederika shouted.

"A liar?"

"He used you for your money."

"And you," the woman shot back. "What did he use you for?"

"I would die for him," Frederika said, her voice hollow. She heard it echo in the room. "I killed for him," she said quietly, her anger spending rapidly as she tasted the dregs of defeat.

"You see. We are both his victims."

"Victims?"

"What else would you call it?"

"I would do it again," Frederika hissed. "How can you know what is between us?" She pounded a fist suddenly into her thigh. "Can't you understand that all you were was a casual fuck? What did it matter to him?"

The tall woman remained calm, in control now, watching her coolly. It was Frederika who was faltering and disoriented.

"At least I had no illusions," the woman said proudly. "He moved me. Like I have never been moved before. That was all that mattered."

"Then why did you want more?"

"It was a fatal error," the tall woman agreed. "I know that now. But it is too late. I should have been satisfied with my share and shut away any other possibilities."

"You screwed up everything," Frederika said. She wondered where Eddie had gone, could understand his agitation now.

"He said he would be back," Frederika said. She felt the chill of evaporating tears on her cheek. They must have come without her knowing, tears of pain. "And he knew you were watching him."

"He knew?"

"I told him. I have been observing you for days. I thought you were"—she swallowed deeply—"the enemy. An agent."

"Believe me. I would rather I was as well." The woman sat down again. "I'm sorry. I really am sorry."

"Who are you?" Frederika asked. The tall woman smiled thinly, but the warmth was visible.

"I am Penny McCarthy." She shrugged. "Anne."

"Anne?"

"He calls me Anne. It is my middle name."

"I'm Frederika Millspaugh." The tears came now, cascading without shame. "Pleased to meet you," she said. She had wanted to be sarcastic, but it had not come out that way. Slivers of light came through the blinds now. The sun was rising. It would be a bright day.

They sat in silence for a long time. Automobiles honked as the traffic rolled past, the beginning of the rush hour. An occasional shout pierced the din, a child's voice.

"So what happens now?" Frederika asked. The onset of morning seemed to symbolize a change in her entire world. It will never be the same again, she thought.

"I've been thinking about that myself." The light removed the shadows from the woman's face, except for the deep blue hollows below her eyes. In the brighter light the woman's eyes were green, incredibly green. Frederika found herself searching for positive qualities in the woman, justification.

"I think he's gone to find you," Frederika said, remembering. "He will want to be certain."

"I saw him leave. But I'm sure he didn't see me."

"What happens when he discovers you're not where you're supposed to be?"

"I have no idea."

The urge for questioning seemed odd. But Frederika did not want the woman to leave. There was more to know, more information required, if she was to survive this. What she really wanted to ask, she dared not. Could she possibly ask another woman how she felt, what she felt? It would be unbearable.

"So he lived with you," Frederika said, deliberately oblique, hoping to catch the woman off-guard.

"No."

"No?"

The woman looked around the room. Compulsively, she rose and opened a closet door. We are two jungle cats, circling each other, Frederika thought, the image embarrassing in its accuracy. Had Eddie reduced them to that?

"See. He didn't live with me either."

"All right, then. Where did he live? Where did he go?"

The knowledge came to them both at the same time, Frederika was sure. There was a sisterhood between them, born of shared humiliation.

"I don't know," she said.

"Is it possible there are others?" Anne asked. The inquiry seemed childlike, naive.

Frederika blanched, since she, too, had been thinking the same thought.

"He wasn't, after all, just hatched from an egg, full grown." She did not try to hide her sarcasm, but it was directed at herself as well.

"Others?" she asked.

"It is not impossible."

She looked at the woman, sure now of the truth, aware of the image that must be in both their minds, the slender body, the power of its sexuality, the electricity of what it could convey.

"No," Frederika said. "It is not impossible." The words were emphatic but without conviction. Despite her reluctance, there was a relationship growing between her and this woman. "You spoiled the whole damned thing," she said quietly to the tall woman, who nodded.

319

"I know."

"And now?"

"I wish it were possible to begin again at square one."

"And where is that?"

"I wish I knew," the tall woman replied.

"It's the place we were before you tried to get more than you were entitled to." Would she really settle for that? Frederika thought. She had blotted out all other possibilities in Eddie's life. Could she abide his consorting with the two of them?

"I could never adjust to it," she decided, the thought articulate. She could sense that the tall woman had understood. "Can you understand that ... " She paused. " ... Anne?" Was she being patronizing? Or taking advantage of Anne's age. There was more than twenty years between them. She was, obviously, even older than Eddie. At that age, she thought, pride might be thwarted. One could accept demeaning.

"Nor me," Anne said. Frederika was not really surprised at her reaction. This woman was not going to accept half a loaf. Nor she. Perhaps it would be better to ignore the possibilities of choice at this point. It was, after all, Eddie's choice. But would they submit to that kind of slave auction? I would, Frederika thought. It would be bearable if I could have him forever. But nothing is forever, she reasoned, confused now by the sudden onslaught of possibilities.

"Do you really think there are others?" Frederika asked. "Like us?" She could suspect the answer to that question.

"I have no doubt about it," Anne said. "Not now."

"But how can we be sure?"

"We'll find out."

Frederika felt in league with the woman now, conspiratorial. Despite her resistance, they were moving toward sisterhood, a thought which she detested. How can I be allied with that woman? I will share nothing with her, she thought. She has no right to know what went on between Eddie and me. What is going on?

320

"We can at least check his whereabouts, between us," Frederika said.

"Yes, that. And we can do what I've done."

"Follow him?"

"Yes."

"Or we could confront him," Frederika said. But, considering the circumstances, we could hardly expect his cooperation, she thought. She could see that Anne had also rejected the idea.

"Between us. If we are clever. If we are careful . . . we could track him," Anne said.

Frederika felt squeamish. It seemed a violation of Eddie's privacy. But he has violated us, she thought, anger rising again, this time directed at Eddie. He has betrayed us both. The bastard! So she could also hate him.

"Yes," she said, her sense of purpose tangible now. "I can do that." Yet her resolve was not quite unencumbered. "And what happens when we do find out . . . discover?"

Anne shrugged, expelling a sigh. "I don't know," she said quietly. "It may not seem as important then as it does now."

They exchanged telephone numbers. When Frederika handed hers to Anne, for a brief millisecond, their eyes met. Anne's green eyes seemed like two blazing searchlights probing her. Could it have been the same, Frederika wondered, the intensity, the joy, the pleasure, the sense of wholeness.

Anne stood at the door, hesitating. Then she turned. "Has he ever mentioned Miranda?" she asked.

Frederika thought, searching her mind.

"No." She waited for a response.

"It was said suddenly. I don't think he realized."

"Another woman? Like us?"

"Another woman yes," Anne said quietly. "But not like us. NO! Not like us." She turned again and let herself out.

Frederika lay in her bed for hours after Anne had left, wallowing in a bottomless void. For years she had felt nothing, was certain that she had died, and then with Eddie she had felt everything. Was she on the verge of death again? The brightness was fading in the room when the telephone's ring shocked her into full awareness. Reaching for it, she wondered if it might be Eddie and she began to compose herself. She had assumed there had been a silent understanding between them. Say nothing. Don't let on.

"He was here." It was Anne's voice. Frederika felt her own resentment. Had they made love? The image was too unbearable to continue and it broke in her mind into a thousand pieces.

"Are you there?" Anne asked, her voice unhurried. Frederika pictured the tall woman in the trench coat, hovering over her.

"Yes."

"I admitted that I followed him. He questioned me. I did not tell him that we have met, nor does he suspect that I know. He is assuming that I think he lives there."

"And he said nothing to clear up the matter?"

"No."

"Did he wonder where you've been?"

"I told him I walked the streets."

"Did he believe that?"

"I don't know. But he is suspicious." She paused. "He made me promise that I would not try to find out more about him. Not now."

"And then?"

"I doubt if any of my explanations satisfied him. I think he will now be more cautious than ever. More secretive." Is she confiding everything, Frederika wondered.

"He was with you all day?" Frederika asked cautiously. The pause that followed telescoped the answer.

"Yes."

What was it like, she wanted to ask.

"I wish I could say I was revolted," Anne whispered finally.

"Nothing was changed?"

322

From my bed to hers, Frederika thought, her heart pounding, punishing herself with the cutting edge of her own humiliation. Was my body smell still lingering on his skin? Were my juices still visible, tastable? The idea of it was a mortification. We must punish him for this, she vowed, touching the nub of a beginning terror. Her question to Anne remained unanswered. So there is still a delicacy between us, she thought, gathering her malice.

"And where is he now?"

"There is no way of knowing. I thought I might follow him, but he is too suspicious now, very guarded. It would not be easy." There was a pause again. "When do you expect him to come to you?"

"Is there ever a set time?"

"Will you call me when you know?"

"Of course." Why should she be spared the pain of it. "And I plan to follow him. I plan to find out. There is no stopping now, Anne. You realize that."

"Yes."

Frederika lowered the phone, heard Anne's breathing, perhaps a sigh, then depressed the connection. Immediately she had the urge to call her back, to find out more about what had happened between them, then fought back the temptation. She dressed quickly and went to work, but her mind was on the street outside and she peered through the windows, searching the passing faces. She wanted, needed, even a brief moment's preparation before any confrontation. That night she worked particularly hard, to drown her mind and body with fatigue.

"You're really pushing tonight, kid," Marcia said.

"I need the money," she snapped.

For the next two days and nights, she reacted like a sleepwalker, passing through her life half-conscious. Only the sound of the telephone restored her alertness.

"Did he call? Have you seen him?" It was Anne's voice. She called at least three times every day.

323

"No." A pause. "And you?"

"No."

"Do you think he suspects?"

"I think he is suspicious, surely. But he cannot know the truth."

"Not unless you told him."

"What purpose would there be in that?"

"I'm not sure."

"You must be more trusting."

"I'm trying. Believe me, Anne, I'm trying."

There seemed, Frederika thought, an edge of hysteria to Anne's voice as the calls persisted.

"He didn't call? You didn't see him?"

"No." Frederika was firm.

"How can I be sure?"

"You can't." Frederika felt her own nastiness. "And how can I be sure *you* haven't?"

"It's maddening."

"How do you think I feel?"

"Please forgive me."

Frederika didn't answer. By the end of the third day, she was frantic and let the phone ring endlessly. Finally she picked it up. Before she could respond, she heard Eddie's voice.

"Will you be there?"

"Of course." She had planned to go to work. Instantly, her plans changed.

"I will be there shortly."

Thankfully, he arrived within a half hour. She was beginning to develop a kind of psychic palpitation as her mind groped through a series of speculations. How would she observe him? Before, her reactions had been natural, inevitable, like the force of gravity. Could she dissimulate now? Could she lie? Was it possible? It was like contemplating death. Then his key was in the door. He stepped into the apartment and, as he did so, her mind went blank and only the primitive force

324

remained. She curled about him, swallowing him, it seemed, as she had once seen a python swallow a pig in an old movie. If he was startled by her reaction, he said nothing, letting her envelop him as if it were his due tribute.

"My God, I love you, Eddie," she said breathlessly. She could feel his breath coming in short gasps as she moved her fingers over his body, undressing him, her animality mindless. She moved herself onto him, bending her torso to insert him, still standing a few feet from the door. He said nothing, the hardness thrusting inside of her, the full force of her body seeking to suck him into her, not only the male organ, the whole of him.

"Eddie. Eddie," she heard herself moan, feeling the great internal explosions, their faraway rumbling, the volcanic force, the lava moving in a hot mass through her body, an eruption of joy. It was joy. She knew. The joy of him. Why?

It was some time before intelligence returned and she lay in her bed watching him, his eyes, she knew, focusing inward, at something that she could neither touch nor understand.

"You think, Eddie," she announced suddenly, seeking an oblique rebuke, some beginning of punishment. "You don't feel." He must have sensed the admonishment.

"That's not true at all." He was protecting himself now, she knew.

"You are governed by your mind." Anne had confirmed that. The idea of Anne emerged, bringing with it the pain that she had successfully kept at bay. Her mind was operating clearly now and she felt she could touch her own cunning. She must be cautious, she decided, remembering Anne's words. I will have to go fishing in his brain.

"I wonder what I really mean to you."

He turned toward her, stroking his chin in an uncommon manner. She had not seen him do that before. He's full of surprises, she thought.

"You mean a great deal."

How could he say that so blandly, she wondered, determined to keep him on the defensive. She wanted to say: Am I the only woman in your life? But the hypocrisy would crush her with guilt. Besides, she would not be prepared for his lies. Not now. She held off asking about the woman who had stood in the cold, waiting, fearful that he would connect the thought with her previous question. Would I really die for him, she asked herself, knowing that something was changing within her.

"Will I be traveling again soon?" she said instead.

"Yes. In a few days."

"To the same place?"

"No. To San Antonio. We have worked out a change in plans."

"And will others die because of what I will do?"

"Yes. But they will be enemies." His thoughts were being deflected now. "The new arrangements have not quite been completed. But everything is moving satisfactorily." He turned toward her and patted her hair. "I am quite proud of you, Frederika."

"What about the woman that I told you about? The one that was watching in front of the building?" It seemed appropriate to broach the subject now, in this context.

He did not blanch or show any sign of sudden intrusion. She observed him closely, watching for signs, but none came. He is a superb actor, she decided, wondering how well she, too, was doing.

"It was nothing," he said. "I had mistakenly thought she might be one of them, an agent. But I checked carefully and now I'm sure it was only a coincidence."

"That must have been a relief."

"Yes," he said. "Unfortunately such things increase one's sense of paranoia. In this business, one always lives with it." He stopped patting her hair. "Did it frighten you?"

"Yes."

"Well," he said offhandedly. "It's all right then."

He seemed suddenly relaxed and, she wondered, perhaps off-guard.

"What is it that you do to me?" she said, her curiosity genuine, although she could feel the tender spot of her humiliation. It was a thought worth exploring, since it contained the kernel of her truth. She had every right to ask why, she decided. For herself. Perhaps he could explain it. She had dared not ask Anne.

"I don't know," he said, frowning, obviously puzzled. It was, it seemed, a thought that even he dared not pursue.

"Do you ever think about it?"

"Yes."

"Has it happened before? With other women?" By his reaction, she knew that the barb had penetrated something inside of him. She hoped there was a wound, that she had drawn blood.

"I cannot say for sure."

"But what do you suspect?"

"How can I answer such a question?" There'd been a brief flash of anger.

"Have you observed it before? A reaction like mine, for example."

"I don't understand."

"Yes, you do," she protested. "Surely there have been other women who have felt this . . . like me, felt the power of you."

She sensed his discomfort. He got up from the bed and paced the room, his smooth body like liquid moving through space. His nakedness began to numb her mind as she watched the tight buttocks reflected in the light, smooth as ivory, and the dangling organ. He is beautiful, she told herself, overwhelmed by the sight of him. How can he possibly explain it? she wondered. I can't explain it myself.

"Explain it, Eddie," she taunted. "Surely you can explain it."

327

"There is no explanation."

"There has to be."

"All right then." He paused, watching her, then shrugged. "It's a mystery. That's the only explanation."

"So there have been others," Frederika said, in full pursuit now, the scent in her nostrils. It had suddenly become more important to know. To know was everything.

"What does all this mean?" Eddie said, turning toward her now, his eyes flashing, brows knitting, his agitation rising.

"I want to know about you, Eddie. You have told me nothing. Surely in the forty-odd years of your life there are things that have happened which have shaped your character. There have been relationships."

He stopped his pacing, shrugged and lifted his arms, palms outward in a typical Latin gesture of mock surrender. He was even smiling, showing the broadest smile she had ever seen him display. Was he mocking her, she wondered, half-expecting him to voice the comedian's stock reaction to contrived feminine triviality ... "Women." Did his eyes search for the ceiling, his head shake with male tolerance, as he expressed the theatrics of exasperation?

"I want to know," Frederika pressed.

"Know what?"

"About you, Eddie. Your life." Her voice rose. "I have a right to know." Did he detect the edge of panic, she wondered, instinctively certain that she had gone too far. She saw his smile disappear.

"Right?" he asked.

"Surely I have that right ... " She felt her voice falter as he glared at her. Did she really? she wondered, remembering Anne and her alleged rights. He is shared territory, she realized suddenly, the reality painful. My God, I will lose him.

"I love you, Eddie. I just want to know." She was conscious of the plea in her voice, the sudden softness. The new attitude seemed to blunt his anger.

328

"I will tell you everything, Frederika." He took a deep breath. "But not now. There are other things on my mind now. There is an important operation in the making. It is intricate."

"Is this what I am part of?" she asked, fearful that her outburst might have caused her cancellation in the plan.

"Of course."

He came back into the bed. His skin had absorbed the chill and he was shivering. She smothered him with her warm nakedness, the touch of his flesh compelling.

"It is a mystery, Eddie," she said, holding him tightly along his back, fitted snugly against her. She squeezed him hard, the pressure making him grunt.

"Yes," he said. "I told you."

It was dark when she heard him moving around the apartment. Hey eyelids fluttered briefly, as she feigned sleep, listening to the familiar sounds. Then she felt his breath on her face, the brief kiss on the forehead, barely touching her skin. He was tiptoeing across the floor. The door opened, creaked slightly, and closed, and she was out of bed in a moment, reaching quickly for her jeans and a sweater. Tying a scarf around her head, she found a pea jacket in the closet. She was sure he had not seen it. Nor had he ever seen her with a scarf around her head. She also had sufficient presence of mind to grab a pair of old unused glasses from a drawer as she sped out of the apartment, running down the stairs and into the street.

Her mind was working quickly now, turning over possibilities. If he had a car nearby, she could not follow him, although she would be sure to take the license number. But he always seemed to be on foot, as if distance was not a problem. Which meant that he lived close by.

It was still evening. The day, as always with Eddie, had sped by quickly. She had thought it might be early morning, sometime close to dawn. But a clock in a nearby storefront told her it was only eleven. She had missed work and had failed to call

329

in, which meant putting an added burden on her co-workers. Perhaps they would fire her. There was a sudden twinge of guilt as she hesitated in the street, looking south toward M Street. She saw him moving across Wisconsin Avenue, turning toward Massachusetts, heading west. There was little foot traffic and she could see him clearly in the moonlit night.

Keeping her distance, she crossed the wide street and kept him in sight. He was moving with swift strides, obviously sure of his destination. Occasionally, he would look behind him. She did not hesitate, secure in her disguise, proud of her cleverness. She followed him tenaciously, thankful that her work had conditioned her legs for speed and distance. She smiled at the idea that her job had, at last, served some useful purpose besides merely providing a living.

She saw him turn and enter an apartment building, making mental notes, sure that she had the identity of the building fixed in her mind. It was a large building, sitting high on a slope overlooking Massachusetts Avenue. She remembered being inside it once, when she was looking for an apartment. When she reached it, her eyes swept the facade. Many lights were on. She could see people moving about inside some of the apartments. She speculated cautiously. One mustn't jump to conclusions. Who lives here? Is he alone? Is there someone else? She waited in the shadows for perhaps a half hour, then proceeded into the lobby of the building. An indifferent young man slumped behind the desk, reading a book. In the moment before she attracted his attention, she had looked over the lobby, checking details, searching for the apartment's directory.

"Is there a pay telephone?" she asked pleasantly. He pointed to a far wall. Nearby were the mailboxes and the directory. It would be too simple. The directory confirmed her instincts. His name was not listed. But that could have been his own choice. It was not simple to rent an apartment in Washington. They checked you out. She cursed her stupidity for not asking the man at the desk a direct question. But they, too, were trained to be suspicious. Then, as she reached the phone, she discovered that she had not taken any money, nor had she bothered to bring Anne's number. You are America's worst detective, she told herself, and for the first time, she felt a sense of risk.

She thought of Anne, tenacious, driven Anne. Let Anne do the dirty work, take the risks, she decided. Why not? Anne was the older, less attractive, more unsure. Her loss was greater, Frederika assured herself bravely, knowing it was a lie. She felt the doorman watching her and picked up the receiver, moving her lips in a charade, then hung it up again. Passing him again, she smiled pleasantly and moved out into the street, noting the address and name of the building on the sign outside. "The Berkshire. 4100 Massachusetts Avenue."

Walking swiftly, her heart pumping heavily, she got to her own building, hurried to her apartment, and dialed the phone. Anne's voice responded quickly, after one ring. So she is anxious, Frederika thought. As well she should be.

"I followed him," she said, her breath still gasping from exertion.

"He was there?"

"Yes."

There was a long pause, a sign. She could feel the tension across the line.

"I followed him to an apartment house on Massachusetts Avenue. The Berkshire. You know it?"

"Yes."

"But I was afraid to ask if he lived there. His name was not on the directory."

She was waiting for direction now, for Anne's will to assert itself.

"What shall we do?" she asked finally. Her own weakness galled her.

"I'll call later," Anne said.

"What are you going to do?"

331

"Find out."

"How?"

"I'm not sure."

There was a firmness in her voice, a resolve. It triggered Frederika's suspicion. She remembered how Anne had persevered in standing in front of her own building. Can I trust her? she wondered. Trust! It seemed suddenly ludicrous.

"You will tell me everything, Anne?"

"Of course."

"We are in it together now, Anne."

"Yes."

"I want to know everything you know. Everything." She had wanted to say "please," but could not bring herself to that. There seemed nothing more to say, but she delayed hanging up, expecting Anne to do so first. Anne's breathing came across the line. Frederika could sense that something was gathering in her mind.

"Was it the same?" Anne asked at last.

Frederika understood instantly. "Yes," she said, hoping that the word could hurt. "The same."

The telephone clicked off and Frederika stood for a long time, the phone still at her ear, until the odd beep began, recalling her sense of place and her emptiness.

XVI

Passion observed is different from passion experienced, Dobbs admitted reluctantly. Such an axiom could take, had taken, the science out of this business, the sense of deduction. It would have had to be instinctive, and he knew he had no instinct for this. You cannot track what you cannot see. Especially what you cannot feel. That had been the secret of his success in this bureaucratic jungle, the feel of something before it occurred. Not that he had never been wrong before. Just not this wrong.

He missed the signposts. He had been contemptuous of the zealousness of the DINA agents, interrogators, analysts, informers. In their reports were embedded the subtleties, the shadings that, taken together, could provide the revelation. And now that he had participated in the full process, was he closer to its key than before? Eduardo, in his place, would have not lost the scent.

Pushing aside the batch of files, Dobbs stood up, walked the length of his office, then sat down again. They were the files that contained the material on Eduardo's political career, to which Dobbs had originally attached so much importance. Eduardo had never run for office. His role had been as a kind of Machiavellian advisor for the Allende group.

After Valdivia, he had returned to his wife, who by then had borne him a son. His son. The seduction had borne fruit. Remembering Miranda's remarks to the interrogator, Dobbs marveled at how she had controlled her contempt. But then, she would be a toady to power. She would always do her duty. Somehow Eduardo had gained the upper hand by his own willed indifference, enough at least to dissimulate, despite the dry rot of their condition. And while he moved in the circles of power, she must have restrained herself, playing the role with him. Yet after Allende's fall, he had been among the first to be interned. He had barely been able to move a block from his home. Without doubt, she had betrayed him. Dobbs had no trouble with that deduction.

Having destroyed the lists, he knew he had outwitted them. They had been hidden in the room behind the wine cellar, easily eliminated by a single match, which quickly created the conflagration, making the room, with its specially constructed flue, one big fireplace. Getting out of the palace was a lucky stroke. Allende had insisted on his martyrdom and had stayed. He had kissed him on both cheeks, stained with the tears of his defeat and self-pity. Continue! That was the only word that had filtered through Eduardo's consciousness. So he had continued by destroying the evidence of the continuity, the lists. Now many of the names were locked in his head, the network of people they could depend on, those who had not surfaced, the cadre that were kept out of the public eye.

It was necessary only to survive, to avoid the demise of his brain, his memory. Above all, he must preserve that.

She certainly must have smelled the smoke. In the breezeless day the ash settled over the roof and the trees, while he stood

334

in the heat of the door, seared but content. If he had not been there to confirm their destruction, he might have avoided the horror of the next few months. An escape route had been carefully mapped in advance, a series of safe places where he could hide until he could cross the Peruvian border.

He had, of course, no illusions. Her revenge would come with his betrayal, and it was quick. Hardly out of the house, in the work clothes disguise he had prepared, he had been whisked into an armored car and brought shackled hand and foot to the barracks, to the whitewashed room without windows, stifling because it was deliberately unventilated. He knew this room, of course. Hadn't they used it themselves? Paranoia was no respecter of ideology. They kept him in the room for hours. A single bulb illumined the starkness. He sat on a stool, in front of a heavy table. Naturally, he knew what to expect. It was all a contrivance. Soon Raoul would come, he knew. The Army was in charge now.

Eduardo heard the door open, then Raoul's snapping military footsteps. He had always been well shod. The cement floor emphasized the perfection of his shiny boots.

"Eduardo." Raoul patted him on the back and stepped around the stool to the chair behind the table. "I feel absurd about this."

Only two weeks before they had stood together clinking glasses of champagne, recalling the old days. It was odd, he remembered, thinking to himself, indulging in nostalgia, as if the end were coming. They were plotting even then. It was, of course, a clue. The country was in turmoil. But they had not realized that it would be the Army that would betray them.

"It is finished, Eduardo," Raoul said, lighting a cigar. "We can get this over quickly and avoid any further unpleasantness. Then I can get you out of the country." His good looks had mellowed. There was gray at his temples. The face had retained its craggy beauty, although the eyes seemed flintier, hardened. Eduardo's back ached from sitting on the low stool.

335

"Allende went too far. We had no choice. You were destroying the structure of the country," Raoul said. It was ridiculous hearing him say this. "I am apolitical," he had always protested. A soldier.

"Burning the lists only complicates things for us," Raoul said.

"Lists?"

"It was known," Raoul said. "We missed it by seconds. It would have made matters so simple. It would have spared this embarrassment. We are friends, Eduardo."

"We were friends."

"Always politics. What is politics? One is as bad as another. You were ruining us all. Even your own family. Were they any better than us?"

"That's all academic now. At least we tried."

"You brought us to the brink of disaster."

"Now it has come."

"A little bloodletting. It is part of our heritage. We must preserve what we have built." Raoul stood up. "All we need now is the names, as many as you can remember. We don't mean to harm them, just to know where they are. We will watch them. Just as you watched your enemies. A simple exchange."

"Do you think that I will simply regurgitate them? That you will charm me out of them? Just as you have always charmed women to give you what you wanted?"

Raoul smiled. "One uses the tools that God has given."

Eduardo could never shake the awesome envy. Had Miranda been one of his conquests? Such a thought had occurred to him before. He had dismissed it then. The bond of friendship was sacred. Considering his present situation, his faith in such an idea was considerably shaken.

"I knew," he said maliciously, wanting to test the assumption.

"Knew?"

336

But his courage failed. It would be pointless to know. Raoul's mindless passion would, as always, make his own seem trivial. Raoul's mouth was open slightly. The cigar jaunty in his teeth. He paced the room, then turned, blowing smoke into Eduardo's eyes. Eduardo observed him, determined to remain numb.

"I will call in a stenographer and you will give us all the names you can remember." He walked toward the door, his heels snapping again on the hard cement.

"Don't bother."

"You're not serious."

"Have you ever known me to lie?"

"Eduardo. This is no game. You know all the devices. In an hour I can have you wishing you were dead. Spare yourself. It is not worth it. We have no time. We are simply protecting what we have won."

"You will kill them. And those you do not kill, you will use. Believe me, Raoul, you will not get any names from me."

"We shall see." He opened the door and left the room.

Knowing what to expect did not make it easier. First they would try to break his spirit with uncertainty, starvation, psychological mischief. Then would come the devices, the dreaded electrical conductors attached to the genitals. It would all be quite businesslike. There would be no real hate in it. The pain would be merely institutional, a brain opener. If that failed, they would inject him with drugs, destroy his will to resist. In the end, he knew, he would tell them something. Yet, above all, he understood the power of the will. Hadn't he willed himself to resist all feeling? Now he must find the will to resist telling them everything, to be selective, preserving what could be useful in the future. They will think they have gotten all of it, although he knew they would be insatiable. But he would make them work for what they got.

The door opened again and he was seized roughly under both arms and prodded along between two broad shouldered guards with expressionless flat faces, their Indian blood a reminder of some forgotten meeting. It was only after they had brought him down a long flight of stairs and thrust him into another room dominated by a long table that he could remember the face of Uno's father. Features which said nothing always put him at a handicap. They made him sit on the table, left him there. Hours passed. Finally he lay on the hard surface, but the light above him was too bright. His eyelids could not shut it out. But when his eyes were closed, he could remember sunlight, lying face upward, hearing the thunder of the distant sea, the rustle of the high grass that edged upward toward the Cordillera and Isabella's soft breathing beside him.

He had not gone back to his parents' house until his father was dying. It was a slow, lingering death, and although he wished he might see the old man, his father had remained persistently adamant. Pride ran too deep in the man that the son had betrayed. In his father's mind, he had committed fratricide. They had called him only when the old man's mind had slipped into chaos. And they had left him to be alone with him. He was a wizened bit of flesh, shrunken, barely recognizable.

"You must make him forgive you," his mother had said, her painted face grotesque beneath henna hair. He imagined he had seen a note of triumph in her eyes, the unmistakable sign of the conqueror's victory. Over the years, as his political ascendency matured, she had written him long, pleading letters to preserve their properties and wealth. Answering, he had gone into long polemics on the reasons for nationalization, land reform, shared property, the destruction of the oligarchs. "You must not betray your blood," she had written in every letter.

His father could not forgive him even if he wanted to. His mind was too far gone, as was his power of speech. Bending over the hollow skull, Eduardo had kissed his forehead. It felt like ice. Only the faint blink of an eye told him that his father was barely alive.

"I forgive you," Eduardo had whispered. He had wondered if his father heard. Did he see a brief nod? He wondered if he truly loved the old man or hated him.

Then, suddenly, the illusion of sunlight dissipated. A tall officer was blocking the naked light above him. Behind him came a young soldier lugging a large tape recorder. He put it on the cement floor and attached a microphone around Eduardo's neck. The officer seemed a pleasant fellow. He smiled. Eduardo, surprised at his own reaction, smiled back. Why not, he reasoned. We are in this together.

"I have no desire to hurt you," the officer said. "I am doing my duty. I have been ordered to get you to provide me with the names of those people who have remained underground and could be a threat against the present regime. A simple request."

"You know I burned the lists."

"Yes. But the assumption is that many of the names have been committed to memory."

"The assumption is incorrect. If I had done that, why would I have needed the lists."

"That is another question." The, officer brushed aside any further inquiry on this point, signaled the young soldier to start the tape recorder, and began his interrogation.

"Let us begin. They need not be alphabetical."

"Alphabetical?" The idea seemed ludicrous. Eduardo laughed. He had not felt such a sense of amusement in years. The officer ignored it. He repeated the question.

"A name. Any name."

"Eduardo Allesandro Palmero."

"That's your name."

Eduardo laughed again. "Now we're getting somewhere."

"A name," the officer repeated. He was no longer smiling.

Eduardo remained silent, closed eyes. He could not tell how long repetition continued. He began to feel fatigue. He must have dozed. When he opened his eyes the officer was gone.

His sense of time faded. His beard began to sprout and a thirst began. At first he had been hungry and then that feeling had disappeared. They were letting him construct a private hell.

The door opened again. He saw the sculptured, handsome face of Raoul. He was smoking a long cigar, elegantly poised in his long fingers.

"What does it matter, Eduardo?" he said. "Who cares?"

Eduardo shrugged. In the face of Raoul he saw the younger man he had envied and adored.

"I would not betray you, Raoul."

Raoul shook his head, lowered his eyes. "I am not asking you to betray me." He took a deep drag on the cigar. The sweet smoke filled the unventilated room. As always, Raoul was casual, collected. How Eduardo envied him this attitude.

"You should have been a poet," Raoul said. "Politics was definitely the wrong profession for you. You always took the wrong road. Especially with women. You never could understand women. You should never have loved Miranda."

He was taunting him now. Perhaps, he is jealous of my courage, Eduardo thought. There was a long silence. Eduardo felt Raoul's eyes exploring him.

"They could kill you, Eduardo."

The boots clicked along the cement. The door closed. Later the officer came back with the young soldier and the tape recorder whirred again. Names? No answer. Names? No answer. The game must have gone on for hours. Eduardo concentrated on other thoughts, seeking to remember the landmarks of his pleasure. They were dim memories and he could not summon them.

Strong arms grabbed him now, bending his body, shackling his wrists to the sides of the table. A huge leather strap gripped

340

his body and he felt his legs being spread and a pinching on his testicles.

"I really did not want to go this far," the officer said. Eduardo opened his eyes. Wires stretched from his testicles to a machine on a little table in the corner.

Whose names shall I give them? he asked himself. Who shall live and who shall die? I am about to play God. There was comfort in the thought of a deity, although he did not believe in God.

"Now I will ask you once more," the officer said. His tone was even, quite businesslike. The litany began again. Names? Silence.

"All right," the officer said pleasantly. "I am going to give you a tiny taste of this, just a little bit. It will indicate how painful a longer jolt will be."

Eduardo braced himself, waiting. The jolt did not come. They were torturing him now without pain. Give me pain, he shouted in his head, while I am ready for it.

When the jolt came, it reached into the heart of him, an animal tearing at his innards, exploding his genitals, destroying his sense of manhood. The explosion radiated upward and downward. No perception of pain escaped. The pores of his body opened.

"Miranda!" he screamed. The current was off, but the pain continued.

"Who?" the officer asked.

He could not believe what he had shouted. Pressing his lips together, he hoped they would seal themselves. The interrogation began once more. Names. He longed for the escape of paralysis, the death of feeling.

Again, he felt the jolt, the accelerated radiation of pain. It seemed endless. He was in hell. His body was burning. How long must he endure this? he wondered, before he would tell them.

"I am just doing my duty," the officer said pleasantly,

forcibly but gently opening Eduardo's eyelids. "Believe me, I understand your pain."

Eduardo remained silent, letting the jolt come again and again, bracing himself, waiting for the moment. Had he been punished enough? Would they all forgive him now? he wondered.

"All right," he whispered finally. He had decided to avoid the drugs. "I will tell you."

"Thank God," the officer said, crossing himself.

Eduardo talked into the tape recorder, giving them names selectively. When he had given them what might be enough to satisfy them, he lay back on the table and closed his eyes. The officer had unfastened the clippers from his genitals with careful delicacy.

"It is awful," he whispered, but it was not intended for Eduardo to hear. He imagined how the young officer would be tonight. Perhaps he would find a woman to prove that he was all right and it would take away his revulsion.

"We could have avoided this," the young officer said. Eduardo felt the burning continue in the center of him. Yes, his mind repeated, I could have avoided this. How could he know I needed this, he thought, feeling a sense of victory now.

Dobbs closed the file in disgust. His eyes ached. It had taken the CIA nearly a year to persuade them to release Eduardo. Did the world really believe it was an act of mercy? He would be their bird dog. He would find all the little birds hiding in the crannies of the trees, the burrows of the fields. It had been a grandiose plan, with Dobbs as architect. It was to be the crowning glory of his long career.

"Damn!" he shouted, banging a fist into his palm. The sound and action seemed so uncharacteristic that he had to pause and listen. Had they heard?

Only Eduardo had heard. Dobbs was certain of that, once

again feeling his spirit pervade the room. Did he detect a faint squeal of laughter on the outer edge of audibility?

He had tracked the women and Eduardo's activities with them. He had known everything. Everything. He had facts. But not wisdom. He looked around the room surreptitiously. Then, reaching downward, he grabbed his own genitals, squeezing them hard. He felt nothing.

XVII

She could be sustained, Marie decided, if she could be with him once a week, perhaps twice. Not that it would satisfy her need for him, that overwhelming addiction to his person. That was the way she could justify the madness to herself, an addiction to his person.

She would endure Claude, endure her children, endure the guilt, endure whatever humiliation to her body, endure anything ... providing she could one day look forward to his possession of her, forever.

"You mustn't flog yourself," Eduardo had said.

"It is unbearable," she had told him, deliberately censoring her mind's picture of it. "I am living a gross lie."

"We cope," he had said, as if the purpose of life was merely to endure. "There is something greater to be considered, beyond our personal desires."

"But my cause is you," she had protested. It was a familiar refrain, and he was expected to understand.

Yet she could not bring herself to tell him how the device

was planted in the ambassador's study. She had wiped the ugliness from her mind. Only the objective was important. The means were trivial. There was solace in such reasoning, tempering her disgust. Not that it had been easy. She had lain awake that night, tossing and turning next to Claude, who slept, finally convinced that he had won her affection again. He might even have been thinking that life had slipped back into its accustomed groove. To him she was surely the great success of the evening, having drawn the attention of the ambassador to the exclusion of others. He could enjoy living in the glow of her success and, of course, the implication that it reflected on him, the husband, for having the power to have won and kept her.

In her hurt body, she carried the reminder of the scene. Was it seduction on her part? Or rape on his? A few months ago, perhaps weeks, it would have been unthinkable. But she had done it. She had done it for Eduardo. She took pride in that. The violation was simply necessary, hardly deserving of more than passing interest. Convincing herself eased her mind, although she slept fitfully.

In mid-morning, Eduardo called. She had dashed to the telephone, hungry for the sound of him.

"It is done," she said.

"Where?"

"In the dust jacket of one of the books in the study."

"Excellent."

"Eduardo ..." Her voice trailed off. She felt her body's sudden need for him. "I need you, darling."

"I will call you."

"Please, Eduardo. Today. Now. I will come to you now."

"You must understand."

"I need you today. Now." She felt the sob take shape, an inflating balloon inside her and soon her body was shaking and she was verging on hysteria. "I can't stand this, Eduardo."

"Please," he said softly. "I feel helpless now. I cannot explain."

346

She tried to bring herself under control, but her breath would not catch and she could barely talk.

"Please," he said again. She knew she was trying to say something, but could not make herself understood, the anguish real, painful. The idea of losing him became suddenly more painful than the realization of her need for him.

He did not call back that day. Or the next. And, as always, the waiting took on the characteristics of a nightmare in which she saw herself as a fly trapped in a spider's web, her wings desperate for flight while her legs moved helplessly, entangled in the sticky strands. Then he called, beckoned her, and the hurt disappeared in his arms.

"It is impossible to convey how much you mean to me," she said, her eyes feasting on his body, transfixed. "It is also a joy to be watched," she said.

"Yes," he whispered.

"Do you feel what I feel, Eduardo?" His hands caressed her hair, stroking as she bent down to implant a long, lingering kiss on his penis.

"You are beautiful," she said, knowing that she had come to uncharted waters. "I live only for you."

He said nothing. In reliving her moments with him, she tried to will in herself a sense of what he felt, what he was thinking. Which was where the abyss began. Do I really know him, she wondered, growing suddenly sad, thinking of the empty moments of her life away from him. Then she drew him inside of her.

"Tell me about your life in Chile," she asked later. She had been greedy for him. Yet there was no surfeit. It was an endless hunger.

"A life," he answered. She could sense his reluctance, but it did not deter her. She would continue to probe, she decided. It was her right.

"And your wife?"

"A wife."

"And your child."

347

"What can I say? A boy, Manuel."

"Do you love them?"

"I ..." He hesitated.

"Is this too painful, Eduardo?"

"It is unnecessary."

"But I want to know about you."

"Later."

"It's always later. What of now?"

"There is no now."

"I am not made from such stuff," she said, entwining her fingers in his. "You are the central point of my life, Eduardo. I can separate nothing. My children, my husband, my other life. All that has no meaning whatsoever." She put her arms around him. "If I died now. In your arms. Right now. It would be enough. Can you understand that?"

He did not answer. She could hear the beating of his heart, strong, rhythmical, powerful. Often at night, in her own bed, she had heard that sound. "Can you understand that?" she repeated.

"I don't know," he said quietly, as if he had given the matter much thought. She felt his heartbeat change its pace. Perhaps there is a message there. And then his heart speeded again as he said suddenly, "Do you think I am cruel, Marie?"

"Cruel?" It seemed an odd characterization.

"Perhaps callous might be a better description."

"You are confusing me."

"I hadn't meant to," he said gently. Then he turned his head and lifted her face. "Whatever do you see in me?"

"See in you?" She rose on one elbow and tried to probe beyond his eyes, which searched her own.

"What is this quality..." He paused, sighed. "It is an enigma."

"Yes, that," she said. "Believe me, I have tried to understand it. One would think there would be a logical explanation. But I have given up on that. You are the sun that gives me life. I would die for you, my love."

348

"Die?"

"Yes."

"I can understand that there are things worth dying for, Marie. That I can understand quite well. For a dream, for an ideal. I would gladly die for the cause of my country's liberation. But to die for me, a person. I think that's quite foolish. Schoolgirl nonsense."

She wanted to be angry, but the heat of rage would not ignite. He does not understand. Perhaps it is because he is not a woman, she thought, giggling suddenly.

"It is funny?"

She let her hand move downward over his bare chest, caressing his penis, feeling the hardness begin under her fingers.

"I was thinking," she said, wanting to be accurate, "that you don't understand because you are not a woman."

He looked downward at himself, the mysterious hardening, perhaps feeling the strange flow of his blood into that part of his body.

"Now there is an absolute truth for you." He smiled and she felt his body suddenly shake with laughter. "It is all so ridiculous, the human body. Why does it do things like that?"

"I am sure there is some scientific explanation." She paused. But I would not want to hear it, she thought, moving her body over his, inserting him, feeling instantly the waves of joy, the sense of life.

The image of their lovemaking was an essential part of her sustenance, a kind of refreshment that, like the reserves of a camel, could keep her alive for long periods in the desert.

"You seem distracted," Claude had said politely a few evenings later at dinner, when the image had been particularly clear in her mind. He seemed carefully polite, avoiding any condescension, as if the wrong phrase, the wrong look might set her off again. If only he could look into her mind, she thought, wondering if the time had come to finally confess it.

349

"Just tired."

"Then perhaps it would not be the time to tell." Understanding was long in coming, as she fought to retain the image. Finally she looked up at him, saw him watching her benignly, smiling.

"Tell?"

"I have a bit of news." He was feigning innocence. It was a familiar pose and she knew that there was, indeed, something about to upset her life.

"It is by way of an announcement." He seemed to want to squeeze the last bit of suspense out of his news.

"Come now, Claude. This is ridiculous."

His face transformed itself from innocence to disappointment. But once again, as he had been doing during the past few weeks of their domestic dilemma, he denied his instincts. She knew he was itching to be sarcastic and she enjoyed his discomfort.

"You are looking at a new ambassador."

"Ambassador." It had been the overriding goal of his life. To be an ambassador before he was forty. In a strange way, she felt jealous of his success.

"Well, aren't congratulations in order?" She got up, as if in a dream, and went over to him, bending, kissing him on both cheeks in the French way. She felt nothing, even when he grabbed her and pressed his lips to her. She endured it.

"You will adore Egypt."

Stiffening, she stood over him, feeling a sudden deep chill. "Egypt?"

"Quite an important deal for us," he said, perceiving nothing of her panic. "It will be in the Mideast where reputations are made. Finally." He paused. "Finally, we are getting the recognition we deserve." He was being the consummate diplomat now, creating the false humility of his trade. I can't bear it, she thought. A few months ago, she might have reveled in the idea of it, prepared the gift of herself for him,

350

the ultimate act of obeisance and worship that he was expecting. Now the thought of what was coming was terrifying. The need for Eduardo overwhelmed her. We are coming to the moment of truth, she told herself. I will never go to Egypt.

Later she let him extract what he might have construed as his "reward" for his success, letting her body be used without apparent purpose, for which she cursed herself, although she told herself that there had to be a reason for postponing the inevitable. Thankfully, it was over quickly.

The next few days were barely endurable, and she hovered on the edge of despair, listening despondently as Claude made his plans known.

"Thirty days," he said. "We will have to start preparing almost immediately. You have to begin the packing, the arrangements."

She said nothing, and when three days had passed and she had done nothing, he said again, "Really, Marie. There are deadlines. Shipping deadlines." The packing crates had already arrived and were cluttering up the hallways.

She nodded as if in affirmation. "I've got to get to it tomorrow."

But when tomorrow came, all she could do was listen to the impending sound of the telephone, and when it rang she rushed to it only to hear the sound of a stranger's voice. This is absurd, she told herself, trying to gather her strength and end the drifting and uncertainty.

By the time five days had passed and Eduardo had not called, her sense of endurance had vanished, and although she had made some halfhearted attempts to fill the packing cases, she knew she was merely buying time, keeping Claude at bay, waiting. He cannot expect me to have that much courage, she decided, taking the car one morning after Claude and the children had left the house and driving to Eduardo's apartment house. Ignoring the attendant, she walked past the desk and, taking the elevator to his floor, knocked boldly at his apartment door. There was no answer. She put her ear to the door, listening. No sound.

She lingered in the corridor, pacing its length, watching his door, knowing how ridiculous she must have looked to the occasional people who passed her on the way to the elevator. She felt their eyes brush over her and sometimes she stared back at them with brazen haughtiness. How could they know her anguish?

Later she waited in her car, watching the entrance, a posted sentry, feeling stupidly helpless, annoyed at her dependency. She watched the shadows lengthen as the sun swept westward in its great arc, feeling the chill as the light faded. She started the motor, waiting for the heat to come. Where was Eduardo?

On the edge of the driveway, leaning against a tree, she saw a tall woman, her face an expressionless mask. Like her, she was watching the entrance to the apartment house, her hands thrust into the pockets of her trench coat. She seemed hawklike, predatory.

Marie had noticed her peripherally at first, and as the day wore on and the woman continued to remain immobile against the tree, she began to inspire greater interest. It was only when Marie had gunned the motor of her car that the woman turned toward her, looking at her briefly, then continuing her vigil.

Darkness descended quickly. The lights in the apartment house, like match flickers, suddenly appeared and the traffic along Massachusetts Avenue thickened. The tall woman's tenacity was compelling, the study of her a distraction. She could see clouds of vapor coming from her mouth as the night chill became more intense. The clock in the dashboard read six o'clock and Marie knew she should have headed home long ago. Vestiges of her old life, the old middle-class programming. The home! Motherhood! How she detested them. Claude would be arriving in a half hour. The children were hungry. By now, they had called Claude at the embassy, wondering

352

where she was. Worry had begun, all the usual anxieties. But she remained strangely calm. Indifferent to their pain. She was waiting for Eduardo.

Then she saw him. He was driving a car into the parking lot, passing in front of her car, his head slightly tilted as he searched for a parking spot. Shutting off the motor, she waited, watched as he maneuvered into a parking space, heard the slam of the car door. She got out of her car and her gaze was pulled suddenly toward the tall woman, who had moved deeper into the shadows, her eyes fixed on Eduardo. He headed for the lobby entrance. Marie moved swiftly, catching up with him as he entered the lobby.

"Eduardo."

"You." He looked beyond her. But her eyes did not waver from his. Eduardo punched the button of the elevator, showing some irritability.

"I had to see you, Eduardo," she said. "I have been waiting all day."

"I told you that you must never do this," he hissed. "They might be watching. It is dangerous." He looked up to check the progress of the elevator, which was moving at a maddeningly slow pace.

"It is important," she pleaded. She watched his effort to control his temper. She felt her throat constrict.

"Claude is being transferred to Egypt," she said. An older couple moved through the lobby, standing behind them, also waiting for the elevator.

"Egypt?" He lowered his voice, obviously trying to achieve a casual air. She wanted to scream, but she held herself in, smothering the urge.

"I cannot go, Eduardo," she whispered. "I will not go."

"We will discuss it tomorrow."

"Now," she pleaded. "Now."

"Please, Marie."

"What can I do? Tell me what to do?"

353

"Tomorrow."

The elevator opened and Eduardo stepped inside and let the elderly couple enter. Then he turned toward her once more, his eyes narrowing, his lips tight.

"Tomorrow?"

"When?"

"At ten. I will be waiting."

Then he stepped in and the door shut. She watched the numbers above the door chart the elevator's progress, felt the weakness in her knees as she tried to move, the feeling of abandonment a terrifying reality. Others had come into the lobby, pressed the elevator button, and waited. She tried to compose herself, confused by her own emptiness and his display of indifference. Surely, he cannot let me go. She fought for the return of logic. Perhaps I have endangered him, his work. The thought seemed to calm her as she moved toward the entrance, remembering the children. She saw a pay phone at the end of the lobby, and dipping into her pocketbook, she put some coins in the box and dialed her number.

"Mommy." It was her daughter.

"Mommy's fine. The car . . ." She cleared her throat. "The car needed repairs. I am waiting for it. Take some cold cereal and tell Daddy I will be late." She did not want to say more, could not, afraid that she would soon attract attention. She hung up quickly and passed through the entrance, moving toward the parking lot again. She groped for her keys, then opened the car door.

The woman was sitting there, watching her, her face shrouded in darkness. She wondered why she was not frightened.

"Is there some mistake?" she asked.

"I'm not sure," the woman said. Marie could feel her eyes probing her.

"I saw you earlier," Marie said. "You were standing there." She pointed to where the woman had been standing.

354

"We were apparently waiting for the same man." The words came through tight lips, but ejaculated in a tone of condemnation. There was no subtlety in it, executed like a missile aimed directly at soft tissue.

"You?" She could not reconcile another woman's image in the context of Eduardo. My Eduardo? They are related in some other way, she assured herself. She could now make out the specifics of the woman's face, older, drawn. Many lines crisscrossed her skin. A sister, perhaps? What else could she be?

"What is he to you?" Marie asked.

"I was planning to ask you the same question," the woman said.

"Who are you?" Marie felt that she was losing the edge of politeness. There was a snap of admonition in her tone.

"Who are you?" the tall woman asked. Marie could sense a touch of rage.

"This is ridiculous," she said with contempt. "You get in my car and then you ask me these impossible questions. You have no right, you know." She paused, glaring at the woman. "I wish you would leave immediately."

The woman did not move, obviously contemplating a new tack. "I have been through this before," she said, a note of reconciliation in her voice. "And it is ridiculous." She seemed to squirm in her seat. "I don't mean to be belligerent, or even rude." The woman paused, marshaling strength. "It is Eduardo ..." she began.

"What are you to him?" Marie snapped. Vague street sounds filtered through the air, but the silence in the car seemed dense, atrophied.

"I am not sure," the woman said, with a tinge of sarcasm. Then came another ejaculation, wrung out of her depths, reluctantly. "A mistress?" she cried. "Is that the right word?" The question seemed rhetorical. It did not escape the stunned Marie.

"What?"

355

"A lover?" the woman persisted. "What does one call it?" A dash of bitterness was creeping into her voice now. "One of three. At least three."

"Three?" It was making no sense at all. "What are you saying?"

"Am I on the target?" the woman said. "Have I hit the mark?"

"One of three." Marie whispered, accepting the inference, but denying the implications to herself. "And you are one?" She looked at the aging woman, who touched her face as if to hide the damage of time.

"Is it so strange?" Malevolence hung in the air again. "I can show you one that is younger than you."

"I really don't understand any of this," Marie said. It was time to run from this madness now. "And I think you had better go. I must get home to my children, my husband. I have had quite enough ..."

"What is that supposed to mean?" the woman asked. Marie's efforts at denial were straining her. There was no place to run, she decided, feeling the emptiness balloon inside of her.

"I think you should come with me," the woman said.

"Where?"

"To meet the other sister."

"Sister?"

"I suppose you think I'm talking in riddles."

"I don't know what to think."

"It is a riddle. I was merely trying to be delicate. But I'm afraid there is no substitute here for the truth, for the brutality of it. Are you prepared to be hurt?"

"I'm prepared for nothing," Marie said, feeling the sense of surrender, still hoping for the miracle of a mistake. "Are you sure we are talking of the same person?" She felt a tug of trepidation waiting for the answer, which came quickly.

"Eduardo Allesandro Palmero," the woman said. "The man you were talking to in the lobby just now. You are only one of the women in his life. There are three of us. Perhaps more."

356

Yes, I can understand that, Marie thought, proud of her logic. He was not, after all, a newborn baby. A man with such power. Naturally, there had been others. She was calming now. She could understand this woman's anguish. An older lover. She was proud of her conquest now. She must be gentle. Sympathetic. I am the victor, she told herself.

"One must learn to accept what is over," Marie said gently.

"Over?"

"He is an extraordihary man," Marie said, flaunting her present possession of him. "But why disturb his tranquillity now? There is much on his mind."

"It still escapes you?" the woman said. "I mean he is my lover now. I mean he is the lover of this other woman now. And you?"

It was a hurled gauntlet.

"I think that is particularly vicious and offensive," Marie said with contempt. "Do you expect me to believe you?"

"Come with me," the woman said briskly, businesslike. Despite her reluctance, Marie put her key in the ignition and gunned the motor, moving the car out of the parking lot.

"Turn right here. The turn south on Wisconsin."

Marie drove the car along Massachusetts Avenue. Briefly she thought of her children, but she continued, gaining speed as the traffic thinned ahead.

"Where are we going?"

"It is futile to speculate at this stage."

Marie darted a glance at the woman, who looked straight ahead, her chin raised in what seemed an arrogant gesture.

"I can understand. Really I can."

"You understand nothing," Marie said belligerently. "How can you understand?"

"You'll see."

The car headed south on Wisconsin Avenue until the woman directed another turn onto Calvert, where they found a parking space. They proceeded on foot to the large apartment house on the corner of Wisconsin. In the elevator, Marie looked at the woman in the light, confirming her age, feeling superior to it. In the polished metal, she saw her own face, the lines smooth, the skin still creamy, despite the lack of makeup. Surely, an old rejected mistress. All right, I am jealous, she thought. I am jealous of his whole life without me.

A young woman opened the apartment door and they went in. The woman was blonde, full bodied, in a tight blouse and slacks. She moved across the room with a youthful grace.

"Another one," Anne whispered. She removed her trench coat, revealing a thin, barely defined figure in a loose sweater and nondescript gray slacks.

"This is Frederika," Anne said. "What is your name?"

"Marie." She had not wanted to give her name and was surprised that it came out. "Marie LaFarge," she said.

"I am Anne McCarthy," the tall woman said. She walked to the couch and sat down heavily. Marie felt the eyes of the younger woman on her.

"I don't know what this is all about," Marie said, actually feeling her sense of superiority. He is my man, she told herself.

"Tell her, Frederika," Anne said. "I have tried. Really I have."

"Faith, hope, and charity," Frederika said. She lit a cigarette and inhaled deeply, the smoke disgorged like a dragon's breath. "That's us. Which one are you?"

"Probably faith," Anne said. "You know that's a marvelous metaphor."

"We are all his lovers," Frederika said. "The three of us. We all share one man. Am I correct, Anne?"

"Well, we are missing one admission." She looked at Marie. "At least three."

"And she is married," Anne said, the sarcasm thick.

Marie felt her knees buckling, the blood draining from her head, dizziness descending. She reached to the wall for support. Frederika rushed to the kitchen and brought a glass of water.

358

"Here," she said, offering the water, which Marie took with shaking hands, trying to hold down a few swallows. Marie felt her strength ebb. She sat down.

"The reality is terribly demeaning," Frederika said. "I'm sure we hadn't meant to be cruel. I've had my shock already and I'm learning to live with it."

"I love him," Marie said helplessly. "He is everything to me." She felt a hand on her back, a gentle caress.

"We know," Anne said, softer now.

"But it doesn't seem possible ..." Marie began. She pictured his body, the surge of strength, the beautiful, graceful sexuality. Can it be the same with them? It is casual with them, she decided.

"It is embarrassing," Frederika said, as if reading her thoughts. Marie could sense her attempt at lightheartedness, although the sadness and resignation beneath the cheer was quite obvious. She moved across the room, then sat down on the bed.

"He was here with me last night. I feel silly saying it. But I feel that we must ..." She swallowed deeply. "... be as accurate, as truthful as possible. I knew then. Anne had told me. And although I could not wash the knowledge from my mind, it was the *same* with him. Can I describe how much I love this man?" She closed her eyes, holding back tears. Her chin trembled. "I feel so naked, telling you both this. But if you could get inside my body, my heart, my soul, you would see how important it is to say this ..." She stopped, gulping for air, breathing deeply in an effort to calm herself.

"It is hateful for you to say that," Marie said, standing up, wobbly, her rage beginning. "It is simply not possible. This is a dream. It is not possible. I will wake up soon."

"There is no point in hating each other," Anne said quietly. "Or bickering. There is a compelling reality here." Her eyes turned from Marie to Frederika. "We are all in love with the same man."

359

"You?" Marie turned toward her, searching for a gesture of humiliation.

"Yes, me too. You're thinking that I'm older, a bit over the hill. Well, maybe more than a bit. But what do either of you know what is inside me? I love him. I am not ashamed of that. What he gives me is more than I ever thought was possible in life. I will give him anything, anything . . ."

"Money," Frederika said. "She gives him money."

"You mean you buy him?" Marie said, thankful for the clue.

"And you, Marie," Anne said. "What have you done for him? We are all doing something. Frederika here is a courier. We have, we know, been responsible for helping him kill his enemies and innocent people, as well."

"Yes, I have delivered information," Frederika said, with odd precision. "Tapes."

"Tapes?" A little scream came out of Marie's mouth, a compulsive cry.

"So you have done something?" Anne said. "Did you think you had a special role here? Come on, tell us. What have you done for him, for the cause, for Chile?"

"What I did, I did for him," Marie said, angry now.

"What?"

"I don't think it's any of your business," Marie said, suspicious now. "You could be agents, enemies."

"Something with the tapes, right, Marie?" Frederika pressed. "You did something with the tapes."

"No. It's not true."

"What are you? Who are you?" Anne pursued. "You are obviously French."

"You have no right."

"No right?"

"You're his enemies." She started to move toward the door.

"Believe me, Marie," Frederika said, gently now. "There is no escape from the reality of it."

"He wouldn't," Marie began. Eduardo, she cried within herself.

360

"He did . . ." Anne said quietly. She looked at the two women, the sense of commonality coming quickly. She was trying to conclude something in her mind, to accept something. She could see the anguish in the other women's faces.

"I planted a device in the embassy" she said finally, remembering what she had done for it, remembering the pain, the humiliation.

"So you see . . ." Frederika said. "You are in it with us."

She turned toward the wall and banged her fists into it, more in anger than despair.

"My God, how I hate him!" she cried, feeling the essence of her life slip from her. How could he betray me? Surely, it was different with them.

"Hate?" Anne asked. "You said hate."

"What else is left?" Marie cried, turning again. "Do you feel as foolish as me?"

"Not foolish," Anne said.

"Used?" Marie asked.

"Not that either."

"What then?"

"I'm not sure," Anne said.

"Nor me," Frederika interjected. "It is too complex to fathom."

Too complex to fathom. A wisp of an idea intruded in Marie's mind. It was the mode of Eduardo. If he did not want to explain it, it suddenly became too complex. And she had accepted that explanation. She had accepted every explanation from Eduardo. Now the truth was emerging, like a chick from a cracked egg. He had felt nothing, nothing. Only the nerves of his body had reacted, mindlessly.

"It is possible he loves all three of us?" Marie asked suddenly, surprised at her own lucidity.

"He loves none of us," Anne said, her lips tight. Her face had paled. There was a long silence. "Perhaps Miranda."

"Who?" Marie asked.

"Miranda."

361

"I never heard her name."

"Nor I," Marie said. "Who is Miranda?"

"Maybe all of us," Anne said. Marie turned to Frederika, echoing her confusion.

"What does it matter?" Marie said bitterly. "He is beneath contempt, a Casanova. One woman is like another." There was never anything beyond "the event," the sexuality, and the way in which they, the women, could be fitted into the master plan, the cause. The words, as they cascaded in her mind, had the ring of truth. But there was something peculiar in her perception of it. The story of Casanova, or what she imagined was the story of Casanova, was never told from the woman's point of view. It is a fraud, she told herself suddenly. She leaned against the wall, watching the other women.

"I am sick in my heart," she said quietly. "I feel unclean." She wanted to say more, hesitated, watched the other women watching her, feeling their pain, as if they were all in the same hospital ward isolated because of the same disease. "I am deeply jealous, as well," she admitted aloud.

"It will curdle your insides," Frederika said. "I have already passed through that valley." She tossed her head. "I am still passing through that valley. The idea of it inflames me, burns me inside. The thought of Eduardo. My Eduardo." She paused. "You think I am cruel and presumptuous. That is the way I think of him. My Eduardo! There, I have said it. Later when I picture Eduardo, my Eduardo, in the arms of each of you, I will ache. I will want to die from the pain of it."

"Yes," Marie said. "I see." There was a stab of compassion as she looked at the older woman, who turned her eyes away.

"I suppose you would think it ludicrous if I were to confirm the same reaction in me ... the older woman." Her fingers worked together nervously. "I am nearly fifty," she said. "And I was under control. I had seen it all, all except ..." She swallowed hard. "... love." Standing up, she faced the blinds. "What a ridiculous stupidity. I had no idea what it was to be a woman until Eduardo. Such a gift demands repayment. What is anything against such a value, the knowledge of oneself? My life was a charade until Eduardo. And yet, despite what I feel, I could not bear to share him. Up till this moment, I thought perhaps I could resolve to do so. Now I am certain. I could not bear to share him. I would rather die."

"Nor I," Frederika said.

Marie felt now the sense of terror. "What then?" she said. Then loudly. "But I need him. I cannot leave him."

"Don't you see, Marie. It is impossible," Frederika said. "He cannot be possessed. He can only be shared. If not with us, with others. None of us know him. None of us have him. We have, all three of us, been betrayed by him."

"But why us?" Anne said. They turned to her, watched her hands move together, her fingers constructing an abstract cathedral. "He must have searched carefully, seeking out the most vulnerable ..." She looked at the two women. "... like us. Smoldering ashes in dead bonfires, waiting for the gift of renewal, of fire. I was ready for him. I was vulnerable ..."

"He was laughing at us," Frederika said.

It's true, Marie thought. Eduardo had cast the line. And we bit like hungry fish. Who could possibly live with that? The bastard. She cursed him now.

"He is a bastard," she said aloud.

"I am not made for a sheik's harem," Frederika said, an edge of humor breaking the tension. "Not me," she emphasized. "The idea is disgusting." Then she laughed. "We could pass him around between us like a credit card. Use his flesh. Treat him as a kind of game, a toy."

"He could never be a game to me," Anne said. The words carried a sense of authority.

"Then there is no solution," Frederika said. She sighed. "Look at us," she said sadly, shaking her head. "Three intelligent women, rendered hopelessly incompetent ... no, paralyzed, by the effect of one man. I don't know how you

363

both feel, but I feel ashamed, ashamed for myself, ashamed for my ... sense of womanhood, that I should even feel this dependence, this lack of control. How dare he exercise such power? How dare he do this to me, to us? I love him, yes. Does that sound so terrible coming from me, knowing how you must all feel?" She paused. "But you know, at this moment, just now, I could kill him and feel no remorse whatsoever."

Marie felt the idea pass into the air, loose and free, a bird suddenly released from its cage, swirling above their heads, a loathsome thing, with a furred beak and little barbs on spindly legs and shaggy wings with an odor that was thick enough to induce nausea. It was her bird, as well, she thought, now that it was loose, her possession as well.

"How can you kill what you love?" she asked, knowing that she was speaking for all of them, certain that they had run to ground on the same track, as if they had suddenly possessed a single heart, a single brain, a single nervous system.

"Better to kill it than suffer with it." It was Anne speaking, softly, but it was their voice now.

"Kill Eduardo?" Frederika asked, her voice low, in the same key as Anne's. "Did I suggest that?"

"I can't believe we are thinking it," Marie said, calmer now, a tranquillity descending over her like a shroud.

"Not thinking it, Marie," Anne said, her fingers entwined, the knuckles white. "Concluding it."

"It was only a metaphor," Frederika said. "A figure of speech."

"Was it?" Anne asked.

"I hadn't meant ..."

"Come now, Frederika," Anne said. "It's hardly the time for dishonesty between us."

Marie forced her mind to darken, to pretend that she was not in this room, that she was not really herself, that she was somehow someone else, watching, merely observing.

"You are serious?" Frederika said. "I think you are both actually serious."

364

"Better that," Anne said, "than living with the truth of him, the knowledge that he will always be shared."

"I'll forget him," said Frederika. "You'll see. In a month, a year, he won't mean a damn to me. Not a damn. Haven't you ever been in love before when the guy meant everything? You couldn't live without him, then poof, it all disappeared, the hurt was gone, and then another guy popped up and it started all over again?"

"Is that the way you expect it will be?" Anne said.

"Yes."

"And has it been that way?" Marie asked. It will never come again, she told herself. Eduardo is mine. I will share him with no one. I would rather have the memory of him than to know the sharing of his flesh with others.

"But to kill Eduardo," Frederika protested, although the power of the protest was fading.

"We have already killed him in our hearts," Anne said.

"I will never love another man," Marie said.

"But how?"

"I have no idea," Anne said.

Silence descended in the room, palpable, thick. Marie could hear the obscene flutter of the bird's wings, the sound creating a cacophony beyond the wave of ordinary hearing. She could not tell how long the odd sound filled the room, only that she was sure that they all had heard it.

"They will think his enemies did it," Frederika said suddenly, obviously contemplating a concrete idea.

"So there is also the instinct of survival present," Marie said thankfully. She had imagined that the deed would mean the death of them as well. And she was secretly preparing herself for it, although she was afraid. Death, after all, would be the end of it. She could endure anything now, she told herself.

"An act of terrorist revenge," Frederika said. "It could be contrived. That is the business he is involved in. It could be contrived."

"How?" Anne asked.

"There are ways."

"Like what."

"Are you both sure?" Frederika asked. "It can only be a decision by the three of us." She breathed deeply and they could see a mist begin in her eyes. "I am so ashamed of my thoughts. I could not bear to know that I was thinking this myself."

"You're not," Marie said, sensing the air of finality, the ritualization of the pact between them.

"I'm scared to death," Frederika said. "My thoughts are frightening me."

"There is no other way," Anne said.

Again the room filled with the sound of the bird. Eduardo! Somehow Marie felt his presence in the room, guiding them.

"All right then. There is one logical way. The weapon is the same the terrorists use. Quick. Loud. There is no pain." Frederika seemed introspective, as if she were talking to someone else in the room.

"I could not bear for him to have any pain," Marie said.

"A bomb." Even the word, as Frederika uttered it, had the force of an explosion. They waited, perhaps sensing that the debris must settle, the psychic blast must be weathered. A bomb, Marie wondered. What did they know of bombs? But the question did not linger long.

"Arrangements can be made." Frederika looked at Anne. "It can be bought."

Even as she recounted it later in the car, Marie could not remember any conversation beyond that, no planning, no confirmation, only the understanding that something was to happen with her concurrence which would mean the end of Eduardo. It was nearly midnight, and as she drove the car toward home, she prepared herself for the inevitable explanations. She was barely in the door when her children and Claude confronted her. The children hugged her.

366

"We were so worried, Mommy," her little girl said.

"Daddy was going to call the police," the boy said. She patted them both on the head, kissed them, marveling at her own hypocrisy, the ability to move in this world with such dissimulation, then dismissed them and passed into the kitchen where she heated some water and prepared some tea. She felt Claude's eyes watching her.

"What was it?" he asked, the sarcasm apparent.

"Some trouble with the carburetor. I had to wait interminably."

"Wait." He paused. "Where?"

"A garage."

"Where?" She had felt her alertness falter. Now it returned with full vigor. It's an interrogation, she thought. He knows.

"Really, Claude, I have been through a lot today. I have no patience."

"What garage, Marie?"

"Someplace near Georgetown. I can't remember the name."

"I called them all. I called almost every garage in the area. Many of them were closed." She turned, saw the redness on his neck, the inflammation of anger. His lips were tight, compressed.

"Where were you, Marie?" His eyes met hers and she turned away.

It is the moment, she thought. The opportunity. The confrontation she had longed for in her heart, the time to lift the burden, to confess. But she could not find the words and she knew they were drowned in fear.

"You simply missed the correct one," she said, her voice a whisper.

"I've been a fool. Haven't I, Marie? A self-centered fool."

"That's absurd." She turned away again and poured the hot water into a teacup. Strike me, she told herself. Punish me.

"You have been betraying me, Marie," he said. His tone seemed gentler or was it merely the air of futility? But the

367

moment had passed. She paused, gathered her strength. I must survive this somehow.

"It is not what you think," she said. She saw her reflection in the polished toaster, distorted, swollen. Her skin was dead white, her hair awry. She saw her lips move. The distortion was the mirror of her own view of herself.

"I'm listening."

"Tomorrow, Claude. I am tired now. I promise. It is not what you think. I will tell you tomorrow." He stood stiffly, his fists balled, then shrugged.

"Tomorrow then." She heard his footsteps depart. Tomorrow. She would think of something tomorrow. Perhaps she might die with Eduardo. The thought seemed a deliverance. Without Eduardo what did it matter?

That night she slept in the spare room, hovering on the edge of wakefulness, her mind dwelling on things of the past, her girlhood in Paris, her school days, her father's face. She sought tranquillity there, finding it in the recall of her mother's touch. She felt her mother's hand braiding her long hair. The process was long and she patiently enjoyed it, each braid tightly made, with that gentle touch, and the soft, velvet voice. Mama!

"My beautiful Marie," her mother's voice said. "There is great joy in being a woman, a beautiful woman. The world will be at your feet." One could face the world with such a thought, a mother's assurance. But she had also said, "You will see. Nothing will disappoint you." It was, of course, the ultimate lie, handed down the generations by mothers braiding the silken hair of beautiful daughters. She could see her mother's face in the reflection of the glass and the fullness of her own adolescent breasts, the nipples pink against the cream of her flesh.

She awoke with a start. The house was quiet. She ran downstairs in her nightgown. There was a note from Claude among the unwashed breakfast dishes.

"Have fed the children. We will talk later."

It was nearly ten. She rushed through her shower, dressed

368

quickly, and without makeup ran into the car and drove quickly to Eduardo's apartment. It was only in the elevator that she focused on the reality of last night's meeting. She knocked at his apartment. The door opened quickly and he drew her in, clasping her in his strong arms, enveloping her.

"Eduardo." It was warm here. It was safe here.

"You're shivering."

"Hold me tight, my darling. Please hold me." She could not seem to chase the chill.

"Are you ill?"

She didn't answer, lifting her face, finding his lips, lingering over the proferred tongue, her hand drifting to his hardening manhood, the mystery unfolding again. She knelt, undid his pants, watched him, feeling the tears come as she kissed him. Then, at that moment, the idea of his control over her gripped her and she felt a sudden urge to kill it inside of her, to disengage. She drew him to the bed. I must feel nothing, nothing, she told herself, willing it as she inserted him, feeling his body rise within her, filling her. Nothing must touch me. I must kill him now, the idea of him.

But the will, her will, diminished as he lingered briefly and she knew instantly that it was hopeless, a vain wish. The waves came, crashing inside of her again, and despite her conscious will to kill it, the pleasure rolled over her again and again. Can it be the same with them, she wondered, waiting for it to begin again.

"Why you?" she said later, as she lay quietly in his arms. They had been the first words she had uttered.

"Why you?" she said again. "Do you understand it, Eduardo?"

"No."

"Do others react this way?" The cunning seemed so pointless. But she persisted. "Other women?"

"I don't think about it," he said. She watched him, tracing the lines of a frown on his forehead.

"How will I ever live without you?" She sighed.

369

"We endure," he said quietly. "The game of life is to endure. To survive."

"Then you are letting me go?" she said, surprised that there was no panic in her voice.

"What can I do?"

"It's a pity," she said.

"What?"

"That you are not a woman." It seemed a joke. She caressed his penis. "No, you're definitely not a woman. How could any of us expect you to understand?"

"Understand what?"

"The meaning."

"Meaning?"

He seemed so dense, so beyond understanding. He is an innocent, she decided. And he must be destroyed for his innocence.

"And you think you will succeed?" she asked.

"One day, perhaps." He had, after all, never been certain.

"And did I help? Was I of any service?"

"Of course. You were instrumental."

"And my reward for that?"

"That is the shame of it. There is no reward."

"I had you. That was reward enough."

He turned toward her, kissed her deeply.

"I hadn't intended to be cruel," he said after he released her, standing up, looking at her, his nude body silhouetted against the window. He is going to tell me now, she thought, to admit his duplicity, his betrayal of us. But he simply stood there, unable or unwilling to be articulate.

"I craved for you to feel as I feel," she said finally when it was apparent that he would remain silent. "You will always be my man, Eduardo." And I, she wondered, sensing a measure of bitterness, will I always be your woman? It was futile to expect more. She got out of bed, began to put on her clothes. Her fingers shook. Perhaps the end of the world will occur right now, at this moment.

370

"I ask only that you accept me. Not judge me." His voice seemed to plead with her, as if he understood what she knew. "I think I am an aberration of time and place . . ." His voice trailed off.

"Who is Miranda?" she asked suddenly. He moved backward, as if the word were a blow, his eyes frightened. She saw him swallow deeply and his chest seemed to labor to breathe.

"We are all her, I suppose," she said finally, reaching for her clothes. He had not heard. Perhaps he had ceased to listen.

Fully dressed, she turned to look at him, a last look. He had moved slightly, and his body was no longer a silhouette, but visibly naked in all its detail, muscular and slender, its grace inescapable as he stood light on his feet, a sculpted male. Beautiful, she thought, he is beautiful. And wanting to remember him in just that way she let herself out the door and walked quickly through the corridor to the elevator. She was surprised that she was dry-eyed, relaxed, breathing easy.

XVIII

Anne had been sitting stiffly in the wing chair in the parlor, waiting for Frederika's call. It was still dark, although she could see the first light changes of the coming dawn through the white curtains. The telephone rang twice, then stopped, the prearranged signal. She got up, put on her trenchcoat, and walked the deserted street toward Wisconsin Avenue, moving northward toward Calvert Street. A policeman standing in a doorway, sheltered from the wind, looked at her curiously. She stared him down with an arrogant glance and moved on, turning on Calvert Street, hearing the click of her heels on the pavement.

In the quickly growing light, she saw the patch of park, the row of benches, the line of leafless trees. Stopping, she leaned against one of them and waited, listening for footsteps, wondering if she had been the first to arrive.

"Anne." It was Frederika's voice, a low whisper behind her. Turning, she saw Frederika emerge from the back of a tree.

Her lips trembled, although the cold was not that severe. Anne came closer.

"I have it," Frederika said.

"Where?"

She pointed to a package, wrapped in brown paper, lying on the ground. It looked innocent, makeshift, the twine knotted in a crude fashion.

"So small?"

"It is quite lethal. I have been assured of that." She looked at her watch. "It is set for 8:45 precisely."

"He is to meet me at the Riggs branch at exactly 8:50, as we agreed," Anne said.

They listened. An automobile's door clicked shut. Then, clearly, the sound of a woman's tread began. Looking toward the sound, they saw Marie moving quickly. Anne stepped out of the shadows to direct her. Marie was red-eyed, her hair awry, her face luminescently pale, almost transparent. A network of blue veins crawled beneath her skin's surface.

"I'm sorry. There was a scene."

"You weren't followed?" Frederika asked.

"No." She hesitated. "I merely said I would end it today, irrevocably. It was all so banal."

"You admitted it? You told your husband?" Frederika looked at her incredulously.

"I said it was brief. I said I would end it now. And that I would be home to see the children off. All very domestic. And quite silly. But it was expected. It is part of the role of the contrite cheat."

"Does he suspect Eduardo?" Frederika probed.

"How could he?"

Frederika shrugged. Anne watched their faces in the quickening light, wondering if her own reflected the same fear. She was surprisingly calm, although when she looked at the package on the ground, she felt a stab of sadness.

374

"There it is." Frederika pointed to it.

"So small?"

"Believe me. It will make a big bang. The person who made it is an expert."

"It is not traceable?" Marie asked.

"I told you. The man is an expert."

Marie shivered visibly. "Do you think ..." she began.

Anne supplied the unsaid words. "If only I could hate him," she said quietly.

"I don't think I can do it," Marie said, her voice cracking. "I am not conditioned to this. I don't think I can do it."

"You think we're conditioned to it?" Frederika said gently, touching Marie's shoulder.

"He said he was an aberration," Marie said. "An aberration of time and place."

"What did he mean?" Frederika asked.

"He was searching for your understanding," Anne said, her insight certain. "He was telling you he is different from other men."

"He is," Marie said pugnaciously. "We all know that."

"What does it matter?" Anne said. "What he is changes nothing."

"No ..." Marie said hesitantly. "I suppose you're right." Her shoulders dropped and her skin seemed to hang on her face, the aging process begun. "I feel like I'm about to go to prison," she said. "Without Eduardo life will be a prison."

"Don't you think you're so unique," Frederika said. "Do you think I can bear the thought of going through life without him?"

"Better half a loaf then," Anne said. She knew she was mocking them and herself. She wondered what they would carry in their memories, and felt her own resolve heighten. There is no other way, she told herself. And yet the plan had never been that definite. The act had been running on its own

375

impetus. Frederika had agreed to find the bomb. She had assured them it would be simple to retrace old contacts, to find a person with this expertise. Terrorism had been institutionalized, and since money was of little consequence to Anne, the means were simple. The bomb had cost fifty thousand dollars. Frederika had merely handed over the bills to a bodiless hand in Baltimore and a voice had instructed her as to the timing device so that it would detonate according to plan. And Anne had, with a casualness that seemed so out of touch with the knowledge of herself, simply made the appointment to pick up the gold in the vaults of the Riggs branch on Dupont Circle. Marie had agreed to put the bomb in the back seat of his car. And they had decided that the moment of impact should take place as close as possible to the Chilean Embassy on Massachusetts Avenue. Simple steps. Simple devices. Hardly a conspiracy. So simple.

"And if we are caught?" Frederika had raised the question, but it had been on their minds.

"So we are caught," Anne said. What did it matter now?

"They are all quite stupid," Frederika had pointed out. "They will think it is the work of his enemies. The DINA."

"Instincts," Anne had said. "What are our instincts? We have all been betrayed by them."

They had parted then. It had been a brief meeting, casual. Three ladies meeting in a park in mid-afternoon, amid the baby carriages and the nannies and the young mothers gossiping on the benches. All so innocent. So pedestrian.

"If there are any second thoughts . . ." Frederika asked now. Morning activity had begun in the area. They heard a car's horn honk, footsteps on the pavement. People were on their way to work. The city was rising.

"I don't have any," Marie insisted, now straightening, but the skin on her face remained slack. "I wish I could accept it as reality, but I can't."

376

Anne felt her own sense of impending emptiness, as if she were feeling the last grains of sand passing through the hourglass of herself. In a way the end of her life was coming as well. Perhaps the other women felt that, too. She could, she hoped, relive the moments with Eduardo, and perhaps that might sustain her in her remaining years. But she was already seeking ways to wash him out of her mind, to grip herself anew. The others were younger. They might find it easier, or harder, since there was statistically at least more time left to them. What had this man done to them? she wondered. Perhaps they should let him live, let him spread his joy. That was what it was, after all. Joy! But the thought of him being with other women was too unbearable to contemplate. It was the point of the exercise.

As she stood there in the chill, she felt the cast of her mind fix itself, like cement, and she was able to observe the two younger women from what seemed like a new perspective. It was passion reversed, forced in upon itself, that made it necessary to attack the life of Eduardo. Was it really only revenge? She wondered if she could touch the nub of hatred in her. What were they all but betrayed lovers? He deserved to die for disturbing what might have been tranquillity and acceptance.

"When you pick that up, Marie," Frederika was saying, "there will be no turning back. I am the only one who has seen a diagram on the method of unmantling it. Then it was destroyed. So you see there is no turning back." She repeated the phrase almost as if she was asking them to stop her. Marie began to fidget with her fingers as she watched the innocent brown-bagged package lying harmlessly on the faded grass.

It had been decided that Marie would put it in the back seat of his car. After all, she knew the geography, had been in the car.

"But only once," she had protested.

"Someone has to do it," Frederika said. "After all, I have done my part."

"And I will do mine," Anne said.

"Will it be swift?" Marie asked, still holding back from reaching for the package.

"As swift as possible. I have been assured of that," Frederika said.

"No pain?"

"What pain could there be in a millisecond?"

Marie wondered if it had occurred to either of them what was in her mind now. Suppose both of them could be eliminated? Would she then have a clear field. Possess Eduardo? Could such captivity be sustained, she wondered, dismissing the thought. It was impossible. The gloom of dawn disappeared and the edge of the sun showed its brightness over a distant point on the horizon, rising from between two large buildings.

"Well." It was Frederika's voice. She was looking at her watch. Then her eyes lifted and a look passed between the women. Anne saw the determination that lay there, in each of them.

"He has made me feel unclean," Frederika said, the words ejaculated like the dying croak of an animal gasping for breath. Then Marie moved, slowly, determined, and lifted the package from the ground.

"Bastard!" Marie cried, and Anne knew it was the most malignant curse that might be uttered. The sound of it congealed her own resolve.

"He is far from an innocent," Anne whispered, knowing it was the truth of it, or at least, what she wished would be the truth. And with him, Miranda would also die.

"I never want to see either of you again," Marie said. It was a mere hiss now. She held the package close to her breast as if it might be some casual purchase. "I will give him your

378

message." She bared her teeth in a heatless smile, then turned and walked away, the sound of her heels on the pavement lingering in the air long after she had turned the corner. Frederika continued to look into the distance, then turning, rubbed the flats of her palms together, a gesture of completion.

"That's that," she said.

"No remorse? No guilt?"

"Not that much." Frederika held up her thumb and forefinger, the space between them narrow, illustrating the meager measure.

No love? Anne asked herself, but she could not bring the answer to her consciousness. There would still be some pain left for her. She had, after all, to confirm the meeting with him, to hear the last sound of his voice.

"If I see you on the street," Frederika said, "I will turn away. If you ever call me, I will hang up. As far as I'm concerned, you don't exist." The words came quick, practiced, and the eyes were misted, but it might have been from the cold. There was no requirement for answering. It was, indeed, over.

Anne was alone in the park now, standing under a leafless tree. A door slammed. A car horn honked. It seemed so ordinary. Why am I here, she wondered, briefly disoriented. Then she started to walk. It wasn't until she had reached her own street that she fully regained her sense of place.

The telephone rang at precisely seven, the agreed-upon time. He was quite precise when it came to these matters.

"It is all ready," she said, when he had acknowledged his identity.

"Then we will meet at 8:50 in front of the bank."

"Precisely," Anne said, looking at her watch. "What does your watch say?"

"Seven-thirty exactly."

"Yes," she confirmed.

"And I will see you tomorrow." He had not changed the pitch of his voice, and for the first time, she sensed its coldness, the calculation that lay beneath.

"Of course, Eduardo." She wondered if it mattered anymore. It is ended, she told herself. But when he had hung up, she seemed to amend the idea in her mind.

It was only after the sounds of Bach filled the house and her body muscles struggled to achieve the perfection of her exercises that she realized contentedly how far back she had put him in her mind.

XIX

Dobbs closed the file on his desk. His eyes stung and he pressed thumb and middle finger into the lids, gently massaging them. Information! It had rolled off the papers like a moving oil slick, drowning him finally. There were facts, supposition, speculation, conclusions, theories, a hodgepodge of bureaucratic justification, heavily layered with the manure of intelligence.

He had, he knew, ignored all that, seeking beneath the surface, into the heart of it. And he had found nests of maggots crawling beneath his own skin. Because he was dead, the fire of life cold, he did not foresee what was coming. What did he know of a woman's ecstasy and how close it was to scorn? Love, he knew now, could be fashioned into a deadly weapon. It was something Eduardo had understood, and that understanding had bested him.

Had he really pieced together the essence of the man from all this litter? Why hadn't he done it before? He had known what was happening. Eduardo's every move was known. The women were also in the net. Had he deliberately let them kill him? He looked around his familiar office, felt Eduardo's presence again. I killed you, you bastard, he hissed. And I would have given anything to have lived and died in your place.

He had, of course, reached the official conclusion immediately, as he had watched them cart off the remains. Now he **was** the CIA man again, the professional.

The official line, spinning now in Dobbs' brain, was that Palmero was wasted by the DINA because of his influence in this country. What an absurdity! The man was a bungler, although the missions he had instigated were quite clever. Yet they could have been aborted by a single word from Dobbs. Let them do it, Dobbs had decided at the time. Shake things up a bit. Sooner or later they would have to intercede anyway.

He looked over the FBI on-scene, quick report. No strange prints. The bomb was traditional, the usual plastic job with the battery operated clock. Simple. Direct. A bit messy, but programmed for overkill, not one of these noisy, just-for-warning pops.

Viewing it dispassionately, Dobbs concocted a number of dead-end theories he could project to the FBI, although he knew he detested the waste of money and manpower. The investigation would be interminable and the poor agents would be put upon, castigated by both their superiors and all those gullible lefties who would beat their breasts and insist that the fellow was done in by the Junta. Wonderful, he decided, shaking his head at the stupidity of it all. He sat down again and studied the photographs of the man under the light, the smooth face, the small moustache, the intense, obsessed look. Then his eye wandered to the photographs taken that morning, the mutilated remains, the abused flesh. Surely, he knew we were watching him? Did he also know what the women would do? And were they really all Miranda?

The instrument was passion, and the death weapon was

passion, the double-edged sword. Which explained nothing to him, since he could not feel it, had not ever felt it. Just give me that power for one week, Dobbs pleaded, mocking himself, and I would submit to the ritual of death.

It was getting late. In the distance, over the treetops, he could see the relentless lights of the rush hour traffic. There was work still to be done. The destruction of records, the death of the information, the reshuffling of personnel, the obliteration and recycling of facts. It annoyed him that he could not do the same with his own brain. He hoped he would forget it someday, but he knew that was now impossible.